DREAM
WATERS

Book One of the Dream Waters Series

Erin A. Jensen

Dream Waters is a work of fiction. Names, characters, places and incidents are the products of the author's imagination or are used fictitiously. Any resemblance to actual events, locales or persons, living or dead, is entirely coincidental.

2017 Dream Waters - Third Edition
Text copyright © 2017 Erin A. Jensen
All Rights Reserved
Dream Waters Publishing LLC
ISBN: 0997171219
ISBN 13: 9780997171211

To Chris. For always believing that my dream was possible, especially when I didn't. I never would've gotten this far without all your love and support.

To Tommy and Johnny. For understanding when dinner was late because I had to finish a chapter and for being the best sons any parent could ever ask for.

And to Missy. For all your encouraging words, pep talks over eggs benedict and for loving my characters as much as I do.

Those who dream by day are cognizant of many things which escape those who dream only by night.

—Edgar Allan Poe / Eleonora

1

CHARLIE

If anyone had told me that my life was about to change forever when I woke up that morning, I'd have said they were crazy and—considering the fact that I woke up in a psych ward—odds are, I would've been right. Parker-Banks Mental Health Facility was basically the human equivalent of the island of misfit toys. We were all a little broken, none of us functioned the way the world wanted us to, we were all there because no one wanted us and we had no place else to go, and every day was more or less the same day over and over again.

It was late afternoon and we were in the middle of a group therapy session. The staff had formed a cramped circle out of folding chairs and herded all of us into the seats, sticking us closer to our fellow mental patients than any of us were comfortable with.

As usual, Frank had volunteered to talk first. "… My head's been full of too many voices today. They all keep whispering at the same time and I can't make out what they're telling me to do." He squeezed his eyes shut and clutched his head in his hands. "I just know it's bad and the demons are gonna be angry if I don't do it."

An old man, who'd blend in perfectly at a Corleone family reunion, hollered his opinion across the circle in a gruff New York accent. "Maybe they're tellin ya to shut the fuck up, so the rest of us can get on with our lives." Anyone who'd ever spent ten minutes in the same room as Bob knew that translated to, 'Shut the fuck up, so I can get back to the television.'

I shifted restlessly in my metal seat, half-listening to them, but mostly just watching Frank flip. That's what I call it when someone's appearance flickers between their form in this world and their form in the Dream World. Frank was ranting about how the demons were coming and there was nothing we could do to stop them. And the more worked up he got, the faster he flipped between weird-old-mental-patient and swarm-of-bugs-in-the-shape-of-a-man. Every inch of his macabre figure pulsed and twitched, like he was nothing more than a single-minded horde of buzzing insects.

Frank kept ranting. Bob kept cursing. Dr. Spenser chimed in every now and then, half-heartedly trying to get Bob to stop interrupting and Frank to take it down a notch. And I tuned out and let my mind wander, until an intoxicating mix of flower and spice wafted through the air and roused my dormant senses. This perfume wasn't just your average ordinary girly scent. It was exotic and delicious and unlike anything I'd ever smelled before, and it lured my attention over to the door as an oafish staff member named Tim stomped into the room. She hesitantly followed him through the doorway, and I suddenly felt like I'd spent my whole life in the dark and I'd just caught my first glimpse of sunlight.

If I could've created a girl by piecing together the best parts of every unattainable girl I'd ever fantasized about, my creation would've been almost as beautiful as her. Long golden hair cascaded over her shoulders and spilled down her back. Perfect delicate features somehow made her look both sweet-and-innocent and devilishly-sexy. This girl was an angel and a siren, capable of capturing a man's heart and of stopping it. Her sleeveless shirt matched the pale pink of her lips and skimmed across the swell of her breast and the curve of her hip, showing just enough of her to leave you aching to see more. But her eyes were what took her from beautiful to breathtaking. Beneath her long lashes, she had the most magnificent green eyes I'd ever seen.

As they moved toward us, she stared at the floor and Tim studied our fully occupied circle of chairs. I had no idea what perverse crime against nature actually spawned the big lump's Dream form but my favorite theory involved a lonely giant, a promiscuous troll and an open bar. And Tim was exactly as intelligent as you'd expect that beer-goggle fueled creation to be. You could practically see the gears turning in his head as he did the math and realized there wasn't an empty seat in the circle. After a vacant glance around the room, he darted to the nearest armchair and clumsily dragged it over. He didn't ask anybody to stand up. He just started cramming the heavy thing into the circle, knocking the other patients out of his way and drawing everyone's complete attention in the process—just in case there was anyone who wasn't staring at the new girl like she was an animal at the zoo, or a meal. She timidly nodded her thanks to Tim and sat down, looking terrified to be inserted into our circle of lunatics.

Dr. Spenser greeted her with a beaming smile. "Everyone, this is Emma," he said, more cheerily than I'd ever heard him say anything. "She just arrived this afternoon. Let's all try our best to make her feel welcome."

Emma glanced up at the deranged group of faces staring back at her and attempted a smile, although it wasn't a very successful attempt. In fact, it was kind of painful to witness.

The session continued, and Frank went on babbling like there'd never been any interruption. I tried not to stare at her, but it was like trying not to look at the sun during a perfect sunset. You know you aren't supposed to, but your eyes keep drifting back. She kept her focus on a large gold cuff around her wrist, tracing a finger over its engraved surface, head bent to hide the tears she was fighting back. And I wished that Frank would listen to Bob and shut the fuck up, so we could wrap up the meeting and give her some breathing room.

Eventually, Frank did announce that the voices in his head wanted him to stop talking. Bob loudly suggested that he listen to those voices more often, and Spenser started going around the circle asking the rest of us if we had anything to share. Normally when the doc asked us to share, I said whatever happened to pop into my head as long as I knew it'd piss him off. Watching him try to stifle his reactions while I described the Dream forms of everybody in the circle was usually good for a laugh, especially when I described him—toad-like face, dark bulging eyes, fat-lipped mouth with long protruding fangs and a pot-bellied body that bloated in size with every tragedy he listened to. Saying something that'd get the paranoid patients all riled up wasn't much of a challenge, but it was another fun way to share. Sometimes I awarded myself points for each one I got to scream or jump out of their seat. Don't judge. Those meetings were absolute coma-inducing torture. I had to amuse myself somehow. But I didn't want Emma to be afraid of me, so when it came to me I just said, "pass." She looked up with an almost imperceptible sigh of relief, and on her turn she followed my lead. Spenser ended the session by announcing that we had some free time before dinner, the end of his sentence drowning in the screeches of metal against linoleum as patients immediately began fleeing the group.

I started crossing the circle to introduce myself to Emma but Spenser beat me to her, his elderly face portraying the perfect mix of kindness and compassion. "I know this is a big adjustment for you, Emma." Brows knit with concern, the doctor paused to exhale a sympathetic breath. "Give it time. You'll get used to it here. In the meantime, if there's anything we can do to make this transition easier for you, don't hesitate to ask."

Her eyes welled with tears, but she forced a polite smile and nodded.

Spenser gently placed a hand on Emma's arm. "Our first private session is scheduled for tomorrow morning. I look forward to getting to know you." The doctor, now in toad-creature form, took one last look at her and puffed a bit more at the sight of her un-spilled tears. Then he smiled an ugly fanged snarl and waddled off.

She stood alone where he'd left her, looking hopelessly lost and frightened. And my heart ached for her. With a nervous glance around the room, she spotted an empty window seat and headed toward it, carefully avoiding any eye contact. Stifling a sob as she reached the seat, she sat down and positioned herself defensively so she could look out the window and still keep an eye on the room.

I started toward the window seat. Across the room, so did Frank. Emma noticed him before she noticed me and the look on her face made it very clear that she wouldn't welcome his company, but picking up on social cues wasn't exactly Frank's strong point. I glared at him as our paths collided in front of Emma. "Go bother somebody else, Frank."

I'd entertained myself on more than one monotonous occasion by telling Frank that I saw insects crawling in and out of his orifices or a demon standing behind him, and every once in a while when I got really bored, I'd let out a bloodcurdling scream just to watch him jump. Ninety percent of the time I was full of shit. The other ten percent? Trust me. You don't want to know. At any rate, greasy old Frank believed every word that came out of my mouth and I terrified him. He eyed me suspiciously for a second, then lowered his head and slunk away.

Eyes full of gratitude, Emma looked up at me—a pretty significant gesture, considering my eyes were the first she'd willingly met. "Thanks for that."

I answered with a grin that probably looked a hell of a lot goofier than I meant it to. "He's actually pretty harmless but he's boring as hell and once he starts talking, it's impossible to shut him up."

She stood up and smiled—a genuine smile, nothing like her painful attempts earlier. "I kind of gathered that from the therapy session."

Walking over, I'd braced myself for the nervous awkwardness I was bound to feel standing so close to such a beautiful girl, but I never felt it. Being with her just felt right. "My name's Charlie." I held my hand out for a handshake. "And if you don't mind me saying so, you look terrified."

Smiling shyly, she took my hand. "That's because I am."

Her unguarded honesty surprised me and I couldn't help but laugh. "Yeah. Well, that'd explain it." I stood there a moment, lost somewhere in the depths of those green eyes, then realized I hadn't let go of her hand yet. Reluctantly, I opened my grasp and let her hand slip from mine, and my heart skipped a beat when she seemed almost as sorry to break the connection. "The key to surviving in a place like this," I confided with an impish grin, "is to find one friend you can always trust to have your back. I actually don't have one at the moment, and it seems like you could really use one."

Her eyes seemed to brighten for a second. Then she answered with warm laughter, the sweetest sound I'd ever heard. "Are you offering to be my best friend?"

Watching her laughter spread to those eyes, it was impossible not to smile. "Yeah. That was the general idea."

"Well, you just saved me from becoming Frank's best friend." Shuddering, she glanced across the room at Frank. "So, I guess I could trust you to have my back." She absent-mindedly stroked a fingertip over her lower lip. If that was a nervous habit, it was the hottest one I'd ever seen.

"Of course I'd have your back, but the deal goes both ways." I nodded toward an old woman sitting in the corner. "If wrinkly Nellie made a move on me, I'd expect you to save me."

She watched the old woman rock back and forth for a few seconds. "Is that really her name?"

"Yeah. Well, actually it's just Nellie. I added the 'wrinkly' for emphasis."

More sweet laughter. "Right. Thanks for clarifying that."

"So what brings you here?" I asked casually, but was instantly sorry I had. Tears glistened in those gorgeous eyes and the smile faded from her lips until it disappeared. "I'm sorry," I whispered, feeling like a complete ass. "It was too soon to ask that." Even swimming with tears, her eyes were incredible. "We've got plenty of time to get to know each other."

Her gaze shifted to the window as she shook her head. "It's alright." She took a few seconds to compose herself then turned back, eyes drier but no less sorrow-filled.

"I forgot to mention," I muttered, wishing I could un-ask the stupid question, "not judging each other's quirks is part of the best friend agreement."

A hint of the smile returned to her lips.

I cleared my throat, thankful she didn't hate me as much as I hated myself for being such an insensitive moron. "You can tell me anything and I promise not to judge, when and if you feel like talking."

"Got it," she whispered, with a smile that didn't quite touch her eyes.

Before either of us could say anything more Tim stomped in and announced that it was dinnertime, putting an abrupt end to our first conversation. She sat beside me during dinner and I kept the monsters away with an occasional glare in their directions. Some of the tension eased from her body and the smile gradually spread to her eyes, but the sadness lingered along with it. After dinner, we laughed and talked like two old friends and before we knew it, it was time to head to our rooms for the night.

Neither of us said a word as I walked her down the hall but it was a comfortable silence, the kind that usually takes years of friendship to achieve. We reached her door and I stopped moving. "Good night, my new best friend. I'll see you in the morning."

She looked up at me from beneath those long lashes. "Good night, Charlie. Thank you for being my knight in shining armor today."

Dork that I am, I actually bowed. "You're welcome, Princess." When I straightened, there were tears in her eyes. I'd obviously said something wrong again. I just wished I had a clue what it was. "I'm sorry."

She leaned back against her door and opened her mouth to answer, but seemed to struggle to find the words.

I wanted to wrap my arms around her and promise her that everything would be alright more than anything. Instead, I raked an awkward hand through my hair. "We've got time. Tell me when you're ready."

Nodding, she whispered, "I'm really glad you're here, Charlie."

"Me too." In my head, I was hollering at myself to reach out to her, comfort her. But my stupid body just stood there, staring apologetically into those green eyes. Whatever I said wrong, I was truly sorry for it.

She opened the door to her room, stepped inside and whispered, "Chase away the monsters for me again tomorrow?"

Something about the timid way that she said it tugged at my heart. "Every day."

At that, she smiled and shut the door.

I pressed the palm of my hand against her closed door and kept it there for a few pounding heartbeats, kicking myself for not being braver. Then I headed down the hall to my room, vowing not to be such a chicken in the morning.

It wasn't until after I shut my door and switched on the light that I realized I'd just spent half the day with her and she hadn't flipped once.

2

EMMA

I woke with the sun in the morning, bound in a tangle of bedding; proof that my first night had been a restless one. Fragments of my dream still lingered and I clung to them, desperate to keep them from slipping away. I could still feel his hands on me. I could still taste his kiss. I stroked a deliberate fingertip over my lips, remembering the feel of his mouth…

…High above us stars had speckled the night sky. A sweet-scented breeze whispered through the darkness, cooling my skin where his touch had heated it. His grasp on me was firm, as though he meant to bind me there with him. It all felt so real. *You are mine.* He'd hungrily rasped the words, the heat of his breath burning them into my flesh as if he was branding me…

...For the first time in my life, I was on my own and that terrified me. No matter how unbearable things got, I had to endure this nightmare alone. I'd never had to function without his strength. I wasn't even sure if I could, and I had no desire to find out. I was going to kill myself as soon as I was alone in my room but somehow, meeting Charlie stopped me. From the moment we shook hands, his friendship felt safe and familiar.

Groggily sitting up, I untangled my limbs from the sheets. Would somebody come and tell me when it was time to leave the room, or was I just supposed to go out there? My stomach lurched at the thought of joining the other patients on my own, and I mentally kicked myself for not thinking to ask Charlie how we could meet up in the morning. I needed something to busy myself with to keep my anxiety from escalating into a full-blown panic attack. Lacking any better ideas, I decided to get up and ready for the day. Slipping out of bed, I showered, dressed and put on make-up, and all the while my heart kept racing. What if somebody came to get me before I was ready? What if I was doing something wrong just by staying in the room? Thanks to my nerves I finished in record time and still, no one had come for me.

After a few minutes of anxious indecision, I decided to wait in the room a little longer. Dropping into a faded armchair by the window, I looked up at the cloudless blue beyond the windowpane. A sky like that used to lift my spirits and fill me with energy, now all I felt was an aching emptiness.

I closed my eyes and let my thoughts drift to him. The image of him pacing and sharing his last words of advice was still so clear in my mind. His anguished expression, the slight slump to his normally perfect posture, the little wrinkles in his untucked shirt, every uncharacteristic detail screamed of exhaustion and defeat. *Tell them what they want to hear.* His hands clenched into fists at his sides. *Tell them that you regret what you did,* a deep breath before adding, *all of it.* He looked so helpless. *Convince them that you're getting better.* I'd never seen him look anything less than confident, to an extent so absolute that most people would mistake it for arrogance. *I'll be doing everything in my power to get you out as soon as possible.*

I was truly sorry for some of my actions, but not all of them. I shook my head and choked back the tears that I wasn't about to let fall. Why did I have to be such a pathetic fool?

I don't know how long I waited in that chair, but eventually I started wondering if anyone would come if I didn't leave the room. I was nervously toying with the idea of venturing out when someone knocked on the door. My heart instantly began thudding. What if it was Frank, or some other patient I wouldn't want to find outside my door? I stood up and took a hesitant step closer, my voice trembling as badly as my body, "Who's there?"

A welcome voice answered, "It's me, Charlie." That familiar British accent calmed me in a way that no sedative ever could.

Exhaling a breath I hadn't realized I'd been holding, I opened the door. Charlie stood in the hall, hands in his pockets, posture relaxed as if this was how we met every day. The twinkle in his hazel eyes added a hint of mischief to the warmth of his smile. Light stubble slightly aged his otherwise youthful face and his hair, a mop of locks that moved as they pleased, fell playfully over his eyes like streaks of multicolored sand. He was dressed in faded jeans and a yellow t-shirt that displayed just a hint of the muscle underneath. On his shirt was a picture of a bowl of cereal and the caption, 'Caution: Cereal killer!' with a spoon for an exclamation point.

I stepped out into the hall, pulling the door shut behind me. "Thanks for coming, Charlie. I was kind of afraid to go out there alone." Hearing myself say it out loud, I cringed at how stupid it sounded.

"Don't mention it. I'm your knight in shining armor, remember? It's my job to keep the monsters away, and your company is all the thanks I need." I must've given him a look because he let out a laugh. "I'm being serious. Do you know how long I've waited to have a coherent conversation?"

He made it sound like he'd been in the facility for ages. "How long have you been here?" I asked, trying not to sound too curious.

He scrunched up his face, exhaled loudly then grinned. "I don't usually delve into deeply personal questions until after coffee."

"I get it," I agreed. "My brain barely functions before coffee."

His grin widened. "I knew we were kindred spirits." The satisfied certainty in his voice made me want to believe that we were. He put an arm around my shoulders, as if physically conveying to anyone watching that he protected me. If any-one else had done it, I'd have flinched and pulled away but Charlie's arm offered safety and comfort, and I needed it. I dropped my head against his shoulder and felt some of the tension seep from my body.

He started toward the common rooms with his arm still wrapped around me, guiding me along. "Let's go join the monsters."

One glance around the main room was all it took to make me feel less stupid about waiting for Charlie. Frank, a man maybe in his fifties, was the first to catch my attention. His dull brown hair was thick and unruly in a mangy-stray-dog sort of way. He wore a brown checkered shirt with every button fastened all the way up to his neck, a beige sweater vest and faded corduroy pants that were inches too short for his legs. White crew socks and brown corduroy slippers that flopped as he walked completed his ensemble. And he was pacing nervously back and forth, repeatedly rubbing his arms and mumbling something about parasites.

The man who'd grumbled loudly the whole time Frank was speaking during group therapy was sitting on the couch. He was probably a good twenty years older than Frank, and a permanent scowl was sculpted in the deep-set wrinkles on his face. His more-salt-than-pepper hair was parted and slicked back; each line the comb had raked through it, still clearly visible. He was dressed in a navy jogging suit and ugly orthopedic shoes, and each time Frank walked by him he'd holler in an unnervingly pissed-off tone, "Shit-for-brains numb nut! Get the fuck outta the way! You're blockin the fuckin television!" I couldn't quite tell whether the fact that the television was off didn't register, or simply didn't matter.

Across the room, Nellie sat in a wooden rocking chair. Her wiry gray hair didn't look like it'd been brushed yet, or anytime recently. Paper-thin skin sagged from her frail old bones and her faded housecoat hung too loosely from her body, making me wonder how much weight she'd lost since being admitted. Bulging blue veins streaked the translucent skin of her legs, socks with worn elastic and grubby pink slippers covered her feet and she was creaking slowly back and forth, staring vacantly at her lap and quietly humming a lullaby.

I bit my lip and looked up at Charlie as we stepped into the room.

His eyes twinkled with amusement. "Glad you waited for me?"

I swallowed the lump in my throat. "Very." I could do this, as long as I had Charlie beside me.

A staff member walked into the room and announced that it was breakfast time. Eager to get our caffeine fix, Charlie and I promptly followed her out. A warm cup of coffee in my hands was a familiar comfort, something I desperately needed—even if the coffee did turn out to be disappointingly crappy.

After breakfast, Charlie and I relocated to the smallest and least occupied of the three common rooms. Five small tables stood in the center of the room. Each was surrounded by four chairs and had some sort of game set up on it. We chose one with a deck of cards stacked neatly on the tabletop.

I smiled at Charlie as we settled into our seats. "Now, can I ask how long you've been here?"

He raked a hand through his hair. He did that a lot. It seemed like a nervous habit, something to do when he wasn't sure what to say. "Or, we could start with your story."

Feeling the all too familiar sting of tears, I bit my lip. "I'm sorry..." I tried to blink the tears back but they kept pooling, clouding my vision.

"It's alright, Em." Eyes on the deck of cards, Charlie combed his fingers through his hair again. Definitely a nervous habit. "I guess I'm just a little afraid of changing your perception of me." He picked up the stack of cards and let them fall from his hand to the table one by one.

"I don't think you could," I whispered, hating the waver in my voice. "I don't feel as hopeless here as I expected to because of you. And if you're going to be my best friend, I'd really like to get to know you."

He chuckled softly without looking from the cards.

"No judging, remember?" I blinked hard, but the tears wouldn't stop pooling. "It's part of our deal."

He tilted his head to look up at me, answering my smile with one of his own.

"Sorry to disappoint you," I continued, "but I think you're stuck with me."

He shook his head, his smile tentative. "You have no idea how much I hope that's true."

I couldn't help but wonder what'd happened to the self-assured Charlie who'd come to my door earlier. "Charlie, if you aren't ready to tell me your story, I get it. How could I not when I can't bring myself to share mine? I just want you to know, your friendship is the only thing getting me through all this. I wouldn't even feel safe here without you."

His smile was sweet and appreciative, and full of sorrow. "I just hope you still feel safe after you learn more about me. I really don't want to scare you away."

"No judging." Whatever he'd done, I knew I could forgive it. I just hoped he could do the same for me.

"Alright." He cleared his throat. "Where should I start?"

Before I could answer, Dr. Spenser walked up to our table and greeted me with a wide smile. "Hello, Emma. Ready for your appointment?"

My stomach churned. I didn't want to walk away when Charlie was about to open up to me, and the thought of going anywhere in the building without Charlie terrified me.

Before I could come up with a response, Charlie answered. "Can we have a minute to finish our conversation first?"

Dr. Spenser scowled at him. "I suppose I could wait a minute if that's what Emma would like." Expression softening, he looked to me.

"Yes," I muttered, "please."

He nodded, but a hint of disapproval glinted in his eyes. "I'll wait in the hall." He turned back to Charlie, brow furrowed, tone much harsher, "Be brief, Mr. Oliver."

Charlie scowled right back at the doctor and answered in an equally harsh tone. "Sure, Doc. I wouldn't dream of upsetting your plans."

For a split second, I thought I saw fear in the doctor's eyes but it vanished so quickly I couldn't be sure it'd been there at all. He kept his eyes on Charlie as he muttered, "I'll be outside the door, Emma. Come out when you're ready."

Charlie gave the doctor a mocking salute and didn't look away from him until he exited the room.

"Honestly, Charlie," I whispered as I slid my chair back from the table, "I don't think there's anything you could say that'd change the way I feel about you."

"We'll worry about that later, alright?" He hesitated, glancing out the door at Dr. Spenser. "I don't trust him, Em. And I don't like the way he looks at you. I'll be in the hall near his office if you need me."

I took a peek at the doctor. "I was nervous enough about this appointment already."

Charlie answered with an apologetic frown. "I know. I'm sorry, but I wanted you to know. He talks to you differently than he talks to the rest of us."

I stood, not wanting to move an inch toward that door. "Walk with me?"

Brow furrowed, Charlie shook his head. "It's probably better if I don't. Spenser isn't exactly my biggest fan."

"Wish me luck then." Willing my stomach to quit churning, I slowly headed to the door.

The interior of Dr. Spenser's office was so remarkably drab, it was almost hard to believe the disheartening aura was unintentional. Aside from the diplomas hanging in cheap wooden frames, the cream-colored walls were bare and in dire need of a fresh coat of paint. Dim lighting gave the room a dismal cave-like feel. The only natural light came from one small window, its frame so crusted with old paint that it must've been years since anyone had opened it. The single window showcased a view of an overflowing dumpster beside the parking lot at the rear of the building. Two lone items sat on his desktop, a metal nameplate with 'Dr. Robert Spenser' engraved in bold letters and my file. Peering at my type-written name on the tab of the manila folder, I wondered just how much the doctor already knew about me.

He sat behind his desk in a standard office chair on wheels—the cloth padding on the armrests, worn and faintly coffee-stained. I sat across the desk from him in a matching chair, minus the stains.

The doctor smiled at me but I didn't trust him, not if Charlie didn't. "You can feel safe in this room, Emma." He leaned forward, resting his folded hands on the desktop. "Anything you share will remain between the two of us and there won't be any negative repercussions, no matter what you have to say. So let me start by asking, is there anything you'd like to discuss today?"

I didn't want to discuss anything with this man, but *his* words echoed in my head. *Convince them that you're getting better.* How was I supposed to do that?

"What's on your mind?" he asked softly.

"I don't know." I shifted nervously in the chair. "I'm just trying to get used to all this."

The doctor nodded. "It's my job to help you through this. You can talk to me about whatever's troubling you."

"Thank you," I whispered, trying my best to sound sincere.

The doctor flashed me that smile again. "While we're on the subject of getting used to it here, I've got a question for you."

I wasn't sure how to respond. So I just nodded.

"You and Charlie seem to be forming quite a bond." Dr. Spenser's eyes drifted to my file. "Has he told you much about himself?"

"He's been kind to me," I muttered. "It's been a comfort having him show me around."

"I'd like you to feel comfortable coming to us if you need anything. I'd be happy to answer any questions and the staff would gladly show you around." He let out a deep sigh as he looked up at me. "Maybe I shouldn't say this, but I don't think spending a lot of time with Charlie would be good for you."

"If you shouldn't say it, then don't." My words surprised me as much as the doctor. I wasn't usually so forward. His voice echoed in my head again. *Tell them what they want to hear.*

"Alright, Emma." The doctor's smile now seemed more forced. "Since you don't want to discuss that topic, let's try another one. Why don't you tell me about your husband?"

A spasm of queasiness hit me like a sudden blow to the stomach. "What do you want to know?"

"Just share whatever comes to mind. I want to learn about your life before you came to us, and your married life seems as good a place to start as any." He leaned back in his chair, arms folded across his chest, settling in for a long discussion.

I didn't want to do this. My relationship with David was none of his business. That's when it hit me. I had no choice. The only way out of the facility was to tell this man everything. *Tell them what they want to hear.* I'd been too numb to really consider the words when he said them, and now I was alone. Heart pounding, I choked back an overwhelming urge to vomit. What was I supposed to do now? The echo of his voice came again. *Convince them that you're getting better.* "When I was admitted," my voice was shaking so badly I barely recognized it, "I was told that David wouldn't be allowed to visit. Is that true?"

"Yes, dear. I'm afraid it is, for now." The more this man spoke, the more I hated that kind smile. "We need to focus on your therapy and figure out what brought you to this point before we complicate things with visitors."

A debilitating wave of nausea crashed over me, leaving a cold sweat in its wake as a desperate need to run screamed somewhere deep inside me. "I don't want to talk about my husband."

"Alright. We'll get to that relationship later," he conceded softly. "Your father passed away recently, didn't he?"

"Yes." I despised this man and his caring smile.

"How have you been dealing with that loss?"

I felt my face flush as panic morphed to anger. "I wasn't close to my father. We hadn't spoken in a long time." The air in the room was growing stagnant and my lungs were beginning to balk at taking it in. If I didn't get out soon, I'd suffocate.

"Still, it must've been difficult, maybe even more so. Your problems were never resolved." The doctor's tone was kind but it felt like he was baiting me. "And you never got to say goodbye."

My stomach gave a violent lurch and I had to struggle desperately to keep from vomiting. "I'm not feeling well," I whimpered. "Could we please stop?"

Dr. Spenser flashed me a sickeningly knowing smile. "You're probably just anxious. Anxiety can make you feel physically ill. We can stop for today. I'll prescribe something to help with your anxiety, and we'll meet again tomorrow. In the meantime, I want you to think about my questions so we'll have something to discuss. How does that sound?"

It sounded horrible, but what did that matter? I didn't have a choice.

3

CHARLIE

I stood in the hall near Spenser's office, far enough away to step out of sight quickly but close enough to hear if Emma needed me. I hoped she wouldn't. I could bust in and protect her if I had to but after that, they'd take me away. In an altercation between a psychiatrist and a mental patient, no one would believe the patient's story. Spenser could restrain me somewhere out of the way or drug the crap out of me, or both. Then who'd protect Emma?

The second she stepped out into the hall, I could tell something was wrong. I ducked around the corner as Spenser followed her out the door. He was a white-haired man, dressed in the stereotypical white lab coat over a shirt and tie. Wire-rimmed glasses perched quaintly on the bridge of his nose. The skin around his pale blue eyes crinkled when he smiled. Everything about the man's appearance assured you that you could trust him. Then he flipped. Long saber-tooth-tiger-like fangs protruded from the creature's mouth, thick nasty drool oozing down the length of them. His grotesque body had inflated considerably since they'd entered his office. He was feeding off her misery, devouring it like a ravenous animal. Every muscle in my body tensed, eager to attack. But I restrained the impulse. Hurting him wouldn't accomplish anything other than taking me away from Emma. Then the kind old gentleman was in the monster's place again. He placed a comforting hand on Emma's arm—smiling warmly, eyes crinkling—but Emma didn't look at all comforted.

The doctor stepped back into his office and Emma headed my way, eyes dazed and brimming with tears. I stepped into sight and waited for her to reach me, knowing she needed to distance herself from that office. When her eyes met mine, she quickened her pace as the tears spilled down her cheeks.

The second she reached me, her body crumpled. I wrapped my arms around her and lowered her to the floor as she leaned her head against my chest, her body convulsing with each soundless sob. She slowly relaxed against me, and I whispered, "Why don't we get out of this hallway?"

With a nervous glance toward Spenser's door, she nodded.

I helped her up and kept an arm around her as we started walking. Most of the patients were in the large common room, so we went back to the small room we were in when Spenser interrupted us. Games were set up on the tables, silently encouraging us to socialize with fellow patients. The only other person in the room was Nellie. She sat in a chair by the window, making hushed soothing sounds, arms cradling a child that wasn't there, staring vacantly outside at something no one else could see.

We headed to a loveseat across the room from Nellie and I kept my arm around Emma's shoulders as we sat down. She shifted, tucking her legs beneath her and resting her head on my shoulder.

I tightened my protective half-hug as she snuggled closer. "Want to talk about it?"

She let out a trembling sigh. "I don't think I can do this, Charlie."

"Do what, exactly?"

"How am I supposed to share the intimate details of my life with that man?" She spoke softly, but the panic was clear in her voice.

"You don't have to," I whispered. "He can't force you to tell him anything."

She looked surprised by my answer. "What do you tell him?"

"Uh," the question threw me a little. I wasn't used to being asked how I did anything. People didn't exactly look to me for advice. "I tell him whatever I feel like saying at the time. Sometimes I make things up, sometimes I tell him what I hate about him and every once in a while, I throw in the truth."

Her eyes widened as she looked up at me, stifling a laugh.

"And as you can tell," I continued, grinning, "he loves me."

Emma chuckled softly. "Uh huh. That was obvious this morning."

I raked my free hand through my hair. "I'm pretty sure I'm his favorite patient."

Her lips curved into a pensive smile. "Your advice is very different from the advice I got before I came here." She said it jokingly, but I could tell the words held some truth.

I smiled back at her. "Well, the person giving you the advice didn't know what a jackass Spenser was."

Her expression hardened. "Spenser said he didn't think spending time with you would be good for me."

"Wow. Just when I think he couldn't be any more of an ass, he tops himself." I really hoped she wasn't planning on listening to him. "It doesn't seem like you're taking his advice."

She shook her head. "I told him that it was none of his business, that you've been really kind to me and I'm glad to have you showing me around."

I gave her a gentle squeeze with the arm around her shoulders. "I'm glad to do it."

She looked up at me. "I do want to share it all with you, Charlie. All the things I don't want to tell him."

"I know, Em. I do, too." I really did. I just hoped I could do it without losing her friendship. "But there's no hurry. I'm pretty sure we've both got time."

She answered with a melancholy smile. "If opening up to Dr. Spenser is the way to get out of here, I'm pretty sure you're right."

We sat there in silence for hours, and all the things she couldn't say kept racing through her mind. People came in and people left but for the most part, the room stayed silent and still—except for the gentle crooning from the old woman by the window, and those softly murmured lullabies only made the room more peaceful—for everyone but Nellie.

4

EMMA

I woke to the sound of rain pattering outside the window. I'd dreamt about David again but the details were hazy. They slipped away the second I opened my eyes. I could still feel him—his kiss, his touch—but I couldn't quite recall the dream. I didn't get out of bed because I was afraid that moving might cause the feel of him to fade, and I wasn't ready to let go. As I watched the rain spill its tears down the windowpane, I mulled over the day before. Charlie sat with me for hours after my appointment with Spenser. I told him the doctor was going to prescribe me something and I dreaded going back to his office feeling foggy and drugged. Charlie suggested I hide the pill under my tongue and spit it out later when nobody was looking. When Tim came around with the evening medications, I tried Charlie's trick and it worked perfectly.

I'd have to meet with Dr. Spenser later. He asked me to think about his questions so I'd be prepared to talk. Not having answers wasn't the problem, not wanting to share them with him was. But he was the key to getting out. I considered the questions. 'Why don't you tell me about your husband?' And 'How are you handling your father's death?' David's words echoed in my head. *Convince them that you're getting better.* He'd be frustrated if he knew I'd accomplished nothing during my first session. Charlie on the other hand said, 'You don't have to. He can't force you to tell him anything.' I couldn't think of a time in my life when I hadn't followed David's advice, but David wasn't with me and Charlie's way sounded so much easier. Maybe I could get away with just sharing fragments of the truth. Dr. Spenser knew what was in my file, but he couldn't possibly know all the details.

When Charlie knocked, it didn't terrify me like the day before. I called, "Who's there?"

And a welcome voice answered, "Your fearless knight in shining armor."

Smiling, I rolled out of bed and hurried to the door in my little blue nightshirt. It didn't occur to me that I should've put something on first, until I opened the door and saw Charlie's face.

It took him a minute to make eye contact as his eyes traveled over me. Judging by his expression, he liked what he saw. He suddenly seemed to realize how obviously he was ogling me. Clearing his throat, he smiled with a bit more twinkle in those hazel eyes. "Is that what you're wearing to breakfast? You must be feeling a lot more comfortable here today."

With a quick glance down at my nightshirt, I realized just how much you could see through the thin fabric and crossed my arms over my chest. I would've felt more embarrassed if his school boyish reaction wasn't so amusing. "I didn't think about it, until I saw your face."

He let out a muffled laugh. "Glad I could help. I'd be more than happy to add judging how see-through your clothes are to my best friend duties." I reached out to slap him but it only made him laugh harder. "Sure you want to do that? You can't exactly slap me and cover yourself at the same time but I'd be happy to help with that, too." Grinning devilishly, he flinched at my playful slap.

I re-crossed my arms. "I'm not ready yet. I still have to shower."

His grin widened. "I'd be happy to help with that, too."

I tried to look offended but not very convincingly. "I think I can manage."

"Suit yourself. I could've helped with the hard to reach places."

I rolled my eyes. "That's tempting but no thanks."

His grin widened. "Is it tempting?"

I stepped behind the door and started to narrow the opening. "I'm closing the door now, Charlie. Do you want to come back in a little while?"

"Nah. I'll wait out here," he answered in the same soft voice he'd used to comfort me the day before, a voice that promised he'd protect me from anything. I watched him sit down on the floor and lean against the wall. When his eyes met mine, he smiled.

"Alright," I answered softly, "I'll be out soon."

"I'll be here," he promised, "for as long as you need me."

5

CHARLIE

I sat on the hallway floor with my head tipped back against the wall as I watched the door to Emma's room close. I'd planned on telling her everything later—about the Dream World and the images I saw—but I wasn't entirely sure if I should. She said she wanted to know me, the real me. But confiding in people about how I saw the world hadn't exactly gone well in the past. I could always see it in their eyes, that exact moment when I stopped being a normal guy and became a raving lunatic. If I scared Emma away, she'd be on her own. And she needed me. If I'm being honest, I needed her just as much.

I was still debating whether or not to tell her when her door reopened. No matter how many hours I spent with her, her beauty still stunned me each time she walked into a room. Silken hair tumbled down her frame, falling around her in golden waves. That exotic gold bracelet still banded one wrist. Her green sleeveless shirt emphasized the magnificent color of her eyes and equally magnificent curves of her body. I grinned up at her like an idiot. "You look nice, but I liked the first outfit better."

She raised an eyebrow. "I'm not sure how to respond to that."

I stood up with a smirk. "You could offer to change again."

"I'm good." There was a whisper of a smile on her lips as she pulled her door shut. "Sorry you had to wait for me."

"You're worth waiting for, Em." I put an arm around her shoulders as we started down the hall. "Have you decided what you're going to say to Spenser today?"

Her perfect lips turned down, in what she meant to be a frown, but on her full lips it looked more like a provocative pout. "I've given it a lot of thought, but I'm still not sure."

I forced myself to stop staring at her lips and focus on her eyes. "You could practice on me. It might help you work through it."

She bit her lip, brow furrowed.

Why did she have to keep drawing attention to those lips? "But I understand if you don't want to. It was just a thought."

"It was a good thought," she muttered. "Talking to you might help because I feel safe with you. I get the oddest feeling with Spenser. I could almost swear he wants to make me hurt. That sounds crazy, doesn't it?"

I half-stopped myself from laughing, turning it into more of a snort. "You do realize, you just asked a fellow mental patient if you sounded crazy."

Her eyes sparkled with amusement. "Right. Sometimes I almost forget where we are."

As if on cue, Frank came running down the hall, bare foot, pajama-clad and hollering hysterically. "The demons are coming! They're gonna get in!" A newly admitted patient followed close behind him, echoing his cries.

Emma stifled a laugh. "I almost forget where we are, when it's just you and me."

I nodded after Tweedle Dee and Tweedle Dum. "Now, *they* sound crazy. Say what you want about Frank, but his timing's spot on."

While the rest of us ate our breakfast in near silence, Frank and his new sidekick sped through the halls followed by two very unhappy orderlies. At one point, Frank zipped through the archway to the cafeteria, grabbed a handful of cereal from one of the serving bowls and chucked it at the two men chasing after them. His new buddy mimicked him and the slower and fatter staff member was panting so hard that he somehow managed to inhale a mouthful. After he finished hacking it up and pretty much ruining everybody's appetite, he marched toward the doorway the other three had just sped through. Slamming the heavy door behind him, he locked it with a key from his belt and a minute later we heard Frank's blood-curdling cry. "YOU CAN'T HIDE FOREVER! THE DEMONS ARE COMING FOR YOU!"

After breakfast and the morning entertainment were over, we were ushered into the largest room for group therapy led by my favorite toad-faced jack-ass. Spenser sat waiting for us at the midpoint of an arc of folding chairs, his clasped hands resting on a binder in his lap. He wore his usual white coat and bullshit smile. Emma and I chose two seats at the outer edge of the arc. As soon as he saw her, Spenser gave Emma a beaming smile. His gaze shifted to me and I gave him the cheesiest grin I could muster, watching with satisfaction as he dropped the smile, his face reddening until he finally surrendered and looked away.

As the last of our group took their seats, Spenser started the session. "Good morning, everyone. I'm sorry to say, Frank and Eddie won't be joining us today."

"Good!" Bob smacked his hand on the empty chair beside him for emphasis. "I've heard enough a that dipshit's belly achin!"

"Bob!" The toad-creature in the doctor's seat scolded. "We all need to be supportive of one an-other here."

Bob rolled his eyes. "I'll be supportive when he stops bein a fuckin DIPSHIT!"

Nellie, who usually never uttered a word during group, pointed a shaky arthritic finger at Bob. "Watch your language! That's no way to talk in front of children!"

"There aren't any fuckin children here, ya crazy broad!" Bob bellowed, standing from his chair. "I'll say whatever the hell I WANNA say! Put that damn finger down before I come over and BITE IT OFF!"

"Bob, you need to control your anger and apologize to Nellie for the threat," human Spenser scolded. "Everyone deserves to feel safe to voice what's on their mind in our circle."

"This ain't a fuckin circle! It's an arc! Ya'd think someone who went to medical school'd be smart enough to know the fuckin difference." Bob was seated again, but he obviously wasn't feeling the whole support circle vibe.

"Bob," the doctor reprimanded, his calm voice requiring visible effort, "apologize to Nellie for the threat or I'll have to remove you from the circle, ah…arc."

"Ha!" Bob guffawed, then scowled at the doc's stern expression. "Alright, for fuck's sake. I'm sorry I offended your imaginary children, ya loony ding bat!"

Nellie answered with a wounded pout.

"Bob," Spenser prodded, "try again, *nicely.*"

"I'm sorry. Alright?" Bob barked. "Can we get on with it? I wanna get back to the fuckin television before that dipshit comes back!"

I was pretty sure that was the closest thing to an apology Nellie was going to get, which was fine since she'd lost interest in the whole conversation and was rocking in her folding chair, humming under her breath and gazing adoringly at her empty lap.

I took a peek at Emma. She was biting her lip, staring at the floor. Feeling my stare, she turned her head and we both stifled a laugh and quickly looked away.

Spenser didn't even attempt to hide his frustration. "Let's get on with our discussion. Since Emma's new here, I think it'd be nice if everyone shared a little about themselves today."

"Give me a fuckin break," Bob interrupted. "I don't give two shits about knowin her, and she sure as shit doesn't wanna know me." Bob nodded at me. "Let Mr. I-See-Dead-People over there share with Barbie." *Thanks Bob. That's just how I wanted to tell her.* "He's the only one she cares about gettin to know. What the fuck do I care?"

Toadish lips curled into a snarling smile, creature Spenser looked at me with drool oozing down his fangs and splatting into thick mucus puddles at his feet. Then he turned expectantly to Emma, but she showed no visible reaction to Bob's comment.

She'd probably just dismissed it as nothing but the meaningless ramblings of a crazy old man.

Sneering, toad Spenser fixed his stare on me again. "Charlie, is there anything you'd like to share with Emma?"

"Nope," I muttered to the old man in the toad's seat, "I'm good."

He turned back to Emma. "Is there anything you'd like to share or comment on, dear?"

She shook her head. "Not today."

"Alright then. Would anyone else like to share something?" The room grew absolutely silent. Looking slightly crestfallen, Spenser nodded. "Why don't we just move on to a group exercise?"

"Why don't we move on to the TV?" Bob heckled.

"There'll be plenty of time for that later," Spenser snapped.

We went on to a few group exercises, all of which failed miserably. If we ever needed to cooperate to survive a life threatening situation, I'd have bet good money we'd all die.

Eventually, Spenser announced that the session was over and Bob hurried to the television only to find Frank already on the couch watching it. Plunking down on the opposite end, Bob greeted the practically drooling and obviously drugged out of his mind Frank with a, "Just keep your fat mouth shut, Dipshit."

Frank answered with a grunt and a slick stream of fresh drool, and Emma and I decided it was time to head to another room.

The quietest room turned out to be the small one we always seemed to end up in. We settled onto the loveseat, sitting sideways to face each other. Emma tucked her legs beneath her. We exchanged awkward smiles as I ran a hand through my hair. "What now, Em?"

She shot me a puzzled look.

"Do you want to talk things through before you meet with Spenser or hear my story, or just play checkers or something?"

She smiled at me. "Good question."

"Thanks," I chuckled.

"I think we're both afraid of the same thing, Charlie," Emma suggested tentatively. "We don't want to scare each other off."

I nodded, but I couldn't imagine how she thought she'd scare me away.

"I know you're worried I won't feel the same after I learn more about you," she said softly, "but I'm not here on vacation. There's a reason I'm here, too."

I was such an idiot. She needed reassurance just as much as I did. Why hadn't I realized that? "Em, there's nothing you could say that'd make me feel different about you."

Eyes tearing, she looked down at her hands folded in her lap. "I feel the same about you. I was going to end my life my first night here, and you're the only reason I didn't. You saved me, Charlie." A tear slid down her cheek. "I need you."

I wrapped my arms around her, drawing her closer. "I need you, too."

A sob escaped her lips as her slender arms hugged me back. I gently tightened my hold and felt her cheek press against mine. "No judging," she whispered, sending a warm shiver through me.

I moved a hand to the back of her head. Her hair was every bit as soft as it looked. "Then we don't have anything to be afraid of." I breathed in the scent of her perfume. The fragrance would always take me back to the day Tim first brought her to our group.

"I can't lose you, Charlie," she murmured by my ear. "I wouldn't make it."

"I promise, you won't lose me." I pulled back from our embrace and tucked a stray strand of hair behind her ear. "I've got an idea." I couldn't seem to get my hand to leave the softness of her skin.

She tilted her head, resting her cheek against my palm. "What is it?"

Distracted by the feel of her smooth flesh, it took me a few extra seconds to process her words. With a conscious effort, I pulled myself from the daze. "Let's take turns sharing."

"Alright," she answered softly, looking perfectly comfortable with her head pillowed in my hand. "Who goes first?"

"Well, it was my idea. So I guess I should." I cleared my throat. "Uh, let's see," I stammered, letting my hand slip from her cheek—not because I wanted to, but because I couldn't focus on anything but the feel of her. "I was raised in England until I was eight. My parents were Americans and I was born here, but my father took a job overseas when I was a baby. Both my parents worked pretty long hours so I mostly learned how to speak from our British housekeeper who sort of doubled as my nanny, and I never lost the accent. It drives my mother crazy."

Emma answered with a whispered laugh.

I grinned at the sweet sound of her laughter. "Your turn."

6

EMMA

My turn. I stared at the loveseat cushion, biting my lip. I knew I should tell Charlie I was married, but for some reason I hesitated. It was such a major part of who I was, and yet the words seemed to stick in my throat.

"Share anything, Em," Charlie murmured. "It doesn't have to be your deepest secret. Tell me your favorite color or something."

No. If I really wanted us to grow closer, I needed to share something personal. Voice breaking slightly, I muttered, "I'm married."

I could hear Charlie's smile in the tone of his voice, "That's not exactly a secret." It wasn't the response I'd expected.

I looked up at him. "You knew?"

"Well, for one thing, you're too beautiful not to have a man in your life." His smile widened as he took my left hand in his. "And for another, the obscenely expensive engagement ring and wedding band were pretty big clues."

I grinned at my stupidity for not thinking of that, feeling curiously relieved by his response. "Right," I whispered, watching him turn the engagement ring on my finger so the conspicuous diamond faced up. "Your turn."

"Come on," he protested playfully. "That doesn't count. You didn't tell me anything I didn't already know."

I flashed him a coy smile. "It still counts. I didn't know that you knew."

He rolled his eyes in mock frustration. "Fine." Then he thought for a few seconds and his expression grew somber. "My father died when I was eight."

"I'm sorry." I hesitated a second before adding, "My father died several months ago." He gently squeezed the hand he was still holding and I shook my head, eyes tearing. "Dr. Spenser wanted me to talk about it yesterday, but I wasn't close to my father. We hadn't spoken since I was eighteen." My voice dropped to a whisper as I added, "I didn't even attend the funeral."

Charlie answered just as softly, "You were eighteen the last time you talked?"

I nodded uneasily. "It's a long story. Maybe another time?"

"Anytime," he whispered.

Movement across the room drew my attention to the door. Dr. Spenser met my gaze and smiled as he stepped through the doorway and headed toward us. Nellie noiselessly followed him into the room like a shadow. He stopped beside our loveseat, but Nellie continued to her usual seat by the window. The doctor's eyes followed her for a few seconds before settling back on me. "Ready for your appointment, Emma?"

Charlie glared at him. "Does she have a choice?" His voice was so harsh and cold that it was almost hard to believe he was the same person I'd just been confiding in.

Dr. Spenser scowled back at Charlie. "Just because you choose not to make progress, doesn't mean you have to encourage Emma to do the same. If you truly care about her, you should let me help her."

Hatred flashed in Charlie's eyes. "What makes you so sure you're the one who can help her?"

Ignoring the question, the doctor turned to me. "Don't let Charlie escalate this into a situation that'd be unpleasant for everyone." He was smiling, but I didn't doubt the threat was real and I didn't want Charlie to suffer for protecting me.

I stood up and smiled at Charlie. "You owe me a game of checkers when I'm done."

Smiling regretfully, he whispered, "Can't wait."

Dr. Spenser gestured to the door. "You know the way."

I nodded and walked away from Charlie, the only security I knew within those walls, still wondering what I was going to say to the doctor.

We walked to his office in silence. Dr. Spenser unlocked the door with a key from his belt, flipped the lights on and ushered me in with a pleasant smile. Pale blue eyes twinkling, he was the face of every kind grandfather. So why didn't I feel comforted?

I sat down in the chair in front of his desk. He walked to the one behind it and dragged the chair to sit beside me, smiling with all the tenderness that a loving grandfather would. "I'm not the enemy, Emma."

I didn't have a response, so I just nodded.

"I'm on your side." He shifted, getting comfortable in the seat. "You need to believe that."

I bit my lip and stared at the nameplate on his desk.

He paused, giving me a chance to respond. When I didn't, he continued. "I know Charlie's shown you kindness, but you need to understand that he's a very delusional young man." He paused again.

I kept staring at the nameplate.

"I want to help you, Emma." He let out a weary sigh. "I know your husband wants that, too."

I tried to recall David's words. *Tell them what they want to hear.* But the memory of his voice was already starting to fade.

Spenser shifted in his chair again. "Let's be honest, Emma. You don't belong here."

That surprised me. I looked up at his sympathetic smile.

"Charlie does. That isn't meant to sound cruel, it's just a statement of fact. The sooner you accept that, the sooner I can help you."

Convince them that you're getting better. I tried to picture David's face but I couldn't seem to recall it clearly. "I'm forgetting David," I muttered. I wasn't talking to Spenser, he just happened to be in the room. "His face, the sound of his voice." Never in my life had I questioned who to trust. At least, not before all this began. But now, I felt lost. My brain whispered that I should listen to Spenser. He was the key to getting out of the facility and back home to my husband. But my heart urged me to listen to Charlie. Was it logical? Maybe not but I felt it so strongly.

Noting my distraction, Spenser seized the opportunity. "Tell me about your husband, Emma."

I had to remember David's face, I couldn't let him slip away. I tried to remember my dream that first night in the facility. His image had been so clear. I answered vacantly, my focus worlds away. "His hair is dark. The set of his jaw is strong. His eyes are a brilliant blue, the most piercing eyes I've ever seen." The memory of his face slowly grew clearer as if describing him out loud could bring it into focus. Almost desperately, I added more detail. "His nostrils flare when he's angry…" Images from my dream came rushing back to me. "…or aroused. There's a fierce intensity to his stare. When he holds someone in his gaze, his chin juts forward, nostrils flared, chiseled lips pressed together tightly. I've watched him shatter a man's confidence with nothing but the intensity of that stare." I exhaled softly, remembering the feel of that gaze. It'd been too long since I'd felt his eyes on me. "That stare alone could bring me to orgasm," I murmured, so lost in recollection that I didn't realize I'd uttered the thought out loud. "Aside from that, he's brilliant, successful and he loves me desperately."

The doctor's voice sounded far off, like a distant echo, barely reaching me. "That seems a strange way to put it. Most people would say, he loves me dearly."

I smiled, still clinging to the memory of that gaze. "I understand that *most people's* passion also dwindles the longer they're together. I've been with David for years and when I walk into a room, he still looks at me greedily, hungrily—the way a man looks at a woman that he desperately wants, but has never touched." My fingertip lazily traced my lips, recalling the feel of his mouth. The sound of a ragged breath drew my attention back to the present, and I clasped my hands in my lap. "If that seems strange, I can live with that."

When there was no answer, I looked up. The doctor's face was flushed, a hint of sweat beaded his brow. He blinked and shook his head slightly. "Are you happy in your marriage, Emma?"

David's voice sounded clearly in my head. *Tell them what they want to hear.* Absentmindedly, I added, "David's British. He lived in England until he moved here to attend college. I could listen to his accent forever and never tire of the sound of his voice."

Spenser smiled thoughtfully. "Charlie has a British accent. Is that what drew you to him, his similarity to David?"

I smiled back at him. "Charlie and David have nothing at all in common, aside from the accent."

"And their affection for you," Spenser added softly.

I sat up a little straighter. "What are you saying?"

"Do something for me, Emma." Spenser straightened, mirroring my movement. "Consider what I have to say before you reject it as wrong?"

I nodded, already opposed to whatever he had to say.

"Could you have missed David so desperately that when you met Charlie, your mind latched on to his one similarity to your husband and made him the rock that you needed? Could you have turned Charlie into more than he was because that's what you needed to feel safe?"

When he put it like that, it sounded so rational. I'd been desperate enough to commit suicide that first day. Had I seen Charlie as something he wasn't, because that's what I needed him to be? No. Every moment with Charlie felt so genuine, and nothing about Charlie had ever even hinted that he was the delusional person Spenser made him out to be. I couldn't have imagined all of it. Could I?

I really needed to talk to Charlie.

7

CHARLIE

Emma said she'd be back for a game of checkers after her session with Spenser. Whether or not she was serious, packing up a game would kill some time while she was gone. There was too much adrenaline coursing through me to sit still and wait patiently. Staying behind while she left with that creature was killing me. I closed my eyes and took a deep breath in a failed attempt to quiet my pounding heart, then I stood from the loveseat. There was a checkerboard all set up and ready on one of the tables in the room, but I told myself Emma might appreciate a change of scenery when she got back, because I needed something to distract myself with until she did. So I decided to pack up the game and bring it into the hallway to wait for her.

Grabbing the box from a nearby shelf, I brushed a thin layer of dust off the cover and wondered how long it'd been since anyone actually played a game of checkers. I set the box on the table and started filling it, tossing each checker a little harder than the last.

Across the room, Nellie stared blankly out the window as she rocked back and forth in her chair. "Hush, child. It'll be alright." Her crooning didn't have the calming effect it usually had on me. "Hush now. She'll be fine. The toad won't hurt her," she murmured in a sing-song sort of lullaby speak.

What the hell? I looked up from the table. Had she just said what I thought she had?

"Yes," she crooned, without looking from the window, "I was talking to you, boy."

Group therapy. Of course. She'd heard me describe Spenser's Dream form during group sessions. Still, I was curious enough to leave the checkers and walk over to her. Sitting down in the chair next to hers, I watched her sway back and forth like her armchair was a rocking chair. I'd never really looked at her up close before. Her gray hair was a frizzy mess, threadbare clothes hung loosely from her wrinkled little body and her vacant eyes were filmy and clouded. Maybe by cataracts? I couldn't say for sure, since I didn't really know what cataracts looked like. Despite my obvious stare, her milky eyes stayed fixed on a point beyond the windowpane.

"He drools when he looks at her," she crooned, like she was singing a demented lullaby. "Thick nasty slime runs down those fangs, plopping on the floor. Her misery must be extra tasty, the way that he hungers for it. Who knows? Maybe her youth and beauty make it sweeter. But he won't hurt her, he thinks his intentions are good. People have a way of believing what they need to, instead of what is."

I listened, stunned and speechless, until she finished. When she did, it took me a minute to find my voice. "Nellie, are you telling me that you see what I see?" Now that I thought about it, I'd never seen Nellie flip. Then again, I'd never really paid any attention to her. She was just a silent presence in the room—no more interesting than a lamp or a chair, something there but not worth noticing—until now.

Nellie's shriveled lips turned up in a hint of a smile without any humor in it, but her glazed eyes stayed focused somewhere distant. "Yes, boy. I'm telling you that I have the curse of Dream Sight, too." She was still speaking in that sing-song voice, as if the cloudy unfocused eyes weren't creepy enough.

"The curse of Dream Sight," I repeated, as much to hear it again myself as to answer, "What makes it a curse?"

Eyes still vacant, she shook her head. "Don't waste my time with foolishness, boy."

Waste her time? Like she had something productive to do with her time that I was keeping her from. I refrained from commenting and listened.

She frowned, looking exasperated, still without focusing on me. "You've lived with it all your life, haven't you?"

"Yeah," I muttered.

"Then I don't need to tell you. You know why it's a curse. Nightmarish beasts find you. Everywhere. There's no escaping them. No way to make them disappear. And if you talk about what you see, you're crazy. If you try to hide it, you might succeed for a while but eventually a nightmare will take you by surprise, one so horrible that you can't stop yourself from reacting and when you do, you're crazy."

Okay. That was disturbingly accurate. "I've never met anybody else who could see what I see. Why haven't I ever seen you flip?"

"Flip? Is that what you call it?" Her grin grew slightly more genuine, but her eyes stayed glazed and unfocused. "I like that."

I raked a hand through my hair. "Thanks."

"You haven't seen me 'flip' because I haven't wanted you to," she crooned.

"Haven't wanted me to? You mean, you can control it?" I still couldn't quite believe this conversation was actually happening. "And by the way, what are you always rocking and singing to? I don't see whatever you're seeing."

Her creepy smile widened. "I haven't wanted you to see that either. Haven't you been listening? You've been living with this for twenty-something years. I'm sure you've learned a few tricks along the way."

I nodded.

"I've been living with it for seventy-something years," she continued bitterly. "Enough time to pick up a few tricks more than you."

"So people with 'the curse' can only see what you want them to?" I pulled my chair a little closer to her. "How does that work? And why haven't you wanted me to see? I would think you'd appreciate having somebody who understood you."

"You'd think wrong." She tried to scoot her chair away from mine, but she was too frail to make it budge. "Best to keep to yourself—hide what you see, hide what you are from everyone—safer that way."

I slid my chair back to give her the space that she wanted. "Then why tell me now?"

"Because I couldn't listen to you getting all worked up any longer. You just make things harder on yourself. It's foolish."

"Thanks," I muttered sarcastically.

"You're welcome," she crooned, either not picking up on the sarcasm or ignoring it, "I can't tell you how to hide things boy—"

"It's Charlie," I interrupted, "not boy."

"Charlie," she repeated, a hint of mockery in her lullaby speak, "I don't know how I do it. I just do.

It's got something to do with the fact that I keep one foot in this world and one in there."

"How the hell do you do that?" I couldn't decide whether to be impressed or skeptical.

"I can't explain it. I just do it. Maybe you'll discover how someday." She said it like she was trying to shut me up, not like she actually believed I would.

"Can you show me what you look like in the Dream World?"

"I can, but I won't," she crooned. "None of your business."

The sing-song voice was really starting to get on my nerves. "Okay. Do you know why Emma doesn't flip? Why she looks the same in the Dream World? I'm thinking maybe it's because she's as beautiful on the inside as she is on the outside. She's got nothing to hide."

She shook her head, her milky eyes filled with disappointment as if her new student wasn't turning out to be as smart as she'd hoped. "You only see what you want to see, Charlie."

"What does that mean?" I'll admit, I was a little hurt by her disappointment.

Her wrinkled hands gripped the arms of her chair. "Are you stupid? It means what it means, boy."

Trying to talk to her was like trying to have a conversation with a fortune cookie. "Are you telling me, I'm not seeing Emma's Dream form?"

She slumped, like she was trying to sink into her chair. "You have to answer your own questions, Charlie. Look harder next time."

"One more question?" If I wasn't seeing other things the way they really were, maybe I was a monster too and I just refused to see it because I didn't want to. "What does my Dream form look like to you?"

She let out a dry cackle. "Now you're just creating things to worry about. You look the same as you do here."

I breathed a sigh of relief. "What do you look like?"

A wistful smile spread across her face. "A younger purer version of me. That's why I keep one foot planted there. If I could exist there and not here, I would."

"Thanks," I muttered. "That's nice and cryptic."

She dropped the smile. "You only see what you're willing to see. I can't change that for you."

"I'm guessing you aren't going to tell me what you see." I wasn't holding my breath for answers anymore.

She looked away from the window and fixed those cloudy eyes on me. I couldn't even hazard a guess at what color they'd once been. I really hoped 'Dream Sight' hadn't caused that. "Not today, boy. Go look harder." At that, she turned back to the window and started rocking and humming like our conversation had never taken place.

Taking that as my cue to leave, I stood up and went back to packing up checkers. When I finished, I grabbed the box and left the room with one final glance back at Nellie but her attention was glued to whatever it was that I couldn't see.

Checker box tucked under my arm, I stood outside the large common room with an unobstructed view down the hall to Spenser's office. Inside the room, Bob was in his usual spot on the couch scrutinizing a basketball game like the safety of the nation depended on his vigilance. Since Bob was practically deaf, the volume on the television was up high enough to make any normal person's ears bleed. I tried to focus on the game's commentary to keep calm. *Look harder.* If anyone had told me a day ago that I'd be taking advice from Nellie, I would've laughed in their face. Had I lost it? Had I spent so many years in mental facilities that I'd started thinking like the rest of them? *Focus on the game* I told myself. Don't create problems. Bob yelled at the television screen every now and then—like any devoted sports fan would—but unlike other sports fans, Bob's comments had absolutely nothing to do with the game.

When I'd about reached the limits of my patience, Spenser's door opened. The doctor came out first, smiling warmly as he spoke. I wasn't close enough to hear what he was saying. Emma stepped out next. *Look harder.* I focused all my mental energy on her with Nellie's words ringing in my ears. *You only see what you want to see.* I willed myself to see it all, and Emma's hair started dancing in some undetectable gust of wind. She wore a flowing gown so white that it practically glowed, long billowy sleeves floating gracefully in that breeze I couldn't feel. Her face was radiant, lit by some brilliant hidden source of light, but her features were the same. If anything, she was slightly more beautiful—if that was even possible. *Look harder.*

The first thing I saw was a ripple in the air, like you see when you look through a wave of intense heat. Then it stepped through the doorway and advanced until it stood with its front legs framing Emma, like the doorway had seconds before. The dragon loomed over her, glaring down at toad Spenser with fire in its eyes. I don't mean that figuratively. Actual flames danced in the creature's eyes, blazing a brilliant sapphire blue. Thick black scales covered the dragon's massive body and beneath those scales, the creature was a fearsome mass of heavily muscled strength with claws and teeth that were solid and powerful and dagger-sharp. The dragon snorted a puff of bluish smoke in the toad's face, and human Spenser squinted and wiped his brow as if he'd actually felt it. The dragon flexed and extended its monstrous wings. They looked leathery like the wings of a bat, but they caught the light from that hidden source and glimmered like thousands of diamonds, constantly transforming from one radiant color to the next. It was the most magnificent thing I'd ever seen. Unfortunately, it was also the most terrifying.

It all happened in seconds, but for me time moved in slow motion. Before my stunned mind could even form a thought, my body reacted. The box slipped from my arm and hit the floor with an echoing crash, sending checkers scattering in all directions as an involuntary howl tore from my throat. It was the hopeless cry of a man facing unspeakable terror, knowing he's about to suffer an agonizing death.

And three sets of eyes fixed on me.

8

EMMA

I stepped out of Dr. Spenser's office, feeling hope-lessly confused. I didn't know what to believe anymore. I needed to talk to Charlie to reassure myself that he was real, that our friendship was real. It wasn't all in my head. It couldn't be.

I looked at Spenser. He was still talking but I had no idea what he'd been saying, and I didn't care. I'd heard more than enough of his opinions. Still, I forced myself to listen, only to hear more of the same. He wanted me to look at Charlie and see him for the delusional psychiatric patient that he really was. "...Try to take a mental step back and observe your friendship from a new perspective. We'll talk more tomorrow."

I nodded, not caring what Spenser wanted me to do. I just needed to find Charlie. The doctor started to say more, but his words were interrupted by a loud crash and a blood-curdling scream. I turned and saw Charlie standing by the entrance to the main common room. A box of checkers lay spilled at his feet. Black and red plastic discs were rolling down the hall in every direction. A look of pure terror was frozen on his face, and his eyes were fixed on something behind me. Heart racing, I whirled around, expecting to see something horrible. Instead, I didn't see anything. Confused, I turned back and watched Charlie crumple to the floor.

I moved to run to him, but Dr. Spenser grabbed my arm. "Look at him, Emma. *This* is Charlie. You can't help him. He refuses to let himself be helped. Stand back and let us handle this."

I didn't want to stand back. I wanted to help my friend, but a swarm of medical personnel armed with stethoscopes and syringes already surrounded him. I'd never get through to Charlie. Heart pounding, I took a step back with a bitter mix of fear and helplessness churning in my stomach.

Dr. Spenser nodded then rushed to join the staff attending to Charlie. Kneeling beside him, the doctor calmly took a penlight from the breast pocket of his white coat and lifted Charlie's eyelids, shining the light at one eye, then the other. "Let's move him."

Two men darted off and quickly returned wheeling a gurney. Together, they lifted Charlie's limp body onto it in a manner so in sync that it was obvious they'd done it countless times before. Then they swiftly wheeled him away with a parade of staff following close behind.

I took a shaky breath and looked around the suddenly empty hallway. I hadn't gone anywhere without Charlie since the moment we met. Slowly, numbly, I headed toward the common rooms. The television was blaring in the big room and Bob was in his usual spot, angrily shouting obscenities at the screen. I passed the room without slowing down and walked until I ended up in the small room Charlie and I always gravitated to. Nellie was sitting by the window rocking back and forth, exactly like she was when I left with Spenser.

I moved to the loveseat and sat down, drawing my legs close to my body and wrapping my arms around them. But the room was too quiet and I was too worried about Charlie to sit still, so I hopped back up and started pacing.

"Relax, child," Nellie's squeaky voice startled me as it pierced the silence, "He's fine."

I moved a little closer to her. "Are you talking to me?"

"You're the only one here." She shook her head, frowning like she thought I was a moron. "Who else would I be talking to?"

I sat down in the chair next to hers. "Right, of course." I didn't think it was such a stupid question, considering she'd never talked to me before and she talked to no one all the time. "Sorry."

Nellie turned to look at me with eyes as worn as her faded house coat. "Charlie's the one you should apologize to."

"What?" Her words stung more than they probably should have. "Why?"

She glared hatefully at me. "You'll break his heart in the end, you know."

I wished she'd go back to looking out the window. Her cloudy stare was making me feel queasy and uncomfortable. "What are you talking about?"

Nellie started rocking back and forth again. "He loves you."

"I love him, too," I muttered defensively.

She smiled, but it wasn't a cheerful smile. It was more of a wicked witch sort of smile. "Not in the same way. Not with your whole heart. Do you really believe this can end in anything other than heartbreak for him?"

I was at a loss for words. Where was this coming from?

Her wicked smile widened. "It's the oldest of fairytales."

Why was I listening to her? "Were you reading a fairytale, Nellie?"

If looks could kill, her scowl would've stopped my heart. "Where do you think fairytales come from?"

"From books," I muttered, phrasing it more like a question than an answer and wondering how to politely exit the pointless conversation.

"Books!" she squawked, "And where do you think the tales in books come from?"

"The minds of the authors?" How had I gotten sucked into this?

"Ha!" she spat. "Minds of the authors! They're nothing but pieces of Dream that the writers stole and sold to this world as their own."

I closed my eyes, wishing I could disappear. "What does that have to do with me?"

"Pay attention, girl!" Half expecting her to slap me, I opened my eyes. "We're talking about your fairytale."

"My fairytale?" Too numb to come up with a polite way out, I tried to take comfort in the fact that I was pretty sure Nellie was harmless.

Nellie's wrinkled hands balled into fists. "A knight and a dragon? How could that possibly end well?"

Maybe I would've been better off watching television with Bob.

"Dreams can quickly become nightmares," Nellie muttered as if I'd answered. "Just remember I warned you, when it happens. This can't end well."

My stomach was churning like crazy. If I didn't get away soon, I was going to throw up but I didn't know how to get away.

Like a knight in shining armor to the rescue, Tim stomped into the room with a dose of medication for Nellie, providing the perfect opportunity for my escape. While Nellie was busy suggesting where Tim could 'stick those damn pills,' I quietly slipped out the door. A few minutes later, Tim stepped into the hall looking equally relieved to get away.

I waited until he took a few steps past the door then hesitantly approached him. "Is Charlie alright, Tim?"

He eyed me with a wide grin as he leaned against the wall. "He'll be fine, Emma. Charlie's done this before."

"He has?" What was I supposed to make of that?

Tim lazily shifted his weight, crossing one foot in front of the other, clearly in no hurry to end our conversation. "He's resting. You can see him tomorrow." He watched me for a minute, almost studying me. When I didn't say anything more, he nodded and started down the hall again.

I spent the rest of the day keeping my distance from everyone and when the day finally ended, I headed to my room. Alone.

9

CHARLIE

One minute, I was staring at the most terrifying creature I'd ever set eyes on. The next, I was plunging into ice-cold water, sinking deeper and deeper, tossing around violently until all sense of direction was lost. Up? Down? I could no longer tell. Slowly, conscious thought disappeared, memories faded and disintegrated one by one, until nothing was left but cold and fear. Defeated, I stopped struggling and gave myself up to the Waters.

I surfaced, gasping for air, sunlight bombarding my unfocused eyes. Blinded and vulnerable, I moved through the Water aimlessly for what felt like forever. When I'd just about given up hope, someone embraced me. Together, we moved quickly and purposefully until my feet hit the soft resistance of sand. Weak and disoriented, I could only help a little as my guardian angel struggled to drag me to shore.

The second we cleared the Water, we collapsed. Clothes plastered wet and cold against my skin, I lay on the hot sand, savoring the warmth of the sun on my face. I took a deep breath. The air smelled of flowers, ripe fruit and a hint of salt from the Water. I squinted and my rescuer leaned over me, blocking the sun's light. At first, the face was a just featureless blur but I kept my eyes on her and watched her face gradually come into focus. She was a young woman, her skin pale and flawless like she'd never spent a day in the sun—which was weird considering how sunny it was. Her features were pretty and delicate and framed by a jumble of rust-colored curls. When she realized I could see, she stopped leaning over me and sat back in the sand.

"Thank you," I sputtered.

She smoothed her soggy green sundress over her knees. "Catch your breath first."

When I caught my breath, I rolled to my side and sat up. "Thank you."

"Don't mention it, Charlie." Her voice was sweet, almost musical. "What was I supposed to do? Sit here and watch you drown?"

I brushed the sand off the back of my head. "You know my name?"

She flashed me a knowing smile. "Of course, I do."

"Well, I'm at a loss," I confessed. How could I have forgotten such an angelic face? "Do we know each other?"

"We do." Her smile widened. "But not here."

"Where is *here*?" I asked, finally taking in our surroundings. Pure white sand stretched as far as the eye could see to either side of us. Flowering bushes and trees met the sand a short distance behind us and in front of us, the sand casually gave way to crystal blue Water. It felt like I'd landed smack in the middle of a 'Wish You Were Here' postcard.

Her naked feet skimmed over the sand in loving caresses. "*Here* is my piece of Paradise."

"Then where did we meet?" As I tried to place her, something about her started to feel familiar. "Near the Dream forest?"

She turned up her nose like I'd asked her to smell a pile of garbage. "I don't go anywhere near that awful place—too unpredictable, too many nightmares."

I tried to brush the wet sand off my shirt, but that just smeared it into streaks. "Where else could we have met?"

She shook her head. "Where else is there, boy?"

Boy? "You can't be."

She flashed me that smile again. "Why can't I?"

"Nellie?" I searched the girl's face for some hint of the old woman.

She nodded, obviously pleased I'd recognized her.

"So, this is what you look like in the Dream World? That is where we are, isn't it?"

"Yup. This is the younger purer me." She raised her eyebrows. "What do you think?"

"I think you're beautiful." Not something I would've guessed I'd ever say to Nellie. "But you only answered half my question."

"I already told you. This is my beach," she repeated, like that explained everything. "This is my Dream."

"Your dream? What does that mean exactly?"

Looking incredibly proud of herself, she chuckled. "I told you I knew more tricks than you, didn't I? This is my piece of the Dream World, my personal paradise."

"Are you saying, you created this place?" I'll admit, I was impressed. "Can people come here from other parts of the Dream World?"

"Yup, I dreamed this place into existence and before you ask, I don't know how I did it. I just did." She stopped to consider my other question. "I don't think people can come here. Nobody ever has before."

I raked my fingers through the matted strands of my damp hair. "If this is your own personal paradise—that you created—and no one else has ever come to it, why am I here now?"

She shrugged her shoulders. "I saw you fall into the Water, so I grabbed you and pulled you here."

Was it even worth asking? "How? Why?"

"How is hard to explain."

Why didn't that surprise me?

"You were close enough for me to grab you, when you fell into the Water." She looked down and watched her feet skim over the sand as she muttered, "And I was worried for your safety, so I did."

Emma. "The dragon."

Her feet stopped moving. "You remember?"

"Why wouldn't I?"

She wrapped her arms around her legs, hands trembling as her fingers wove together. "You didn't jump into the Water on purpose. It pulled you in. I wasn't sure where you'd land or what you'd remember."

Why did she suddenly seem so nervous? "Were you afraid I'd land near the dragon?"

"No," she abruptly dismissed the possibility, as though she was desperate to be done with the subject. "Finding the dragon couldn't be that easy but when you fall into the Waters without trying, you never know what might happen. Are you wondering why you didn't land near Emma since you were near her when you fell into the Water?"

I nodded.

"The 'flipped images' we see aren't visions of what's actually happening in the Dream World when we see them."

I massaged my temples. This was all starting to make my head hurt. "They're not?"

"No," she whispered. "Think about it. When you're awake in one world, you're asleep in the other one. If you weren't, you'd miss things in both worlds. While people are up and around in the other world, they're asleep in this world."

I really wished I had an aspirin. "So, what are we seeing?"

"Visions of the person in the Dream World— glimpses of moments that happened in the past, or moments that'll happen in the future."

"Okay. I can grasp that, but I don't get what I saw with Emma."

"What don't you get?" she asked impatiently, drawing her feet closer to her body and yanking her sundress over them.

"I looked harder like you said to."

Nellie smiled, obviously pleased I'd taken her advice. I didn't imagine people listened to her words of wisdom all that often.

I fought the urge to smirk. "I saw Emma. She basically looked the same as always, but I saw the dragon at the same time. I've never seen two images when somebody flips. Why did Emma have two Dream forms?"

Nellie frowned. "I can't answer your questions for you. Why do you think you saw two?"

What was she, my Dream psychiatrist now? "I don't know. Does she have a split personality?" I blurted the guess out in frustration, but it'd actually explain a lot. It'd explain why Emma was in a mental facility and it'd explain why one person would have more than one Dream form. "Are you going to tell me if I get it right, or are you just going to watch and laugh while I fumble through this blindly?"

Nellie looked genuinely hurt. "I brought you here. I'm trying to help, but it's not my place to give you answers. Isn't discovering the answers what life's all about?"

Seriously? "Where were you afraid I'd land when I fell in, and why did you say finding the dragon wouldn't be easy?"

She started drawing waves in the sand with her finger, and I got the distinct impression she was doing it to avoid looking at me. "Honestly, Charlie, I wasn't sure where you'd land. It's unpredictable when you don't jump on purpose. You could end up anywhere the people you've met have been. You're a mental patient. Can you imagine the sections of Dream some patients might inhabit?" Her finger stopped drawing mid-wave. "Trust me, boy. There are Dark places in the Dream World, places you should never go. Venture too far into them, and you risk losing a part of yourself to the Darkness."

I was really getting tired of the cryptic shit. "Great. Thanks for the vague ominous warning. I was afraid you might give me an actual answer for a second there."

"I've already said too much." Even at a whisper there was a waver to her voice. "Just thank me for keeping you safe and jump back into the Water."

"I don't know which world I find you more annoying in." It wasn't the nicest thing to say to the one person who understood me, but I said it out of frustration and maybe a little out of fear.

Nellie was about to snarl something back, but the leaves of some bushes just off the beach started rustling and I hopped to my feet to get a better look. "Something's over there."

Nellie stood up with a weary sigh and as she turned toward the bushes, I saw the scars—large deep identical scars—marring the flesh on both of her shoulder blades.

I took a step closer to her. "What happened to your back?"

She turned and gave me a hard shove toward the Water's edge. "It's time for you to go now, Charlie." It caught me by surprise and knocked me off balance, back into the surf.

And the icy Water pulled me back in.

10

DAVID

Lord only knows how much time I'd wasted lying in bed, trying to ignore the subtle taunts from the clock on the mantle. Each new tick was a whisper in the dark, mocking me—announcing one more second lost, one more second she'd been kept from me, one more miniscule sound— quietly fueling my rage. I'd personally see to it that barring me from visiting my wife became the biggest regret of that doctor's miserable life, but thoughts of future retribution did little to console me as I lay alone in the dark. I'd never fall asleep like this. I was too full of anger and my bed was too empty. Tossing the covers aside, I stood from the bed with a frustrated sigh.

I made my way through the darkness to the bedroom door, wrenched it open and squinted at the light that came spilling into the room. Barely noticing the cold of the hardwood beneath my feet, I stepped out into the hall and marched to the top of the winding staircase. Drawing a slow deliberate breath, I turned to the portrait of Emma on the wall to my left. The sight of my lovely young bride standing on the beach in her wedding gown made my heart pound all the more furiously. The picture had always been one of my favorites. If she'd been focused on the photographer when it was taken, I'd probably be less fond of it. But she'd been looking over his shoulder at me—hungrily, the way a starving woman might eye a five course meal—and she knew exactly how that stare affected me.

With a sigh that bordered on a groan, I descended the mahogany staircase and headed straight to the wet bar in the lounge. I grabbed a glass and a vintage bottle of Absinthe from the bar and a bottle of water from the refrigerator beneath it. Pouring myself a generous portion of liquor, I added a slow trickle of water and watched the liquid gradually cloud. Giving it a quick swirl, I raised the glass to my lips, took an appreciative sip and relished the feel of it in my mouth for a moment. Then I swallowed, savoring the warmth as it slid down my throat while its licorice aftertaste burned on my tongue. It was a ritual I'd performed often lately in a futile attempt to dull the insatiable need that consumed me. I took another slow sip and closed my eyes. I missed the taste of her, desperately.

She was mine. The fact that some other man possessed the power to keep her from me was maddening. If any man there laid a hand on her... Enraged by the notion, I threw my glass across the room, jaw clenched fiercely as I watched it shatter.

Dropping into a leather chair by the fireplace, I couldn't help but muse that my recent drinking went against everything I'd ever taught Emma. This turned my thoughts to a wedding reception years ago...

...I sat at our empty table, slowly nursing a single malt, my gaze fixed on Emma. She was on the dance floor, as were all the young girls. But the rest of them might as well have been sitting down. Emma was the one that stood out. She was dressed in a little silver cocktail dress that sparkled as she moved beneath the lights. Her hair was twisted loosely atop her head and delicate curls fell from the twist, gracing the sides of her perfect face. She wore silver heels with straps that wound around her ankles, drawing my eyes up her supple legs. I watched hungrily as she moved her lithe body, every dance move a seduction. Now and then, she'd turn as she danced and give me a look that begged me to pounce. And I would. Later. When the rest of the world disappeared. But for the moment, I was content to sit and watch her greedily. I kept my gaze neutral, as far as any onlooker could tell. But she knew I was watching her. As she writhed to the music, I knew that she could feel my eyes on her body as surely as she'd feel my hands later...

...As I drove home from the reception, she pouted. "Why wouldn't you buy me a drink tonight?"

I grinned, silently letting her sulk as I pulled into the garage and parked the car.

We entered the foyer and as I closed and locked the door, the loud click of the dead-bolt slipping into place declared the obvious. We were finally alone. With an almost predatory swiftness I grabbed her, spun her and pinned her body against the door with my own, entwining my fingers with hers. I slid my left leg between her thighs, coaxing them apart and pivoted so that she could feel my arousal press against her own.

She let out a startled gasp.

"Do you feel that?" I whispered in her ear.

"Yes," she moaned.

"Alcohol dulls what you feel," I rasped, grazing her earlobe with my lips as I spoke. "It makes you feel less."

She exhaled a ragged breath.

"If you feel nervous," I tightened my grip on her fingers slightly, "or frightened," a labored breath escaped her lips as I breathed the words in her ear, "or aroused," I ground against her and she tipped her head back and moaned. "Then feel it—surrender to the sensation, or overcome it—but never dull what you feel."

I trailed lingering kisses from her ear along the line of her jaw, hungrily noting the rise and fall of her breasts as her breathing grew needier. She squirmed anxiously beneath me and my mouth moved greedily to hers, teasing her lips apart, hungrily pushing my tongue into her sweet mouth.

"You are mine," I whispered between kisses, not wanting to part from her mouth for too long. "And if you ever dance like that for anyone but me," I kissed her hard, pushing my tongue deeper, "you'll regret it." I pulled my head back to gaze into those magnificent green eyes.

"There IS no one but you," she purred. Then she leaned forward and kissed me wantonly, biting my lower lip as she writhed against me.

I groaned and pulled back just far enough to yank that little cocktail dress up to her waist, slip my hands beneath the thin lace of her panties, tear them off and undo the front of my pants. Without hesitation I thrust inside her hard and fast, and found her wet and ready for me, like she always was.

She cried out as I gripped the smooth flesh of her thighs, lifting her off the floor, crushing her body between my own and the door as I moved inside her, harder, deeper.

"Who do you belong to?" I growled in her ear.

"You, David," she murmured, "Only you."

Then spoken words escaped us both as a chorus of our gasps and moans echoed through the foyer until we came in unison and her exhausted body collapsed against mine.

"You will always be mine, Princess," I whispered, pulling out of her and tugging at our clothing, adjusting

it just enough to get us to the bedroom. I scooped her into my arms and moved to the staircase...

I must've drifted off to sleep at some point during the recollection because halfway up the stairs, I looked down and found my arms empty. Heart racing, I bounded up the remaining steps. When I reached the top, I looked to my right. Emma's picture was gone. I rushed on to the bedroom, threw the door open and found her lying naked on the bed with her golden hair spilling around her like a halo of silk.

As I stepped through the door, the room melted away and she lay in sweet grass beneath a star-filled sky. Behind her, the reflection of the waxing moon shimmered on the glass-like surface of a lake. I turned my head to glance at the door I'd walked through. It was gone. The entrance to a cave stood in its place.

Her eyes met mine with a look of panicked desperation. "I couldn't remember your face. I was losing you."

I stepped toward her slowly, fearing that if I moved too quickly she might disappear. When I reached her, I knelt in the grass to kiss the lips I so desperately missed and whispered, "You'll never lose me, Princess. You will always be mine."

11

CHARLIE

I knew where I was before I opened my eyes. The air was saturated with the harsh chemical scent of hospital disinfectant and the mattress beneath me made even the lumpy bed in my room seem luxurious. I was in the infirmary. Spenser would be somewhere nearby. The kind old doctor would want to keep an eye on his patient and the toad-man would want to gloat because I'd screamed like a little girl in front of Emma and passed out, or had a seizure, or whatever explanation he'd use to explain my loss of consciousness. I didn't feel like talking to either Spenser, so I kept my eyes shut and my breathing steady.

Emma saw me freak out. How was I going to explain that? She probably thought I was crazy after witnessing my 'episode' in the hall, so I didn't have a whole lot of options. I had to tell her about my Dream Sight. What was the worst that could happen? I'd tell her about the Dream World and confirm what she already believed. I was a lunatic.

Assuming by some miracle that Emma still wanted to be anywhere near me, my next problem would be the dragon. Thanks to all the nightmarish creatures I'd encountered over the years, I was pretty good at not reacting when people flipped. Dr. toad-face flipped constantly, Frank was in bug form at least half the time and I never even blinked at their flips, but the dragon would be a little harder to ignore—not just because the thing was monstrous, but because it scared the living shit out of me. I'd have to get really good at acting calm in the face of terror really quickly but again, what did I have to lose? Either I could do it, or I couldn't—in which case, Emma wouldn't want to get anywhere near me and it wouldn't matter.

So, what the hell was the dragon? The more I thought about it, the more the split personality theory made sense. People with split personalities usually didn't know about their other personalities, at least I thought I'd read that somewhere. That'd explain why Emma seemed so normal but was in a mental institution, but what could've caused her split personality? Wasn't it usually brought on by some sort of trauma or abuse? Her father? Emma said she hadn't spoken to him since she was eighteen. She didn't even go to his funeral, and his death was one of the first things Spenser wanted her to discuss. Could her father have hurt her enough to make her form another personality to keep her safe? Nothing could protect her better than the dragon I'd seen looming over her. That beast looked at Spenser like it wanted to tear him apart. If my split personality theory was right, I could accept the dragon. It wanted to keep Emma safe. So did I. So there shouldn't be a problem, unless the dragon saw me as a threat.

I'd be stuck in the infirmary for the rest of the day. I knew the drill. Even if I woke up and acted perfectly fine, Spenser would insist that I stay for observation until morning. If talking to Emma in this world wasn't an option, I might as well look for her in the Dream World, but I didn't have a clue where I'd end up if I jumped into the Water. I doubted I'd find Nellie's beach again since she'd seemed pretty anxious to get rid of me. What didn't she want me to see behind the bushes, and what caused those scars on her shoulder blades? Whatever the answers were, hiding them was important enough to shove me back into the Waters she'd just saved me from. What did Nellie say? Finding answers is what life's all about, or some bullshit like that. It was time to look for some answers. I focused all of my mental energy on calling the Waters, the ripples of clear blue materialized and I held my breath, braced for the cold and jumped.

The Water was just as cold and disorienting as it had been hours before, but this time I could still form rational thoughts because the Water hadn't overtaken me. I'd chosen to enter it. If Nellie could control things in the Dream World, I probably could too. Right? What if all it took to find somebody was to think of them? It was worth a shot. *I want to find Emma. Take me to her.* The second I finished the thought, my body started rising, faster and faster, as if the Waters couldn't get rid of me soon enough.

Blinding light assaulted me as I hit the surface, but this time I was ready for it. I'd kept my eyes shut. I lifted my eyelids a little, letting in just a fraction of light. Little by little, I opened them wider until they were all the way open and adjusted to the light. And all the while, I swam toward the blurred smudge of land up ahead.

Dripping wet and painfully cold, I waded out of the Waters as I eyed the shoreline. There were no signs of life and the surroundings weren't at all familiar. It was bright. It could be where Emma was, but so could a thousand other places. That's when it dawned on me. If my split personality theory was right, I could find ethereally beautiful Emma but I could also find scary as hell dragon Emma, and the dragon wouldn't be just a vision here. That beast could rip me to shreds in this world. Why hadn't I thought of that before I jumped?

I kept a cautious eye on the edge of the forest as I walked along the shore. Weathered pines stood like an ominous horde of gatekeepers, warning me not to come any closer. The longer I eyed them, the more

I doubted my original assessment that there were no signs of life. The pines didn't have faces and their trunks and branches weren't at all human or animal-like, but a hateful cognizance resonated through them so fiercely that I swore I could hear their ugly whispers in the breeze. I was seriously considering jumping back into the Waters when a man boldly emerged from the trees. He was young and muscular, and if I was a girl I'd probably also say he was handsome. He had dark wavy hair, strong rugged features and a welcoming smile. Dressed in armor that glinted in the sunlight, a sword proudly belted at his side, he carried himself with an air of sturdy confidence. If you were being chased by a monster, this was the guy you'd want next to you.

"Hello, friend." He extended a hand in greeting as he reached me. "When did you arrive in my stretch of the forest?"

I took his hand and shook it. If I had any doubts about his strength, his crushing grip definitely would've eliminated them. I tried not to let concern that he might've just crippled me show on my face. "Right before you did."

He eyed my wet hair and sopping clothes. "Where's your boat?"

If Nellie had a trick for staying dry when you jumped through the Waters, couldn't she at least have shared that? It'd sure save me a shitload of embarrassment. "Would you believe, I swam here?" I asked in a tone sorely lacking conviction.

He answered with a hearty laugh. "That'd be impressive. The nearest land is nowhere near here."

"Would you believe, I fell out of a boat and then swam here?"

The man's smile widened. "I'd believe, it's not my business and you don't feel like talking about it. I can respect that."

"Thank you," I muttered, more than a little relieved to be let off the hook. "I'm looking for a dragon. I don't suppose you've seen one?"

He shook his head. "That's not a creature I'd easily forget."

No kidding.

His eyes moved along the shoreline. "I can't say that I've ever seen one here, and I can't imagine why you'd be looking for one."

I stifled a laugh. "That, my friend, is a long story." *And if you didn't believe the swimming story, you sure as hell won't believe that one.*

He frowned. "I'm afraid I can't point you to your dragon, but I can offer a fellow knight a fire to warm up beside before you continue your search."

I couldn't stop myself from cracking a smile. "Fellow knight?"

He nodded. "I can always spot one. Knights are confident, brave and the only men crazy enough to go looking for dragons," he added with a hearty chuckle.

I raked a hand through my dripping hair. "Well then, I guess I'm a knight. My name's Charlie by the way."

Dark eyes twinkling with amusement, the knight smiled. "Good to meet you, Charlie. My name's Robert, but please call me Bob."

"Huh," I muttered. "I didn't recognize you without the couch and television."

He raised an eyebrow. "Come again?"

Flipped images never ceased to amaze me. Who the hell would've guessed that Bob was a knight? "Never mind, Bob. Let me help you start that fire."

12

EMMA

I shut the door to my room, leaned back against it and closed my eyes. The world was slowly caving in on me and my sanity was crumbling beneath its weight. Could Dr. Spenser be right? Was I so broken that I'd invented my own reality to replace the one I couldn't face? Would it really be such a shock to discover that I was wrong about Charlie? I'd been a pathetic fool outside the facility, why should things be any different inside? What'd happened to Charlie in the hall? I hadn't been allowed to see him since he'd collapsed. There'd been no chance to 'step back and look at him.' So many questions filled my head, overwhelming me so entirely that when Tim dispensed our evening medications, I took the pills he gave me without giving it a second thought.

I could picture David's disapproving stare. He wouldn't be pleased to learn that they were drugging me. Memories of the night he first shared his opinion on chemically dulling your senses came rushing back to me, and I was instantly aroused. Even now, as hopeless and confused as I was about everything, my body reacted to him. Just the thought of him left me aching to be touched. Despite every uncertainty, I still desperately wanted to trust my husband. I'd give anything to feel his arms around me and know that I was loved. Without him, I didn't want to go on living. Could he possibly feel this lost without me?

I shook my head. That line of thinking would only fuel my anxiety. I needed to clear my head, not obsess over unanswerable questions. Hoping a hot shower might help, I wandered into the bathroom in a trance-like daze. The drug was clearly beginning to take effect. I absent-mindedly stripped off my clothes, leaving them wherever they happened to land. Then I started the water running in the shower and hazily watched it spill through my fingers as it warmed. I stepped in and as the rush of warm water spilled over me, my thoughts drifted to a simpler time…

…I sat on the living room carpet, drawing pictures at the coffee table, dressed in my favorite lacy pink dress— the one I called my 'princess dress'. My parents were busy getting ready for some fancy corporate dinner. I didn't know what it was for exactly. I was five years old, too young to understand or care about the event's details. All that mattered to me, was the tea party my babysitter and

I were going to have while they were out. I'd been looking forward to it for days.

The heavy stomp of my father's footsteps entered the room, followed by the hurried click of my mommy's heels.

"Damn it, Judy. Why the hell do you have to make everything so difficult?" My father was angry. "Why can't we just ask one of the neighbor girls to come over?"

"Albert," my mommy pleaded. I could tell she'd been crying. "I can't just leave her with some teenager we barely know."

I kept my eyes on my drawing but out of the corner of my eye, I could see my father's hands start to shake. I hated it when they fought. "I swear to God, you do this on purpose. Don't I deserve a night out with my wife by my side? Do I ever come first?" The babysitter wasn't coming, and my father blamed me for ruining their plans.

"What do you want me to do?" My mommy was getting louder. I took a quick peek up at her. Her make-up was beginning to streak down her cheeks with her tears.

I heard the door in the foyer open and close, then confident footsteps approaching the room, but I didn't look up from my picture. I didn't want to remind my father that I was in the room.

"Damn it, Judy," my father barked, "I want you to be by my side for once. Choose me over—"

My father's words were cut off midsentence, "Is there a problem?" I loved the sound of that British accent.

"David." My father looked surprised. He'd obviously been too distracted to hear him come in.

"Hello, Albert," David responded curtly, then nodded to my mommy, "Judy."

My mommy smiled, but it was painfully obvious that she'd been crying.

"We can't go. At least, Judy can't." My father's voice was getting loud again. "The babysitter cancelled and God forbid we try to find another one." He threw his wallet and keys at the couch.

My mommy's tearful voice answered, "I won't leave my little girl with a stranger."

My father took a deep breath, gearing up to yell again.

But David hindered whatever he was about to say. "How about with a friend?" He sat down on the couch beside where I sat on the carpet. "I wasn't all that excited about the dinner, and I heard that a princess is having a tea party here this evening." I knew he was talking to me as much as them now. His tone was much softer and gentler than the harsh tone he'd interrupted my father with. "I think that sounds like much more fun. Why would I want to be a boring old lawyer, when I could be a king having tea with a princess?"

My mommy dabbed at her cheeks with a tissue. "Don't you have a date for the dinner, David?"

David reached down and brushed a stray curl from my cheek. "Yes, but she's nowhere near as special as Princess Emma."

"Thank you, David," my mommy whispered. "We owe you one."

"Nonsense," he replied dismissively. "I owe you, for allowing me to spend some one on one time with my favorite girl."

Nodding, my father clapped David on the back as my mommy hastily touched up her makeup and gathered her coat and purse. "You are one of a kind, my friend."

David smiled. "Get out of here. Go do your boring grown-up stuff and let us get on with our tea."

I looked up at David as the front door closed. He was watching me with more love than either of my parents ever did.

We spent the evening wearing paper crowns and drinking juice from little plastic teacups. I was pretty sure I was the only girl in town who'd ever had a British king attend her tea party.

When it grew late and I started to yawn, David put on one of my movies. I curled up—safe and warm, beside the most sought after bachelor in town—and fell asleep in his arms to the singing of a cartoon princess...

...By the time I finished showering, the medication had taken full effect and I was feeling dangerously unsteady. I almost toppled out of the shower reaching for a towel. Luckily, I managed to break my fall by grabbing the edge of the tub. I dried off as best as I could, leaning against the wall to keep my balance. Then I stumbled to the dresser in the bedroom, yanked a drawer open and bent to pull out a pair of pajamas. But leaning made the room start spinning, so I dropped the clothes and shuffled to the bed. I half-laid, half-fell on top of it. I just needed to rest a minute. Then I'd get dressed and crawl under the covers. A second later, I was asleep...

...I opened my eyes, expecting to see the bedroom ceiling. Instead, a canopy of stars adorned the sky above me. I brushed a lazy hand over what should've been a blanket and felt a soft bed of grass. A warm breeze danced across my naked skin, playfully toying with wisps of my hair as nocturnal tones echoed through the stillness—the melodious chirp of a chorus of insects, a soft rustling as leaves frolicked in the breeze and the distant song of a lonely night bird calling for its mate.

I'd dreamt of being in this clearing with David. I tried to remember the dreams but where the memory of him should've been, I only found emptiness—a nauseating feeling that something vital that'd once been there now was lost. I couldn't recall a single moment we'd spent together. Terrified, I called his name out into the night, "David!" My desperate voice echoed through the silence unanswered and I felt an unbearable ache in my heart.

Then he stepped from the mouth of a cave. For a brief moment, I thought I saw our upstairs hallway behind him, but I blinked and saw nothing but rock and darkness. It didn't matter. Nothing mattered but the fact that he'd come. His brilliant blue eyes brimmed with as much love for me as they ever had. They also seemed to shimmer with tears, but that was probably just a reflection of the moonlight on the water. I concentrated on the features of the face I'd loved all my life. How could I have forgotten him? "I couldn't remember your face," I whispered. "I was losing you."

He moved toward me tentatively and knelt beside me in the grass. His warm breath sent a shiver through me as he whispered, "You'll never lose me, Princess. You will always be mine."

He kissed me gingerly at first, like he feared I might break but as I kissed him back with every bit of want and need that I felt, his kiss deepened. He slipped a hand in my hair, cradling my head in his palm, holding me to his mouth. Somewhere in the back of my mind, Dr. Spenser's words echoed and I couldn't help but wonder if this was just a dream. I pulled my head back to look at him. A hint of sorrow glinted in his blue eyes as he returned my gaze. I touched his face and a tear slid down my cheek. Dream or not, I needed him. "I've missed the feel of you," I whispered. "Show me that you're real."

He took my hand from his cheek and kissed it. Then he pulled back to crouch above my naked body. Hunger glinting in his eyes, he rasped, "I've missed the taste of you."

A twinge of excitement flared through flesh that ached to feel his touch.

He kissed my lips, then started moving lower at a torturously unhurried pace. He'd always known exactly how to tease my body until the need became excruciating and the only thing in the world that I wanted was the feel of him inside me. His lips trailed slowly… whispering over my neck… slowly lower… lingering on my breasts… with strong hands… and a hungry mouth… arousing places lower down… trailing his tongue… with agonizing slowness… down my belly… heating flesh that screamed for him… to my belly button… lower still… he lifted his head as he reached my thighs… and parted them… staring wickedly into my eyes… then he dipped his head… the slightest whisper of his tongue stroked over me… and a wave of pleasure pulsed through me… he confidently set a rhythm … matching his moves to my desires… perfectly… teasing, torturing… delighting in the power he held over me… surges of pleasure coursed through me… intensifying… until the need to feel him inside me… became desperate and fierce… strong fingers pushed inside me… unraveling me… until an explosion of ecstasy convulsed through my body… a sensation so intense… I could barely stand the feel of it… overwhelming me to the point… that I had to pull away… but his hands held me firmly in place… forcing me to surrender… driving me beyond conscious thought… until I became nothing… but nerve endings… I felt nothing… but pleasure… there was nothing… but him.

As my senses came back to me, his body lowered and a frantic need to feel his skin against mine consumed me. I tugged at his clothes and he hastily helped me tear them off. "I need to feel you inside me," I pleaded.

With a deep throated sound that was almost a growl, he thrust inside me—filling me, completing me—and we cried out together. I clung to him, urgently gripping his body, needing him as close as possible and he lowered his weight so that his flesh pressed so firmly against mine, I could barely sense where I ended and he began. His kisses grew deeper and hungrier until he began to moan. The start of his climax ignited mine and together we shattered the night's silence, overtaking the peaceful sounds of nature with our carnal cries until both of us were spent.

Dropping his head between my neck and shoulder, he nuzzled my ear and whispered, "I'll never let you go."

"Promise me," I begged.

Lifting his head to look into my eyes, he brushed his thumb across my bottom lip. "I swear it to you, Emma. You will always be mine." He planted his palms on either side of my body to lift himself.

But as his chest started rising, I wrapped my limbs around him. "Not yet. I want to stay like this."

Locking his eyes with mine, he gently lowered himself back down. "My Princess, I would stay like this forever."

13

CHARLIE

It was morning and I was back in the infirmary on that uncomfortable mattress with the stench of chemical disinfectant burning in my nostrils. I didn't remember jumping back through the Waters. I must've fallen asleep in the Dream World and woken in our world, the 'other world' as Nellie called it. It was weird. The way she saw the dreams as her primary world, like this one was the dream to her. Who the hell knew? Maybe she was right.

Bob and I had talked for hours in the Dream World while the fire warmed me and dried my soggy clothes. Bob was an honest to goodness knight in shining armor. It was his sworn duty to keep anyone who happened upon his shore safe from harm. I considered asking him what it would cost to hire a knight to help me search for a dragon, but figured it'd be hard to explain why the dragon couldn't be hurt. I could just imagine that conversation. *Would you believe, the dragon is a beautiful girl in this alternate reality where you're a crotchety old jackass?* Yeah. Involving Bob probably wasn't the best idea, but I would've loved to learn the story of the grumpy old man who was a noble protector at heart.

Footsteps approaching the bed snapped my attention back to the present. It had to be the toad. Might as well get the conversation over with. I couldn't pretend to be asleep forever. I opened my eyes to a heavy-lidded squint and the toad's bloated face leaned over me. I was sorely tempted to shut my eyes and hope he hadn't noticed, but I didn't.

I blinked, adjusting to the light and human Spenser stood next to me with a look of concern etched on his aged face. "You gave us a bit of a scare yesterday, Charlie."

"Sorry," I croaked, cleared my throat, then added, "How rude of me." I was in serious need of a drink of water. My throat felt like it'd been lined with sandpaper.

Spenser wheeled a stool up to the bed and sat down with a tired sigh. "Everything has to be a joke with you, doesn't it? You and I both know that's a coping mechanism. Do you want to tell me what you saw?"

"It was nothing. Sometimes I just forget how ugly you are. You caught me off guard and it scared the shit out of me. I'll try harder not to let it get to me next time."

I cleared my throat again as my eyes drifted to the bedside table. There had to be some water somewhere.

Spenser stood up with a disappointed frown, crossed the room and opened the door to a full-size refrigerator. Trays of medicine bottles, little glass vials and syringes full of God-knows-what neatly lined the shelves inside. The doctor opened a drawer at the bottom of the fridge, took out a bottled water, nudged the door shut with his elbow and carried the bottle back across the room. "One of these days, I'm going to get you to realize that I'm not the bad guy. I'm here to help you." He handed me the water then settled back onto his stool.

I hesitated briefly as I stared at the bottle, wondering whether it'd been laced with something. Shit. I'd been spending way too much time around paranoid mental patients. Shaking my head at my own stupidity, I twisted the cap off and eagerly downed half the bottle.

Spenser waited patiently until I stopped drinking, then he continued, "If you made an effort to accept your hallucinations for what they are, we could actually make some progress. With therapy and medication, we could get these delusions under control and you could attempt to live a normal life. Or would you rather stay here forever? Sometimes I think deep down you've given up on yourself." He exhaled, looking exhausted and every bit his age. "We can tackle this together, Charlie. Let me help you."

"That's a tempting offer. Maybe some other time." I wasn't in the mood for his psycho-babble. I was too anxious to find Emma and see if she'd still talk to me. "Am I free to go?"

The doctor rolled his eyes. "I'm going to hold you to that, Charlie. 'Maybe some other time.' We are eventually going to make some progress."

I shot him a phony grin. "Is that supposed to give me hope or make me feel threatened?"

"It's supposed to eventually penetrate that thick skull of yours." He straightened a little, leaning toward me. "I'm going to ask one more time. What did you see in the hall yesterday? Even for you, that was a pretty major episode."

I sat up so Spenser couldn't loom over me and shrugged. "You looked bored. I wanted to give you something to do after you were done talking to Emma."

His brow furrowed with a look of genuine concern. "You should give her some space. She has enough to work through without you complicating things."

"Why don't you give her some space? She seems to like talking to me more."

Spenser flipped back to toad form and glared at me, hatred flashing in his bulging eyes. "You won't like the consequences if you interfere with her therapy."

I feigned a look of shock. "I'm pretty sure that was a threat."

"You're free to go, Charlie," the toad croaked. "Just watch yourself."

"Of course, Sir." I gave him a one-fingered salute. "I'll be on my best behavior."

I stopped walking in the middle of the hallway and looked through the window into the large common room. Bob was in his usual spot on the couch, sporting khakis and a dark blue button-down shirt. It was the first time I'd ever seen him wearing anything other than a jogging suit. It suited him, made him look more respectable or maybe I just perceived him differently now that I'd seen his Dream form. The television was off, but Bob was staring at it anyway. He must've felt me watching because he turned his head and looked at me. I smiled and waved to the old knight and to my complete shock, he nodded. For a flicker of a second, he was young and handsome and dressed in armor. Then old Bob was back, scowling at the dormant television. "Stupid sons of bitches!"

I shook my head as I started toward the small room Emma and I spent most of our free time in, hoping I'd find her there. But Nellie was the only person in the room. She was sitting at one of the tables, playing a game of checkers...with herself. I watched her as I walked toward the table. She moved a black piece, sat back and studied the board, moved a red piece then repeated the process. Each time her invisible opponent moved, she scowled like the move surprised her.

She glanced up as I stopped beside the table. Returning her attention to the checkerboard, she greeted me in a squeaky monotone, "You're awake. That's good."

"Yeah, I made it back. Thanks for pushing me." I hoped the sarcasm wouldn't be lost on her.

"You're welcome," she muttered. Apparently, she hadn't picked up on the sarcasm. "And you're welcome for pulling you out in the first place." Or, maybe she had.

"Right. Thanks for that."

She moved an 'opponent' piece, then sat back and studied the board as she muttered, "Damn it." Then she looked up at me. "Can't you see I'm busy? Emma's not here. Isn't she the one you're looking for?"

"You know she is, Nellie. Don't waste my time with foolishness." Maybe it wasn't nice to throw her own words back at her, but I couldn't resist.

She shook her head as she studied the game, then she jumped an 'opponent' piece and smiled triumphantly as she removed it from the board. "She's fine, boy."

"Charlie," I corrected.

"She's fine, *Charlie*," she repeated mockingly.

I ignored the taunt. "So, did you look out for her last night?"

"Do I look like a bodyguard to you?" She hunched closer to the table to study her 'opponent's' options. "I did have a little talk with her though."

I moved the next 'opponent' piece for her, jumping and removing two of her checkers from the board. "Would you mind telling me what you said?"

She scowled up at me. "Yes, I would mind. I'm in the middle of something."

I turned and started walking away. I didn't have the patience for her bullshit. "Sorry, Nellie. What was I thinking, expecting you to actually help a fellow Dream see-er out?"

Her chair screeched angrily as she pushed back from the table. "You can be a real ungrateful bastard! You know that?"

I didn't even break my stride. "Yup, I'm an ass."

As I stepped out into the hall, I decided to head to Emma's room. There weren't a whole lot of places left to look for her, and the fact that I hadn't run into her yet was starting to make me nervous. As soon as I started walking, the door to the hall bathroom swung open and a twitching man-shaped horde of insects swarmed out, watched me pass, then fell into step behind me.

I stopped short and spun around. "Do I look like I want a shadow, Frank?"

Barely avoiding running into me, human Frank studied me with absent confusion like I was talking in a language he didn't speak. "I don't know. Do you?"

"No, dumb ass. I don't. Go annoy somebody else."

With a wounded pout on his bug-infested face, Frank swarmed off.

In a few more steps, I found myself at Emma's door. Only this time, it didn't feel perfectly natural to be there. Swallowing the lump in my throat, I knocked.

"Who's there?" She sounded groggy, but I also detected a hint of fear. Was that because she was afraid it wasn't me, or afraid it was?

I hesitated a second before answering, "It's me, Em."

"Charlie!" She sounded happy to hear me. Thank God.

"Yeah, I'm back," I announced to the closed door. "Any chance you missed me?"

"I'll be right there." That didn't answer my question, but she was talking to me. That was a good sign. At least, I hoped it was.

Emma opened the door in more modest pajamas than the day before. A little pink t-shirt subtly hugged her perfect curves and pink plaid pajama shorts hung low on her hips. She was sporting a just-rolled-out-of-bed hairstyle, probably because she had. I didn't see any hesitation in her gorgeous eyes. In fact, she smiled like she was really happy to see me.

I was searching for the right words to say when she flipped. This wasn't like the usual flip. Emma was suddenly lying naked on the grass and I was kneeling beside her, unblinking, unable to draw a breath. The sky above us was covered with stars, moonlight shimmered on the quiet surface of a lake behind her and a cave loomed in the darkness off to our side. It was as if we'd fallen straight into the Dream World. Real as it all seemed, I knew this was just a vision— a glimpse into someone else's dream—but she was staring up at me with a look of desire so fierce that I'd almost describe it as desperate. I'd never been so turned on in my life. Unfortunately, my expression probably made that obvious and so did another part of me that I had no control over. I couldn't seem to stop gawking or speak or form a thought. Compared to this, plunging into the Dream Waters was nothing.

She flipped back to Emma in pajamas and we were standing in the hall just like before. I took an unsteady breath and wiped the sweat off my brow.

"Charlie?" Her voice was timid and shaky. "Are you alright?"

I stared at her, trying to remember how to think and speak. In other words, trying to ignore the massive erection that was diverting all the blood away from my brain. "Yeah. I'm fine." But I didn't sound fine.

She put a hand on my arm. "How can I help?" Then she flipped again and we were back in the Dream World. With her perfect naked body lying next to me, I was painfully aware that she was still touching me.

"I just need to sit down." I was still standing wasn't I? "Why don't you go get dressed while I sit a minute?" *Close your eyes,* I told myself. But I couldn't look away.

"Do you want to come sit on the bed while I change?" Her eyes were hungry and wanting, *pleading.*

More than anything. "No, uh...thanks." I backed up, feeling strangely detached from myself since my body still appeared to be kneeling in the grass. A distant sensation told me that my back had met the wall and I clumsily slid down it, struggling to reconcile what I felt with what I saw until I vaguely detected the floor beneath me. "I'll be fine out here."

"Tell me what to do," she whispered.

The smell of her perfumed body was intoxicating and all the suggestions that came to mind were pretty pornographic, but I could only feel faintly guilty while staring at her naked body. She stared back at me with an irresistible come-hither look gleaming in those eyes. *She wants me.* I drew a shaky breath. *Stop being an idiot* my brain dimly scolded. *She's not yours.* "Go get ready, Em. I just need a minute."

"Did I do something to upset you?" she whispered.

Damn it. "No. Never." I forced a weak smile. "I guess I'm still a little shaky this morning, but I'll be fine."

She flipped again and Emma in pajamas was sitting next to me on the hallway floor. She looked so scared and childlike as she smiled at me. "I don't want to drive you away, Charlie. I need you."

Please don't say that now. With a swift mental kick, my brain finally managed to regain control. "I'm not going anywhere, but we'll miss breakfast if you don't go get dressed."

She nodded, searching my eyes. "Promise you're alright?"

I let out a heavy sigh. "I swear it, Em."

Eyes widening, she inhaled sharply. "I'll go get dressed then." Looking dazed, she stood up, walked into her room and shut the door.

"Take your time," I muttered to the closed door as I dropped my head back against the wall.

14

EMMA

I stood in the bedroom, gripping the doorknob. *I swear it, Emma.* When Charlie spoke those words, images from a dream had come flooding back to me. *I swear it to you, Emma. You will always be mine.* David's voice echoed clearly in my head, as if I'd just heard him say the words. The dream was so vivid. *I was lying in the grass beneath a sky full of stars with a lake behind me and a cave in front of me. I was panicking because I couldn't remember David's face.* That made sense. I'd been terrified that I was forgetting him the day before. *Then David stepped from the cave.* A rush of images came pouring back. *David crouching over me, kissing me, his mouth everywhere, his body pressed against mine.* It felt more like actual memories than fragments from a dream. He said he wouldn't let me go. I begged him to promise me. *I swear it to you.*

I shook my head. What was I doing? That was just a dream. I'd been thinking of David before I went to bed. It was only natural for him to find his way into my dreams, but this was reality. Charlie was out in the hall and something was wrong. I should be out there with him.

I hastily grabbed some clothes from the dresser, shed my pajamas and slipped into them. According to Dr. Spenser, Charlie suffered from delusions. I didn't want to believe that because Charlie was my rock. Spenser was right about that much. But something was obviously wrong. What was he reacting to just now, and what was he reacting to before he collapsed? Had I been deluding myself about Charlie? I had to admit it was a possibility, but I wanted it to be untrue so badly…for both of us. Even if Charlie was delusional and I'd imagined a connection that wasn't there, I'd still want to help him. He'd been a friend when I desperately needed one. It was time to return the favor. When I finished dressing, I took a deep breath and opened the door. Charlie was still sitting on the floor with his eyes closed and his head tipped back against the wall.

I sat down next to him. "Charlie?"

Without opening his eyes, he smiled and whispered, "Hey, Em." Then he turned his head and looked at me.

Resting my head against the wall beside his, I smiled back at him. For a minute, we were both quiet.

Charlie finally broke the silence. "Did you miss me?"

"Terribly," I whispered.

"I was afraid you'd want to keep your distance after my outburst." He chuckled, but I saw the apprehension in his eyes.

"Dr. Spenser wouldn't let me near you after you passed out," I whispered, "I'm sorry."

A tear slipped down his cheek as he squeezed my hand. "I'm sorry I left you alone. I promised I'd always have your back."

"I didn't know what to think. Spenser said our connection was all in my head..." my voice broke and I couldn't hold back the tears.

Charlie scooped me into a bear hug. "It isn't, Em. I don't usually connect to people easily, but I felt our connection the moment we met."

I wrapped my arms around him, hugging him back.

"If you don't want to be around me because of my behavior, I'll understand," he murmured, "but don't let Spenser ruin our friendship."

"He couldn't," I whispered. "You mean too much to me, Charlie. I couldn't make it through any of this without you."

He touched his head to mine. "I'm sorry I wasn't there for you yesterday."

I sank against him, closed my eyes and felt safe.

He tightened his squeeze a little. "We should probably get to breakfast before they come looking for us."

Breakfast was more than half over by the time Charlie and I walked in, but I couldn't have cared less. We ate quickly then headed straight to our usual spot.

Neither of us said it, but I think we were both relieved to find the room unoccupied. My last exchange with Nellie had been pretty unsettling, and I wanted to talk to Charlie without worrying about her inserting comments into our conversation. I wanted to find out what'd frightened him so much the day before, why he'd lost consciousness, what'd happened in the hall this morning. I guess a part of me still needed to justify his actions to prove to myself that Dr. Spenser was wrong about him.

We sat on our loveseat, facing each other. Neither of us had said a word since we walked into the room and the longer the silence dragged on, the more awkward it felt. Charlie usually broke our uncomfortable silences, but I knew he needed me to end this one. "Can I ask what happened yesterday?"

He ran a hand through his hair. "Yeah. I don't think we can avoid the subject."

"You can tell me anything, Charlie. I won't judge."

He nodded and I watched his anxiety turn to resolve. "What's the right way to start a life story?"

"It's your story," I whispered. "It starts however you want it to."

Smiling, he closed his eyes and took a deep breath. "According to Dr. Spenser, I'm a schizophrenic who suffers from paranoid delusions...but Spenser's wrong."

I wanted Spenser to be wrong about a lot of things. Charlie didn't seem schizophrenic—until yesterday, he'd never acted the least bit unusual—but what'd happened yesterday, and this morning?

"I know every paranoid schizophrenic would probably say that." He opened his eyes and looked at me, waiting for a response.

"If Spenser's wrong, what's right?" I whispered.

He looked up at the ceiling. "I don't see the same things you see when I look at people."

"What do you see?"

"I see this world but I can also see another one." He took another deep breath. "It's hard to explain to someone who can't see it."

I ignored the churning in my stomach. "Take your time."

He seemed surprised by my encouragement, but he went on without commenting on it. "Everyone has another form in the other world, and I can see people flip from one form to the other when I look at them."

Why was I so shocked? Charlie was a mental patient, a diagnosed schizophrenic. I'd known all along that delusion was a very possible explanation for his actions. "What is this other world?"

"The Dream World. It's where we go when we sleep. All my life, I've watched everybody around me flip to their Dream forms—my grade school teachers morphed into monsters, bums on the sidewalk turned into knights and elves—and when I reacted to the changes that nobody else could see, people thought I was crazy." He lowered his head. "And I'm sure you agree with them now."

"Dream World," I repeated, liking the sound of it. "Do you meet other people in this world of dreams?" Was I humoring him or was I so delusional that I was willing to accept his delusions, rather than confront my own?

Charlie looked up, studying me curiously. "Yeah. That's why you wake up and remember dreaming about other people."

Of course I knew the idea was absurd. Didn't I? I found myself thinking of the vivid dreams I'd been having of David every night. I woke up almost hearing him and feeling him. I smiled at Charlie. "Why do you look so surprised?"

"Because you're still here," he muttered. "This is the point in the conversation where people usually back away looking for an exit."

"No judgments, remember?" Foolish as I knew it was to even consider the possibility of his Dream World, the idea made my skin tingle. Besides, I'd already resigned myself to sticking with Charlie no matter what. "Can you actually go to this Dream World or do you just see glimpses of people's Dream forms?"

"We all go there when we sleep, but I can go when I'm awake if I want."

"Is that what happened yesterday?"

"Kind of. I don't usually go quite like that, but I didn't go on purpose yesterday. I was sort of sucked in." He paused like he didn't know what else to say.

"Have you ever seen me in the Dream World?"

"No," he whispered sheepishly. "I've tried to look for you, but I don't recognize the place where I see you."

"So, you've seen my Dream form?"

He hesitated a second before answering, "Yeah."

"What do I look like?" I prodded, curious to hear how he pictured me.

He combed his fingers through his hair. "You look exactly like you do here, maybe a bit more beautiful if that's possible."

I felt myself blush at the compliment. "You said you don't recognize where I am. Do you see people in a particular place?"

"Sometimes," he answered softly. "Most of the time, all I see is the person's flipped image but every once in a while, I can see the area around them."

"Where did you see me?"

He focused somewhere distant. "In a clearing in a forest."

"Tell me more," I whispered.

"I was catching clear glimpses of it this morning." His face reddened. "The sky was full of stars, there was a lake and a cave."

I stopped breathing. *Could last night have been real?* I looked at Charlie's flushed cheeks and re-membered lying naked in the grass—David walk-ing toward me, his mouth on my body, his body pressed against mine. If Charlie really could see into dreams, how much of mine had he seen? I was embarrassed to ask, but far more enchanted by the idea that this place might actually exist and that I could meet my husband there. Impossible as it was, it seemed equally impossible for him to imagine a place exactly like the one in my dreams. "What was I wearing when you saw me?"

He let out an unsteady breath. "Nothing."

Could I really have been with David? Heart racing, I looked at Charlie. He'd just shared his deepest se-cret, now he sat next to me completely vulnerable. If these visions of his were real, he'd spent his whole life being written off as crazy when he wasn't.

I slid closer and wrapped my arms around him. "I'm still here, Charlie. I'm not going anywhere." I felt him shudder as he dropped his head to my shoul-der and began to cry.

I held my friend until he spilled every tear he'd kept inside for so long, and found myself longing to believe in a world of dreams.

15

DAVID

The aches in my body cruelly wrenched me from sleep long before I'd have chosen to wake and as the bleariness of slumber faded, I found myself still uncomfortably hunched in the chair by the fireplace. Across the room, shards of glass—bathed in a glistening puddle of vintage Absinthe—littered the floor. The jagged pieces sparkled brilliantly as they caught the light of the rising sun, streaming through the window. Standing groggily, I brushed a hand over the stubble on my face and a rush of images from my dreams bombarded me. I could still feel the softness of her skin against my lips, and the taste of her still seemed to linger on my tongue.

Rage welled up from deep inside me but I quickly suppressed. Allowing emotion to control my actions would accomplish nothing. Anger channeled into calculated efforts to bring her back could achieve far more than blind fury. I had to proceed one well thought out step at a time, and abolishing the visitation restriction was the first step. Revenge would have to wait.

Stepping over the spilled liquid and shattered glass, I exited the lounge and headed toward the staircase. This wasn't the first time that another man possessed the power to keep her from me. However, this was different. Emma belonged to me now and truth be told, it'd been much easier to steal her away back then.

My thoughts wandered to earlier in the evening of that wedding reception years ago...

...The bride and groom beamed as they danced their first dance as husband and wife, but it didn't particularly interest me. Attending the wedding reception of a client was more an obligation than a pleasure. The only upside, was that it was an evening with the Reeds and since Albert and Judy Reed were quite close to the groom's family, their daughter had been invited as well. The groom's younger sister was around the same age as Emma and over the years, the two teenagers had endured countless gatherings in each other's company.

As waitresses flitted about serving coffee and cake, our foursome watched the happy couple twirl around the dance floor. Emma absent-mindedly pushed the cake around her plate with a fork as she watched them dance.

"For God's sake, Emma," Albert snapped. "You're seventeen years old. At what age do you plan to stop playing with your food like a child?"

Emma dropped the fork to her plate and neatly folded her hands on the tabletop. "Sorry. I guess I'm not that hungry."

"Speak up when I talk to you," Albert barked, scrutinizing his daughter disapprovingly, "and sit up straight."

Judy placed her hand on top of his, a silent plea to let it drop.

Scowling, Albert pushed back from the table. "I'm going to get a scotch. Would anyone else like a drink?"

Emma shook her head without meeting his eyes.

He raised an eyebrow to me, and I cleared my throat. "No thank you."

Judy looked up at Albert as she slid her chair back from the table. "I'll come with you. I'm not sure what I want yet."

Albert smiled at his wife as she took his arm, and they headed toward the bar.

As I watched them walk away, I placed a hand on the back of Emma's chair and leaned in closer to her. "One of these days, I'm going to snap when he speaks to you like that," I murmured, noting her slight shiver at the warmth of my breath with silent satisfaction.

She looked up at me from beneath her long lashes. "Will you dance with me tonight?"

"No. I will not," I answered with a stern stare.

Uncertainty flashed in her eyes as she whispered, "Why?"

"Because," I answered softly, "I don't believe I could have you in my arms, without giving away the fact that I've had you in my bed."

Her cheeks flushed with color at my words.

"You give yourself away as well, Princess," I murmured. "It would be foolish to bring attention to ourselves."

Green eyes sparkling beneath hooded eyelids, she looked up at me and purred, "I miss the feel of you."

Nonchalantly knocking a fork to the floor with my elbow, I bent and slipped my right hand between her knees beneath the tablecloth while retrieving the utensil with my left. As I straightened from the floor, my hand slowly advanced up the smooth flesh of her inner thigh. I felt her body tense to keep from reacting and suppressed a wicked grin. When I reached the lace of her panties, I leaned in close to her ear and rasped, "I miss the taste of you." She breathed a ragged sigh as my fingers slipped beneath the sheer fabric.

Lightly brushing a fingertip over her sensitized flesh, I reveled in her struggle to keep silent and still as she stifled a reflexive shudder. With a throbbing need to penetrate her, I slid my fingers possessively inside her and a soft moan escaped her lips as her eyelids drooped.

Feeling how deliciously ripe she was for me, a low growl rumbled deep in my throat and I ached to pull her to my lap. Well aware that I was dangerously approaching the limit of what either of us could refrain from reacting to, I grudgingly withdrew my fingers and trailed them back down the softness of her thigh. Through all of this, I kept a subtle eye on Albert and Judy as they laughed at the bar.

"I need to be with you," Emma pleaded breathlessly.

Though I was just as painfully aroused, I regarded her with detached coolness. "Patience, Princess. Go dance."

"I want to stay here with you," she protested softly.

"I cannot appear disinterested if you stay this near to me," I rasped, watching Judy walk away from her husband and exit the room. "It is all that I can do not to lift you onto this tabletop and take you in front of the entire wedding reception."

Her lustful expression suggested that she wouldn't resist if I actually did, arousing me all the more.

"Patience," I reiterated as Albert approached the bar again. "Go dance."

With a slight pout to her lips and a lovely blush to her cheeks, she stood and discreetly lowered her dress where my hand had swept beneath it. I watched her move to the dance floor to join the other girls and stifled a groan as her slender hips began to gyrate to the music. I knew the sensuality of her movement was due to the way I'd just aroused her and that every seductive writhe was not only for my benefit, but also designed to frustrate me because I'd toyed with her and sent her off.

I drew a cleansing breath as I stood from my chair, then made my way over to the bar. Albert was standing beside it, downing another scotch.

I made a quick show of glancing over the faces in the room. "Where's Judy?"

"Bathroom." He raised his glass and took another sip.

I'd lost count of how many drinks he'd consumed—as I'm sure, had he. "How are you planning to get home?" I inquired, my voice conveying a bit more irritation than I intended.

"I'm driving. How the fuck else would I get home?" There was a subtle but unmistakable slur to his words.

My heart began to pound. "You aren't in any condition to drive, Albert."

"Well, it's too damn far to take a cab."

I took a deep breath, reigning in my fury. "I am not about to let you drive drunk with your daughter," as an afterthought I added, "and your wife in the car."

"Well, Mr. Fucking Boy Scout, what would you suggest I do?"

Though I wanted to suggest that I knock some sense into that brainless head of his, I calmly replied, "Get a room here for the night. Surprise Judy with a romantic evening and a leisurely brunch in the morning."

"A romantic evening?" he echoed sarcastically. "Just me, Judy and Emma? You are aware that not everyone has a carefree do-whatever-the-fuck-you-please lifestyle, right?"

Jaw clenched, I carefully restrained my anger. "I'll drive Emma home."

"She doesn't like being home alone at night." Albert's words were drenched in bitterness. "Judy wouldn't leave our precious little pain in the ass all alone and frightened."

I managed to unclench my jaw enough to reply, "Then I'll bring her to my house. You can call me when you're on your way back tomorrow, and I'll drive her home."

"Alright, I'm sold." Albert shook his head. "We're going to owe you big when you're married."

"All part of my brilliant plan," I replied with a forced smile, which sufficed since he wasn't sober enough to tell the fucking difference.

Albert went off to see about getting a room whilst I ordered a single malt from the bar. Then I slowly made my way back across the room, eyes fixed on Emma. Sitting down at our empty table, I nursed my drink and maintained a guardedly neutral expression as I watched her dance.

It wasn't long, before Albert and Judy returned to inform me that they had a room and were calling it a night. Judy thanked me emphatically for my generosity and waved goodbye to Emma as they left, neither of them stopping to say a word to her.

Emma returned to the table and was ready to leave the moment I informed her that she'd be coming home with me but I told her to go back and dance some more, reminding her that we ought not to appear in a hurry to leave together the moment her parents disappeared.

Her lips curved into a coy smile. "If we have to stay, will you buy me a drink?"

"I would do anything you asked me to," I replied huskily. "What would you like?"

"Something I'm not old enough to have," she whispered mischievously.

I raised an eyebrow. "That would be me."

Smirking, she whispered, "Buy me a drink."

"I will buy you a soda," I responded sternly, "but I will not buy you alcohol."

"So, I'm old enough to take to bed. But I'm not old enough to buy a drink for?" she questioned playfully.

"It has nothing to do with your age," I whispered, "and legally speaking, you're not old enough to do either with."

"But that won't stop you from taking me to your bed."

"No, it won't," I replied in a guttural whisper. "I can't help myself where you're concerned. I want you desperately, all the time."

"Never mind the drink. Take me home," she purred. "I want to feel you inside me."

And that was the extent of my feeble self-control. "I'll get our coats," I rasped, stifling the overwhelming urge to put my hands on her right then and there.

16

CHARLIE

I pulled off my t-shirt, flung it and watched it briefly connect with the chair across the room then drop to the floor. Shaking my head, I flopped down on the bed and sprawled across the mattress. It felt good to be back in my own bed after lying on that lumpy excuse for a mattress in the infirmary. As I tugged the blankets up to my chin, a million thoughts raced through my head. I figured my odds of drifting off to sleep, just because my head was on a pillow, were somewhere in the range of slim to none.

I did it. I told Emma about my Sight, and she didn't run away screaming. Was it possible for somebody without Dream Sight to believe it all anyway or was she just amazing enough to accept her friend, quirks and all, like we'd promised since we met? I wasn't sure. But she didn't look at me like I was a psycho, and that alone amazed me. There was just one monstrous detail that I still hadn't shared with Emma. When she asked what her Dream form looked like, I couldn't bring myself to tell her about the dragon. I didn't exactly lie. Her Dream form really did look the same as her form in this world. I just left out the part about her also having a dragon form. If by some miraculous leap of faith, Emma actually believed in the Dream World and my ability to see it, it seemed wrong to tell her about the fiery-eyed beast that lurked behind her. That thing scared the living shit out of me. I couldn't do that to her.

After sharing my secret, I'd cried like a baby and while I was blubbering on Emma's shoulder, a shadow had descended over the room. I'd looked up and found myself face to face with the dragon. The beast was a hundred times more terrifying up close than it'd seemed from a distance—which is saying a lot, considering I practically shit my pants the first time I saw it at a distance. Nellie said Dream images were just memories of the past or visions of the future, but those fiery eyes bore straight through me. I would've sworn that dragon was watching me. At least I'd managed to keep it together this time, instead of screaming and passing out.

I punched at my pillow with a frustrated sigh. I wasn't going to fall asleep anytime soon. If I wanted to get to the Dream World, I'd have to jump. If Nellie hadn't been such a crotchety bitch earlier, I might've asked her for pointers on ending up where you wanted to when you jumped into the Waters, not that I'd have held my breath for answers. Nellie had figured it out on her own. If she could do it, I could too. Right? Shoving my chaotic thoughts aside, I concentrated on calling the Waters until the clear blue ripples appeared. I pictured Emma, hoping that'd help me find her. Then I braced for the cold and jumped.

Plunging through the icy depths, I focused my thoughts on Emma and ignored the biting cold. *Emma.* I pictured the clearing I'd seen her in. *Emma.* I thought of the lake and the star-filled sky, refusing to let the Waters strip the memory from me. *Emma.* I pictured the cave. *Her naked body. Those hypnotic green eyes filled with lust.* It was impossible for me to picture that starry night without seeing her perfect body lying naked on the grass. *Emma.* I held the thought. *Emma.* I lost all feeling to the cold. *Take me to Emma.* I fought the disorientation and ignored the pain, clinging desperately to the thought of her. The Water seemed to knock me around for longer than usual, like it knew I was holding onto something and was determined not to let me. Maybe my resolve was growing stronger or maybe it was just the visual of Emma's naked body that my stubborn mind refused to part with. Whatever the reason, I kept the thought of her from slipping away until the Waters finally admitted defeat and tossed me to the surface.

I emerged gasping for breath and blinded by sunlight. I'd been so focused on remembering Emma that I'd forgotten all about keeping my eyes closed. Somewhere in the distance, a voice cried out and I paddled blindly toward the noise, hoping it'd lead me to shore. Slowly, my eyes adjusted and a blurred smudge of shoreline took shape up ahead.

When I reached the shore, I dragged myself out of the Water, crawled until I reached dry ground, then dropped to my belly. Not far from me, a thick line of trees marked the edge of the forest. Emma's clearing could be somewhere inside those trees, but I doubted it. If I'd landed where I wanted to, I would've emerged from that lake by her clearing. This place looked familiar, but it wasn't because of Emma. I'd walked this shore before, I was almost sure of it. I dropped my head with a frustrated sigh. I'd been so freaking proud of myself for holding onto Emma's image, but it hadn't done me a damn bit of good. The Water had still carried me wherever it felt like. So, why did this shore feel so familiar?

I spun toward the Water and quickly discovered that I wasn't alone. A short distance down shore, a man sat at the edge of the forest—knees drawn up to his chest, arms folded on top of his knees, bent head resting on his arms. I remembered the cries that'd led me to shore, and felt like a moron for forgetting. The noise must've come from that guy. *But what made him cry out like that?* I did briefly debate whether to walk over to him or dive into the Water and get the hell out of there, but I'd come this far. What'd be the point of jumping right back out? This wasn't Emma's clearing, but maybe that guy knew how to get there. Maybe the clearing really was inside those trees. *Maybe the dragon made him howl like that.* That'd mean I'd found Emma, but it'd also mean I could be facing the dragon at any second. *Facing it in the Dream World, its world.* After seeing it up close, I was pretty sure that was a position I never wanted to be in.

If I was staying, lying on my stomach probably wasn't the best defensive position. So, I hopped to my feet and studied the man as I walked toward him. He was wearing sturdy leather boots that reached more than halfway up his calves, the legs of his pants tapered and tucked into the boots, and he somehow managed to make that look manly and not at all ridiculous. No way could I pull that off. His tunic was blue, detailed with darker blue stitching and belted with a braided gold cord. Thick brown waves of hair spilled from his bent head, over the blue of his tunic. When I was almost close enough to touch him, he lifted his head.

"Charlie?" The sorrow in Bob's eyes hinted at the sort of anguish that'd make such a strong man cry out in agony.

"Hey, Bob," I muttered, feeling like an idiot for not coming up with anything more appropriate to say to someone in such obvious grief.

He smiled, but the heartache in his eyes was unmistakable. I sat down next to him and waited for him to speak. Clearing his throat, he blinked the tears from his eyes. "I'm afraid you've caught me at a vulnerable moment."

"Sorry." I started to push myself up to my feet. "I could leave if you'd rather be alone."

He drew the sorrow inward with a loud sniff. "Nothing to be sorry for. I welcome your company." He eyed my wet hair and clothes, and his smile brightened. "Swam here again?"

Grinning, I sat back down. "Sure. We'll go with that." I took a deep breath, filling my nose with a mix of damp scents—old moss-covered trees, decaying pine needles and a musky odor that I couldn't quite place. "Everything alright?"

Bob shrugged. "Just a bad dream."

"It must've been a pretty bad nightmare to make a tough guy like you cry out like that." I hated how dumb that sounded as soon as the words were out of my mouth.

He chuckled softly. "Thank you. That's very flattering."

I nodded, feeling only slightly less stupid.

"It's a recurring dream. I wouldn't want to bore you with the details." He leaned forward, picked up a stone by his foot and started absently tracing a finger over its smooth surface. "You'd probably think I was crazy if I did."

"I'm pretty sure I wouldn't, Bob. If you don't think I'm a lunatic for showing up sopping wet from God knows where and claiming that I swam here..." He let out a hearty chuckle. "...why would I judge you for a dream?"

Eyes on the stone in his hand, he shook his head. "Because it's more than a dream to me. I could almost swear I've lived it. I'm beginning to wonder if I'm losing my mind."

"You aren't, Bob. If it feels real, on some level it probably is." What else could I say? If I tried to explain the other world, he'd think I was the crazy one.

He chucked the stone into the Water. "I don't know what to think anymore. There are times when the dreams feel more real than this. That sounds ridiculous, doesn't it?"

Insightful actually. "No, it doesn't. Do you want to talk about it? I can be a pretty good listener when I want to be."

Chuckling softly, he shook his head. Then something made him change his mind and I watched his gaze turn inward as the misery drifted back into his eyes. "The place in my dreams is a prison of sorts. My body's trapped there. My thoughts are all jumbled. I can't keep my memories straight, can't control what comes out of my mouth." He stopped, shaking his head again. "I can handle all that. I don't like it but I can tolerate it. It's the flashes of memory that wake me up screaming."

"What kind of memory?" I asked quietly.

"The world in my dreams is different than this one. People dress differently and speak differently. There are tools and gadgets I couldn't even begin to describe." He paused, looking to me for a response.

"I can imagine it pretty well," I assured him.

Smiling, he continued, "In these memories, I'm a protector. Sort of like I am here but different, if that makes any sense. There's a group of us who've dedicated our lives to protecting others. We don't wear armor. We wear blue shirts and hats and medals that mark us as protectors. I only remember flashes but I know I loved it. I protected the innocent. I stopped those who did wrong. My life meant something. But then I see flashes of a day..." choking up, Bob stopped to take a deep breath, then went on, "flashes that wake me in a cold sweat with my own screams ringing in my ears. I can never remember all the details when I wake, but I remember the face of a woman. Her eyes hold so much misery that I can barely stand to look at her. I can feel her heart breaking when I look in those eyes." Bob took another deep breath. "I remember running toward a row of trees, cradling a child in my arms. I remember walking away and him whimpering, begging me not to leave." Bob shook his head. "I remember a small broken body, lying motionless on a bed. My heart pounds when I see it. I can barely keep from vomiting and I'm overcome with a desperate need to help, but I'm trapped inside my own head and my actions are beyond my control. Every day, I see that woman's grief-stricken face, I see that boy shake with fear as I walk away, I see that small lifeless body, but I'm no longer me and there's nothing I can do." At that, Bob dropped his head in his hands and started to sob, but it didn't take long for his tears to die away. "That's all the detail I ever remember when I wake." His last words were spoken with an absoluteness that left no doubt he was finished speaking. They seemed to hang in the air as he turned to look at the Water.

I felt the heavy silence like an ache in my chest, but I had no idea what to say so we both sat in silence, watching the Water.

He was the one who finally spoke. "What does it matter? It's just a dream. Right?"

"I don't know, Bob. Dreams can hold a lot of truth." What more could I say? Then a thought occurred to me. "Hey, this might sound crazy but what if I could find out more about that dream for you?" He must've been a cop. *A protector dressed in blue.* If those were real memories, I had a strong hunch that the missing parts would explain how he went from fearless-policeman to television-obsessed-old-man.

"Charlie," he answered softly, "when we met, I had the strongest feeling that I already knew you. If you say you can do it, for some absurd reason, I believe that you can."

From out of nowhere a warm breeze swept onto shore, heavy with the scent of Emma's perfume. *"Charlie,"* a voice whispered in the breeze. I turned to see what Bob made of it, but he didn't seem to have noticed. Did I imagine it?

The warmth of the breeze engulfed me as it whispered my name again, *"Charlie."* It was Emma's voice. *"I'm sorry to bother you."* Without knowing why, I reached out and I actually felt her. I pulled the feel of her closer. *"Charlie, please wake up,"* the breeze whispered. *"Please."* Her tone was more urgent each time she spoke.

I reached up and felt the softness of her cheek. "Shhh. It's alright, Em. Everything's going to be alright." I drew the feel of her closer, fully aware that it made no sense. Maybe things didn't need to make sense in a World of Dreams or maybe I felt her because I'd carried the thought of her through the Water with me. Her scent in the air was so heavy that I could practically taste it and the feel of her in my arms was so real. I turned to get Bob's take on it, but he was gone.

I sat alone on the shore, holding onto the feel of Emma. One by one, the trees of the forest faded and disappeared, then the ground beneath me started shrinking. Stupid as it sounds, I held on tight to the feel of Emma's body, determined to keep her safe. I wasn't about to let her dissolve with the scenery, so I held her close and watched the shore get smaller and smaller until I was back in the Water. But this time it was warm and smelled like Emma's perfume. Baffled and disoriented, I clung to the feel of her as I slowly drifted up...

17

EMMA

I slipped an arm underneath my pillow and fixed my eyes on the night sky outside the bedroom window. When did life get so complicated? *You know exactly when.* I shook my head as if I could shake away the memories, but I couldn't. I could dream of David every night. I could spend every waking hour daydreaming of the moments we'd shared, earth-shattering moments. He was my world. He always had been, but nothing could undo the things we'd done. *Don't let your thoughts go there.* Slowly, maliciously, panic was tightening its grip on me. Each new breath that I took came quicker and shallower than the one before it. With each new beat, the pounding of my heart grew louder and faster. Pain and heartache screamed somewhere deep inside me and a desperate aching need to flee burned in the pit of my stomach, but there was no escaping my own skin. I needed someone to hold me and tell me everything would be alright. *But it won't. It never will. You've lost everything.*

The pounding of my heart echoed in my head—giving voice to the panic, urging me to run, until lying motionless became absolute torture—and an all-consuming need festered inside me to rip out my hair, bang my head against a wall, hurl my body through the glass window, anything to dull the internal torment for even a minute or two. If it was daytime, I could turn to Charlie. He'd wrap his arms around me and I wouldn't feel quite so hopeless. *Go to him.* I sprang out of bed, hurried to the door and stood there with my heart pounding, staring at the knob. The air in the room suddenly seemed too thin to breathe.

I yanked the door open with a ragged inhalation and stood in the doorway, peering out into the hall. It was dimly lit and eerily silent, not a soul in sight. They obviously didn't leave the patients unattended at night but there were less people working at this hour, and they'd be stationed at the desk near the entrance. I could see Charlie's door at the far end of the hall. I wouldn't have to pass the desk to reach it, but I could still get caught and I had no idea what the repercussions would be. I honestly didn't care what they did to me. *But if they told David...* If my husband learned that I'd been caught sneaking into a male patient's room in the middle of the night, to put it mildly, he wouldn't react calmly. But in that moment, I didn't care. I wanted to hurt David as much as I wanted to hurt myself—maybe more. *Go to Charlie.*

I couldn't be alone anymore. *Go. Curl up in Charlie's arms.* I stepped into the hall, silently closed the door and started toward Charlie's room. When I reached it, I just stood there hesitantly staring at the knob. Any sound that I made would alert whoever was at the desk that I was out of my room. If Charlie was sleeping, knocking loud enough to wake him would probably get me caught. *Just go in.* Hand trembling, I grabbed the doorknob. I shouldn't be doing this. *Go.* Turning the knob, I slipped inside and noiselessly shut the door.

The room was dark. Moonlight cascading through the window provided the only hint of light. My unadjusted eyes couldn't make out the shape of Charlie in his bed, but I could hear him breathing, deep steady breaths. He was asleep. It didn't seem right to disturb him, but standing in his room—in the dark while he slept—basically made me a stalker. *You're here, stupid. Do something.* Had I completely lost my mind? I should tip-toe back to my room before I got us both in trouble.

I turned back to the door, but something stopped me before I touched the knob. I was filled with a desperate aching need to hurt something, mainly myself. I didn't want to be alone so I moved to the bed, sat down and whispered, "Charlie?" He took a deep breath and smiled without opening his eyes. Close to tears, I leaned over his sleeping body and whispered in his ear, "Charlie, I'm sorry to bother you." Rolling to his side, he wrapped an arm around me and pulled me closer. "Charlie, please wake up," I pleaded through tears that I couldn't hold back any longer. I needed him to wake and reassure me that this wasn't completely insane. "Please."

He touched his hand to my cheek. I knew he was dreaming, but I tipped my head against his palm and took comfort in the gesture. "Shhh," he whispered, "It's alright, Em. Everything's going to be alright."

He was going to wake up and think I'd gone completely insane, and I'd be the first to agree with him. I sagged, letting him pull me closer and soundlessly began to sob.

His arm tightened protectively in response and he inhaled sharply as his head turned on the pillow. "Emma?"

"Yes," I whispered.

"Am I still dreaming?" I looked up at his sweet boyish face bathed in moonlight. He looked disoriented and utterly confused to find me on his bed, although he didn't seem to mind.

"No. You're awake," I whispered. "I'm sorry to bother you." It was a stupid answer, but I was at a loss for words and feeling completely pathetic now that he was awake.

Locks of sand-streaked hair fell over his eyes as he shifted, propping himself up on one arm. His other arm stayed wrapped around me and his smile widened. "Bother me? I wouldn't exactly call waking up to find a gorgeous girl on my bed a bother." He brushed my cheek with his hand, and his brow furrowed. "You've been crying. What's wrong? I didn't hurt you in my sleep, did I?"

I lifted a finger and brushed the wayward strands of hair back from his eyes. "No, of course not."

He breathed a sigh of relief. "Then what's wrong?"

You're here. He's awake. Say something. "I couldn't sleep. I thought maybe if I curled up in your arms I might feel safe for a while. It was stupid. I'm sorry I woke you..." My voice trailed off as I moved to leave with whatever small shred of dignity I had left.

But he held me and kept me from slipping away. "My arms are all yours, and there's nothing to be sorry for." The tenderness in his voice brought fresh tears to my eyes. He dropped down onto the mattress so that he was lying on his side and tilted his head to rest on top of mine. "It's alright, Em."

In his arms, panic loosened its crushing grip on me. I sagged against his chest and sobbed, the urge to hurt myself gradually faded and I almost believed that everything could be alright. When I stopped crying, I looked up at him. There was so much affection in the way he was smiling at me. Only one other person had ever looked at me like that. Thinking of David conjured memories of his body pressed against mine. *Like Charlie's is now.* I crawled into bed beside him in the middle of the night while he was sleeping. Had I completely lost it? I let out a shaky breath. "You must think I'm crazy."

"Never." He stroked my cheek with his fingertips. "I'm glad you came. I hate the thought of you hurting and alone right down the hall from me."

"I should go," I muttered.

His arms held me tight. "Stay."

"Charlie..." I hesitated, not sure what to say.

"Emma, if you're uncomfortable then yeah, you should go. But if you're going because you think it's what you're supposed to do, stay. No one else ever has to know that you did. I want you to feel safe."

"I do, too."

"Stay," he whispered. A tear slipped down my cheek and he brushed it away with his thumb. "Don't worry about what anyone else would think. Do what you want to do."

"I want to stay with you," I whimpered. He gently tugged the blankets out from under me and pulled them up so that I was under the covers beside him. "Is this a bad idea?" I whispered.

"No," he promised. "You're safe with me."

Beside him, the panic melted away and I drifted off to sleep, wrapped in the warmth of his arms.

18

DAVID

The sun having set on another tiresome day, in a seemingly endless string of days without her, I settled into my empty bed. I'd done all I could to ensure that the judge ruled in my favor. Anyone could be convinced to see things the way that you wanted them to—a subtle threat, the granting of a favor, a monetary offering—it was simply a matter of determining what would best persuade the particular individual. The fellow I'd entrusted to determine what would best persuade our judge had been in my employ longer than anyone else, and I trusted him implicitly. Benjamin had shadowed me for so long and was so attuned to my intentions that I practically considered him an extension of myself. He was willing to do whatever was necessary, in any given set of circumstances, and he'd never failed to successfully complete a task. It hadn't taken long for

Benjamin to pinpoint the judge's Achilles heel or for me to subsequently convince the judge to sympathize with my plight. There was nothing left to do but wait for the court date, and get some sleep. Which was easier said than done lately.

With a frustrated sigh, I turned toward Emma's pillow. Her empty side of the bed was a painful nightly reminder that she'd been taken from me, making it difficult to relax enough to fall asleep. If it weren't for the dreams once I finally succumbed to sleep, I'd have gone completely mad. Those dreams sustained me. I trudged through my days, anticipating the moment when I'd drift back to sleep and hold her in my arms again. My need to see her, to be with her, grew more desperate each day that she was kept from me. I stroked a hand over my wife's pillow. I would not end each day slumped in a chair with a glass of liquor in hand. I refused to be that man. I simply needed to occupy my mind with a distraction until exhaustion claimed me and carried me off to sleep. Instead of fixating on the fact that she wasn't with me, I needed to remember a time when she was…

…I sat at my desk, drafting my summation for the next day in court. A knock on my office door interrupted me mid-thought. "Come in," I called, ready to make whoever disturbed me sorry that they had.

The door swung inward and Benjamin stood there for a moment, framed by the doorway's mahogany trim. He stepped to one side and gestured toward the interior of my office. *Emma gave him a warm smile as she slipped through the doorway, and all thoughts of the closing statement swept from my mind with her entrance. Just the sight of her was all that it took to arouse me.*

Eyes cast downward, she ventured a bit further into the room. Giving me a subtle nod, Benjamin closed the door, leaving the two of us alone.

I watched her with anticipation as she stood there, hesitating. "What brings you here today, Princess?" Her cheeks took on a lovely blush at the sound of my voice, and I gave her a sinful smile.

"My father said that you offered me an internship to see if this is something I'd be interested in doing."

My smile widened. "Have you decided to take me up on the offer?"

She peered up at me from beneath her long lashes. "If you still want me."

Nostrils flaring, I replied, "I'll always want you, but you're standing awfully far away to carry on a conversation. Why don't you come closer?"

I eyed her hungrily as she slowly approached my desk. Her skin had a lovely sun-kissed glow as if the sun itself had marked her as its own. Her lips were glossed a delicate shade of pink to match her outfit. A pale pink sleeveless dress wrapped around her slender body, hugging each voluptuous curve and tying at the hip. A feral desire to grasp the ties and yank the dress undone made it difficult for me to concentrate on much of anything else.

As she stopped directly in front of my desk, I ached to sweep everything on it to the floor and drape her supple body across the wooden surface. "How close did you want me to come?" she murmured, a hint of mischief glinting in those dazzling eyes.

"Closer than that," I replied wickedly.

She slowly rounded my desk and my body ached to pounce, but I held back. I wanted to make her come to me...

...Fatigue cruelly chose that particular moment to carry me off to sleep, leaving the rest of the memory frustratingly unfinished. I'd go back to it another time. That was the last wisp of conscious thought to cross my tired mind...

... A warm breeze caressed me like a lover's heated breath as I stood, eyes closed at the mouth of the cave. The steady hum of nocturnal creatures whispered through the silence, making it feel more absolute. Drawing a deep breath of the fragrant night air, I opened my eyes. An elegant veil of stars cloaked the night sky. The lake sparkled brilliantly, reflecting the radiance of the moon above. But she wasn't there.

Stretching my back as I stepped from the cave, I couldn't help but smile. My last thoughts had been of wanting to make her come to me, and now she was making me wait. Relishing the feel of the dew-drenched grass beneath my feet, I headed toward the lake.

Hours had passed at a sluggish pace, a hint of the rising sun glimmered on the horizon and the moon had all but faded. Still, I sat in the grass at the water's edge, alone—my sentiments oscillating savagely between worry and anger. Being left in the dark, completely ignorant of where she was or how she fared, was maddening.

Overhead, thick dark clouds began to choke what'd been a perfect cloudless sky. The sky opened and the heavens spilled their swell of tears. Streaks of lightning lit the sky, followed by deafening cracks of thunder. I stood and stared at the wrath of the sky and fed it all of my fury. If someone had kept her from me, my pain would be nothing in comparison to theirs. I closed my eyes, the rains washed over me and I began to melt away...

...I woke with a massive headache, finding it a struggle just to open my eyes. It was only five o'clock, but I'd never drift back to sleep. I needed aspirin and caffeine so I sat up, dragged myself out of bed and groggily made my way down the hall, barely pausing at Emma's picture. I listlessly descended the staircase and shuffled into the kitchen. Normally, the smell of freshly brewed coffee greeted me when I came downstairs in the morning, but the new house-keeper wouldn't be in for another hour and that was too long to wait. I started toward the refrigerator to fetch the coffee, but a throbbing in my temples reminded me that I'd also come down for aspirin so

I headed to the cupboard, retrieved the aspirin and popped a few into my mouth. The day had barely begun and I was already in the foulest of moods. I decided to forget the coffee and go take a shower, hoping it might get me feeling halfway human.

After shaving, taking a long hot shower and dressing, my mood still hadn't improved in the slightest. At least enough time had passed that coffee would now be waiting for me. Deciding to finish a journal article I'd begun the day before while drinking my coffee, I headed to the lounge to fetch it. Two steps into the room, something sharp pierced the sole of my foot. Lifting it with a loud, "Fuck," I found a sliver of glass embedded in my sock and carefully removed it with an aggravated sigh.

Sara, our incompetent new housekeeper, came timidly scampering into the room. "Is something wrong, Mr. Talbot?"

"Not at all," I growled. "I just find hollering random obscenities a delightful way to begin my day."

"Sorry, Sir," she squeaked. "That was a foolish question."

"Well, at least we agree on something. Tell me, when did you plan on cleaning up the entire mess on my floor? Did you run out of time yesterday and decide to leave some of the glass shards for today?

Some notice might've been nice before I sliced my foot on one." I moved to the waste basket behind the bar, tossed the glass sliver in then looked up at the housekeeper. Her eyes were tearing, but I didn't give a damn. I didn't pay her to do half her job.

"I'm sorry, Sir," she sniveled, her voice little more than a whisper.

"Speak up for Christ sake," I barked. "I don't have time to ask you to repeat everything you say."

Straightening, she looked me squarely in the eye and replied, "I'm sorry, Mr. Talbot. I'll clean it up thoroughly after I'm done with your breakfast."

"That wasn't so hard now, was it? No breakfast this morning. Just coffee."

"Would you like me to bring it down to you?" she squeaked, already reverting to her meeker tone.

"I would. Before the morning is half over please."

She nodded, looking close to tears again and scurried from the room as though she couldn't get away fast enough.

I had scant patience for that woman's timid meekness and none for her half-assed job performance. I couldn't recall Isabella having ever been so useless. Perhaps it wasn't fair to compare the new housekeeper to our previous. After twenty-plus years of working for me, Isabella knew exactly what was expected of her and usually went far above and beyond it cheerfully. Even on her first day, she'd been a hundred times more capable and pleasant to be around than the new housekeeper.

Perhaps I should've gone easier on Sara, considering my wife wasn't around to counter my temperament with her own. Emma had always been the voice of kindness in the Talbot household. I didn't do sweet and patient. There was only one person I was willing to be patient for. For Emma, my patience had no limits. I'd wait for her forever and forgive her anything without a moment's hesitation.

19

CHARLIE

I drifted lazily, higher and higher, clutching my tangible memory of Emma. I'd focused my thoughts on her when I jumped into the Waters, hoping it'd lead me to her clearing. It hadn't, but somehow I'd carried this invisible echo of her to the Dream World with me. I'd been able to hear her and feel her. I'd even smelled her perfume, and now I held her invisible body as the Waters carried me toward the surface.

I emerged into darkness with only a whisper of moonlight to light my surroundings. I was back in bed, but I could still feel Emma in my arms and smell her perfume. Was this another dream? Nellie had created her own paradise in the Dream World, maybe this was mine. I couldn't imagine a more perfect dream than lying in bed with Emma in my arms, but she was crying. I turned my head and realized I could see her. "Emma?"

"Yes."

"Am I still dreaming?"

"No. You're awake," she answered softly. "I'm sorry to bother you."

Bother me? I promised her that finding her in my bed was anything but a bother. *More like a dream come true.* But I kept that thought to myself. Emma was hurting and she needed me to reassure her that everything would be alright. It took some convincing, but eventually she agreed to stay with me. I was pretty sure she'd wanted to all along. Why else would she have come? I pulled the blankets over us—drawing her closer, hoping the gesture would comfort her—and a darkness gradually settled over the room.

I glanced down at Emma, breathing peacefully in my arms. It hadn't taken her long to fall asleep once she decided to stay. I looked up and jerked convulsively as I caught a glimpse of blazing sapphire eyes. Luckily, Emma was sound asleep and the movement didn't wake her.

Aside from that initial jolt and the terror-stricken thudding of my heart, I managed to keep surprisingly still as I studied the creature. The dragon's monstrous fully-extended wings had encircled my bed, enclosing the two of us in a brilliantly sparkling dome that was somehow radiant without lessening the darkness. If anything, it enhanced it. The beast's head was bent and flames flickered wildly in its intensely blue eyes as it held my gaze. I wanted to close my eyes, but I felt paralyzed beneath the weight of that burning stare. I don't even think I blinked.

If my theory was right, this beast was the Dream form of Emma's split personality, created to watch over her in times of abuse. If her abuser had been a man, the dragon probably wouldn't trust men and wouldn't be too thrilled to see Emma in my bed. I just prayed it could sense that I wanted to keep her safe. *Why the hell was I worrying?* Dream images were just visions. Right?

A thought suddenly occurred to me. I hadn't had any luck finding Emma in the Dream World so far, but Emma's body was snug in my arms and her dragon was hulking over us. If I jumped now, would I be more likely to find them? I was so eager to find out that I didn't even have to summon the Water. It just appeared, anxious to help. Heart fluttering, I looked down at Emma, concentrated on her perfect face and the feel of her body in my arms and jumped.

Bitter cold struck me like an unexpected slap to the face. I'd been too distracted by my enthusiasm to remember to brace for the shock. Holding Emma tight, I focused on her beautiful face as the Waters knocked us about. Then her eyes snapped open, wildly panic-stricken and filled with terror. I tried to give her a reassuring look as best I could while being tossed around underwater. She looked like she really needed air. *Damn it. Don't let this hurt her. I'd never forgive myself.* As soon as I finished the thought, the Water hurled us to the surface.

Sunlight blinded me as Emma gasped and flailed in my arms but I held her tight and once I caught my breath enough to talk, I did my best to calm her down. "Em, I jumped through the Waters to the Dream World. I didn't know you'd get pulled with me." Her only answer was more gasping and thrashing. "I promise I'll keep you safe. First, I need to get us to shore. Just try to relax, okay?"

She stopped flailing and conveyed all her panic with one trembled word, "Okay."

Holding her with one arm, I pulled us through the Water toward a blurry shoreline with the other. Several exhausting minutes later, we crawled from the surf and collapsed on the sand.

Chests heaving, wet clothes plastered to our bodies, we silently waited for our breathing to slow. I absently watched a trickle of water fall from her hair to the sand until I noticed that her green eyes were wild with panic and fixed on me. I confidently returned her gaze, wordlessly assuring her that everything was alright and watched the fear fade from her eyes as wonder took its place.

Smiling faintly, she rolled to her stomach and I did the same. The sun's warmth embraced us, dulling our memory of the Water's hostile chill as she surveyed the landscape, admiring the tropical trees and bushes at the edge of the beach. I sat up and turned toward the surf where a picture perfect sunrise poised above clear blue Water.

Following my lead, Emma sat up and shifted to look at the Water. "It's beautiful."

"This is Nellie's beach," I muttered.

"Nellie?" she echoed doubtfully. "Our Nellie?"

I nodded.

"You've seen her in dreams?" Emma asked softly.

"Yeah. She can see Dream forms, too. But she doesn't want anybody to know, so you probably shouldn't mention it."

"Sure," Emma replied absently, eyes glued to the sunrise.

I stood and held a hand out to her. "Walk the beach with me?"

Smiling, she placed her hand in mine. I gently pulled her to her feet and we started walking hand in hand, admiring the sunrise.

After a minute, she broke the silence. "You found me."

I stopped walking and she stopped beside me. "I did." I raised my eyebrows. "So, what do you think?"

"I think it's amazing."

As we stood face to face with a picture perfect sunrise painting the sky, I felt an incredible urge to kiss her. "Thank you for believing me." This was just a dream, right? If I kissed her, it wouldn't be real.

She looked up at me, biting her lip, transfixing me with the magnificent green of her eyes.

Even the sunrise had nothing on their brilliance. I tipped my head, touching my forehead to hers. *Kiss her. It's just a dream.* But I knew better. It was more.

A high-pitched scream from the bushes startled us both. **"What the hell are you doing?"** And the moment was lost.

"Nellie," I muttered disappointedly as I watched her run toward us.

Emma squinted at the young girl. "Nellie?"

I nodded. "That's her Dream form."

Nellie didn't stop until she was practically standing on top of me. "You stupid bastard! I trusted you!" she screamed in my face. "And this is how you repay me?" Nellie let out another blood-curdling scream, also in my face.

Her reaction seemed kind of extreme. All this, just for landing on her beach? "I'm sorry, Nellie." I tried my best to sound sincere even though I didn't feel it. "I didn't come back here on purpose. The Waters tossed me to your beach."

She shook her head frantically. "You jackass! You're even dumber than I thought! You think I'm upset because *you* came back to my beach?"

Okay. Now I was at a loss. "If you aren't mad about me coming back here, what are you so upset about?"

"You brought *her* here, you stupid ass! How could you risk my beach?" Dropping to the sand like her muscles couldn't support her any longer, Nellie broke down in tears.

"We can jump back out," I offered quietly.

"It's too fucking late!" Nellie sobbed. "You've already exposed my home!"

"I'm sorry, Nellie," I muttered. "I don't know what to say."

Nellie glared up at me. "You lured a dragon to my paradise! You might as well keep it now! It's no good to me anymore!"

A small part deep inside me was a little unnerved by the severity of Nellie's reaction. Just how dangerous was dragon Emma? I pictured those blazing sapphire eyes fixed on me. Maybe it was time to get out of the Dream World before the beast made an appearance. "Nellie," I whispered, "how concerned should I be about running into the dragon?"

"YOU SHOULD BE TERRIFIED!" she shrieked. "I'd take my own life before I'd let that dragon find me!"

Shit. So...pretty concerned. I looked at Emma, and she raised an eyebrow. "Em, it's probably time for us to go."

Emma nodded as she crouched down next to Nellie, her expression portraying equal parts confusion and regret. "Your beach is beautiful, Nellie. I'm not sure what's going on, but I'm sorry we upset you."

Nellie answered in an oddly calm tone that was far more ominous than the screaming, "I told you this fairytale wouldn't end well. Why couldn't you just listen?"

Emma didn't say anything, but she looked hurt by Nellie's words.

Nellie took Emma's hand with a tired sigh. "It's not your fault. Believe me, I understand that. Just stay away from me. I beg you." Then something behind us distracted her and she dropped Emma's hand.

I turned to see what'd grabbed her attention. The sky was rapidly darkening as heavy storm clouds smothered the sun, then the sky erupted—streaks of lightning lit the sky, claps of thunder shook the earth under our feet—and suddenly we were standing in the middle of a merciless downpour with raindrops pelting us like tiny angry fists. Too stunned to act, Emma and I exchanged bewildered looks.

"Run!" Nellie screamed above the thunder. "Jump back into the Water!"

Emma gawked in horror at the violently crashing waves. "Jump into *that*?"

"Go!" Nellie shouted, giving Emma a hard shove toward the Water.

I knew where this was going. We needed to make our exit before Nellie made it for us. Grabbing Emma, I headed to the Water's edge as I shouted in her ear, "Trust me, Em." Then I jumped, gripping her tightly in my arms.

20

EMMA

This wasn't right. Charlie and I were back in the Water. I didn't know how, but I knew that when we surfaced, I'd be awake. And I hadn't seen David yet. I still needed to find our clearing. This couldn't be the end of my dreams.

As the Waters continued to batter us around, my panic grew. How would I make it till bedtime tomorrow if I didn't see David tonight? Charlie held me firmly in his arms. He'd promised to keep me safe, and he asked me to trust him when we plunged into the Water. I couldn't explain why I had to leave until we left the Water, and by then it would be too late. I closed my eyes, silently pleading that Charlie would understand what I had to do. Then I pushed against his chest as hard as I could. It caught him by surprise, and I broke free of his hold. He watched me, shocked and wounded, as the Water pulled him away and swallowed him up. Then I was alone.

I shouldn't be here. This was a place most people couldn't go. A place I couldn't go. I closed my eyes at night, fell asleep and dreamt. I didn't jump into Dream Water. I didn't even know what Dream Water was. What if I couldn't get out? The longer the current jostled me, the more I regretted my decision to push away from Charlie. It'd been a foolish impulsive thing to do, and he'd looked so hurt.

I tossed about aimlessly until I began to forget. All I knew was fear and all I felt was cold. Where had I been trying to go? I'd been desperate to get there. But why? I belonged to the Water. *No.* I belonged to something else. *Someone else.* A strong voice echoed deep inside me. *YOU ARE MINE. YOU WILL ALWAYS BE MINE.* I didn't know who the voice belonged to, but I knew that I needed him. It was a desperate aching need and it tore at my heart. The pull of that voice was stronger than the pull of the Water. Silently, I screamed, *I belong to him.*

The Water expelled me violently and for a brief frightening moment, I was airborne. As quickly as I'd breached the surface, I began to plummet down. Raindrops pummeled me as I fell and streaks of lightning, followed by deafening claps of thunder, filled the sky. Just before I hit the surface, I screamed at the top of my lungs, "You can't have me!" I felt stupid yelling at Water but after all the bizarre things I'd seen, it seemed worth a try. I barely made a splash as I touched the surface of the lake. A gentle lapping motion carried me to shore, and I marveled at how strange it was that the Water was so tranquil when the storm above was so fierce. For a long while I sat on the shore, letting the rain pelt my body as I watched the angry sky.

Slowly, my thoughts came back to me. I remembered where I'd come from, who I was and who I needed to see. *David.* The memory of his voice had saved me from losing myself to the Water, I was almost sure of it. I looked around with a clearer mind. This was our lake. Our clearing. I stood and headed toward the cave, slowly at first but my pace steadily quickened until I was running. Panting and desperately hoping to find my husband inside, I reached the mouth of the cave but something made me hesitate. With a shake of my head, I brushed the hesitation aside and stepped in.

As I entered the darkness, a rush of memories flooded over me. I turned to look at the clearing, but I no longer saw what was there...

... A pretty blue blanket was spread out over the lush green grass. The lake behind us was so still and perfect that it looked like it was made of glass. I wore a pink dress that sparkled as it caught the sunlight. My favorite doll and stuffed animal were sitting on the blanket with me, laughing and talking and drinking tea, as if those were the most natural things in the world for toys to do. I

served tea from a china tea pot with an elaborate hand-painted floral pattern, and my guests drank from cups with the same design.

We were waiting for someone to join us, and he was late.

"It's perfectly acceptable for a gentleman to arrive fashionably late," announced a sock monkey with a red bow tie, my oldest and dearest plaything.

The beautiful china doll shook her lovely head, making her dark ringlets bounce. "He could've let us know he'd be late."

The monkey's eyes narrowed. "Where else do you need to be?"

"He's right," I agreed cheerfully. "How can anyone complain on such a perfect day? I can't think of anywhere I'd rather be."

The doll crossed her little arms over her chest. "It'd be better if he was here."

"He will be, as soon as he can." There wasn't a doubt in my mind…

…It was night, but the sky didn't glisten with stars like it normally did. It was thick with storm clouds. Rain poured down steadily as I stood barefoot in the wet grass in the middle of the clearing. My hair was drenched, my pajamas were too. The water-soaked fabric clung miserably to my shivering torso.

He was in the cave. I could only see darkness beyond the entrance but I knew he was there, and he wanted me to leave. I was staying anyway. "Please come out," I called into the darkness. "I'm afraid."...

...The memories faded as quickly as they'd come and were lost the moment they slipped away.

"David?" I called into the darkness. There was no response, so I ventured a few steps farther into the cave's dark interior. "David?" I called again, a little louder and more desperate than the first time.

Faint sounds echoed deep inside the cave, like whispers from very distant voices, answering my call. I tried to make out what they were saying, but couldn't pick any actual words out of the myriad of sounds.

"Hello?" I called. "Is someone there?"

The voices stopped and there was absolute silence.

This was starting to seem like a really bad idea. I took a couple steps back toward the mouth of the cave. The whispers started up again, and my heartbeat quickened. Did I dare call out again? Faraway laughter echoed deep within the cave, and a chill crept down my spine.

Then a wave of icy Water came crashing out of nowhere and carried me away.

21

CHARLIE

One second Emma was safe in my arms, the next she was pushing me away. It caught me off guard and broke my grip before I could even register what'd happened. Powerless, I watched the Waters pull her away and swallow her up. She'd come to me for comfort in the middle of the night and I'd promised to keep her safe. Instead, I dragged her into the Waters while she slept in my arms. She'd trusted me, and now she was gone.

A growing sense of dread churned in my stomach as I focused my thoughts on nothing but Emma. I pictured her face and hollered her name in my head. *Emma!* I thought of the feel of her in my arms and the smell of her perfume. *I won't let you take her!* The Waters tossed me around violently, trying to make me forget—forget that I'd lost her, forget her completely—but I refused to let go and eventually, the Water gave up and propelled me to the surface.

Gasping for air, I emerged into darkness. I waited for my eyes to adjust and my lungs to fill, and I prayed for Emma to come back to me.

A pair of blazing sapphire eyes flashed above me.

"I'm sorry," I whispered to the beast in the shadows. "I lost her."

The dragon dipped its head toward my arms. *An echo of a past movement?* I didn't know, or care. I looked down. And there she was, safely tucked in bed beside me. I looked back up at the dragon. "Thanks."

The beast blinked its monstrous eyes.

I looked down at Emma. It didn't look like she was sleeping peacefully. Wherever the Waters took her, she didn't seem to like it. I touched her cheek. "Em."

Beads of sweat glistened on her forehead as she whimpered softly, twisting in my arms.

"Emma," I spoke a little louder this time, closer to her ear, "wake up."

She whimpered and thrashed again. She didn't fall asleep like she normally would've. Well, she did but then I pulled her into the Waters. What if she couldn't get back out? Desperate, I looked back up at the dragon. "Is she trapped? What do I do?"

The dragon just stared at me.

Thanks for nothing, I thought. But I didn't say it out loud. Whatever it was, that beast still scared the shit out of me. Damn it. I'd officially lost what little sanity I'd had. I was talking to a Dream form and as if that wasn't bad enough, I'd just asked it for advice.

Emma whimpered again.

I had to do something, I couldn't just watch her suffer so I called to the Water but this time, it resisted me. In my head I howled, *Show yourself!* And the Waters appeared, sparkling before me in answer to my silent roar. Nellie pulled me out when the Waters swallowed me. If she could do it, I could too. I had to. "Let Emma go," I demanded to the rippling blue depths. "Give her back to me." The rippling of the Water swelled to a raging frenzy. "She doesn't belong to you!"

For a flicker of a second, I saw her body tossing through the Waters then Emma bolted upright in my arms, gasping for breath, eyes wide with terror. As she caught her breath, she slowly seemed to get her bearings. "Charlie?"

I breathed a sigh of relief. "Hey, Em. Why did you push me away?"

Her brow furrowed. "I'm sorry. Did I push you in my sleep?"

She didn't remember. Right. People without Dream Sight only remembered flashes of their Dream lives, if anything. "No," I lied. "You were just sort of thrashing around. What were you dreaming about?"

She pulled her hair back from her face, twisted it and flipped it over her shoulder. "I think I was having a nightmare."

I took the hand that was still fidgeting with her hair and gave it an affectionate squeeze. "What was it about?"

She winced, like it pained her to think about it. "It was dark. I remember hearing whispers and laughter."

I slid back against the wall, pulling her along with me. "Do you remember anything else?"

She sagged against me and muttered, "No. Should I?" Then she tipped her head back and frowned at me. "Did you see me in the Dream World?"

I hesitated, wondering if it was wrong to tell her about a dream she couldn't remember.

"You did," she whispered, shifting to look me squarely in the eye, "Didn't you?"

"Yeah." I picked up the end of her makeshift ponytail and smoothed the silky strands between my fingers. "I was kind of hoping you'd remember."

"I wish I could," she murmured, tilting her head toward my hand. "Tell me about it?"

"It was sunrise and we were on a beach."

She shook her head, and I let her hair slip from my fingers. "I wish I could remember."

"I found you, but then I lost track of you," I muttered, figuring that sounded better than 'you pushed me away.'

"I remember feeling panicked," she said softly as she toyed with the tip of her ponytail. "Do you think that's why?"

I doubt it, since you pushed me away on purpose. "No. You didn't seem too worried about getting separated."

Some of the hurt that I felt must've shown on my face because she dropped her hair and whispered, "Did I do something wrong?"

"No." I couldn't be upset about something she'd done in a dream. Dreams weren't the same for people without Dream Sight. They couldn't control what they did. They just acted on impulse. *And her impulse was to push me away.*

She bit her lip, brow furrowed. "Something's bothering you."

"You were just a little hard to wake," I whispered, "and I didn't like seeing you stuck in a nightmare."

She twisted to look out the window. "I should get back to my room before it gets light." Turning back to me, she smiled. "Thanks for making me feel better last night, Charlie. I don't know how I'd survive this place without you."

I smiled back at her. "You don't have to know. I don't plan on leaving you here alone."

Still grinning, she slid to the edge of my bed. "See you soon?"

I nodded. "I'll be the guy waiting outside your door."

She stood up, walked to the door, opened it without making a sound and slipped out into the hall.

As my door closed, I looked up where the dragon had been. It was gone of course. There wasn't a hint of light outside. Since it was too early to go out to the common rooms, I wondered if I should go back to the Dream World and do some damage control with Nellie.

That's not true. I knew I should. I just didn't want to.

22

DAVID

I sat in the chair by the fireplace, shifting my weight with a frustrated sigh. I'd read the same line of the article at least five times over. The coffee hadn't helped my attention in the slightest— at least, not for mundane topics that didn't concern me. With another heavy sigh, I tossed the journal to the coffee table. The aspirin had done nothing to ease my headache, and my mood was still just as foul. I looked up at the clock on the mantle. It wasn't quite seven o'clock and I had no early morning appointments. I leaned back in my chair, propped my feet up on the coffee table and closed my eyes...

...A moment later, I opened them and found myself standing in the middle of the clearing. The storm still raged above me—raindrops furiously pelting the surface of the lake, violent bursts of lightning flashing across the sky, the ground beneath my feet reverberating with each crack of thunder.

I started toward the cave and stopped when I reached the entrance. Murmured whispers echoed deep within the cave's cavernous belly as I stood at its mouth and watched the clearing. The thunder and lightning gradually faded, the rain eased and eventually stopped entirely. The storm clouds withered, and once again the sun dominated the sky.

I turned at the sound of movement behind me in the cave and watched a stuffed monkey wearing a red bow tie step from the shadows. I couldn't help but chuckle at the absurdity of the sight.

The monkey's little black eyes narrowed. "Thanks for laughing."

I stifled another chuckle. "Sorry. I couldn't help myself."

His yarn brows furrowed in a ridiculous attempt at a glare. "Laugh it up. Don't mind me."

"I don't mind at all," I answered, smiling despite the frown on his stuffed face. "It's the first laugh I've had in quite some time."

His yarn brows furrowed deeper.

"I'm sorry. It's a bit difficult to take you seriously. Perhaps, if you lost the bow tie?"

"Right," he snapped, "because a walking talking sock monkey without a bow tie commands loads of respect."

With a bit of effort, I lost the smile, cleared my throat and banished the amusement from my voice. "You had something to tell me?"

The look of irritation vanished from his face. "She was here."

I took a step closer to him. "When?"

"Right after you had your tantrum and left."

"You don't want to piss me off this morning," I responded with a stern glare.

The toy's mouth drew down in an apologetic frown. "Sorry, boss."

I dismissed the apology with a wave of my hand. "Tell me more."

The monkey cocked his head to one side, choosing his words carefully. "She came flying out of the lake."

"Flying?" I echoed skeptically.

"Well," the toy amended, "it was more like she was thrown out."

"What did she do, once she was here?"

The monkey's gaze shifted to the clearing behind me. "She sat by the lake, watching the storm for a long time and then she came to the cave."

I took another step toward him. "Did she come in?"

The monkey nodded. "She stood at the opening for a while. I was going to come out and talk to her, but she looked pretty deep in thought and

I didn't want to interrupt whatever she was working through."

"Go on," I prodded.

"Then she shook it off and walked in. She called your name a few times." The monkey futilely straightened his sewn-in-place bow tie. "She sounded pretty distraught."

"Damn it." Why hadn't I stayed longer?

"Then a wave came out of nowhere and washed her away." The monkey watched me, waiting for a response.

I answered with a frustrated, "Fuck," then frowned at him. "Forgive my foul language, little one."

The monkey stiffened. "Hilarious."

I grinned down at him. "Since when are you so sensitive?" Dropping the smile, I added, "Thank you for the information."

He smoothed a hand over the top of his stuffed head. "You're welcome."

I nodded toward the shadows. "How's she doing?"

The monkey shook his head. "The same."

I gave another slight nod.

The monkey nodded in return then disappeared back into the shadows.

I walked a few steps further into the cave, and the murmured whispering that'd begun when I entered ceased entirely. "She is mine," I declared. "Do not forget that."

23

NELLIE

I sat in the sand at the Water's edge, watching the storm. I hadn't moved a muscle since they jumped back into the Water, but my heart was still racing and I couldn't catch my breath. I should probably leave while I still could, but where the hell would I go? I didn't have the strength to do this again, not at my age. My reflection in the Water showed a lovely young girl, but who was that fooling? She'd faded away a lifetime ago, along with my happiness, my dreams and my sanity. What'd I done to deserve any of this? *You know exactly what you did.*

"Shut up!" I screamed, but I regretted it as soon as the words were out of my mouth. What if the dragon heard me? I shouldn't call any more attention to my beach.

I never should've pulled that clueless fool to my shore. I should've let the Waters take him. My life would've gone on being quiet and simple. Why the hell had I even cared? *Because the boy reminded you of yourself at that age.* "Leave me the hell alone!" I screeched, then remembered I shouldn't make noise.

Wet leaves rustled behind me and I turned toward the bushes at the edge of the beach. "Stop moving." I couldn't take it if the dragon found her. She was all I had. *She's nothing but an echo of a dream, you old fool.* "Shut the FUCK UP!" A monstrous streak of lightning lit the sky in answer to my cry. "Strike me down! I dare you!" I shrieked, then added in a whisper, "Just please don't find her."

I looked back at the Water just in time to see something surface. I squinted, curiously studying the object until I realized it was that idiot's head. I should just sit back and watch the waves pull him under and swallow him up. *But you won't.* "Shut up!! Damn it, SHUT UP!" I screeched. "I will! I swear!"

Charlie was already making his way to shore and it wasn't long before he was crawling from the angry Waters and collapsing on the wet sand, not far from where I sat.

I stood up and watched him struggle for breath as I moved toward him. "Fuck you!" I shouted over the storm and as soon as I was close enough, I kicked his ribs. "FUCK YOU!"

Charlie doubled over, hugging his side as he coughed and gasped for breath. I stood over him, watching him suffer with morbid satisfaction.

When he finally caught his breath, he sat up, coughed one last time and looked up at me with that obnoxious smartass grin of his. "I knew you'd be happy to see me."

I lifted my foot to kick him again, but he snatched it mid-kick. "If I let go, will you be nice?"

I shook my foot but couldn't free it from his grip. "Be nice? Is that what you were doing when you lured evil to my beach?"

The boy raised an eyebrow. "Evil? Isn't that a little dramatic?"

"No. That's being nice!" I hollered, still trying to shake my foot from his hand. "I should've let the Waters have you the night you fell in! I hope that dragon tears you apart!"

"Ouch." Charlie let my foot drop to the sand. "Tell me how you really feel."

"You're such a fool, Charlie. Everything's a joke to you." I turned my back to him. I didn't know if he could see my eyes tearing in the middle of a downpour, but I wasn't taking the chance. "It won't be a joke when you're left broken and alone." Wiping my nose with the back of my cold wet hand, I started to walk away.

I heard Charlie stand up behind me. "Nellie, wait." Soft footfalls padded toward me through the rain-soaked sand. "Please."

I stopped but didn't turn around.

He circled me so we were standing face to face and for once, he looked sincere. "How can I make it up to you?"

I dropped to sit on the sand. "You don't understand. You can't ever make it up to me."

"Then make me understand," he insisted, dropping down next to me.

"I can't, Charlie. I'm too busy trying to figure out where to hide. There's no safe place left for me."

"Nellie," he muttered, "what if I could find you a safe place?"

"What the fuck are you talking about?"

"If I found a safe place for you to go, would you follow me there?" he asked eagerly.

"How are you going to find a safe place? You don't even know what's not safe."

"Could you trust me enough to at least give it a look?" he pestered.

I shook my head. "I don't have time for your stupidity."

He flashed me a sarcastic grin. "Thanks for the vote of confidence, Nellie, but you should really tone down the flattery. I don't want to get a swelled head."

"You're welcome, Charlie," I answered with equal sarcasm, "and thanks for taking away my only happiness and ruining my life."

He smirked at me. "You know, forgiveness is not your strong point."

"Neither is good judgment," I muttered. "I never should've talked to you. You're going to destroy me in the end. I just know it."

He dropped the smirk. "Or maybe, I'll save your miserable old life."

I was done with this. I stood up and started walking away. "Get the fuck off my beach, Charlie. You're not welcome here."

I heard him stand up and start to follow. "Yes, I am. You gave this beach to me. Remember?" He raised his voice to a high-pitched squeak. "You might as well keep it! This beach is no good to me now!"

"You're an ass," I hollered over my shoulder without slowing down.

I heard him stop moving. "And you're a miserable old bitch! But I don't hold it against you."

I just kept marching through the rain.

"I'm going to fix this, Nellie," he hollered over the storm. "I'm going to put a smile on your miserable old face and when I do, you're going to thank me!"

I turned and scowled at him. "And I'm going to watch and laugh when that dragon rips you to pieces."

Smartass grin plastered on his face, he shook his wet mop of a head as he moved to the Water's edge. "You're going to thank me." Then he jumped into the Water and washed away.

24

EMMA

I managed to sneak back down the hall and into my room without anyone noticing. Absent-mindedly shutting the door, I moved to the bed with a lingering sense of dread from the nightmare I couldn't recall. Charlie said he'd dreamt of me. If everything he told me about this dream world was true, I'd dreamt of him, too. If I did, I didn't remember. Was it all in his head? He'd described the clearing in my dreams of David perfectly. How could he have done that if he hadn't seen it? *But how could he have seen it?* The dream images and the world he described, it all sounded like a delusion. Did that make me delusional for even considering the possibility?

I crawled into bed, pulled the blankets up to my chin and closed my eyes. What had I dreamt about? The memories felt just beyond my grasp. There'd been darkness, whispers and laughter. Evil laughter, like something out of a horror movie. *The movie you watched when you were a teenager, the one your mother wouldn't let you see.* I tried to picture the darkness and hear the whispers and laughter. *The clearing.* I remembered standing in the dark, looking out at the clearing. It was storming and I was alone.

My head throbbed as pieces of it came back to me…

…I stood in the rain, wet and cold and alone. Eerie laughter from that movie echoed somewhere distant. I was afraid and I didn't want to be alone. I looked to the cave. I wanted David to come out. He told me to go to my room and stay away from him, but I didn't want to. The movie had me spooked and my imagination was playing tricks on me. It felt like things were lurking in the shadows, watching me. I called out to him, told him I was frightened. The only response was the patter of the rain, and still I stood there. Alone…

…The pain in my head was almost unbearable.

If I was remembering the nightmare I'd just had, why was I mixing it up with old memories? I hadn't thought about the night we watched that movie in ages. What'd made me think of it now, and where did that memory of me standing in the rain come from? It felt like a recent dream, but why would real memories from years ago be jumbled up with it?

Maybe my mind was reverting to another time when I'd needed to be near David because I wanted to be with him so badly now. *Do you?* Part of me didn't. That part was still confused. That part hated him, but he hadn't hated me—not for a second—even after everything I'd done. Was it because he loved me unconditionally or because he felt guilty...or both?

Maybe I'd be better off not even trying to figure it out. Dr. Spenser could keep giving me pills to make me forget, make me stop feeling. I had too many unanswered questions and no way to find the answers. That was one of the worst parts about all of this, not knowing if it'd all been for nothing. How could I keep on breathing if that was the case? *You don't deserve to breathe, either way.*

Clutching my aching head in my hands, I squeezed my eyes shut tighter. I couldn't take this anymore. I didn't want to live if he'd lied to me. *You don't deserve to live.*

I opened my eyes and lifted my arm up in front of me. The intricate design on my bracelet glinted in the moonlight. It was a gift from David, not to commemorate a happy memory, to block a horrible one. Hide the scar, bury the memory. That was the idea, but the bracelet was no less a reminder than what it covered. As I slipped the gold cuff off and traced a finger along the vertical scar that ran up my arm from my wrist, the memories came flooding back. *If he hadn't found you, you'd be in the ground.* I wasn't sure if that'd be worse, or better.

I pictured David's face as he walked into our kitchen that night. His pained expression was so full of fear and grief, as if it was his flesh I'd cut into.

I slipped the bracelet back on my wrist. *Hide the scar, bury the memory.* With each passing day, it seemed harder to make myself forget. When all was said and done, did it even matter whether he was lying? I didn't deserve to walk or talk or breathe. If I had a knife, I'd finish what I started in the kitchen that night. I just wanted to stop thinking. Stop remembering. *Stop breathing.*

25

CHARLIE

The sun was coming up by the time I got back from Nellie's beach, which meant I could go check on Emma soon. I eagerly jumped out of bed, showered and dressed in my usual, t-shirt and jeans. I still couldn't quite believe Emma had tiptoed to my room in the middle of the night.

Once I was dressed and ready for the day, I sat down on the edge of my bed. Was it too early to go knocking on Emma's door? She hadn't exactly gotten a full night's sleep, and I didn't want to disturb her if she still needed rest. Either way, I didn't feel like sitting alone in my room so I got up, walked to the door and opened it. Drumming my fingers against the doorjamb, I looked down the hall at Emma's door. Deciding I should probably give her more time to sleep, I stepped out of my room, pulled the door shut and headed toward the common rooms.

The largest room was the most populated and since I didn't really feel like being alone, I walked in. Frank was shuffling around the room, wringing his hands and mumbling to himself, floppy slippers accentuating his every step. He narrowed his eyes at me as I stepped in the room.

I greeted him with a cheerful, "Morning, Frank."

He kept walking without even acknowledging that he'd heard me.

Bob was sitting on the couch, dressed in gray pants and a dark blue button down shirt. His eyes were glued to the morning news, like the safety of the planet depended on his diligence. I walked over and sat down next to him. He looked at me but didn't say anything.

I smiled at him. "Morning, Bob."

He turned back to the screen. "Keep it down. I wanna hear this."

"No prob, Bob."

"Shut up, kid," he grumbled, without looking from the screen.

I promised young Bob that I'd get some answers about his past. How the hell was I going to do that? Old Bob wasn't exactly a chatter box. It was also very possible that he couldn't even remember his own story. Spenser sure as hell wasn't going to fork that information over to me. Nellie was probably the best one to ask, at least she would've been if she wasn't so pissed at me. So, why not give talking to old Bob a shot? Worst case scenario, he'd start swearing and yelling and I'd leave. I turned to the grumpy old man sitting next to me. "So what's your story, Bob? What'd you do before this place, and what brought you here?"

He looked away from the television. "What the fuck's with all the questions, kid?"

I got his attention. That alone was a major accomplishment. "You seem like an interesting guy. I just thought it'd be nice to get to know you better."

He looked at me like I'd sprouted a second head. "Get to know me *better*? You think you know me now?"

"Not really... I guess I should've said, I'd like to get to know you...not better...just a little," I rambled. "How's that?"

"How's what?" he asked, still looking at me like I was a circus sideshow freak.

I shrugged. "I just meant, does it sound better if I phrase it that way?"

"What am I, your fuckin teacher?" he grumbled. "What do I care how you say it?"

"Right." I tried hard not to let my amusement show on my face. "Let me change the question. Tell me a little about yourself."

Bob scowled at me. "That ain't a question."

"I thought you weren't my teacher."

To my complete amazement, Bob grinned. "I'll tell ya somethin about myself, kid. I like to watch the television without gettin interrupted by stupid questions."

"It wasn't a question, remember?"

Bob actually chuckled. "Kid, what do I have to say to get you to go away, so I can watch my TV?"

Now we're getting somewhere. "Just answer one question. What did you do for a living before you ended up here?"

His wrinkled face contorted, like he was physically struggling to recall the information. After a painfully long minute of that, he frowned. "I can't remember. I don't think I've ever been anywhere but here, kid." He looked genuinely upset that he couldn't remember.

I decided it was probably best to let it drop, for the time being at least. "I'm not sure I ever have either, Bob."

That seemed to appease him a little. He looked back at the television but as he did, he had one last thing to say, "Nice talkin with ya, kid."

I couldn't have stopped myself from smiling if my life depended on it. "Nice talking to you too, Bob." With my investigation at a temporary standstill, I got up and headed for the door. That's when Nellie walked into the room and stopped, blocking my exit. Hair an even more tangled mess than usual, she just stood there scowling up at me with her bony hands on the hips of her faded housecoat.

I flashed her a cheesy grin. "Morning, Nellie."

She answered with a squeak that was meant to be a growl. "Fuck off."

My cheesy grin widened. "Thanks. You have a great day, too."

"Get outta my way, Dream-squasher."

"Giving me a nickname? I knew you cared. Dream-squasher has a nice ring to it."

She reached up and slapped me but she was so frail, it hurt about as much as a swat from a fly swatter. Witnessing the assault, Tim rushed across the room to my aid. "Nellie, be nice," he reprimanded, like he was scolding a naughty kindergartener.

"Fuck off, troll boy!" Nellie snarled.

Tim looked like he wasn't sure how to react to that.

The poor guy was so stinking dim-witted, I usually couldn't help but feel sorry for him. "We're good, Tim," I gave him an appreciative nod. "Thanks for the backup though."

He nodded to me, then turned to Nellie. She stuck her tongue out at him and he shook his head, apparently concluding she wasn't as big a threat as he'd originally feared. With one final demeaning, "Be nice," he walked away.

"Troll," Nellie muttered, as he moved out of earshot.

"You're even more of a ray of sunshine than usual this morning, Nellie."

"You took my fucking sunshine and suffocated it." Her scowl deepened as she stepped around me and headed for the nearest table.

I'd done all the socializing I could take for one morning but thanks to all the time it'd killed, it was probably late enough to go see Emma. I headed out the door toward her room and miraculously made it all the way there without any more exchanges with fellow patients.

I knocked lightly on her door, hoping it wouldn't wake her if she was still sleeping.

She answered instantly, "Charlie?"

Good. I obviously hadn't woken her. "Hey, Em."

She didn't answer, but I heard soft footsteps approach the door. It opened slowly and I never would've guessed I'd utter these words, but she looked terrible. Her posture was slumped, her expression dismal, red puffy eyes made it obvious she'd been crying and her normally silky hair was a tousled mess.

"What's wrong?" I whispered.

"Everything," she sobbed.

I wrapped my arms around her, and she dropped her head against my chest. Not really sure what to say, I tried to lighten the mood a little. "Wow. One night with me and you're miserable."

She looked up at me with a sigh of relief. "So, it did happen."

Okay. Now I was really starting to worry. "It did. Don't you remember coming to my room last night?"

"I do, "she answered softly as a tear slipped down her cheek. "I just wasn't sure it was real. I don't know what to believe anymore."

This was breaking my heart. "Then just believe you can lean on me," I whispered, lowering my head to rest on top of hers, "and we'll figure the rest out together. Alright?"

"Alright," she half-sobbed, half-whispered.

26

EMMA

I numbly followed Charlie's suggestion to go back into the room and get dressed, barely registering the sound of him closing the door behind me. Normally, I'd shower before dressing but this morning it didn't seem worth the effort. Trance-like, I walked to the dresser, pulled out the first clothes my hands touched and stripped off my pajamas, letting them drop to the floor at my feet. I shrugged into the clothes I'd grabbed without a thought about if they matched or how they looked. Then I shuffled into the bathroom to use the facilities and drag a comb through my hair, but I didn't look in the mirror. I didn't care how I looked, and I hated the girl the mirror reflected.

Ready as I cared to be, I walked back to the door and opened it. Charlie stood in the hallway exactly where I'd left him.

He took my hand in his and gave it a gentle squeeze. "Ready?"

I nodded, afraid that if I spoke I'd start to cry again. He put an arm around my shoulders and started walking. I moved along with him, my thoughts a million miles away. I didn't deserve comfort from anyone, especially not someone as good and kind as Charlie.

I stopped walking and he stopped beside me. "What is it, Em?"

"I can't do this anymore," I muttered without meeting his eyes.

"Can't do what?" he whispered.

"All of it—walk, talk...breathe. I don't deserve to be alive."

Charlie tipped his head and touched his forehead to mine. I met his gaze and watched the tears pool in his eyes. "Talk to me, Em." He sighed, almost as if it pained him. "Let me help. If you stopped walking and talking and breathing, I don't think I could take it."

The pain in his voice reminded me of David's reaction the night he found me. Though, I don't think any other voice could ever match the depth of despair that'd been in David's. Self-loathing gripped me as my body started to fall and my mind slipped back...

...With a strangled cry, David rushed across the room to me. Bright red stains smeared the front of his perfectly tailored suit as he cradled my limp body, gripping

a blood-soaked kitchen towel to my wrist. There was so much blood. Even the tears sliding down his cheeks were tinged with the red of my blood, as if punctuating the absoluteness of the anguish in his eyes. I looked up at his grief-stricken face and felt my life draining from me...

...We were on the hallway floor. Charlie was holding me in his arms, like David had. I looked up at his worried expression. I could see that he was talking, but I couldn't make out his words. Then someone was lifting me, laying me on a stiff mattress. I looked back at Charlie. He was trying to stop them from taking me, but the bed started moving. I watched the ceiling scroll by as they rushed me down the hall. Then Dr. Spenser's face was hovering over me, full of grandfatherly concern as he spoke. But his words were lost to me. I felt something puncture my skin and prayed that he was cutting me, ending my misery. Then everything went dark...

... Brilliant sunlight bathed my skin in warmth as a gentle breeze wafted over me, carrying the mingled scents of meadow grass and wildflowers in bloom. I opened my eyes. The sky above me was a perfect cloudless blue. I lay on sweet grass, listening to a jubilant chorus of birds and insects. And I felt at peace.

Was this the afterlife?

I heard a bellow not far from me, then footfalls quickly pounding nearer. Someone knelt beside me but for some reason, my eyes stayed fixed on the blue of the sky. Strong hands scooped me up, cradling me to a warm body but I was frozen, completely at the mercy of the figure holding me. I felt him lean over me, still I only saw sky. A welcome kiss caressed my lips...

...I opened my eyes, expecting to see him. Instead, florescent light shone too brightly in my face. The chemical stench of hospital disinfectant hung heavy in the air and the doctor's face hovered over me, hazy and unfocused.

"Emma," a voice called from far away.

I looked up at Dr. Spenser. His mouth was moving again, had he been talking to me? *Who called my name?* I tried to sit up but Dr. Spenser shook his head, gently guiding my shoulders back to the mattress.

"Doctor?" I asked groggily.

"Relax, Emma," his voice sounded through some unseen tunnel.

"Where am I?" I managed to mumble.

"You're in the infirmary."

"Where's David?" I shifted, searching the room for him.

"Your husband isn't here, dear," his voice calmly echoed.

My head hurt. "I felt him."

"Just rest, Emma."

I closed my eyes...

...The sun's warmth enveloped me as a gentle breeze blew across my skin. I felt his arms around me, but I didn't dare open my eyes. I was too afraid it'd all melt away and I'd see Spenser's face again.

"Emma," his voice whispered.

I squeezed my eyes tighter to keep myself from slipping from the dream.

"Open your eyes," he whispered, his mouth not far from my ear.

"I'm afraid," I whimpered.

"Of what?" His whispered words were drenched in sorrow. "Of me?"

"No," I murmured. "Never of you. I'm afraid I'll open my eyes and you'll be gone."

He sighed softly. "Look at me."

I reluctantly obliged, dreading—yet fully expecting—to see the doctor's face again. His blue eyes returned my gaze. A single tear slipped down my cheek, and he tenderly brushed it away with his thumb.

I was afraid to even blink for fear of losing him when my eyes reopened. "I can't do this anymore."

"I'm so sorry," he murmured, heartache brimming in his beautiful eyes.

I hesitated a second before muttering, "For what?"

"I failed you," he whispered. "You should never have had to go there."

"I want to come home to you." I wanted it so badly that my heart hurt.

"There's nothing I want more," he answered softly. "I promise, I will bring you home soon. In the meantime, remember what I told you. Tell them what they want to hear."

"I'm so tired," I muttered.

He stroked my cheek with his fingertips. "Then rest, and never forget how much I love you."

"I love you," I whispered as my eyelids grew heavy. I closed them and felt safe for the first time in a long time, cradled in the warmth of his arms...

..."Emma," the doctor's voice echoed.

No. It was too soon. I didn't want to leave, but I knew it was already too late. I couldn't feel his arms anymore. All I felt was the uncomfortable mattress beneath me. I hated the doctor for pulling me away. Resentfully, I lifted my eyelids.

Dr. Spenser was sitting beside me. "How do you feel?"

"I want to go home," I whimpered.

The doctor gave me a sympathetic smile that only made me hate him more. "I'm afraid I can't make that happen yet, dear."

My eyes welled with tears.

"Are you ready to talk about what brought you here, Emma?" Spenser coaxed. "That's the first step you can take toward going home, or at least seeing your husband."

"Why are you keeping him from me?" A horrible thought occurred to me and dread churned in the pit of my stomach as I whispered, "Does he not want to see me?"

The doctor flashed another sickening smile. "If there's one thing I can tell you with absolute certainty, it's that he wants to see you very badly. Your husband is an incredibly," he seemed to struggle for the right word, "*persistent* man."

I smiled, despite my heartache. I knew exactly how persistent David could be. "What do I have to do to see him?"

"Talk to me," the doctor answered. "Open up about what brought you here."

I let out a weary sigh. I couldn't remember ever feeling so exhausted. "Right now?"

He answered with another patronizing smile and it vaguely crossed my mind that if I didn't feel like such a zombie, I would've slapped it off his face. "No. Right now you need to rest and when you feel up to it, you can go out to the common rooms."

"I'd like that," I whispered flatly, thinking how worried Charlie must be.

27

CHARLIE

One second, Emma was talking to me. The next, she was collapsing and I was getting pushed aside as medical staff rushed to her aid. Tim lifted her onto a gurney and promptly wheeled her away. No one would let me follow. As far as they were concerned, I was nothing to Emma. I wasn't family, I wasn't a spouse or significant other. Maybe that did make me nothing. I needed to stop being such an idiot. I was something she sorely needed in this place, a friend. But a fellow patient, friend or not, had no right to sit by her side in the infirmary. Now I knew how she must've felt the night I first saw the dragon and fell into the Waters.

I don't know how long I sat there in the hallway after they took her away, to me it felt like hours. Eventually I started thinking rationally enough to realize no one would be coming back to tell me how she was, so I picked myself up and started walking.

I had no idea how to help Emma or even what was wrong for that matter. How much did I really know about her? I suspected she had a split personality, but I didn't know for sure. I knew a dragon followed her, or was a part of her, or was her split personality's Dream form. I knew she had a husband but beyond that, she was really still a mystery.

My aimless wandering eventually took me to the small common room. Our room. Figuring it was as good a place to wait as any, I sat down on our loveseat and stared blankly at the door. I didn't realize I wasn't alone until I heard hushed sounds across the room. Nellie was in her usual seat by the window. When she noticed me looking at her, she stood up and headed over. But Nellie was the last person I felt like dealing with. I went back to staring vacantly at the door, hoping she'd take the hint.

Without a word, she sat down next to me. I kept looking straight ahead, ignoring her. After several minutes of uncomfortable silence, she let out a weary sigh and shifted toward me. Out of the corner of my eye, I watched her mouth open to speak twice. Both times, she stopped before making a sound, which was fine with me. I didn't care what she had to say.

"I'm not up to a fight right now, Nellie," I muttered flatly.

She shook her head. "I wasn't going to start one." When I didn't answer, she exhaled a slow deliberate breath. "Walk away, Charlie." Her tired voice was laced with hints of sorrow and regret.

I turned to look at her. "What are you talking about?"

"Emma," she whispered, "she'll never bring you anything but hurt."

"I didn't realize you were psychic in addition to all your other talents."

Her shoulders sagged. "Not psychic, just experienced."

"Really?" I snapped. "You were once a guy who was friends with Emma?"

"Don't be an idiot. I was once a blind fool like you're being now."

I turned to stare at the door again. "I don't have the energy for this, Nellie."

She let out another weary sigh. "Why do you refuse to listen to me? You know I'm more than just a crazy old lady."

"What've you done for me?" I asked bitterly. "You tell me you have all these tricks, but you don't share them with me. You give me vague fortune-cookie-ish warnings of impending doom, and you yell at me. According to you, I'm even responsible for blotting out the sun. I squash dreams, remember?"

"Dragons squash dreams." From the corner of my eye, I watched her nervously search the room like she was worried a dragon might be hidden some-where, listening.

Despite everything, I was curious. "What did dragons do to you?"

I felt her shiver beside me. "Dragon," she corrected softly, "singular. Deceived me. Used me. Destroyed me."

I turned toward her and she shifted away from me, but not enough to hide the tears her milky eyes were trying to blink away. "It's a long story."

Suddenly, being left alone didn't seem as important as hearing Nellie's story. She was the only person I knew with any information about dragons, and I really wanted answers. "What else have we got to do?"

She sniffed back the tears. "It isn't a story with a happy ending."

I fought the urge to laugh at the obviousness of that statement. "I kind of figured that."

She closed her eyes and shook her head. As she did, she flipped several times very quickly. Snarled gray hair flipped to rust-colored ringlets, saggy wrinkled skin transformed to a pale flawless complexion and her ratty old housecoat became a bright green sundress. She was still partially turned away from me, and as her shoulders flipped—from faded cloth to youthful flesh—I saw the scars on her shoulder blades. "What are the scars from?"

Young and angelic, she turned to me. A tear slid down her porcelain cheek as she started to answer, but we were both distracted by something moving on the floor beside the loveseat.

"What was that?" I whispered.

A small bare foot poked into view around the corner of the loveseat. "Please…" Young Nellie choked back a sob as she shook her head. "Don't say anything."

Before I had time to decide if I even had anything to say, a very young girl with curls like Nellie's peeked out from behind the loveseat. Then Nellie flipped, and the child disappeared.

"Is that who you're always rocking and singing to?" I whispered, stunned by what I'd just seen.

Old Nellie nodded, looking painfully tired. I'd learned her secret and her ability to keep her Dream form hidden appeared to be failing her.

"Why can I see you now?"

Nellie's eyes were still glued to the child that I couldn't see. "You've always been able to see me. I told you, you only see what you want to see."

That didn't make any sense. Before that first time Nellie spoke to me, I hadn't cared enough to make an effort one way or the other. "Why wouldn't I want to see that?"

"I don't know," she whispered hoarsely, "maybe a part of you sensed the danger, or maybe you didn't want to see how broken I was."

"You don't look broken."

"You see my scars." Young Nellie was sitting in the old woman's place again and the toddler was back on the floor, staring up at me with wide innocent eyes.

Feeling oddly spellbound by the child's gaze, I whispered, "Who is she?"

Nellie reached down and lifted the girl to her lap. "My daughter."

I was at a loss for words.

Young Nellie smoothed a hand over the child's curls. "Her name is Lilly." The little girl blinked at the sound of her name.

"Hey, Lilly," I whispered, then looked up at Nellie. She was old and frail again, cradling a child that wasn't there. "Nellie, you said flipped images were nothing but memories and visions from the Dream World. How can you pick up a memory and put it on your lap?"

Nellie flipped back to her younger self. "She's REAL!"

I'd obviously hit a nerve. Was she lying when she told me they were just memories and visions, or was she lying to herself about the child? I seriously doubted she'd answer that question, but I'd learned more from this conversation than from any other we'd had. If I asked different questions, maybe I could learn even more. "Who's her father?"

She hugged the child a little closer. "She doesn't have one."

The little girl reached out to me, and I extended a tentative hand toward her. Nellie promptly swatted my hand away. "You can't touch her."

I dropped my hand to my lap. "Because you won't let me or because I wouldn't be able to?"

Old Nellie scowled at me. "Both, stupid."

I ignored the insult. "Then why can you pick her up?"

Young Nellie rolled her eyes at me as Lilly reappeared on her lap. "Because I have a foot in both worlds. Don't you remember anything I teach you?"

"Stop being so mysterious. A foot in both worlds, what the hell does that mean?"

She smoothed the wrinkles from Lilly's dress. "I really can't explain it. I don't know how I do it."

"Alright." There was no sense in wasting time with questions she couldn't or wouldn't answer. "Will you tell me about the dragon that hurt you?"

Fear flashed in her eyes as she cautiously searched the room again. "I can't."

"Why not?" I followed her eyes and didn't see anything out of the ordinary. "Is there another dragon that I'm not seeing?"

Her eyes widened. "Dear God, I hope not."

"Sorry," I muttered sheepishly. "I just meant, why are you so afraid to tell me?"

The tension in her body eased, but only a little. "Do you remember me telling you that there are dark places in the Dream Forest, places you shouldn't go because you'll leave less than you were?"

I nodded.

"I was speaking from experience," she whispered.

Just once, couldn't she give me a straight answer? "Cryptic and unhelpful."

She frowned, like she was truly hurt by my comment. "Very helpful if you'd listen. *Dragons* come from those dark places."

"So, Emma lives in a dark place in the Dream forest?" I asked skeptically.

Nellie nodded, looking pleased that I'd understood.

I watched Lilly's little fingers play with the hem of her dress. "Is that where you met the dragon?"

"No," old Nellie muttered, looking extremely frail in contrast to her Dream form, "I met the dragon in a place like this."

I raked my hair back from my face. "Like I met Emma."

"I met him in the Dream World shortly after I met him in this world, and he befriended me in both worlds." A dreamy tone crept into her voice as she whispered, "He showed me things and taught me things I never could've imagined in my wildest dreams, and I fell in love with him in both worlds."

Okay. I hadn't seen that coming. "You fell in love with a dragon?"

"I told you, Charlie, I speak from experience. I was as foolish as you once." She stopped to think for a second. "More foolish, I think."

"So what happened?" I asked, genuinely curious.

"Trust me." Young Nellie hugged the child on her lap. "You don't want to know."

"I do actually."

Nellie seemed to consider telling me more but when she opened her mouth to speak, something across the room stopped her.

I turned to see what she was looking at. Emma was shuffling through the doorway, leaning heavily on Tim for support. It was painfully obvious that she'd been drugged. Behind them sauntered the dragon, glaring furiously at everyone and everything.

I looked back at Nellie, old and shriveled and cowering with fear. Could the dragon touch her since she had 'a foot in both worlds'?

Suppressing my own fear of the beast, I stood up and headed toward Emma. She smiled drowsily when she noticed me.

"Hey, Em." The dragon's shadow eclipsed us both and I felt the heat of its breath on my face, but I didn't look up. I just nodded to Tim. "I can take it from here, buddy."

Tim nodded back and slowly let go as I put my arm around Emma. Then he turned to her with a big dopey grin. "You let me know if you need anything, Emma."

She flashed him an appreciative smile and groggily muttered, "Thank you, Tim." And he turned and left the room, grinning like a giant who'd just feasted on the tender flesh of a princess.

I suppressed a shiver at the thought. "To our usual spot?"

Emma nodded, and old Nellie scrambled away from the loveseat as quickly as her frail old body could manage.

We moved slowly, our path darkened by the dragon's enormous shadow. I ignored it. I had two feet in this world—if it could touch me and it wanted to, it would've by now—at least, that's what I told myself.

We sat down and the dragon lumbered around the loveseat to stand guard behind us. Again, I felt its scorching breath on my neck. Emma slumped against the back of the couch. I watched her, feeling the dragon's burning stare as I considered what to say.

"I'm sorry," she whimpered.

The pain in her voice was like a knife to my heart. "For what?"

"Everything," she whispered.

"You don't have anything to be sorry for, Em."

She smiled, but it was a sorrowful smile. "I wish that was true."

"Talk to me," I encouraged softly.

Eyes fixed on the extravagant gold band around her wrist, she drowsily lifted her arm and turned to me.

"Talk to me," I whispered.

She slipped the cuff off, revealing a deep scar that ran up her arm from her slender wrist.

I leaned back, slouching close to her and ignoring the blast of heat to the top of my head. "Want to talk about it?"

She tilted her head to touch mine. "What would I say?"

I reached up and tenderly traced the scar with a fingertip. "Tell me what happened." Then I took her hand in mine and placed it between us, earning another blast of heat to the head.

We sat in silence for a while, with her hand in mine and our bodies slouched together. After a few minutes, she muttered, "You'll hate me."

"I could never hate you, Em."

She bit her lip as her eyes filled with tears. "You don't know what I did."

"Doesn't matter," I whispered, "There's nothing you could do to make me hate you. Best friends don't judge, remember?"

She made a soft sound that was almost a laugh but without any joy. "I almost forgot."

"I promise," I whispered. "You can tell me anything."

Her breath hitched. "If I lose you, I'll never make it in here."

"Could never happen. Talk to me."

She gave a slight nod. "I tried to kill myself and failed."

"That's not telling me any more than your arm already did," I whispered.

"I don't know where to start," she sobbed.

I gave her hand an encouraging squeeze. "Start with whatever you think of first."

"My husband has always been the most important person in my life," she whispered reverently. "We've been together since I was sixteen."

I gave her hand another squeeze. "That'd make you high school sweethearts."

She smiled faintly to herself. "Not exactly. I've known David all my life. He was my father's business partner and closest friend."

"Oh," I muttered, wondering how to respond to such an unexpected statement. "Your father was okay with that?"

She didn't even hesitate to consider the question. "Not at all."

"Does the reason you hadn't spoken to him in years have anything to do with that?"

"It has everything to do with that." She wiped a tear from her cheek with her free hand. "But my relationship with my father was a small price to pay. We were never close."

I got the feeling there was a lot more to that story.

She gave my hand a slight squeeze, more reflex than purposeful gesture. "David was more loving than my father ever was."

"So your husband's a pedophile." *Shit. I really needed to filter what came out of my mouth.*

She didn't seem offended. "I can understand why you'd think that, but there was nothing even slightly inappropriate about our relationship when I was a child. I was like the daughter he never had, and he treated me with the loving devotion that my father never did. Our adult relationship didn't start until I was old enough to be in that kind of relationship."

"With another teenager, not a man old enough to be your father." *Why the hell did I keep blurting things out without thinking?*

"A pedophile is a person who preys on children," she stated absolutely, shaking her head, "a man who desires to be with children, sexually. David is a man who has always desired to be with *me*, to love *me*, but he's always loved me in a way that was appropriate for my age. When I was a little girl, he loved me like a father. When I grew up, he kept on loving me. Our relationship just evolved. I get how that might sound wrong. I don't know how to explain it so it makes sense to someone else."

"Let's just assume I understand," I whispered.

"Even though you don't," she replied softly.

I hesitated a second, then nodded.

I guess she decided that was good enough. "I can't even begin to cover all the history between us, but he's the center of my universe and I'm his. That's how it's always been."

"If things were so wonderful, what made you try to take your own life?" *Jesus. What the hell was wrong with me?*

She looked down at her arm and muttered, "The thought of losing him."

"Go on."

She started to cry and barely managed to whisper, "I can't."

Spenser walked through the door and headed our way before any more stupid comments could pop out of my mouth.

28

NELLIE

The boy was a damn fool. I tried to warn him, but he wouldn't listen. I'd even tried to warn the girl. She wouldn't listen either, but I couldn't really blame her. She wasn't Sighted. To her, I was just crazy old Nellie—blathering on about fairytales and nonsense—but fairytales are real. Folks without Sight can't grasp that. All those stories of fairies and dragons and giants and trolls are nothing but fantasy to them, but those of us with Sight know they're more like history. At least, we should. Which brings me back to my first statement. Charlie was a fool.

To be honest, I couldn't really fault him either. I'd been just as clueless as Charlie once upon a time. I didn't know anything about our world back then. I'm not talking about the world we're in now. I'm talking about *our* world, the one that belongs to those of us with Sight. Most people are born into this world, oblivious to the Dream World. They're the Unsighted. They close their eyes when their head hits the pillow and drift off to the World of Dreams. To them, it's nothing but a lovely escape from reality. But to those of us with Sight, it's every bit as real as the other world. We remember the Dream World clearly when we wake, and we catch flickering glimpses of a person's truer self in this world.

Our Dream forms shape who are in both worlds— all of us, Sighted or not. There are too many different Dream forms to name, but every creature in the World of Dreams fits into one of two categories: they're either a creature of Light or a creature of Darkness. It's what we are at our core and there's no changing it.

The lucky Sighted, both Light and Dark, are born to a Sighted parent. They're taught from birth to ignore the images they see in this world because not everybody can see them. But not all Sighted are born lucky. Some are born to Sightless parents, no one sees what they see and nobody's around to teach them to pretend not to see it. And in this world, if you see things that nobody else does, there's only one explanation. You're a fucking lunatic.

I was one of the unlucky Sighted, back in the days when crazy folks were sent away and kept hidden. All my childhood years were spent in loony bins, and the images that only I saw were my waking nightmares.

The doctors fed me all sorts of pills to make my 'hallucinations' disappear, but I still saw it all. I was just too drugged out of my fucking mind to react.

I sympathized with Charlie right from the start. He was unlucky, too. He'd never met another Sighted person, not as far as he knew anyway. It'd taken years for a Sighted person to find me and years more for him to teach me. I knew I could've been that sort of guide to Charlie, but I was too afraid to reach out. The first lesson that every Sighted person learns, is to ignore what you see no matter how much it disturbs you. I might've learned the lesson later in life than most but it was just as deeply ingrained in me, probably more. I would've gone right on ignoring all of Charlie's stupidity, but everything changed the day *she* showed up.

Charlie ignored a lot of what he could see. He didn't pretend not to see it. His mind just ignored it altogether. Maybe his brain was overwhelmed by all the images around him or maybe subconsciously, he ignored the ones that scared him the most. Whatever the reason, Charlie didn't see the dragon at first. In fact, he refused to see the beast for days. But I saw it. The very first time that girl walked up to our circle, her dragon strolled right along with her. Even after Charlie finally saw it, he seemed to choose when to notice it and when not to, but it was always there. Every time she walked into a room that dragon followed her. Charlie had no idea how much danger he was putting himself in. I probably should've kept my fat mouth shut and stayed the hell out of it. After all, I had more reason to fear dragons than just about anybody, but how could I sit by and watch that dragon destroy the boy? Fool or not, he didn't deserve to suffer the sort of living hell that I did. Nobody deserved that.

Those were the thoughts that went through my head while I sat by the window like a cowering fool. When that dragon walked into the room, it took every bit of courage I could muster to get off the loveseat and scurry away. I wanted to run out of the room and get as far away as I could but the dragon stood between me and the door, and it was angry. So I snuck to my chair, shaking like a leaf and praying not to bring any attention to myself. I couldn't let that Darkness see my daughter. So I stayed quiet and still and watched the beast breathe down Charlie's neck. I wanted to help, but what could I do?

While I was concentrating on making myself as invisible as I could, the doctor walked in and headed straight to Charlie and the girl, the sweet old man's face masking the toad's. He wasn't a particularly quiet man, so I could easily overhear their conversation.

The doctor knelt down in front of the girl, pulled a penlight from the pocket of his white coat and checked her eyes. "How are you feeling, Emma?"

"Alright," she muttered sluggishly. It didn't take a medical degree to tell they'd drugged the shit out of her.

The doctor turned to Charlie, without scowling for once. "Would you two be up to joining us for a group session in a little while?" The question was directed more to Charlie than the girl. "Emma's having a hard time opening up. She needs to feel safe in order to share what's troubling her and you obviously make her feel safe, Charlie. I think it might be easier for her to start talking if you were with her."

I was as shocked by the toad's words as Charlie looked. The boy knew exactly how to push the doctor's buttons, and he did it all the time just for the fun of it. Dr. Spenser usually struggled to hide his true feelings toward Charlie. The toad-man just couldn't understand why Charlie hated him so much because he wasn't Sighted. He had no idea what a monster he was.

Charlie looked at Emma. "What do you think?"

She blinked at him with a dopey look on her perfect face. The wheels in her pretty little head obviously weren't turning full speed. "I'd feel better talking with you, than without you."

That was all Charlie needed to hear. "We're in, Doc."

The toad nodded then walked away grinning, from what was easily the most pleasant conversation he and Charlie had ever had.

Charlie stood, helped Emma up and steadied her as they started walking. And the dragon snorted more heat at the back of his head as it followed them out the door.

I needed to find a place to hide. I couldn't sit in a circle near that dragon. I couldn't risk letting it see my daughter but before I could find a place to tuck away to avoid group therapy, that half-witted troll came in to drag me to the session.

29

EMMA

With each step Charlie and I took toward the large common room, I regretted agreeing to participate in the group session a little bit more. How could I possibly share my story with a circle full of people? It'd taken me this long just to work up the courage to start opening up to Charlie alone. I stopped moving. "I don't think I can do this."

Charlie raked his hair back from his face. "Should I tell Spenser you aren't up to it?"

David's words echoed in my head. *Tell them what they want to hear.* And I let out a defeated sigh. "If I don't join in, Dr. Spenser will just want me to open up to him in private, at least this way I won't be alone."

"I'll be right next to you," Charlie promised. "Just say the word and we'll make our exit."

I nodded and we started walking again.

When we stepped into the big room, the folding chairs were already arranged in a semicircle on the far side of the room. Dr. Spenser was seated in the center chair, flipping through the pages of a binder and periodically pulling a pen from his pocket to jot something down. But the rest of the seats were still empty.

Bob was in his usual spot on the couch, watching the evening news or at least staring at the screen. It was kind of hard to tell with Bob. Charlie led me to the couch, sat me next to Bob and sat down on my other side. As usual, Bob's attention stayed fixed on the screen.

To my surprise, Charlie greeted him with a friendly, "Hey, Bob."

Even more surprising, Bob answered, "Hi, kid." But his eyes stayed glued to the screen.

I was still feeling foggy from whatever the doctor had injected me with, but a familiar name coming from the television still managed to grab my attention. "...In local news, forty-five year old divorce attorney Sophie Turner was found dead in the bedroom of her penthouse apartment this morning. Turner was employed by the law offices of Talbot and Associates, a prosperous local firm that has long provided counsel to many of the community's most prestigious and affluent members. A confidential source from the police department informed us, that at this time the cause of death remains undetermined and the possibility of foul play has not been eliminated.

According to friends and neighbors, Ms. Turner was in peak physical health and given Ms. Turner's notorious reputation for ensuring that her clients' demands were always generously satisfied by the close of court proceedings, there's been some speculation as to whether revenge might've provided a motive for murder. David Talbot, owner and co-founder of the law firm under its original title, Talbot and Reed, was not available for comment. But co-workers, still grappling with the shock of Ms. Turner's sudden and unexpected death, told us that she will be greatly missed…"

I did my best to keep looking drowsy and unfocused as I fought the urge to vomit.

Charlie noticed but didn't make it obvious. "Walk with me for a minute before group gets started?" I'm not even sure I managed a nod but he stood up, held out his hand and helped me from the couch. Almost as an afterthought, Charlie looked over his shoulder. "See ya later, Bob."

Bob nodded without looking from the screen and I groggily glanced around the room, relieved to see that he was the only person anywhere near us. Unless Charlie and I were actually on the screen, I was pretty sure nothing that we did would draw his attention.

We went back to the small room as quickly as I could manage in my altered state, headed straight to our loveseat and sat down. Thankfully, we had the room to ourselves.

"Talk to me, Em," Charlie whispered as he sunk back against the cushions, "Something about that news report upset you. Talbot is *your* last name, isn't it?"

I dropped back against the cushions beside him, let out a shaky breath and nodded. "That's my husband's law firm."

"Your *husband's* firm?" Charlie echoed. "*David Talbot* is your husband?"

I nodded again. "And Albert Reed was my father."

Charlie raised his eyebrows, looking more than a little impressed. "I knew you had money, but I didn't realize you had *that* kind of money."

I smiled, despite my rising panic. "So now you like him?"

Charlie shook his head without missing a beat. "No. He's still a pedophile. He's just an impressively wealthy pedophile."

I opened my mouth to defend my husband, then realized it wasn't important at the moment. "Not now, Charlie."

"Right. Table the pedophile debate until later," Charlie muttered. "Did you know that lawyer who died?"

The contents of my stomach surged, but I needed to talk this through. "Yes," I whispered, before my nerves could get the better of me.

"Can you elaborate?"

"Are you sure you could never feel differently about me?" I winced. "No matter what?"

Charlie nodded. "You can tell me anything, but you'd better talk quick because group'll be starting soon."

I swallowed, steeling my resolve. "Sophie Turner is the reason I'm here."

Charlie frowned, almost apologetically. "Can you explain that a little more?"

"I was taking an antidepressant because I was having trouble coping with my father's death," I whispered, barreling past the voice in my head that was warning me to keep quiet. This would be the first time I'd ever told the whole story to anyone. "We were at the firm's Christmas party and I really wasn't supposed to drink while taking the medication, but I only planned on having one. The trouble is, once I have one, I lose all good judgment and forget I shouldn't have more. It usually isn't a problem because David always reminds me when to stop, but he was busy mingling with clients that night and people kept getting me drinks." I stopped, dreading what came next.

Charlie touched his head to mine. "Go on."

I took a deep breath. "One minute, I was fine and the next, the combination of the drug and the alcohol had me feeling really fuzzy, so I went into the ladies' room to collect myself. I was touching my lipstick up at the mirror when I looked up and saw Sophie standing behind me, grinning"…

...As I told Charlie the rest, it all came rushing back as vividly as if it'd happened hours ago...

Sophie smiled at me. "Enjoying the party?"

I smiled politely back at her reflection. "I am. And you?"

She chuckled softly to herself. "I'd be enjoying it a lot more, if you'd stayed home."

"Excuse me?" I wasn't exactly sure what she was implying, but I was sure I didn't like her tone.

"What I enjoy," she rasped wickedly, "is your husband."

Her words were making me feel dangerously queasy. "What are you talking about?"

Her filthy smile widened as she raised an eyebrow. "I think you know." Her reflection's gaze traveled to my necklace. "David certainly does love to mark what's his, doesn't he? You're lucky. You get to wear yours all the time. He only lets me wear mine when he fucks me."

The ground beneath my feet was beginning to crumble but I couldn't seem to remember how to move or speak, so I stood frozen as she shattered my heart.

"He says it's a fabulous change of pace to be with a woman instead of a girl. You see love, he's getting rather tired of playing Daddy while his little wife cries on his shoulder."

I desperately needed to vomit, but I fought it. I couldn't give her the satisfaction.

"You should thank me for showing him a few new moves," she murmured, stepping closer. "He really is an

amazing lover, the best I've ever had. But you don't have anyone to compare him to, do you?"

My eyes welled with tears, but I refused to let her see me cry so I tore myself out of immobility and sped to the door.

"Nice chatting with you, dear," she taunted behind me as I pulled the door open.

I wandered back into the party in a devastated haze. The room was too full of people and music and laughter. Every festive detail turned my stomach a little bit more. I scanned the room and found David standing at the far end, talking to a client. I watched him for a minute, feeling more of the floor crumble beneath my feet. Then I rushed toward the exit as quickly as I could without drawing attention to myself, avoiding eye contact so I wouldn't get dragged into any conversation.

Thankfully, I reached the door without anyone stopping me. I pushed it open and a winter breeze hit me like a slap to the face as I stepped outside, but I didn't care. My coat was checked, David had the ticket and I couldn't stand the thought of going near him. Heart throbbing, I rushed toward the parking lot.

It wasn't long before Benjamin appeared at my side. "Mrs. Talbot?" I must've looked awful because he sounded really worried. "Emma?"

"Take me home please," I pleaded in a hollow whisper without meeting his eyes.

"Of course." Benjamin took off his jacket, wrapped it around my shoulders and led me the rest of the way to

the car. When we reached it, he opened the back door and ushered me in. I crawled inside, desperately fighting back the tears.

When we got to the house, Benjamin offered to come inside with me but I gave him an empty promise that I'd be fine and insisted he return to the party so David wouldn't be left without a ride home.

I walked into the house in a trance-like daze. All my life, there'd been one absolute certainty—David loved me—I'd never doubted that, not for a second. I didn't understand how he could've touched another woman. If I'd been thinking clearly, I would've confronted him about it but I was altered and my whole world was crumbling out from under me. I went into the kitchen, grabbed the biggest sharpest knife I could find and dragged it up my wrist. I stared at the cut for a minute, numbly watching the trail of thick red blood deepen and spread. Then I switched the knife to my other hand to slice the other wrist. I didn't realize anyone else was even in the house and dazed as I was, I didn't hear her come into the kitchen. She startled me... I couldn't say the rest out loud.

"What happened?" Charlie whispered.

"Isabella, our housekeeper, snuck up behind me. She tried to grab the knife from my hand, but I wasn't thinking straight. I'm not even sure exactly how it happened, it was all so fast..." I looked up at Charlie and finished in a broken whisper, "I stabbed her."

30

CHARLIE

I sat next to Emma in stunned silence. She'd just shared her darkest secret with me. *I stabbed her.* What was I supposed to say to that? It only took me a matter of seconds to accept her words as simple fact. It'd already happened, she regretted it deeply and she'd trusted me enough to tell me about it, even though she was afraid of losing my friendship because of it.

It was my job to reassure her that I didn't feel any differently about her. "You didn't mean to do it. You weren't yourself."

Crying without making a sound, she closed her eyes and shook her head. I wrapped an arm around her and drew her closer. That only made her cry harder but maybe that was exactly what she needed, a shoulder to cry on. A thought occurred to me and

I wondered why it hadn't sooner. "What happened to your housekeeper? Was it fatal?"

"She was still conscious when David got home," Emma whispered through her tears, "but she lost consciousness before the paramedics got there and she never regained it. She's been in critical condition ever since."

"How long did it take for your husband to find you?"

"Not long," Emma whispered. "Benjamin went straight back to the party after dropping me off. He found David and told him that he'd driven me home and I'd been pretty upset. David knew something wasn't right because I hadn't come to tell him I was leaving, so he left the party right away."

"What happened when he got home?"

"I'll never forget the look on his face when he walked into the kitchen and found the two of us..." Emma took a shaky breath. "When he saw the gash on my arm and all the blood, he looked like he was in pain. To look at his face, you'd have thought I'd just cut him instead of me." She stopped talking and closed her eyes.

"What'd he do?" I prompted softly.

"He looked at Isabella lying on the floor, the front of her blouse soaked in blood, blood pooling around her on the floor," Emma let out a broken sob, "and he walked *past* her to me."

"You're the one he loves," I whispered, not even sure why I was defending him.

Emma wiped a tear from her cheek. "She was obviously hurt worse than I was but he grabbed a kitchen towel, wrapped it around my wrist and scooped me into his arms. I'd never seen him frightened before. Ever."

I brushed another tear from Emma's cheek as she went on. "David wanted to call our private physician for help and leave the police out of it, and I was shocked when Isabella agreed that it would've been the best solution, but she told him it was too late. I'd already called 911. I must've been in shock when I called because I didn't even remember doing it."

Not sure what I could possibly say to comfort her, I tightened my half-hug around Emma's shoulders, wordlessly encouraging her to go on.

"David looked crushed when he heard that I'd called the police," Emma whispered. "I'd never seen him cry before that either. It wasn't long before we heard the sirens but by the time the police and paramedics came into the kitchen, Isabella had lost consciousness. A couple of paramedics rushed her off to the hospital and another paramedic tended to my arm while the police questioned David. I was starting to fade by then, but I heard David tell them he wouldn't answer questions until his lawyer was present. I vaguely remember wondering why the police were only questioning David when he hadn't even witnessed what happened.

The paramedics put me on a stretcher. When David saw them moving me, he walked away from the police and insisted that he needed to be with his wife. He told them that they could ask him questions at the hospital after his attorney arrived. The police agreed and he started walking next to me but the image of Sophie's face, sneering at me in the mirror, popped into my head and I just lost it. I started screaming that I didn't want him anywhere near me. David looked devastated. The police made the paramedics take me away, and I hazily remember them saying something about taking David to the station.

No one ever gave me the details of what happened after that but from the bits of conversations that I overheard, I know that after my hysterics, the police suspected David of stabbing Isabella and cutting me. David didn't correct their assumptions. He let them believe he was guilty until the police eventually figured out that he hadn't come home until after the stabbing.

When I was discharged from the hospital, I should've been taken directly into police custody but David paid an insane amount of bail and made arrangements for me to come home under the care of an in-house psychiatrist and physician. Our bedroom became my hospital room and David kept a respectful distance by sleeping in a guestroom.

He was the lead attorney defending me in court. Other lawyers at the firm suggested that it might be better to let someone else handle my trial, but David didn't trust anyone else to defend me. My doctors testified that I'd been under tremendous stress due to the recent death of my father and the combination of stress, medication and alcohol had resulted in an altered mental state, in which I was incapable of rational thought. David fought desperately for a temporary insanity verdict with the allowance that I be held under house arrest and treated by a psychiatrist from home." Emma's voice broke on her next words, "But obviously, we lost. During all of it, David never once asked why I'd done it or why I'd suddenly turned against him but he begged me to leave the country with him lots of times, to disappear to a tropical beach somewhere far away. But I hated him for what he'd done, and I hated myself for hurting a woman who'd never shown me anything but kindness. We didn't deserve to sneak away. I didn't even deserve to live and at the very least, I deserved to be punished.

The night before my verdict, we knew there was no hope of house arrest. I'd either be sent to jail or if we were lucky, sentenced to a psychiatric facility. We were in David's study and he was pacing the floor, giving me last minute advice. He stopped, knelt on the floor in front of me and whispered, 'Why did you do it?'

I said, 'I could ask you the same thing.'

And he gripped the sides of my chair and pleaded with me to explain what I meant, until I whispered, 'Sophie Turner.'

But David just looked confused.

I told him how she'd come to me in the ladies' room that night and confessed to being his lover, and every word that I spoke broke my heart a little more.

At first, David just looked stunned but as I went on, his grip on the sides of my chair tightened so much I thought he'd pull it apart. When I finished, he growled, 'I'm going to kill that bitch.' Then he told me she'd propositioned him at the party and he'd laughed in her face, told her she was drunk and suggested she go home and sleep it off. He said he offered to call her a cab, and he swore that was the extent of anything that'd ever happened between them. He'd hurt her pride and she wanted to hurt him back. But I didn't know what to believe," Emma whispered. "If Sophie was telling the truth, he wouldn't necessarily admit it...but he seemed so sincere."

I considered it all for a minute before saying anything, then I cleared my throat. "Your husband said he was going to kill Sophie. If she did lie to you, I almost couldn't blame him. I'd want to kill her, too." I dropped my voice to a whisper, "Would he actually do it?"

Frowning, Emma whispered, "I'm not sure."

"Em, the police need to know about this."

She looked up at me, her green eyes wildly panicked and swimming with tears. "Besides David, you and I are the only ones who know about Sophie and we don't know anything for sure. Let the police figure things out on their own. Please."

"I must really be crazy," I muttered, "but alright."

Emma let out a sigh. "Thank you, Charlie. For everything."

Then Tim came in to collect us for group.

31

BOB

Group therapy was a load a horse shit. I had more important things to do, but that big dumb ox turned off my fuckin television and said the jackass doctor told him everybody had to go. So I sat down to waste an hour, listenin to a bunch of assholes snivel about every fuckin problem they'd ever had. I was the first schmuck to get dragged to the group, so it was just me and that sorry excuse for a doctor, sittin in foldin chairs, waitin for more idiots to join us.

The doctor grinned at me like a fuckin retard. "Hello, Bob."

I just scowled at him.

"We're going to try something a little different tonight."

I almost suggested he try shovin that binder up his ass but I settled for, "How long is this bullshit gonna take?"

"As long as it needs to," the doc answered, still smilin like a fuckin moron.

"Since you're the only jackass here, besides me," I growled, "why don't we turn on the TV till the pissin and moanin gets started?"

The doc dropped the phony smile for a second then quickly plastered it back in place. "It shouldn't be long. Let's just wait. Okay?"

"Do I have a choice?"

His fake smile slipped again. "Well, no."

At least that was honest. I had no patience for people actin like somethin they weren't. He was a jackass, so he should just act like one. "Do the other idiots know they're 'sposed to be here?" I growled impatiently.

"Yes, Bob. They're coming." He wasn't pretendin to be cheery anymore, which was fine by me. As he finished talkin, the ding bat with the imaginary kid shuffled into the room and took a seat across from me.

The jackass plastered the retard smile back on his face. "Good evening, Nellie."

"Fuck you!" she snipped. "What's good about it?"

I stifled a laugh. "I'll second that. Why don't we all just agree, this is bullshit?"

The doc's phony smile dropped again as he stood up. "If you two will excuse me, I'm going to go see about gathering the others."

"Why don't you turn on the TV while we wait for you to do your fuckin job?"

"It won't be long, Bob," the jackass promised as he walked away. "Just sit tight."

"I was sittin tight on the damn couch in front of the TV, ya stupid fuck," I grumbled.

Nellie giggled. "Damn waste of time. What does he think it matters?"

"It doesn't," I agreed. "There's more important shit to worry about, like takin care a your invisible baby."

The old bat narrowed her eyes at me.

But I was too tired to bicker. "Relax. I just tell it like I see it."

"You don't see *shit*," she spat.

"I see a fuck of a lot more than you."

"Give me a fucking break," she squeaked.

I smirked at her. "You know, you've got a hell of a mouth on ya, lady."

She shot me a pouty little scowl. Then somethin behind me grabbed her attention. The way she was cowerin, you'd think it was a ghost.

I turned to see what'd upset the old goat, but all I saw was that annoyin kid walkin into the room with his Barbie girlfriend. The poor girl looked shaky as hell and her eyes were all glazed over. Somebody'd

obviously drugged the shit outta her. The kid practically had to carry her to keep her upright. I turned
back to the ding bat. "What the hell's your problem?
You look like ya've seen a ghost."

She was shakin like a leaf. "A monster. Not a
ghost."

I couldn't resist. "Is the monster here to steal
your baby?"

Her milky eyes got three times bigger and instead of bitchin at me, she muttered, "I hope not!"
Then she did a little double-take and looked at me
like I'd just turned into Cary fuckin Grant. Lookin
away real slow, like it was hard to take her eyes off
me, she glued her eyes back on the kid and his girl.
The closer they got, the wider her eyes got and
when they started movin to her side of the circle,
she scurried over and plopped down in the seat
next to me.

"What the fuck's up with you?" I whispered.
"You're actin loonier than usual." She didn't answer
so I turned and watched Barbie and the kid take
their seats across from us, wonderin which one the
crazy bat thought was a monster. This was almost
entertainin enough to be worth the waste a time.

More numbskulls filled in the circle until the doc
and the dipshit who was always blockin the TV took
the last two seats. The doc glued his plastic smile in
place. "Hello, everyone. Thank you all for joining
us."

"What the hell are you thankin us for?" I grumbled. "We didn't have a choice."

The doc's smile dropped a little. "Well, thank you anyway. For cooperating and participating."

"Who the fuck said we were gonna do that?"

The doc didn't acknowledge my comment. "We're going to try something a little different tonight. We're going to go around the circle and each of you is going to talk about the same topic."

"World peace or what we wanna be when we grow up?"

The doc ignored me again. "No one is going to pass tonight. I want all of you to take your turn. Give us a little background about your life before you were admitted, then tell us what brought you here."

Nellie shook her head and muttered, "This is horseshit." God help me. I was startin to like the little ding bat.

The dipshit who made a hobby outta blockin the TV was sittin next to the doc, so he talked first but I couldn't tell you what he said. I tuned out as soon as he opened his fuckin mouth and passed the time by watchin the rest of the morons. Blondie was droopin against the kid, but he was obviously okay with that. The boy got a dopey grin on his face every time that girl walked in a room. He sat with an arm around her shoulders and a look that challenged anybody to even think about gettin near her. The ding bat cowered at my side, watchin the two kids like a hawk. For once, she wasn't rockin back and forth like a freak show. Maybe her imaginary baby was already asleep or maybe she really was afraid a monster was gonna eat it. I wondered why the hell she'd moved next to me. I wasn't plannin on fightin the kid or his Barbie doll for her.

More whiny bastards shared their sob stories, but I didn't listen to them either. Whenever I did tune in, they were spoutin some crap about their feelings or their shitty life.

The whiny little shit on the kid's other side finished snivelin, which made it the kid's turn. I was actually curious to hear what he had to say because he usually made up a bunch of bull about monsters and unicorns and shit. If I couldn't watch my TV, at least he was entertainin.

Usually, the doc looked at the kid like he wanted to punch him in the face and you almost couldn't blame him. The kid knew how to get under his skin and loved to get him goin but this time, the doc kept smilin. "It's your turn, Charlie."

Charlie nodded and grinned at Tranquilizer Barbie. "Let's see, my life before I became a certified lunatic. We lived in England when I was little because my Dad's job was there, but he died when I was eight. We were Americans, so my mom and I moved back here. Mom worked a lot, she kind of had to since she was a single parent, and she got really overwhelmed really quickly. She couldn't handle the stress and the heartbreak, and she couldn't handle me," the kid muttered with a sad smile. "I've always seen things that nobody else does," he shot a glance across the circle at the old bat. "I'd see the woman in front of us at church or the waitress in a restaurant morph into a monster, and I was just a kid. It scared the hell out of me, so I freaked out. A lot. In very public places. I'd throw things at very proper-looking ladies or walk up to crack-heads on the street and bow to them because to me, they were knights in shining armor." The kid looked at me and smiled, and the old prune next to me fidgeted in her seat. "My mom didn't know what to do with me. She took me to different so-called doctors." That was said with a nod in the doc's direction. Doc didn't smile at that. "But the doctors were all demons and freaks. I needed someone to chase away the monsters, not more monsters to terrify me. The doctors pumped me full of all kinds of drugs and the drugs turned me into a drooling zombie, but the monsters didn't go away. When I turned sixteen, my mom finally decided she couldn't take it anymore, so she shipped me off to a place like this. You can imagine what kind of hell it was for a teenage boy to find himself locked away in a prison full of monsters." He smiled to himself but it wasn't a happy smile. "And that was my life from then on. They'd keep me locked away and drugged up for a good long time, out of sight out of mind I guess. My mom would come and visit just often enough to satisfy her guilty conscience, which wasn't often, and I stopped trying to contain my reactions to what I saw. I mean, what was the point? Even my own mother had given up on me. Every so often, my mom's guilt would eat away at her enough that she'd check me out of the facility I was in, but she never kept me for long." He cleared his throat. "That's pretty much my story. This is just one prison of many and my mom has apparently gotten over her guilt or gotten better at ignoring it because she hasn't visited once since she put me here." The kid stared at the floor, teary-eyed and obviously done talkin.

It was more honest than the kid'd ever been. Even the doc was silent for a minute before he shook his head. "Thank you, Charlie." Then he smiled at the kid's girlfriend. "Emma, it's your turn."

Emma looked up when the doc said her name but once she started talkin, she only looked at the floor. "My father died not all that long ago. It really shouldn't have mattered that much because we hadn't spoken in years and I hated the man. But for some reason, his death hit me really hard. My doctor put me on an antidepressant to help me through it and I wasn't supposed to drink alcohol while on the medication, but the night of my husband's Christmas party, I did anyway." She was lookin at the floor but her mind was a million miles away. "The combination of the medication and alcohol together with my depression had me feeling worse than I'd ever felt in my life, so I left the party without telling my husband and went home to kill myself." She slipped a big gold bracelet off her tiny wrist, held up her arm and traced a finger over a thick scar that ran up her arm from her wrist. "I took the sharpest knife I could find and did this, but our housekeeper snuck up behind me when I was about to slit the other wrist. I think she was trying to catch me off guard so she could grab the knife, but I was so out of it..." She stopped again, closin her eyes, tears slidin down her cheeks. "It all happened so fast. I'm not even sure exactly how, but I spun around and stabbed her in the chest before I even realized what I was doing." She broke down in sobs. The kid pulled her closer and she leaned into him, buryin her face against his shoulder.

"Thank you for sharing, Emma," the doc said quietly.

More fruitcakes told their stories and I tuned out again. I didn't give a shit what they had to say. When I looked up again, everybody was starin at me.

"Bob," the doc said, "It's your turn."

"My turn?"

The doc nodded. "To tell us a little about your life before coming here and share what brought you here."

Life before coming here? The kid'd asked me the same question. What the hell had I done before? I tried to think back. *Trembling little boy.* Damn it. My head was killin me. *Lifeless body in my arms.* What'd it matter? I just wanted to get back to my TV. Why the hell couldn't they just skip me? "Fuck," I muttered under my breath, "I can't seem to remember."

The doc shot me that plastic grin, and I really wanted to knock it off his fuckin face. "Bob, I know it's hard for you to remember. Would you like me to help you?"

All I thought was, *what an asshole.* But I nodded.

The doc smiled. "Bob's a retired detective." *Sirens.* "And he's a true hero." *Lifeless body in my arms.* "He was injured in the line of duty." *Gunshot.* "He survived a gunshot wound to the head. Unfortunately, his long term memory was affected and his ability to control what he says is extremely limited now so he requires assistance, which is why he was admitted here."

My head was achin like a son of a bitch. "Can I get back to my TV now?"

The doc smiled. "Sure, Bob. You can be excused from the rest."

"Wait," the kid chimed in, before I could even stand up.

The doc grinned at him. "Yes, Charlie?"

"Tell us how it happened?" Why the hell had the kid taken such an interest in me?

The doc nodded. "He was investigating the disappearance of two children, a brother and sister, and he'd tracked the man who abducted the children back to the house he was keeping them in. Bob called for backup, but the kidnapper was planning to move the kids. He'd already put the boy in the van and gone back into the house, so Bob retrieved the little boy and snuck him to his police car." *Trembling little boy begging me not to leave.* "Then he went back and climbed through a window into the house to get the girl. She'd been severely injured, but Bob managed to sneak her out and get her to his car. *Lifeless body in my arms.* He put the girl in the car next to her brother but when he moved to pull his head out of the car, a second kidnapper pressed the barrel of a gun to the back of his head." *Gunshot.* "Bob reacted fast enough to get the kidnapper away from the car and the kids and shoot him in the chest, but the man's gun fired and shot Bob in the head."

No one said anything for a while.

Charlie was the first to talk. "What happened to the kids, did they get away from the other kidnapper?"

"Yes." The doc smiled—a real smile, not the plastic fake one. "The backup Bob had called for showed up and the children were returned to their mother." *Woman in agony.* For some reason, that made my head feel better.

"Was the little girl okay?" Charlie asked. I wondered why the hell he had more questions about my story than Barbie's, but I wanted to hear the answer.

"Eventually," the doc answered. "She was in intensive care for quite a while."

"But she healed, eventually?" Charlie asked.

Doc nodded. "Yes and she grew up and became a police officer. She's happily married and has two children, two boys. She named her older son Robert and they call him Bob."

I looked down at the floor, hopin nobody'd notice that my eyes were tearin.

"They come to visit you every Thanksgiving, Bob. She says your sacrifice is what she's most thankful for because without you, her family wouldn't exist." A tear slid down my cheek and I sniffed and wiped it away. I didn't look up but a pair of wrinkled little hands started clappin next to me. A second later, the room was full of applause. I nodded, still starin at the floor.

When the clappin stopped, doc talked for a couple minutes then group was over. All around me, people scooted outta foldin chairs and shuffled outta the room.

A pair of sneakers moved into my line of sight. "You're a hero, Bob." I looked up. The kid was grinnin away like the cat that ate the fuckin canary.

"Why're you so interested, kid?"

"It isn't every day I meet a knight in shining armor." The kid held out his hand. "I just wanted to shake your hand."

I gripped his hand, gave it a firm shake and the kid's smile got even wider. He clapped me on the back, then he left with Barbie and I went back to my TV.

32

DAVID

I sat at the desk in my study, glaring at the phone in my hand. I'd just finished a conversation with Emma's doctor, a foolish ass of a man who thought far too highly of his own opinion. Under any alternate set of circumstances, I'd gladly demolish the dolt's overinflated sense of self-worth but as it stood, the man had the power to keep my wife from me so I had to play nice and my patience with that was growing ridiculously thin.

Like a principal phoning to report a child's good behavior to a parent, the doctor had called to inform me that Emma was making splendid progress in her therapy. I held my tongue and agreed that this was good news. In a way, it was. It meant that he was one step closer to permitting me to visit, but the fact that it was necessary for my wife to share her deepest thoughts with that condescending buffoon in order for me to see her, made me want to rip his beating heart from his chest.

Setting my phone on the desktop, I considered the view outside my window. The sun was beginning to sink below the horizon and the water brilliantly mirrored the sky's palette of pastel hues. It was exactly the sort of picture perfect sunset that Emma loved…

…She sat beside me in the sand, not the least bit concerned about defiling the unsullied white of her sundress. Strands of her golden hair danced in the breeze as she alternated between staring out over the surf and scribbling words into the notebook propped on her knees.

I studied her with all the admiration that she studied the sunset. "Poetry?"

"I prefer to think of it as capturing transient visions onto an unfading canvas of words," she answered softly.

I smiled at her, savoring each word as it left her lips. "You have the tongue of an artist."

"If you say so," she replied in a deliciously velvet tone, flashing me a seductive smile.

I grinned wickedly at her. "Will you share some of your words with me?"

She gave me a look that defied me to resist pulling her into my arms. It didn't matter how recently I'd touched her, she always left me wanting more. "What will you give me in return?"

"Anything you want," I rasped.

She looked at the setting sun, then back to me. "Dangerous words. What if I want more than you're willing to give?"

Leaning close to her ear, I whispered, "Impossible."

She turned those hypnotic eyes from me to the notebook and began to read:

"Wisps of cotton candy clouds
streak the slowly melting sky
as warm brown sugar sand
relents to the persistent touch
of her salt water lover's tongue."

She looked up at me as she finished. "What do you think?"

I smiled at her. "I think your words make me hungry."

Mischief glinted in those gorgeous green eyes. "Is that all?"

"No," I rasped. "I also think that I've never found a sunset so arousing."

"What do I get in exchange for my words?" she purred, obviously pleased by my answer.

"Well," I whispered, leaning close to her ear again. "You aren't the only one with a talented tongue." I drew back and regarded her with a devilish grin. Then I placed the slightest whisper of a kiss on her earlobe and began trailing my lips ever so lightly along the line of her jaw, then down her neck.

She dropped her notebook to the sand with a breathy sigh as my lips leisurely traced over her collarbone, each kiss a bit hungrier than the last. I drew a hand along the strap of her sundress, slipping it from her shoulder and following the movement with my mouth and she sighed softly as I lowered her to the sand.

My palm traveled lazily down her side, over her hip, down her thigh and her breaths grew audibly heavier. When my fingers reached the soft flesh of her outer thigh, I slowly slid my hand higher, drawing her hem up with it.

She moaned softly as my lips neared her perfect breasts and I withdrew my mouth and halted the progression of my hand along her thigh, gazing reverently into those dazzling eyes for a moment. Then I lowered my mouth so close to her ear that my lips skimmed it as I spoke. "Have I done enough to pay for your words yet?"

"Absolutely not," she rasped, laughing as she clutched the back of my neck and pulled me closer, bringing my lips to hers.

Tightening my grip on her thigh, I kissed her greedily and slid my hand up to her waist, lifting her dress along with it. When I pulled back, she lifted her head, not wanting our lips to part. I hastily dragged the dress up and over her lifted head and tossed it to the sand beside the forgotten notebook.

I eyed her sun-kissed flesh hungrily as she lay beneath me, a pair of lace-trimmed panties her only remaining garment. I slid my palm over her belly, stopping to brush my fingertips across the lace at her hips as her breathing grew deeper, needier. Lowering my mouth, I placed a soft kiss below her navel and trailed my fingers along *the lace at her inner thigh and she squirmed expectantly beneath me.*

As my lips slowly whispered lower, I slipped my fingers beneath the thin cloth, making her whimper softly. Then I tore the fabric from her body and she gasped and writhed beneath me, her breathing ragged and desperate as my mouth moved lower...

...An unwelcome knock at my study door snapped my thoughts back to the present.

"Come in," I called, without moving from my chair.

The door opened and Brian—my firm's most talented attorney, excluding myself—walked in looking utterly spent.

"You look worse than I feel," I observed, with a dry smile.

"Thanks, boss." He flashed me a sarcastic grin, then quickly dropped it. "I'm assuming you heard about Sophie?"

Nostrils flaring, I nodded. Just the mention of that woman was enough to get my blood boiling.

Brian sighed. "I held the press off all day but they want a statement from you."

"I don't give a damn what the press wants," I growled.

He shrugged. "I can deal with it. I just need to know what you want me to say."

I stood from my desk and walked to the window to observe the setting sun. "Say that we'll miss her terribly. Say that she was a miserable cunt and we're glad to be rid of her. Say whatever the hell you want to say."

"The miserable cunt statement is probably the most accurate," Brian mused, "but I think I'll refrain from using that one. Does soul sucking she-devil sound more respectful of the dead?"

"Probably not," I answered vacantly, watching the waves roll onto shore. *The persistent touch of her salt water lover's tongue.*

He cleared his throat. "Do you want me to have flowers sent to the funeral home from the firm?"

"Do whatever you feel is appropriate. What I want is an entirely separate question." I turned away from the window to face Brian. "I certainly won't be shedding tears at her graveside."

"I don't imagine many people will." He took a step toward the door. "I'll take care of things. I just wanted to get your go ahead."

"Go ahead," I replied dryly. "Leave me the hell out of it."

"Consider it done, boss." He hesitated, trying to decide whether to say something more.

"Out with it," I prompted. "What else is on your mind?"

"Are you all ready to argue against the visitation restriction?"

My hands involuntarily clenched into fists. "I've been ready since the moment it was imposed."

Brian nodded. "If I can help in any way..."

Emma had always liked Brian. For her sake, I refrained from taking my frustration out on him. "Thank you. I appreciate all the effort you put into her case, and so did Emma."

He answered with a melancholy smile. "Is there anything else I can do for you?"

I turned back to the sunset. The sky was ablaze with color. "Nothing at the moment," I replied absently.

"Good night then," Brian replied as he exited the room.

"There's nothing good about it," I murmured to the darkening sky...

... Our naked bodies still entwined, we lay in the sand as the sunlight gave itself up to the darkness. I brushed a wayward strand of hair away from her eyes. "Can I consider my debt paid now?"

Smiling, she purred, "Very well paid." Then she scowled at me with mock frustration. "But I won't have any underwear left if you keep destroying it."

"I'll buy you more." I drew her head to mine and kissed her pouting lips. "Lots more," I added, with a mischievous grin.

She laughed as I kissed her again. Pulling her mouth back from mine she murmured, "I'll hold you to that."

I rolled to my back in the sand, holding her close so her body rolled on top of mine. "Please do."...

33

CHARLIE

All alone and wide awake, I stretched out trying to get comfortable. She'd only been in it for a matter of hours, but my bed felt empty without her now. Outside the window, specks of starlight spattered the darkness, a full moon hung low in the sky and the absolute blackness of the sky itself brought to mind the scales on Emma's dragon.

So much had happened since she left my room. Emma's mind had finally reached its breaking point, and I think her heart had too. When we first met, we'd both been afraid to share our secrets. We'd each assumed that once we exposed our worst, the other wouldn't want anything to do with us. She told me she'd 'done things to get here, too' and at the time, I couldn't imagine what she could've done that she thought would make me feel differently about her. Now I understood, but she'd accepted my Sight as just another detail of who I was and I felt the same about what she'd done. The act that brought her here didn't define who she was. It was just a detail.

As if Emma's guilt wasn't enough of a burden, she was also tormented by unanswered questions. Was her husband unfaithful? Did he take a woman's life to cover it up, or because that woman had wrongfully shattered his marriage? The shocking thing wasn't that Emma broke down, it was that she'd held it together as long as she had. I wished I had a way to help her find some answers.

Thanks to an unexpected stroke of luck, I'd actually gotten some answers for Bob. It turned out that he'd been given the answer lots of times. *But not in the Dream World.* The thought of ending this exhausting day by bringing some peace of mind to young Bob made me smile. The tricky part would be getting the Waters to take me where I wanted to go. So far, my record for succeeding at that was pretty unspectacular. Still, it couldn't hurt to give it a shot.

I pictured the rippling blue Waters and they instantly appeared. Taking a deep breath, I braced for the cold and jumped in. As I plunged through the icy depths, I pictured old Bob bowing his head to hide his tears.

The Water tossed me around roughly, pulling me through its frigid depths as the bitter cold numbed me to my core. But I kept my thoughts focused on Bob. I pictured everyone clapping for his bravery.

Bob was a hero. There was an entire family that wouldn't exist if it wasn't for him. He'd sacrificed his mind and all his memories for those two kids. He at least deserved some closure. I silently howled, *Take me to Bob!*

I surfaced quickly and violently, gasping for air but for once, my eyes didn't have to adjust. The sky was dark and star covered, and I didn't have to exhaust myself to reach the shore. The Water gently swept me there and deposited me right on the bank.

Sitting up, I took in my surroundings. The moon hung low and impossibly large in the star covered sky and a thick tree line stood a short distance behind me. This was Bob's section of the Dream forest. *Holy shit.* I did it! I actually landed where I wanted to. Now I just had to find Bob.

Feeling pretty damn proud of myself, I stood up and started walking along the shore. I'll admit it, Nellie had me a little leery of entering the forest. Her ominous warnings about dark places that'd drain your soul had me a little spooked. Alright, maybe more than a little. I wasn't going into those trees unless I absolutely had to so I walked along the forest's edge, hoping Bob would emerge from the trees like he usually did.

It felt like I'd been walking for miles. Eerie whisperings from the forest permeated what would've otherwise been absolute silence. A chorus of chirps and buzzes announced the presence of hidden frogs and insects, or pixies and gremlins for all I knew. Unseen creatures that I didn't even want to identify scampered through the underbrush and the ethereal calls of what I seriously hoped were night birds, echoed through the trees. Even without entering the woods, I was starting to feel like I was walking through a nightmare.

Just when I was considering giving up, a familiar voice called out behind me. "Charlie! Is that you?"

I turned and started toward him. "Hey, Bob!"

He greeted me with a welcoming smile. "It's a little late for night swimming and falling off of boats, isn't it?"

I had to love this guy. His willingness to accept the bizarre without question was utterly endearing. "What can I say? I missed you."

Bob grinned. "It's always good to see you." Then his expression grew serious. "Are you tracking your dragon again?"

I shook my head. "I came to talk to you this time actually."

He looked surprised by my answer and that's saying something, considering all the things that didn't faze him. "I'm pretty sure I saw your dragon here tonight."

"You did? Where was it?" Why would Emma be in Bob's stretch of the forest? Then again, maybe that wasn't strange at all. Maybe sitting on the couch next to Bob and listening to his heroic story had left him on Emma's mind when she fell asleep. I guess anything was possible in a Dream World.

Bob's eyes swept over the shore. "It was walking the shoreline. I kept out of sight in the forest and followed it for a while, but I lost sight of it."

"Any idea where it might be now?" I asked, not at all sure I wanted to find it. Maybe it was the darkness that had me feeling less brave, or maybe I'd just heard Nellie's warnings about dragons one too many times.

Bob shrugged. "Hard to say. It could've entered the forest, or it could be farther up ahead in the direction you were just walking."

"What would you've done if it saw you?" I asked curiously.

Bob considered the question for a second, then answered with a hearty chuckle. "That's a good question. I didn't really think that far ahead. You know, brave and smart don't necessarily go hand in hand. I guess I would've figured it out as I went along."

The more I talked to young Bob, the more I liked him. "Brave and smart probably don't go together because smart people stop to think about how stupid an idea is before they actually do it. Maybe it's not a bad thing that you lost it for the time being."

Bob let out a sound somewhere between a chuckle and a snort. "You said, you came to talk to me. What about?"

That's when I realized I hadn't considered what I was going to say. Like Bob said, brave and smart aren't always a package deal. How was I going to explain this without sounding completely insane? "Remember when I offered to help find out the details of your dream?"

Bob raised his eyebrows. "Of course I do. You're the only company I've had in a very long time. I'm not likely to forget our conversations."

"Right." I cleared my throat. "You told me that you felt like we knew each other, from somewhere else. Remember?"

Bob nodded.

"Well, that's because we do and my swimming stories are going to sound completely logical compared to this but I swear, it's all true." I stopped, wondering how bad an idea this was.

Bob gave me a reassuring smile. "I consider myself an excellent judge of character, Charlie, and I've had a good feeling about you since we met. If you say it's true, I'll believe it."

"Thanks." But I wasn't holding my breath that he'd still feel that way after hearing what I had to say. "You know me in another world. Those crazy dreams of yours that feel like more than dreams, they're memories from that world. Still with me?"

"Go on," he muttered.

"You were a police officer in the other world. They're protectors who dress in blue and wear a gold badge like you described in your dreams and they protect people, just like you do in this world. They uphold the laws and stop people from doing wrong. Anyway, your job led you to search for a sister and brother who were taken from their mother. You found them, but the kidnapper was going to move them somewhere else before your fellow officers could get there to back you up."

Brow deeply furrowed, Bob seemed to be hanging on every word.

"You didn't want to risk letting him get away, so you snuck the kids out but a second kidnapper snuck up behind you before you could leave. You shot him with a weapon called a gun, but he had a gun pointed at the back of your head. It went off and he shot you. You survived, but you lost the ability to remember things from the past and you aren't completely able to control your actions." I looked up at Bob, expecting him to laugh in my face.

"You weren't kidding. That's pretty unbelievable," he said quietly, brow still deeply furrowed. "But as outlandish as it all sounds, it actually explains a lot of what I see in my dreams. I trust you, Charlie. If you say it's true, I believe you. Somehow, it feels right."

I was shocked and relieved by Bob's response. I'd spent a lifetime having people dismiss the things

I said as nothing but crazy rambling but recently, three separate people had actually listened to me and believed me. "I swear to you, it's all true. You're a hero."

Bob cleared his throat. "What happened to the children? Did they find their way back to their mother's arms? A grieving woman often haunts my dreams. She has to be the mother."

I smiled, happy to deliver some good news. "The other officers showed up and returned them to their mother. The little girl was injured, so she had to stay in the hospital for a long time but eventually she got better and went home to her mother. She grew up to be a police officer, got married and had two sons. She named the older one Robert and she calls him Bob. They come to visit you every Thanksgiving because without your sacrifice, their family wouldn't exist."

For a long while, Bob just watched the Water mirror the star-filled sky. Gradually, his brow un-furrowed and his mouth curved into a smile. Finally, he looked at me. "I'm not sure what to make of this other world, but hearing that the tortured souls who haunt my dreams are safe is a tremendous comfort. I am truly grateful to you for bringing some peace to my troubled mind."

As I listened to him, an idea started forming. It was crazy but so far, crazy had worked for us. "Bob, you said that you're lonely. I'm the only company you get?"

"Sadly, yes," he answered quietly, "unless you count that dragon earlier."

"If the dragon approached you, do you think you could defend yourself?"

He flashed me a confident grin. "I'd certainly give it my best shot. I've defeated some terrifying creatures in the past."

"I don't doubt it," I muttered. Bob was one fearless protector in both worlds. "Do you think you could defend yourself against it without hurting it?"

"May I ask why you'd want to know?" Bob looked intrigued. Maybe when you spend all your time alone, you welcome *any* conversation, no matter how ridiculous. That'd sure explain a lot.

I grinned at him. "If you can believe it, I have a soft spot for the dragon."

He let out a laugh. "I think we've established that I'll believe just about anything. I'm fairly confident I could—at least, I've got as good a chance as anyone else, possibly better."

"Better for sure," I agreed. "And how would you feel about not living alone anymore?"

He raised an inquisitive eyebrow. "Are you thinking of moving here?"

I shook my head. "No. I've got things to do in other places, but what if I knew of a person or two who'd like to join you? How would you feel about having others to protect again?"

Young Bob's face lit up like a Christmas tree. "I can't think of anything I'd like better—except, maybe the company of a beautiful woman."

I grinned at him. "Bob, I just might turn out to be your best friend."

He chuckled. "That wouldn't be too difficult to accomplish, considering you're my only friend."

I shook my head and grinned at him. "I should go. I'll get back to you as soon as I can. Hopefully, I'll have more to tell you next time."

"I look forward to it." He gave me a manly clap on the back, which—I'm embarrassed to admit—almost knocked me off balance. Young Bob was packing some serious muscle.

I started toward the Water, feeling more hopeful than I'd felt about anything in a long time. Maybe I could do some good for once in my life. Stranger things had happened. Just ask Bob.

34

NELLIE

I sat on my beach, admiring the night sky while Lilly slept peacefully beside me. If only I could be so at peace. Fear was always in my mind and in my heart. Where were we supposed to go now? This tiny pocket of Dream was the only safe place left—that is, until Charlie brought it to the dragon's attention. He had no idea what he was messing with. I kept trying to warn him but he just refused to listen. He was too distracted by that beautiful face, but nightmares were more than capable of hiding behind perfect features. I knew that all too well.

I looked down at Lilly's angelic face and stroked a hand over her curls. Drawing a deep breath of the crisp night air, I looked up at the oversized moon that hung low and full in the star speckled sky. It'd be a perfect night if it weren't for the terror in my heart. As I was admiring the way the moon made the Water glow, something surfaced in the distance.

Heart pounding, I scooped Lilly into my arms and took off running. I didn't slow down until we were off the beach and out of sight behind the bushes. I laid Lilly down on a soft patch of earth, she stirred and whimpered in her sleep but one stroke of my hand against her cheek was all it took to soothe her back to oblivion. With Lilly safely tucked away, I needed to draw attention away from her hiding place.

I ran from the bushes, searching the Waters, hoping the intruder had been too focused on emerging to notice my child. With my heart still slamming in my chest, I spotted the unwelcome visitor. *The dragon. It'd finally come for me.* I dropped to my knees in the sand, closed my eyes and prayed for a miracle. If my time had come, at least let my daughter be spared. Too afraid to watch the beast, I kept my eyes squeezed shut until it was so close that I could hear it moving through the Water.

When I opened my eyes, the monster I expected to see wasn't there. The boy was. Normally I'd have yelled at him for barging into my paradise uninvited but I was so relieved to see him and not the dragon, I was almost tempted to hug him. I watched Charlie wade from the surf, move to dry ground and collapse. Then I slowly headed toward him, giving him time to catch his breath but when I reached him, he wasn't the least bit winded.

He looked up. "Nellie! I'm glad you found me. I'm not sure I had the energy for another long search tonight."

"What are you talking about? I didn't find you. You came to my beach. Uninvited. Again." I didn't have the heart to put any real anger into the words. I was still so relieved to see him and not the dragon.

He frowned, looking genuinely apologetic. "Yeah. Sorry about that. I wouldn't have come again, but I had an idea I couldn't wait to share with you."

I was almost intrigued, but I wasn't about to let him know that. "Have you decided to stop acting like an idiot?"

Charlie flashed that smartass grin of his. "Nope. I'm still the same idiot. Admit it. You wouldn't want to see me any other way."

"If only I didn't have to see you at all." Since he wasn't getting up, I sat down beside him.

"You'd miss me if you didn't, Nellie. You don't have to admit it. I know it's true."

I shook my head, but I was having a hard time not smiling. Finding out that I wasn't about to be devoured had put me in a wonderful mood.

"I just might have the answer to your prayers," he declared, looking quite pleased with himself.

I let out a very unladylike snort. "The day you're the answer to my prayers will be the day they declare us both perfectly sane and throw us a party!"

"Sounds great. But let's try my idea first."

I narrowed my eyes at him. "What the hell are you rambling about?"

"I want to take you someplace, Nellie." He was still grinning away like a kid at a carnival. "Just come see it before you say no."

I let out a tired sigh. "What would I do about Lilly? I don't exactly have a forest full of babysitters to call on."

Charlie looked around. "I almost forgot about her. Where is she?"

"She's sleeping peacefully," I grumbled, "and I don't feel like waking her up to go traipsing all over the Dream World."

He combed his fingers through his hair with a frown. "I don't suppose you could just leave her here to sleep?"

"Well, you'll make a wonderful parent some day!" My joy must've been wearing off because he was starting to irritate the crap out of me. "You can't just up and leave a small child alone. Even for you, that's a stupid thing to ask."

"Let me ask you something," he insisted, ignoring the insult. "If I wanted to show you another place in the Dream World, could you follow me? And if you can, could you bring Lilly?"

"You're exhausting," I muttered, rolling my eyes. But I answered anyway. "If you jumped into the Water and I followed holding Lilly, we could all go together. The real question is, could you actually go where you wanted to? I thought you didn't know how to do that."

"I'm learning. Now come on. Let's wake Lilly up and go before the night's over!"

I wasn't sure why I was even considering it. Charlie was certainly no expert at controlling where the Waters took him. Lord only knew what Light-forsaken place we might wind up in, but he did have me curious. "Could we do it another time, so I could keep Lilly awake instead of disturbing her?"

"She'll love it," Charlie promised. "I'm trying to do something good here, Nellie. Help me out a little."

"You're such a pain in the ass. I don't know why I ever opened my mouth and talked to you in the first place." I stood up and took off toward Lilly's hiding spot.

He hopped up and hurried after me. "Now that's just hurtful."

We found Lilly curled up and sleeping content-edly behind the bushes, just the way I'd left her. Grinning, Charlie whispered, "She looks so peace-ful, like a little sleeping angel."

I hated to end whatever sweet dream had put that smile on her face, especially since I hadn't had a sweet dream of my own in ages. "I really don't want to wake her. Could we wait until tomorrow?"

Charlie let out a sigh as he watched my little cher-ub. "For Lilly, I guess we could."

I was surprisingly touched to hear the boy speak so tenderly about my daughter. "Well then, I guess we're going on an adventure tomorrow."

35

EMMA

I couldn't bring myself to lie down or even turn off the lights, so I sat on the bed with my knees pulled up to my chest and my arms wrapped around them in a death grip. My heart hurt—it was an actual physical ache—and I didn't know how to make it stop.

I'd shared my story with all of them, a version of it anyway. That was what they wanted, wasn't it? *Tell them what they want to hear.* But the only one I'd shared the whole story with was Charlie. I revealed the darkest part of myself to him and he didn't turn away. I didn't deserve to have anyone care about me after what I'd done to Isabella. Yet for some reason, David and Charlie still did.

I'd been refusing to remember what'd happened because I couldn't live with the truth, but I couldn't lie to myself anymore. In all the time I'd known her, Isabella had never treated me with anything but kindness. She'd been almost like a mother to me. How could I have hurt her? I'd also been blocking the memory of my encounter with Sophie. If her words were truthful... I couldn't even finish the thought. Without David, I had nothing. I was nothing. Our connection was a part of me. I didn't know how to exist without it. I wanted so badly to believe that Sophie had lied, but how could I ever know for sure? Sophie was dead. She'd crippled our marriage and shortly after David learned what she did, she stopped breathing. Was my husband capable of ending her life? *Yes.* The answer whispered somewhere deep inside me. I knew he was, but why? Was it a punishment for exposing their secret or an act of rage, directed at the woman who'd caused so much destruction with one ugly lie?

It was possible that David had nothing to do with her death, but I didn't believe that to be the case. It was too big of a coincidence and yet, I didn't want to direct any suspicion toward him. He'd been willing to take the punishment for a crime I'd committed even after I asked strangers to keep him away. He quietly took the blame until the police uncovered the truth, then he fought desperately to keep me out of jail and he did it all with no idea why I'd pushed him away.

And he was still being kept away because of my actions. I didn't want him near me when the paramedics took me and I wouldn't let him near me in the hospital after he was released and came rushing to be by my side, but I never told any of them why. No one knew about Sophie, except David and me—and now Charlie. So, the doctors were left to speculate as to why I'd wanted to keep my husband at a distance and Dr. Spenser suspected spousal abuse. He believed he was protecting me by keeping David away, but David would never physically hurt me. I knew that with absolute certainty. Unfortunately, Spenser had no way of knowing for certain. Just like I had no absolute way of knowing if Sophie had lied.

I sat in the chair on wheels, staring vacantly at the name plate on Dr. Spenser's desk. When I broke down, he said that if I really opened up I'd be allowed to see David, although I still wasn't entirely certain I wanted to see my husband. That wasn't true. I wanted to. I just wasn't certain I should want to. I turned my head to look at the doctor, sitting beside me in the other chair on wheels. I hadn't slept at all the previous night and the lack of sleep was making it difficult to focus. "I'm sorry. What was the question again?"

Dr. Spenser smiled. It was a kind smile but there was something hollow about it. "Why were you so insistent that David be kept away from you when the paramedics took you to the hospital, and why didn't you want him near you at the hospital? There had to be a reason that the man you'd been married to for years suddenly frightened you."

"I never said he frightened me," I answered flatly, sounding as detached as I felt.

"Alright." The doctor shifted, crossing his legs. "Then why did you want him to be kept away?"

How was I supposed to answer that? *Tell them what they want to hear.* I couldn't answer truthfully. I might've considered it before, but telling the doctor about Sophie now that she was dead could lead him to suspect David and even if he was guilty of killing her, I couldn't betray my husband. Maybe that made me a fool. If he'd been unfaithful and murdered to cover it up, what exactly was I trying to protect? *The man I loved.* That was it, plain and simple. No matter what he'd done, I couldn't stop loving him. I didn't know how. I could hate him just as passionately, but I'd always be his. "Could you repeat the question?"

The doctor placed his hand on top of mine. "You seem awfully distracted today, Emma. Are you feeling alright?"

Am I feeling alright? "I tried to end my life but failed, I was committed to a mental institution for wounding a woman I've loved since I was a child—possibly fatally—and I haven't been permitted to see my husband since being imprisoned here. No! I'm not feeling alright! None of this is alright!"

"Good," the doctor replied with a nod.

I jerked my hand away from his, absently noting that mine were trembling as I folded them in my lap. "Why is that good?"

Dr. Spenser smiled. "Because you're venting about what happened. You're opening up and talking about what's hurting you. That's progress, Emma."

"If I'm making progress, can my husband visit?" I asked flatly, almost certain the answer would be 'no.'

"We can talk about it after you answer my question, the one you keep conveniently forgetting. Why did you want your husband to be kept away from you after Isabella was stabbed?"

I couldn't help but notice he'd phrased it *after Isabella was stabbed*, instead of *after you stabbed Isabella*. What answer could I give that'd satisfy him, other than the truth? He asked about my relationship with David the first time we met, but he'd also asked about my father. "I'd been drinking and I was confused," I answered hoarsely. "My father's death had hit me hard, and I blamed David for destroying my relationship with my father." It was such a filthy lie, I could barely choke out the words but if it made these questions stop and led the doctor to believe I was making progress, it was worth it.

Spenser took off his glasses and carefully wiped the lenses with the sleeve of his white coat. "What about now? Do you still blame David for ruining your relationship with your father?"

I let out a shaky breath. "Of course not. Like I said, I was confused."

He held his glasses up to the light to inspect the lenses, then slipped them back on. "Well in your confusion, why did you blame David?"

I figured I might as well follow Charlie's example and 'throw in some truth.' "Because once I moved out of the house and in with David, my father and I never spoke again."

"Your father didn't approve of the relationship?"

"David was my father's business partner," I answered matter-of-factly. "My parents came home early from a weekend away and found us together."

"Found you together?" Spenser asked, as if he didn't know exactly what I meant.

"Yes," I answered flatly. "My father came home to find his partner in my bed."

"And how did your father react?"

"I was eighteen years old," I snapped, "and he found me in bed with his best friend, a man more than twice my age. How do you think he reacted?"

"You need to work through this, Emma. That's what therapy is all about. You can't keep bottling everything up inside you, it's not healthy. So, you tell me what his reaction was."

"He was furious!" I shrieked. It was more truth than I'd meant to offer and yet, I felt oddly compelled to finish. "He didn't yell at David, just me. He called me a whore and he grabbed me and started choking me." My eyes welled with tears as I remembered the strength of his grip around my neck.

"What happened next?" Spenser coaxed, nudging his glasses up the bridge of his nose.

"David hit him. Hard. He knocked my father to the floor. Then he stood over him and told him that if he ever laid a hand on me again…" I'd been so caught up in the painful memory, I realized a moment too late that I shouldn't have said it.

"Go on," Spenser prompted.

"He'd kill him," I whispered. "Then he scooped me up and took me away. When we were almost to the front door, my mother came rushing down the stairs. Her eyes were full of tears but she didn't cry. She just looked at David and whispered, 'Take care of her.' He promised he would, always. Then we walked out the door and I never spoke to either of my parents again." I looked up at Spenser with tears streaming down my cheeks. I didn't wipe them away. They'd waited years to be shed. I wouldn't dismiss them as nothing.

Dr. Spenser gave my hand what he intended to be a comforting squeeze. "It sounds like your husband loved you very much."

I yanked my hand back. "Why do you say *loved* instead of *loves*?"

"I didn't mean anything by it, Emma. Your story occurred in the past, so I spoke of him in the past tense." Spenser cocked his head to one side. "Do *you* feel the past tense is more appropriate?"

"My husband *loves* me," I whispered through my tears, "present tense."

"Fair enough," the doctor patronized.

"He *does*," I sobbed. "Why do you insist on keeping him from me?"

He let out a sigh and shifted in his seat. "Because *you* insisted on keeping him away, right after you attempted to kill yourself and then stabbed a woman you'd known and cared about for years. Why was that Emma? The story you just told paints your husband in a very favorable light, but it doesn't explain why you pushed David away the day you hurt yourself and almost killed someone else."

I cleared my throat. "I don't want to do this anymore."

"We can continue tomorrow if you need a break."

"Have I shared enough for my husband to visit?" I whispered, stifling a sob.

Dr. Spenser shook his head. "We're not there yet, Emma."

Feelings of rage bubbled up from deep inside me. I hated Spenser and I hated myself for ending up in this position but most of all, I hated the woman who'd started it all. I was glad Sophie was dead. She deserved to die.

36

CHARLIE

She was slipping deeper and deeper into darkness; that was my first thought as I watched Emma come down the hall after her appointment with Spenser. That radiance that'd mesmerized me since the moment I first saw her had noticeably dulled and her striking eyes now brimmed with despair. Her slumped posture, her listless movements—and pretty much everything about the way she carried herself—conveyed a sense of hopelessness.

Behind her, the dragon appeared out of nothingness. Maybe it was my imagination, but the shimmer and vibrantly shifting colors of its massive wings seemed more dazzling than ever. I imagined a man could easily become transfixed in a mix of awe and terror, right up until the moment the beast devoured him.

As Emma neared me, I shrugged off the dragon's spell. "Hey."

"Hey," she echoed vacantly.

"Walk with me?"

Tears swam in her eyes, threatening to spill if she spoke so she bit her lip and nodded.

I put an arm around her shoulders, and she moved beside me in a trance-like daze. "We're going to get you through this, Em," I promised softly.

A tiny sob escaped her mouth. "I'm not sure you can, Charlie."

The dragon exhaled, scorching the back of my neck and my heart skipped a beat. The dragon was just a vision, right? So why did I keep feeling that? Was I imagining all those fiery breaths? While I was tossing around possible explanations, another pulse of heat blasted me and I reflexively spun around to face the source.

"What is it?" Emma asked flatly, like she'd asked to be polite but didn't really care.

The beast's massive head bowed down to us. Its sapphire eyes blazed even more furiously than I remembered, and its monstrous nostrils flared and exhaled a puff of bluish smoke, clouding our surroundings. It looked every bit as real as smoke from a campfire, except for the fact that it was blue, but the scent was a far cry from campfire smoke. It was a heady blend of exotic spices, somewhat reminiscent of Emma's perfume. I turned back to her. "I'm sorry. What'd you ask?"

My distraction seemed to pull Emma out of hers. "What made you turn around?"

"I thought I heard something," I muttered, ignoring the heat searing the base of my neck and the aroma of smoked spices that accompanied it, "but I guess I was wrong."

Emma wasn't buying it. "Charlie, you're the only person here that I can trust so please be honest with me. You see something from the Dream World, don't you? And you've seen it before. I notice how you look behind me and above me and your eyes widen, but you pretend nothing's there. Are you seeing my Dream form?"

I swallowed, considering how to dance around the question, then noticed we'd reached the door to the yard. The perfect diversion. Normally the door was locked for obvious reasons, but visiting hours had just started and because of the gorgeous weather, they were letting us venture outside. I pressed the palm of my free hand against the door and grinned at her. "Want to take a walk outside?"

Eyes brightening, she whispered, "Yes."

I pushed the door open, the sun's warmth embraced us as we stepped out onto the lawn and I breathed in with a satisfied smile. "The smell of freshly mowed grass is almost as amazing as the smell of your perfume."

Emma shot me a puzzled look. "I don't wear perfume."

"What are you talking about?" I muttered, sounding as confused as she looked. "It was the first thing I ever noticed about you."

She stared at me for a few seconds, but we were interrupted before she could answer.

Either they'd approached us in stealth mode or we'd been too intent on the bewildering turn in our conversation to notice, either way, I looked sideways and found Tim standing beside me with a tall impeccably well-dressed black man in his late fifties or early sixties. His graying goatee was precisely trimmed and a charcoal gray cap covered his bald head. His black suit was perfectly tailored, even the man's black rimmed glasses looked stylishly expensive and behind those glasses lurked the darkest eyes I'd ever seen. Calling them black would be an extreme understatement. They were more of an infinite dark that left you shivering and feeling painfully cold on the inside. His strong features—coupled with the fierce set of his jaw—hinted that under different circumstances, he'd be terrifying but he'd clearly come to see Emma, and the expression he regarded her with was one of sincere affection and concern. As his gaze shifted to me, his expression lost every trace of warmth and his glare grew so hostile and cruel that I found myself irrationally fearing it might stop my heart. Not only was I positive that this man was capable of inflicting excruciating pain, I'd bet big money that he occasionally did and he enjoyed it immensely. A savagely displeased glance at my arm around Emma's shoulders made it very clear why he was less than thrilled with me. I let my arm drop to my side and the man's unforgiving glare eased, but not by much.

The man flashed Emma a smile that left no doubt they were old friends. "Hello, Emma." The darkness in his deep rich voice sent a shiver down my spine.

"Benjamin," she whispered his name like a contented sigh.

"How are you, my dear?"

Eyes tearing, Emma whispered, "Happy to see you."

He moved closer and she let her tears fall as they embraced. I took a few steps back, not wanting to intrude on the moment. I remembered Emma mentioning a Benjamin. He was the one that drove her home from the party after her run in with Sophie. I'd figured he was the Talbot's driver or something, but the fondness Emma regarded him with suggested that he was much more.

Until he cleared his throat, I completely forgot that Tim was still standing next to me. "Emma, do you know this man?" he asked, obliviously after the fact if you asked me—which of course, no one did.

Emma and Benjamin dropped their hug. "Yes," she answered, smiling faintly. "He's an old friend."

"I'll leave you two to visit then," Tim mumbled as he walked away.

"Thank you," Emma called after him. She turned back to Benjamin and gestured toward me. "Benjamin, this is Charlie. He's been a wonderful friend to me here."

Benjamin smiled at me but it wasn't a friendly smile—it was more the sort of smile that a lion might give its prey right before it became dinner—and Benjamin wasn't the only one staring daggers at me. The dragon still loomed above Emma, glaring down at me. Another hazy puff of blue billowed from its flared nostrils and I had to stifle the urge to cough.

Emma didn't seem to notice the coldness of Benjamin's smile. "Charlie, this is Benjamin. He's my husband's dearest and most trusted employee."

"Thank you," Benjamin replied, "But I'm not sure Mr. Talbot would gush over me quite so much."

Emma smiled at him. "Well, he should."

I extended my arm for a handshake. "Nice to meet you, Sir." The formality seemed appropriate. I didn't get the impression this guy would want to be on a first name basis with me.

Staring icily at me and ignoring my outstretched hand, Benjamin nodded.

I turned to Emma. "I should give the two of you some privacy."

"That'd be appreciated," Benjamin stated frigidly.

"Alright then," I muttered, lowering my hand and stepping a few more paces back.

Emma's eyes searched mine, questioning whether I minded leaving. "Find me later?"

"Yeah. Of course." I smiled then walked away, wondering what to make of Emma's visitor.

Benjamin hadn't exactly given me a warm fuzzy feeling. Then again, if he was close to Emma's husband, it was understandable that my arm around her shoulders wouldn't make him happy. I figured it wouldn't hurt to stay outside and keep an eye on them.

37

EMMA

As I watched Charlie walk away, I hoped his feelings weren't too hurt. Benjamin hadn't looked pleased to see Charlie so close to me, and David definitely wouldn't be pleased to hear about it. I didn't want to make Charlie feel unwelcome, but it was probably better that he give us time to talk alone. I turned back to Benjamin.

He regarded me with a somber smile. "David's a mess without you."

I fought the urge to smile, feeling desperate and pathetic for wanting to. "I've been trying to tell the doctor what he wants to hear, but he keeps saying it's not enough for David to visit."

Anger flashed in Benjamin's eyes as he shook his head. "He's doing everything he can to get the visitation restriction dropped but for now, he sent me to find out how you're holding up."

"I've been better," I whispered hoarsely. "I'm starting to wish we'd run off to a tropical beach when we had the chance."

Benjamin smiled but his eyes were full of sorrow. "I'm afraid he'd come storming in here to break you out if I told him that."

I chuckled but I wouldn't put it past him.

He drew a deep breath, then exhaled loudly. "Are you still angry with him?"

The question caught me off guard. I had no idea how much Benjamin knew.

"He'd turn the world upside down for you, Emma. I've never seen him so much as glance in another woman's direction since the two of you were first together," voice dropping slightly, he added, "before anyone knew about the two of you."

I wouldn't have expected David to share that. Back then, it would've meant jail time for him if anyone found out about us. Loyalty or not, that was placing an extreme amount of trust in Benjamin's silence. "I didn't know David told you."

Benjamin smiled. "He didn't. The way he looked at you gave him away. He was extremely guarded whenever anyone else was around but when I was the only other person there, he lowered his guard just enough that his feelings for you were obvious to me."

I dropped my eyes to the lawn. "Did he tell you about Sophie?"

"About what she said to you at the party that night?"

I stared at Benjamin's shoes and nodded.

"The day you were sentenced, I went back to the house with him. He was nothing but blind rage at first. Anything breakable that was in his path ended up shattered, but eventually I got him to stop breaking things and start drowning his sorrows and after an obscene amount of scotch, he alluded to what she said. If Sophie had crossed his path that night, I can only imagine what he might've done."

I looked up at him. "And now she's dead."

"Yes, she is," Benjamin agreed, without a trace of sympathy.

I didn't ask if David killed Sophie. I was too afraid of the answer. "That doesn't prove she was lying. He could've been just as angry if they had an affair and she exposed their secret. How can you know for sure?"

"I know." There wasn't a hint of doubt in his voice. "Trust what you feel, Emma. David lives for you. He'd never betray you, or hurt you in any way. That, I know for sure."

"I'm falling apart without him," I whispered, tears spilling down my cheeks. "I need to see him."

Nodding, Benjamin wiped the tears from my cheeks. "Then that's what I'll tell him and he'll find a way."

38

CHARLIE

I sat on a bench near the flower garden, far enough away that it wasn't completely obvious I was spying. A few of the patients were feeding bread to the birds, so I pretended to bird-watch while I kept an eye on Emma and her visitor—and her dragon. Emma was obviously fond of Benjamin and clearly trusted him, but he worked for her pedophile husband so I wasn't all that sure I wanted to trust him, which was probably stupid. Benjamin was somebody from her life—*her real life*, not the surreal one we were trapped in—and what Emma truly wanted was to go back to her old life, the life that made sense to her. Except, it didn't anymore. I wished I could jump into the Dream World and get some answers from Sophie for her, but Sophie was conveniently dead, which made Emma's husband a murderer. Unless it was a freak coincidence but that didn't seem very likely.

I studied Emma's body language as she talked with Benjamin. She was more at ease around him, some of her glow had even returned after just a few minutes with him. It made me wonder how she would look talking to her husband. Despite the fact that he might've cheated on her and might've murdered the woman he cheated with, Emma still loved him. That was blatantly obvious whenever she talked about him. Even when she was talking about the bad stuff, there was this look of reverence on her face when she said his name.

While I was busy spying on Emma's visit, someone sat down on the bench beside me. I turned and found young Nelly sitting next to me with Lilly on her lap. Silky ringlets gleaming in the sunlight, Lilly reached for the bread in Nellie's hand as birds gathered at our feet.

Nellie held the bread higher. "Be patient, child." Smiling, she tore a piece from the slice and placed it in Lilly's hand. I noticed Nellie's hand stayed touching her daughter's while she tossed the bread.

When I first asked about Lilly, Nellie had gotten incredibly defensive. At the time, I just chalked it up as one of her many quirks, but now I wondered. *You only see what you want to see.* Did she see this daughter because she existed or because Nellie wished she did?

And if that was the case, had she ever been real? It didn't make sense for Nellie to have another Dream form with her all the time, or did it? Was it any different than the dragon that followed Emma around? To answer that, I'd have to know what the dragon actually was and I still didn't, not for sure.

I greeted my bench-mates with a cheerful smile. "Hello, ladies."

Young Nellie grinned at me. She looked lovely bathed in sunlight too, dressed in her green sundress with her bare feet dangling just above the ground. Lilly looked up at me, wide-eyed and innocent like a little angel dressed in white.

I held my hand out. "Can I have a piece?" I was so tempted to reach out and try to touch Lilly's little round arm, but I was too afraid of upsetting Nellie to actually do it. I didn't have the heart to spoil the illusion, if that's all Lilly was. I looked across the lawn at Emma's threesome. The dragon stayed firmly positioned with its massive front legs framing Emma. Whenever she moved, the beast moved with her. Watching the dragon shimmer in the sunlight, I wondered if I'd be able to feel it if I tried to touch it. Not that I'd ever try. Even my stupidity had limits.

With Lilly's hand nestled in hers, Nellie eyed me warily as they dropped a chunk of bread in my hand.

"Thank you, ladies." Did it even matter if Lilly was real? She was Nellie's only happiness. I couldn't take that away from her.

Lilly giggled, but Nellie's eyes fixed on Emma's threesome. "So much Darkness."

I knew she was talking about the dragon but chose to pretend I didn't. "I think those cataracts are clouding your vision. It couldn't be brighter out."

Eyes fixed on Emma and her visitors, Nellie shook her head. "Someday you'll open your eyes, boy. For your sake, I hope it won't be too late."

Lilly twisted on Nellie's lap for a better view of the chickadee that'd settled on the bench next to ours. It hopped closer and she giggled gleefully.

I grinned at Lilly. "Wow Nellie, you sure know how to darken a sunny day."

"I give up," Nellie muttered. "Find out the hard way like I did."

"Don't give up on me," I whispered, "not before our fieldtrip tonight. You're still coming, right?"

"If you're still in one piece."

I winced. "Ouch."

Nellie handed Lilly another piece of bread and cradled her tiny hand as she dropped it. "Spying on shadows is asking for trouble."

If Emma's dragon was a shadow, wasn't Lilly the same? "So assuming I'm in one piece," I whispered, watching Lilly try to squirm free to get down and play with the birds, "are you still planning on coming?"

Her gaze returned to the threesome across the lawn. "As long as you won't be inviting any dragons."

"Wouldn't dream of it," I promised. "I'm surprised you haven't run inside to hide from the dragon. You must be feeling brave today."

Nellie turned toward me. "Sauntering recklessly into a dragon's sight isn't brave, it's suicide."

I watched the dragon move with Emma as she walked with Benjamin. "Isn't that a little dramatic? I've been close to Emma since she got admitted and she hasn't killed me yet."

Nellie hugged Lilly a little tighter. "Walk too far into the Darkness and you'll never find your way back out." As she finished the sentence, her melodious voice grew feeble and squeaky, Lilly vanished and wrinkled old Nellie sat next to me, her milky eyes following the dragon.

The beast turned its massive head in our direction and a puff of bluish haze from its nostrils trailed across the lawn. As the colorful smoke wafted toward us, Nellie's trembling jostled the bench.

"Why don't you go inside?" I whispered, watching the smoke drift toward us. It'd clearly been aimed at us. As used to Emma's dragon as I was becoming, that was still the stuff of nightmares. With a little effort, I looked away from the beast and turned to Nellie. She seemed paralyzed with fear, so I snapped my fingers in her face to break the trance.

She whipped her head toward me with a look of pure terror in her milky eyes. "What are you doing? Do you want to die?"

I was about to say something about her being paranoid when I noticed movement out of the corner of my eye. Benjamin was walking toward us and Emma was heading back inside. I was a little surprised she wasn't coming to get me, unless she knew Benjamin was coming over to threaten me or stab me or something. I wouldn't put anything past David's right hand man. For all I knew, he'd killed Sophie for his boss. For a minute the dragon lingered, watching us instead of following Emma to the door. By the time Benjamin reached us, I half expected the dragon to bolt across the yard and devour us but it turned and followed Emma into the building.

"So, I'll catch up with you later. Bye." I elbowed Nellie and nudged my head toward the door, hoping she'd take the hint and go inside. I didn't know what Benjamin wanted, but I doubted he'd come over to make small talk. Nellie stayed frozen next to me and her head tilted up to look at Benjamin. The fact that he was standing while we were sitting seemed to magnify his menacing aura, and it didn't need any magnifying.

Benjamin glared at old Nellie. "Walk away, woman. I have no business with you."

Scurrying from the bench without standing fully upright, Nellie dashed for the door without saying a word.

Benjamin towered over me, peering down and the longer I looked up at him, the larger he seemed to be. "What are your intentions toward Mrs. Talbot?"

Okay. I wasn't prepared for that question. "Um, my intention is to be her friend and watch out for her," I muttered, relieved that my voice sounded much more confident than I felt.

Brow furrowed, Benjamin sat down next to me. "You don't desire to become *more* than friends?"

Well sure, I've got desires. But I wasn't about to admit it to this guy. "No, of course not."

His eyes narrowed. "Why do I find that hard to believe?"

Because she's the hottest woman I've ever seen. "I don't know, Sir. My intentions are pure. I swear."

Benjamin let out a lingering sigh and coming from him, even that sounded menacing. "I'm not eager to be the messenger that tells Emma's husband about your friendship but let me warn you, you don't want to make an enemy of Mr. Talbot. He treasures his wife above everything else. You think I'm frightening?"

I nodded before realizing it was a rhetorical question, so much for coming across as confident.

Benjamin continued as if he hadn't noticed. Probably, because it was no great surprise. "*He* is what frightens *me.*"

39

BOB

For once, I didn't have to strain to hear the television. All the numbskulls that usually flapped their gums while I was tryin to concentrate were out frolickin in the sunshine. I had the couch to myself and there was no pain in the ass tryin to talk to me. The boy was the worst of them lately. For some reason, he'd decided to make a hobby outta askin me goofy questions. To be honest, I didn't mind too much. He was a good kid. Still, a break from all the fuckin noise was like Christmas come early. If my head didn't hurt like a son of a bitch, everything'd be perfect.

I dropped my head in my hands and shut my eyes. Those dipshits were startin to rub off on me. I was wastin valuable silence, interruptin myself with pointless thoughts. I tried to concentrate on the television. A classy broad with blond hair and a tight body had a microphone in her hand and a plastic smile on her pretty face. She stood in front of a burnin apartment building while officers and firefighters fought thick smoke and spreadin flames to get everybody out and put out the fire. It made me proud to see my boys in blue makin the city a safer place. They switched back to the anchorman with gray at his temples and a stick up his ass, sittin all safe and comfy inside. If you asked me, that skinny no-balls prick needed a swift kick in his lazy ass for hidin inside while a woman risked her safety to get a story for him. I couldn't tell you what the yellow-bellied bastard said because the wiry-haired ding-bat with the invisible kid came rushin in right when he started talkin. She scurried to my couch and plopped down next to me, too fuckin close for my comfort but I was already up against the armrest, so I couldn't put any distance between us. The old bat was pantin like she'd just got done sprintin a mile.

I frowned at her. "What the fuck's got you all wound up? Boogie man chasin you and your invis-ible baby?"

Her cloudy eyes narrowed. "Just watch your tele-vision, ya old jackass, and let me worry about what's chasing me."

"I could let you worry about it a lot better if you'd go take your crazy someplace else," I growled. "How the hell am I 'sposed to concentrate?"

"On what, you darn fool?"

I nodded at the television. "The news, woman. You're actin batty *and* stupid and I gotta tell ya, it ain't a great combination. I know you can't help bein batty, but you might wanna work on the stupid. Sharpen up with some word games or somethin."

She growled, which was just comical in her squeaky little voice. I smirked, not so much on purpose. I just couldn't fuckin help myself.

Her milky eyes narrowed. "What the hell's so funny, jackass?"

I think she meant it to sound intimidatin but she didn't exactly have the voice for it. "Can you hear how ridiculous you sound?"

She clenched her bony little hand into a fist. "Don't you get it, you big dummy? I'm in danger. Just watch your damn television and let me sit here."

The laugh I tried to hold back came bustin out in a snort. "Danger of what? Lookin like a fruit loop?"

She shook her fist at me then turned to look out the window. The kid was out there sittin on a park bench, talkin to a tall colored fella. I felt the old bat start shakin the second she looked at him.

"Shit. You really are scared, aren't you? Did that thug out there threaten you?" I liked to give the dingbat a hard time, but that son of a bitch had no right to scare her. I had no patience for goons who preyed on people weaker than themselves. "You want me to go out there and clock the bastard?"

She turned and looked at me. "You'd do that for *me*?" By the expression on her wrinkled face, you'd think I'd just offered to take her to a fuckin dance.

The sudden change in the way she was lookin at me made me nervous. "Don't get all hot and bothered, woman. I'd do that for anybody who was gettin bullied by some jackass."

She grinned at me like she was about to go bust out her dancin shoes. "Thanks."

At least she'd stopped shakin. Even loony old broads had a right to feel safe. "You're welcome. You didn't answer my question though. Am I goin out there to set that shit-bag straight, or what?"

Her goofy grin got even bigger. "No. This is good. Just let me sit here. Okay?"

I shifted, wishin I could put some space between us. "Just keep it down so I can hear my television."

"Deal," she squeaked, still grinnin like a goofy school girl.

She kept her word and stayed quiet the whole time the news was on. Turned out, havin some company wasn't such a terrible thing. If I'm honest, it was kinda nice to be needed. It felt good havin someone to protect again.

40

NELLIE

I'd been catching glimpses of the old windbag's Dream form since the last group session. One minute, he was a crabby old bastard and the next, he was a handsome knight in shining armor—and just when I'd get used to the strapping young hero's chiseled features, he'd turn back into an old jackass—but old fart or fetching young man, I stayed close to him.

He sat next to me with his eyes glued to that stupid television set. Lord only knew what his scrambled mind thought he was doing that was so damned important. As the television reporter droned on about a bombing in some foreign country, I watched the twosome in the yard and wondered if Charlie could feel himself slipping into the shadows. As long as that golden-haired beauty was ahead of him, I doubted he'd notice until somebody removed the blinders from his foolish eyes and he found himself immersed in Darkness. If somebody had warned me in my youth, would I have listened any better? Probably not.

With a shiver that had nothing to do with the temperature, I turned away from the window. There was only so much Darkness my poor old heart could take. Shutting my eyes, I hugged my baby girl closer. I wouldn't cry. Shedding tears was pointless and weak. My aged mind would just have to let those memories be. I focused on the stream of noise coming from the television. The news was full of gut-wrenching stories of hatred and violence and my old heart couldn't handle all that, so I concentrated on tuning out the words and listening to the drone of voices. I focused on the feel of Lilly in my arms, the warm comfort of the body sagging next to me, the steady rumble of his inhales and exhales. It'd be alright. The Darkness wouldn't get me here. As for Charlie, he'd just have to fend for himself. I had no defense against shadows. All I had were the gaping holes that Darkness had left behind.

I thought of my beach, my beautiful paradise lost. My choices now were to leave it behind for the dragon to claim or cling to it until the beast devoured me right along with it. In his naïve eagerness, Charlie had promised to make things better. As much as I knew it'd be best to distance myself from the boy, I found myself drawn to his optimism. Despite all the pain life had doled out to him, he still believed in happily-ever-afters. If anyone was a Dream squasher, it was me, not him and despite all my griping and bitterness, the boy was still trying to help me.

A snore that could've come from a hibernating grizzly bear ripped from the throat of the old man slumped beside me. Smiling, I opened my eyes and looked at him. His eyelids were heavy and motionless, his mouth was open wide enough to catch every fly out in the yard, his head was flopped against the back of the couch at an angle that guaranteed a stiff neck when he woke up and big buzzing snores resonated from his mouth and nose with the steady rise and fall of his chest. Careful not to make a sound, I reached over and tilted the old fart's head to a more comfortable position. He sighed contentedly as his wrinkled lips turned up in a smile.

I wondered what the old bastard's Dreamscape looked like. He was a hero in this world before he lost his mind. Hell, even that was because of his bravery. I'd seen his Dream form so I knew he was a man of courage and honor in the Dream World, too. I found myself surprisingly tempted to jump in and pay him a visit but just as my curiosity had about gotten the better of me, footsteps entering the room made me jump.

"Sorry," lilted a honeyed voice near the door, "I didn't mean to startle you." Some of the girl's glow was back. Apparently, the visit from Darkness had agreed with her.

I scowled at her. "What do you want?"

She walked into the room, eyes briefly darting to the conversation in the yard as she sat down on the coffee table in front of us. "Why do you hate me so much?"

"It's nothing personal." Talking over the television was a pain in the ass so I reached over Bob, grabbed the remote and turned it off. "If it's any consolation, I hate cancer, too."

Her brow furrowed, and I took guilty pleasure in picturing it permanently wrinkled. "You're comparing me to cancer?"

"Or poison. I hate that, too."

Frowning, she whispered, "That's hurtful." I imagined deep frown lines creasing that perfect face as her porcelain skin thinned and sagged.

I smiled at her. "Life can be painful. You of all people should know that."

She shuddered so slightly that I could've easily missed it. "Why do you say that?"

I narrowed my eyes, blurring her flawless features. "How much pain have you caused? The boy's tender heart is swelling and it'll keep on swelling until you make it burst, and what brought you here? You tried to off yourself and when somebody tried to stop you, you almost killed her, too. Your father's death caused you pain, so you hurt another. Just because you've chosen to fill yourself with Darkness, doesn't mean you have to infect the people around you, but you choose to because you're toxic and vile. You're cancer. You're poison." I was so engrossed in chastising her that I didn't hear the footfalls of expensive shoes entering the room.

"Perhaps I have business with you after all," a Dark voice murmured behind the couch.

I turned to face the Darkness, waking the old man next to me from his catnap. "No. Please. Forgive me. That was uncalled for."

Charlie walked into the room at that point, stopping just inside the door. He stood motionless and made no move to speak, obviously aware he'd interrupted something.

Bob turned to see who I was talking to and glared at the Dark man. "You. Do we have a problem?"

Charlie motioned for Bob to shut his mouth, proving he wasn't completely stupid.

I looked back at the girl's Dark friend, who was eyeing Bob stoically. "Relax, old man. There's no problem. Your lady friend just forgot her manners, but I'm sure she's remembered them now." He looked into my eyes and I felt the Darkness bore into my soul. "Isn't that right? You were just about to apologize and in the future, I'm sure you'll remember to hold your tongue."

Trembling, I nodded. "Of course."

His Dark eyes pierced straight through me. "You didn't apologize."

"Of course," I muttered. "Forgive me. Please. Sir."

"Not to me." The man nodded toward Emma. "To her."

Though it pained me to turn my back to the man, I looked at Emma. In a shaky voice, I hardly recognized as mine, I begged, "Please forgive me, child."

Tears glistened in Emma's lovely eyes as she whispered, "It's alright."

"No," the man demanded, making me jump. "It most certainly is not alright."

I turned back to face the Darkness. "Of course."

"You're damn right, it's not alright." I looked at the man sitting next to me on the couch. He was young and rugged and fine looking. Eyes twinkling with vigor, he smiled at me.

The Dark man studied Bob, nothing but slight curiosity apparent in his expression. Then he smiled at me with pure Dark amusement. I imagined having your blood ice in your veins would feel about the same as being the recipient of that smile. "How nice for you to have a knight in shining armor to protect your virtue."

"How about you and me step outside, ya big slab of meat," Bob grunted.

The man turned that Dark smile on him. "I think I'll pass for now. However, if your lady friend continues to insult my mistress, I may take you up on that."

Old Bob was on the couch again. I probably should've been touched that he was still sticking up for me, but it was hard not to miss the virile young stallion that'd defended me seconds ago. He turned to look at Emma, voice full of awe, "Your mistress? How the hell did you bed *her*? If you don't mind me askin."

"I do mind," the man replied coldly, "and it's 'mistress,' as in my boss's wife not my lover, you old fool."

Eyebrows raised, Bob turned back to the Dark man. "Too bad for you."

The man now wore no smile, icy or otherwise. "I think we're done here." He looked at Emma. "Walk me out?"

The girl just sat there stunned for a few seconds then she snapped out of it, stood and nodded at the man.

Smiling, he walked around the couch and held his arm out to her. She took it as they turned toward the door, and Charlie bolted to a corner of the room.

On his way out, the man turned his head to us one last time. "I trust you'll remember your manners in the future."

"We will, if you will," old Bob growled.

Apparently, that was good enough because the man turned back to the door and left the room with Emma on his arm.

Bob looked at Charlie, then me, a puzzled look on his sour old face. "What the fuck was that about?"

Charlie shook his head. "Trust me, Bob. You don't want to know."

41

DAVID

I sat on the terrace, viewing the sun's colorful descent toward its inevitable fate—to slip from the heavens, only to be swallowed by the voracious waters patiently lying in wait below. Drumming my fingers atop the half-finished single malt on the arm of my lounge chair, I mused at the absurdity of the unceasing cycle. Why bother to climb the sky each dawn, to avoid a predator that you know will overtake you in the dusk? What point was there to fleeing one who pursued so tirelessly—night after night—driven by such maddening passion to devour you? In the end, such a predator always consumes what it desires.

Another day without her was drawing to a close. Tomorrow was my day in court, and I'd done everything possible to ensure that the judge would overturn the restriction barring me from visiting my wife. Normally, Benjamin handled any necessary cajolery prior to a court date but in this case, I'd handled everything personally. Benjamin's powers of persuasion were nothing short of remarkable, but mine exceeded his. I should never have left any task in other hands during Emma's trial. Fear of losing her had nearly incapacitated me and I'd allowed panic to cloud my judgment. I would not make the same mistake again.

In lieu of assisting with preparations for court, I'd sent Benjamin to pay a visit to Emma. I needed to know how she fared and I wasn't about to trust the word of that imbecile doctor at the facility. After visiting with Emma, Benjamin planned to stop at the hospital to check on Isabella. Sipping scotch in a futile attempt to dull the ache in my heart, I impatiently awaited his return. Everything was out of my hands at the moment. I wasn't accustomed to feeling powerless, and the uncertainty of it all was weighing heavily on me. My eyes threatened to tear but I held them wide, refusing to show any sign of weakness even in private. I had to stay strong. Emma was depending on it, on me. So I stared wide-eyed at the brilliance of the sunset until it became nothing but a magnificent blur of color.

I didn't realize my eyelids had drooped until Benjamin's voice roused me. "Evening, boss."

I twisted in my chair, partially to face him, partially to stretch. Too much time spent slouched in a lounge chair had left me feeling less than refreshed.

Drawing a deep breath to shed my grogginess, I gestured to the seat opposite mine and lifted a bottle of Chivas from the table, tilting it so the rich liquid sloshed to one side.

Eyeing the bottle greedily, Benjamin headed to the table, flipped a glass upright and served himself a sizable drink. He took an appreciative sip as he sank into the chair facing mine, then he closed his eyes and let out a slow deliberate sigh.

"How is she?" I prodded, my tone only slightly more demanding than I'd intended. I was too impatient to waste time on pleasantries.

Benjamin opened his eyes and fixed them on me. "She's handling things about as well as you are," he reported glumly, shifting in his seat to face the sunset. He wasn't exactly a rainbows and sunsets sort of fellow, which made it somewhat obvious that he'd turned so as not to display emotion. Subtle as the movement was, it wouldn't have been evident to most but we'd known one another long enough to hear what wasn't said. The man seated before me had been described numerous times as emotionless. It was often said that his heart was made of stone, so the fact that his grief for Emma's suffering was difficult to conceal was like a dagger straight to my wounded heart.

I pushed up from my chair and moved to lean against the rail. Watching the water spill over the sand, I tried to picture Emma's body lying naked and entwined with mine on the beach below. "She would love the view tonight," I stated absently, as much to myself and the setting sun as to Benjamin.

"She would," he agreed softly. His voice was harsh by nature, which made the tenderness that he spoke of her with all the more meaningful. "She was out in the yard when I showed up today," he added, obviously intending for the statement to comfort me. But it didn't.

I sighed, hesitating a moment before asking, "What did she say?"

He didn't hesitate to reply, "She said that she needs to see you and she's falling apart without you."

I turned toward him, searching his face for any flicker of dishonesty. My deepest fear was that our time apart had allowed her hatred for me to grow. A sugar-coated version of the truth was the last thing I wanted. I didn't need false hope.

"Her exact words," he assured me, as if reading my mind.

I studied him doubtfully. "What else did she say?"

Sorrow glinted in his eyes as he held my stare. "Isn't that enough?"

I turned back to the sunset to conceal my own emotion. "Of course not. It won't be enough until I bring her home."

"You will," he answered softly. "It's just a matter of time."

"I've lost too much time already." I turned from the rail to face him. "I'm not a patient man."

A melancholy smile tugged at the corners of his mouth. "No. You aren't." He spoke in a gentle tone, quite unnatural for him, obviously attempting to keep me calm—an effort I did not appreciate. "We *will* bring her home soon."

"Not soon enough." I looked back at the sand, lying in wait for its lover's next touch. "How is Isabella? Has there been any change?"

"I'm afraid not." The disappointment was clear in his voice. "She's stable but she still hasn't regained consciousness. They're starting to consider options if she doesn't wake up," his voice broke as he finished. Benjamin and Isabella had worked closely together for many years. She was far more than just a co-worker to him.

I found myself fighting tears again as I watched the ebb and flow of the tide. The sun had almost finished slipping from the sky, but the sand and surf remained oblivious. To them, nothing existed but the touch of the other. "Was Mark there?"

"He was," Benjamin replied brusquely.

The answer surprised me. Isabella's son wanted everyone connected with the Talbots kept far away from his mother. No one could blame him really. A Talbot had almost killed her. In his place, I'd hate us, too. "How did you find anything out with him there?"

"He didn't show up until after I'd already spoken to one of the nurses," he answered, almost smugly.

Benjamin's deep dark voice had undoubtedly seduced the poor girl into divulging medical information that she shouldn't have.

"Did he see you?" I asked curiously.

Benjamin nodded. "I told him it pained us to hear that there was still no change and I offered to pay for her medical expenses but as usual, he refused our assistance."

I shook my head. "Foolish boy." As much as he refused to believe it, we loved his mother dearly. Isabella wasn't just an employee, she was a member of our family but he couldn't comprehend that.

Mark had confronted me shortly after Isabella was hospitalized, when he discovered I'd arranged for her medical bills to be sent to me. He insisted that his family had 'no need for our blood money' and told me he'd always suspected that my adult relationship with Emma had begun when she was a minor and I'd coerced Isabella into 'keeping her mouth shut'. I was sorely tempted to ask the dolt how he thought his college tuition had been paid for but for Isabella's sake, I refrained. I also kept the fact that I helped hide his mother's secrets to myself. Despite what Mark chose to believe, I loved the woman dearly and I'd never betray her confidence—even after her death, which I prayed was still far off—and Emma would never forgive herself for what she'd done in a haze born of ingested chemicals and a broken heart. She loved Isabella every bit as much as the rest of us.

Dread knotted in my stomach. "Do you have any idea what he's planning to do if Isabella doesn't wake?"

"No," Benjamin answered quietly, "but if he chooses to end her life, I'll be sorely tempted to end his."

I smiled. "I don't believe that'd help anyone concerned."

"Maybe not," he answered coldly, "but if that boy pulls the plug on her, I won't give a fuck what it will or won't help."

"He won't," I assured Benjamin. "He may be an idiot but he loves his mother. All of his rage and stupidity stems from that love."

"And from stubborn fucking ignorance," Benjamin added icily.

"And stubborn fucking ignorance," I agreed, "but that's not really his fault."

The night air had cooled significantly now that the sun had disappeared. From down below, came the steadily repeating sound of waves crashing over the sand as moonlight bathed their embrace in an eerily enchanting glow. Behind me, Benjamin cleared his throat. There was something more that he was hesitant to share.

I returned to my chair. "What is it?"

"Emma has made a friend at the facility." He flinched involuntarily on the word *friend*.

Jaw clenched, I gripped the arms of my chair. "Tell me about him." My voice was low but there was no mistaking the barely contained rage.

"I didn't say it was a 'him'." Benjamin's voice remained steady and strong, but he was nervous.

"You didn't have to," I replied in a semi-restrained growl.

Benjamin shifted in his seat. "There's a boy there who's taken it upon himself to protect her."

I tightened my grip on the chair. "Did you inform him that was unnecessary?"

Benjamin swallowed. "No."

"Tell me why," I insisted.

Benjamin's heart was racing. "The boy insisted his only intention was to keep Emma safe. He said he only intended to be a friend."

Voice low, I growled, "And what did you expect him to say?"

"He sounded sincere."

"That doesn't answer my question," I snarled. "Did you expect him to tell you if his intentions were," I choked the next words out venomously, "*less than pure?*"

Benjamin flinched at the fury in my voice. "What would you have had me do?"

Heavy heart thudding madly, I drew a sharp breath. Too much madness coursed through my veins to sit still any longer, so I stood and started pacing. "Did he lay a hand on her?" I spat the words as if each one were poison.

And was answered by silence.

Jaw clenched all the tighter at the silent admission, I growled, "I'd have had you tear him limb from limb."

Standing slowly, Benjamin sighed. "There's one more thing I need to tell you."

42

EMMA

Once again, I was alone in my room. Charlie had walked me to my door and wished me good night. After closing the door, I stood directionless and purposeless in the center of the room. I'd obediently downed the pills that Tim handed me, but I wasn't the least bit tired. Maybe my body was becoming immune to the effects, or maybe my mind no longer cared enough to sustain my body and sensed no point in rest. I moved to the bed, dropped onto it and curled up in a ball above the covers. There was no need to switch the lights off. I hadn't bothered to turn them on. Outside the window, I only saw darkness. If there were stars in the sky, they hid themselves from me.

Charlie had been sullen for the rest of the day after Benjamin's visit. I could only imagine what Benjamin might've said to him after I went inside.

I could've insisted on staying while they spoke, but it would've been pointless. When Benjamin meant for something to happen, somehow it always did. Besides, despite Benjamin's intimidating nature, I knew Charlie would be able to handle himself. The difficulties that he'd overcome in his lifetime were remarkable. If it'd been me—left and forgotten in sterile facilities all my life—I wouldn't have survived. At least, not with my optimism intact. But Charlie had.

I wondered what kind of mother could desert her child like that. Then I remembered my own parents. What kind of father would choke his own daughter? The man had never cared about me, but I'd always had David to make it alright. Charlie never had anyone. Dr. Spenser said that I didn't belong in the facility. Charlie didn't either but no one seemed to see that and unlike me, he didn't have anybody outside the facility fighting to free him. All Charlie had was a woman hoping to keep him contained. How could she have known Charlie all his life and not seen how beautiful he was? Imagining what his childhood must've been like made my heart ache for him.

At least that disproved my morose suspicion that my heart no longer functioned. All I'd felt in its place lately was a painful emptiness, and Nellie's words had only deepened that void. *I was cancer. I was poison.* I loved Isabella dearly, but somehow I lost myself in those seconds that I hurt her. For the life of me, I couldn't remember how it'd happened. The memory was just a blur of darkness and hurt. Maybe Nellie was right—I was cancer, I spread darkness—maybe I would only hurt Charlie in the end, but what was the end? Was it my own end, or would I eventually be freed from the facility only to leave Charlie behind to the darkness?

I slipped the gold cuff off my wrist. Of all the gifts David had given me over the years, why did I bring this one? I left behind the one I treasured most, a pendant he gave me for my sixteenth birthday. It was a brilliant heart-shaped ruby, elaborately caged and bound by intricately intertwining metal vines. David had unceremoniously given a small box wrapped in black and white silk ribbons to my father at work, apologizing that he couldn't attend my party and asking him to deliver the gift. When I unwrapped the present, my mother's eyes grew wide with envy. Her own extreme fondness for jewels bordered on obsession. No matter how many my father bought her, she always wanted more and she made a point of knowing exactly how much each was worth. When she eyed the necklace, she remarked that it was worth more than every piece in her jewelry box, combined. *Much more.* At that, my father decided the necklace was 'too much to give a sixteen year-old child' and insisted that we return the gift. At the time, I wasn't sure if my father was angry because his friend had given his daughter such an extravagant gift or because any gift that he could afford to give his wife could never possibly compete. Now that I was older, I knew it was the latter. It was so long ago, the rest of the details were a blur but somehow in the end I got to keep the pendant. And I never took it off, until the night my world came crumbling down around me.

I took it off just before cutting my wrist.

When I came home from the hospital, I found the necklace draped across my pillow—but I couldn't bring myself to put it back on—and the day I was sentenced, I left it on my pillow before we headed off to court.

As I stared at the bracelet that conjured nothing but painful memories, I wished with all my heart that I had that pendant. Whenever it hung around my neck I felt like David was close, even when he wasn't. I let the cuff drop from my hand and fall to the floor with a dull thud. Then I closed my eyes and wept—tears of regret and heartache and emptiness—and somehow in the midst of those tears, I drifted off to sleep...

...A brilliant array of stars was scattered across the sky, the cool night air carried the mingled scents of meadow grass and exotic flowers in bloom and a hidden chorus of nocturnal creatures harmoniously threaded through the silence of the evening. I lazily rolled from my back to my stomach. The lake at the edge of the clearing shimmered as if it was laced with diamonds. I breathed a contented sigh at the tranquility of my surroundings.

Soft footfalls sounded behind me, but I didn't dare turn around. I was too afraid that the footsteps weren't his. As the steps drew nearer, my heartbeat quickened and the sound of the unseen soul dropping to the grass beside me caused an actual physical ache in my heart. I closed my eyes and held my breath. The body shifted closer, planting strong hands in the grass on either side of my shoulders, but I was afraid to open my eyes.

"Can you not bear to look at me?" The sorrow in his voice made my heart throb.

"I don't think I could take it, if I opened my eyes and didn't find you here." Even in a whisper, desperation filled my words.

A hand brushed the hair from the side of my face, and familiar lips kissed the flesh he'd exposed. "I'll always be here, Princess." The warmth of his breath heated me, and I felt it everywhere. His body pulled away and strong hands rolled me onto my back. He lowered himself to the ground beside me, pressed against my side and slid a hand across my waist. Still, I kept my eyes shut.

"Stubborn," he whispered in my ear, sending a heated shiver through me.

His lips touched mine—tentative at first, seeking permission—but as I kissed him eagerly back, his mouth moved hungrily against mine. His lips dominantly coaxed mine apart and a powerful tongue thrust deep in my mouth, as if he meant to devour me. His hunger ignited my own and I thrust my tongue greedily back, kissing him with every bit of desperation and need that I felt. The hungrier and needier my kisses grew, the deeper and stronger his became.

A confidant hand slipped into the hair at the back of my head, weaving deft fingers through the strands, grasping the back of my head and holding me to that hungry mouth. And the ache in my heart became an ache in places lower down. I opened my eyes, the brilliant blue eyes of the only man I would ever love stared greedily back at me and the fire in his eyes heated those dark empty places inside me. I was no longer heartache or emptiness, I was hunger and fire. And this man was the only one who could temper the flames. Unable to bear the ache any longer, I wrapped my arms around him, desperate to draw him down to me.

Pulling his mouth back from mine, he answered my grasps with a ravenous growl. With a hurried combination of hands and mouth he savagely tore at my clothing and as soon as he lowered near enough to reach, I tugged at his. Nostrils flared, he greedily watched me struggle to shed his clothes then he nimbly helped me remove the last of them. Fixing his eyes on mine, he stayed perfectly still for several audible breaths. As he watched me, that fire in his eyes consumed every thought and every feeling I'd ever had until all that I knew was a desperate aching need.

His desire every bit as feral as mine, he lowered his body and with a look of all-consuming lust, he thrust inside me and I cried out at the feel of him. As he moved inside me, sensation devoured conscious thought. I no longer saw. I no longer heard. Light filled the darkness, quelling the void, making me whole, satisfying every need I'd ever had until the both of us were spent and he collapsed, his powerful body melding perfectly to mine...

...Bolting upright in the dark, I awoke with a gasp. I was alone in the room they called 'mine.' It was only a dream but my body didn't seem to realize that. My flesh still tingled as if it'd just felt his touch, and I still felt like he'd just been inside me. What before was void, now burned with an unquenchable fire. If he'd been in my bed, I'd have straddled him and begged for more but I was all alone in the darkness. Outside the window, stars sparkled in the sky like diamonds. And I lay naked and panting and aching for more.

43

CHARLIE

Having just walked Emma to her room, it was time to head to mine. My mind barely registered where I was going, but it didn't matter. My feet knew the way, which wasn't necessarily a good thing. Neither was the fact that I referred to that generic institutional bedroom as 'my room.' Those were just small testaments to the fact that too much of my life had been spent locked in places like this. Until I met Nellie—I mean *truly* met her—somewhere deep inside, I'd always figured the rest of the world must be right. It only made sense that the one person who saw images that no one else did was the crazy one. Turns out, I wasn't. But where did that leave me? It wasn't like the rest of the world saw things any differently, to them I was just as crazy as I'd always been. I couldn't exactly call my mother up, tell her everything I saw was real and ask her to come get me. None of what

I'd learned changed what I'd accepted long ago, my mother didn't love me—at least, not enough to make an effort when things got tough.

I reached 'my door,' turned the knob and stepped inside. As I flipped the light switch, I mentally shoved the self-pitying thoughts aside. I had plenty of other things to think about. I wasn't sure what to make of Emma's visit from Benjamin. He hadn't flipped once the whole time he'd visited, which wasn't all that unusual. Plenty of people didn't flip very often. I'd spent months occupying the same space as Nellie and Bob and until recently, I'd never seen either of them flip. Whatever Benjamin was in the Dream World, he was a walking talking nightmare in this one and at the end of his visit with Emma, he basically walked over and threatened me. But his threat didn't involve him doing anything. He just warned me not to make an enemy of David Talbot. *He is what frightens me.* I'd seen more than my share of nightmarish creatures over the years. My second grade teacher was a leathery demon with yellow eyes, jagged teeth and filthy razor-sharp claws and my mother went through a zillion babysitters because most of them had Dream forms that scared the living shit out of me. One especially memorable sitter was a nasty goblin that drooled and licked her fat lips every time she looked at me. I could go on, but you get the point. By the time I grew up, I didn't scare all that easily and yet—even without seeing Benjamin's

Dream form—I got the feeling that if I met him in a dark alley, I'd piss my pants if he so much as looked at me. I stood my ground during our conversation and walked away with my pants unsoiled, a fact I'm ashamed to admit I was actually proud of. Benjamin was just David Talbot's messenger and according to the messenger himself, he was nothing compared to his boss. *He is what frightens me.* I was starting to think Emma must be wed to the devil himself.

Benjamin made it sound like he wasn't going to mention me to Mr. Talbot. Then again, who was I to Benjamin? Why would he risk hiding information from a boss he feared? It seemed more likely that he *would* mention me, in which case there was probably a price on my head. Maybe I should learn to sleep with one eye open, or 'a foot in each world' like Nellie.

Speaking of Nellie, we had big plans for the night. I plopped distractedly onto my bed. The exchange between Nellie and Bob earlier was interesting. They seemed to have gone from crotchety enemies to very close friends pretty quickly. The way Nellie looked at Bob, I figured she must be seeing his Dream form. I had to admit, young Bob was a handsome guy and despite all her craziness, young Nellie was an angel—at least, until she opened her mouth.

I reached over and flipped off the light switch then burrowed down under the covers. There was no chance I was going to drift off to sleep. I had way too much on my mind and I didn't want to waste valuable Dreamtime attempting the impossible, so I pictured the rippling blue waves, silently called out to them and they obligingly appeared. With a satisfied grin, I took a deep breath and plunged into the Water.

The only thoughts I held onto as I sunk through the frigid depths were of where I wanted to go. *Take me to Nellie's beach.* I pictured her postcard-worthy shore. *Nellie.* I pictured young Nellie's pretty face, though I couldn't seem to picture her features wearing any expression but a scowl. Even in the midst of the Water's assault, I smiled at that. *Nellie.* I focused on her name. Her face. Her tropical paradise. *Nellie. Nellie. Nellie.* I continued the chant as I started rising toward the surface. My head emerged and my mental picture of Nellie's beach was replaced by the actual thing. The sky was dark, and the moon hung low and full and radiant as if it was there just to light my way. The realization that I didn't have to adjust to the atmosphere fluttered through my mind and was quickly forgotten. My focus was on reaching the shore and finding Nellie as soon as possible.

I moved almost effortlessly through the Water and quickly found myself on the shore. Sitting up, I scanned my surroundings. I didn't see anybody, but Nellie was expecting me so she shouldn't be too hard to find. Feeling no need to rest, I stood up and started walking the beach.

In a couple of minutes, I found the spot where Lilly had napped the night before and a twinge of hesitation struck me. As I walked toward the bushes, I prayed that this idea was as good as I thought it was. I moved closer and the leaves started rustling, closer still and a tiny giggle emanated from the foliage. Grinning, I rounded the bushes and found Nellie sitting cross-legged with Lilly on her lap. Lilly looked up at me with those big beautiful eyes and clapped her hands in delight, but Nellie was shaking.

Seeing Nellie—looking so timid and frightened—I felt more compassion for her than I ever had before. "Hey," I muttered as I sat down next to her, "Everything alright?"

Nellie nodded, nervously searching my eyes. Even in the dark, I could see the tears in hers. "Just fine," she whispered.

I smiled at her as Lilly reached her arms out to me. I raised an eyebrow at Nellie and when she nodded, I lifted Lilly off her lap and sat her down on mine. Lilly reached up and touched the stubble on my chin. Being secluded on a beach with just her mother all her life, I guess she'd never encountered facial hair. I stared cross-eyed at her hand on my chin and she giggled as she slid her hand up to my cheek. I made another silly face and she giggled even louder.

Nellie's trembling had eased a little, so I figured it'd be okay to ask about it. "What's wrong?" I asked as Lilly continued amusing herself with my face.

"I thought you were the dragon," Nellie answered in a trembling whisper.

A tiny finger poked up one of my nostrils, and I gently brushed Lilly's hand from my nose. "You knew I was coming. Why did you think it was the dragon?"

Nellie drew a deep breath. "I always think it's a dragon. Every time a head breaches the surf, I think the worst."

Lilly tugged at my ear and giggled at the pained expression on my face. "I can't imagine what it'd be like to live with that much fear."

Nellie barely refrained from breaking into sobs. "I've spent my life cringing at shadows."

Lilly tugged at my hair and squirmed to reach more, each time I freed a handful from her little fingers. "What happened to you?"

"I told you," Nellie whispered as she searched my eyes, "I've told you so many times. A *dragon* happened."

I tipped my head and shook my hair at Lilly, and she giggled enthusiastically. "You never say more than that. What did the dragon do?"

"Unspeakable things." Smiling morosely at her little cherub, Nellie lovingly smoothed a hand over her curls. "Don't let a dragon break you, Charlie. Their hearts are full of venom. If you let one close, it'll destroy you. Darkness sinks its teeth into anything it likes and devours what it treasures most."

Nellie seemed so petrified, I didn't have the heart to point out that her words were just more cryptic nonsense. She seemed to genuinely be trying to open up to me, but she was obviously terrified of doing anything that might draw the dragon's attention. Whatever the dragon did to her, it must've been the stuff of nightmares but none of that pertained to me. Emma couldn't be the sort of dark creature Nellie was warning me about, it just wasn't possible but I'd save that debate for some other time. "Maybe a trip will help take your mind off your worries."

Nellie shook her head. "You still won't listen."

Tired of playing with my head, Lilly reached out to Nellie and I sat her back on her mother's lap. "That's not true. I am listening. I just don't think Emma poses the same kind of threat that your dragon did."

Nellie let out an exasperated sigh. "You still only see what you want to. I don't know how to open your eyes."

"Why do you want to open my eyes so bad?"

Nellie looked at me like I was a moron. It was a welcome sight. So far our exchange had been so atypically cordial, it was almost uncomfortable. "Because, you big idiot, I'm starting to care about what happens to you. Crazy right?"

I was surprised at how touched I was by her words. "No, you old hag, it's not crazy. I'm actually starting to care about you, too."

She smiled, looking as pleased by my statement as I was by hers.

"Which is why I wanted to take you somewhere tonight," I continued. "So, are we going on this trip or what? Because I'll stay in bed until Tim drags me out if I have to. Either we go now or we go later, but I'm not leaving this world until we've gone."

Nellie rolled her eyes, but she was smiling. "Why the hell not, it's not like my dance card is full for tonight. You're the only one who ever comes calling and no offense, but you're not my type."

"How am I not supposed to take offense at that?" I wondered aloud, not caring at all. She wasn't exactly my dream girl either.

A twinkle of amusement glinted in her eyes. "You're just a boy. I prefer someone whose diapers don't need changing."

I raised an eyebrow. "I've been potty-trained for quite a while, old woman. If anybody needs diapers, it's more likely you than me."

She shook her head. "Come back and talk to me when you're an old fart, and we'll see how funny that is then."

I stood up. "So, you're not denying it."

Holding Lilly in her arms, she stood up and gave me a playful swat to the side of the head. "Let's take this fucking nonsense to the Water."

"Enough with the language, Nellie." I flinched as that earned me a second swat. "You've got a serious case of potty-mouth." Lilly let out a gleeful giggle as she slapped me, mimicking her mother.

Nellie took Lilly's hand and attempted to give her a scolding frown, but she couldn't do it without laughing. "I'll be sure to take that up with the toad next time we sit down for a session." As we talked, we moved toward the Water's edge with Nellie following my lead.

"I think you should." My toes touched the Water and I turned to her. "How do we stay together?"

Nellie hugged Lilly to her chest, then reached a hand out to me. "If we stay connected we'll end up in the same place. Just hold on tight and concentrate on where you want to go."

I almost couldn't believe she was placing so much trust in me. Being taken seriously was still a fairly new concept for me. An image of the Water pulling Emma away from me popped into my head. I'd been terrified of where she might end up and powerless to help her. *She pushed you away, remember?* I shook my head. There was no point in scaring Nellie by sharing that story now. Besides, Emma hadn't understood what was happening. But Nellie had Dream Sight. "I promise, Nellie. I won't let go." Damned if I would. Let the Waters pull my fucking arms off. That was the only way they'd escape my hold.

"I know," she whispered. "I trust you, Charlie."

I wrapped my arms around Nellie, firmly including Lilly in the embrace, we took a deep breath in unison and jumped into the surf.

44

BOB

For some odd reason, the sun had set unusually quickly and light succumbed to darkness in the blink of an eye. But maybe my perception of time was just warped. It was difficult to separate one minute from the next when nothing existed to fill those minutes. How long had I walked this shore? How long had I been alone? Minutes. Days. Years. Decades. Time had lost its meaning a long time ago. It almost felt like nothing else had ever truly existed, except in my dreams.

On his last visit, Charlie spoke of another world, one he claimed I belonged to. I was a protector in this other world—or rather, I had been. According to Charlie, my act of bravery saved the lives of those children who haunted my dreams, but that same act left me a prisoner—trapped within my own skin—words left my lips without my mind's consent and my actions weren't necessarily ones I'd consciously choose. Years of my life had apparently been wasted in this waking hell and I was an old man now in this other world. If everything Charlie said was true, where was I now? How was it possible to be a helpless old man in some other world and the capable man the waters reflected in this one? One of those worlds must be false. Charlie was a man of character. I could trust him to speak truthfully. I'd been sure of it since the moment we met. No matter how far-fetched his story sounded, I believed it—which meant that this empty forest I guarded, only existed in my fractured mind.

Too distracted to find a more comfortable place to sit, I sat down on a cold uneven patch of earth. This forest was my prison, not my home. What purpose did I serve here? I was glad that my courage had saved innocent lives, but I wished I had died a hero's death because now I was nothing but a burden in that other world and in this world, I wasn't sure what I was.

I looked out across the dark expanse of water, shining like smooth black glass in the moonlight. The starry sky above was reflected so perfectly, as if a looking glass floated atop the tranquil surface. In fact, there seemed to be an uncanny stillness to every detail about the night, even the chirping sounds coming from the forest seemed unnaturally muted.

Somewhere deep within the trees, a creature howled. I couldn't identify the cry but it was undoubtedly the bellow of a predator. Prey didn't announce itself like that. I pushed myself up from the uneven ground and started toward the forest. What was there to fear if none of this was real? And if it was, all the better. I could end this sorry existence, gloriously locked in battle with some Dark creature. Maybe I'd even be fortunate enough to come upon Charlie's dragon. He'd asked me not to harm it. A strange request, yet out of respect for Charlie, I'd honor it. But that didn't mean I couldn't provoke it. Perishing in the jaws of the world's darkest beast seemed a much more fitting end than dying old and feeble in my sleep. *But if Charlie was right and this was my sleep, would it even matter?* Life just seemed so pointless now, with nothing left to protect or even care about.

Just as I was about to penetrate the forest, a splash sounded behind me shattering the stillness of the water's glassy surface. I spun around and started toward the water, searching the darkness for whatever had defiled the evening's pristine stillness, but I didn't have to search for long. Not far from shore, the heads of two figures protruded from the water. As I caught sight of them, my pace quickened to a run and the moment I reached the water, I dove in. A bitter chill enveloped me, robbing the breath from my lungs, but I barely noticed. I just kept pushing through the water, never taking my eyes off the figures up ahead.

As I approached, the features of the closer figure gradually coalesced into a familiar face. Happening upon Charlie in the water was no great surprise. It wasn't the first time he'd mysteriously found his way to my shore. "Do you need help?"

"No." He nodded toward the figure farther out. "Help them."

Not bothering to waste time answering, I kept on swimming. The second figure was nothing but a shadow, but my heart was pounding as I witnessed the silhouette's frantic movements. I pushed myself to move quicker and realized somewhere along the way that two heads protruded from the water. The one I'd missed from a distance appeared to be the head of a small child, and the adult was clearly struggling to keep afloat and hold the child. I could sense panic tightening its grip on the figure as the water whispered promises of a dark and icy grave. I pushed on, but the faces of the twosome remained shrouded in darkness until I got near enough to touch them and discovered the adult was a woman. Even in the throes of panic, there was a look of unshakable determination on her lovely face. I wrapped an arm around her and pulled her close, careful to hold her so the child stayed afloat. "It's alright. You're safe now."

She twisted in my arms and seemed stunned as her eyes met mine, but she calmed and stopped floundering.

ERIN A. JENSEN

"We'll meet you on the shore," I hollered ahead to Charlie.

"See you there," he called back.

In the next moments, I only focused on getting to shore. Once the water was shallow enough, I lifted the woman and child and carried them to dry ground. Setting the woman down on the grass, I sat down beside her. Sopping wet, struggling for breath, eyes wild with panic, she was still the most beautiful creature I'd ever set eyes on.

"You're safe now," I whispered, surprising myself with the tenderness in my voice. As she watched me, her breathing slowed and the panic drained from her eyes. I glanced down at the child cradled protectively in her arms. Her wide eyes regarded me with youthful curiosity and I marveled at how calm she'd been the entire time. Even her own mother's frantic display of terror hadn't fazed her in the slightest.

"I'm fine too, Bob," Charlie muttered. "Thanks for asking."

I'd been so focused on the woman and her child that I hadn't noticed Charlie dropping to the ground near us. Quite honestly, he didn't even enter my thoughts until he spoke. "I wasn't worried about you," I replied, without taking my eyes from the child's inquisitive gaze. "You've proven you can handle yourself in the water. What brings you here tonight? Did you fall out of your boat again?"

"What are you talking about?" the woman asked, her voice sweet and lyrical.

Charlie shot me a knowing grin. "Just go with it. Bob and I do."

I smiled at him, then returned my attention to the woman. Wet clothes coupled with the cool night air had her shivering convulsively, but I was just as drenched as she was. "I'm sorry. I don't have anything dry to offer you."

"It's alright," she assured me. Though her shiver seemed to deepen. "Thank you for helping us." The melodic quality of her voice conjured images of sunshine and colorful fields of wildflowers in bloom.

"I wouldn't dream of doing anything else," I murmured. "My name is Robert by the way, but please call me Bob."

The woman smiled as if we were old friends. "Pleased to meet you, Bob. My name's Nellie and this is my daughter, Lilly." As her trembling fingers smoothed the child's damp hair, I noticed that Lilly wasn't shivering. At the sound of her name, the girl lifted a tiny hand to my cheek.

"Hello, Lilly." Returning my attention to her mother, I added, "It's a pleasure to meet you."

Nellie smiled, and Lilly slapped my face.

Charlie stifled a chuckle. "She learned that from her mother."

I frowned at him. "I don't believe that for a second. I can't imagine this charming woman swatting anyone."

Charlie smirked at Nellie. "Give her time."

She shot him a pleading look, but I pretended not to notice the exchange and quickly changed the subject. "So what brings you to my forest?"

"We came to see you," Charlie replied cheerily.

I turned to Nellie. "I'm honored." Even in the dark, I could see her cheeks take on a lovely blush.

"Bob," Charlie muttered, "is there any chance you've got some dry clothes or a blanket?"

"Of course, my satchel is just within the trees," I replied, wondering why that hadn't already occurred to me.

"Walk with me?" Charlie muttered as he stood up, his expression making it clear that he wanted to speak in private.

I nodded then looked at Nellie. It saddened me to walk away from her even for a few moments. When would I get another opportunity to visit with such a lovely woman? I was painfully aware that the answer was most likely, never. "Please excuse us."

"Of course," she whispered.

Reluctantly, I stood and headed toward the trees. Charlie fell into step beside me and unlike Nellie, he didn't seem exhausted at all. As soon as we were out of earshot, Charlie stopped moving. "Remember when I said I might know of someone who needed protecting?"

I felt my heart skip a beat. "Yes."

"Nellie's in need of protection," he confided in a hushed tone.

I turned to look at her, half-afraid she wouldn't be there. But there she was, sitting in the grass just where I'd left her. "What about the child's father?" I asked, trying not to let my hopes soar too high. "Where is he?"

"I don't know," Charlie whispered as he glanced at the twosome, "Nellie's never said a word about him. All I know is that Nellie and Lilly live alone on her beach, but Nellie thinks the safety of her home has been compromised."

"Poor thing," I muttered, "What does she need protection from?"

"A dragon," Charlie whispered, "She believes one is after her."

So that's why Charlie had asked all those questions about whether I could fend off a dragon on his last visit. "The same dragon you've been searching for?" I asked, wondering how Charlie could possibly be fond of a creature that would threaten that sweet woman.

"Maybe." Charlie ran a hand through his hair. "It's complicated."

Anxious to bring Nellie something dry, I started toward the forest again. "What's complicated about it?"

Charlie moved alongside me. "I don't completely understand it myself, Bob. If I did, I'd explain it."

"Give it your best try," I insisted. "Help me comprehend why you would want to protect a beast that'd harm that lovely woman."

We crossed the tree line and entered the forest. My leather satchel sat propped against the trunk of a weathered pine, right where I'd left it. I grabbed it, slung it over my shoulder and headed back toward Nellie and her daughter without waiting to see if Charlie would follow. I walked alone for a few paces before he fell into step beside me.

"How can I help you understand something I don't understand myself?" The strain in his voice emphasized the degree of his frustration. "Honestly, I don't know what the dragon is but somehow it's connected to a girl I'm fond of."

I stopped for a second, observing him closely. Fond was too mild a word, I could see it in his eyes. "You love the girl," I muttered as I started walking again.

Moving along with me, Charlie shook his head. "It doesn't matter if I do or I don't. She belongs to somebody else."

"I'm sorry to hear that, Charlie." I truly was. "But what does the dragon have to do with this girl?"

Charlie considered the question for a moment. "An image of the dragon shadows her in the other world. I know that sounds crazy—"

"No crazier than half the other things you've told me."

Eyebrows raised, he muttered, "Does that mean you believe me?"

"Haven't I always?" Pretending not to notice the tears in his eyes, I added, "What do you think this dragon shadow is?"

Charlie let out a frustrated laugh. "I have no idea. I've been trying like crazy to figure it out, and I've got theories but no actual answers. I think the dragon might be the form she takes in this world, and I'd never forgive myself if anything happened to her."

"The dragon is your girl?" Of all the odd things I'd heard from Charlie that had to be the oddest.

"She's not *my* girl," he contested, a bit too emphatically, "and I don't know for sure. The dragon might be her. She's gone through some tough times. One of my theories is that whatever trauma she suffered caused her personality to splinter in the other world and the dragon is a personality that her mind created to keep her safe. It'd explain a lot of what's happened, but I honestly don't know for sure. What I do know—at least, I think I do—is that the dragon exists to protect her."

"So harming the dragon might harm the girl," I muttered.

"Yes," he agreed, sounding thoroughly uncertain.

"What's this girl's name?" I inquired, as we reached Nellie and Lilly.

A hint of sorrow crept into his features. "Emma."

Nellie looked up at Charlie, voice trembling, "Don't speak her name here! Destroy yourself if you have to, but don't drag everyone else into the Darkness with you!"

I dropped to my knees, pulled a blanket from my satchel and wrapped it around Nellie's shoulders, being sure to include Lilly in its warmth. A smile spread across Lilly's face as her fingers explored the frayed edge of the blanket. "Charlie has no intention of hurting us, Nellie. What harm could speaking a name do?"

Looking utterly exhausted, Nellie sighed. "He's already exposed my beach, and he'll lure the dragon to your home too if you give him the chance."

"You look so tired," I said softly. "How long has it been since you slept?"

She shook her head. "I don't need sleep. I'm asleep in the other world."

So Nellie knew about this other world. "You at least need to rest."

"I need to stay alert," she insisted, panic bleeding into her words. "I need to watch over Lilly and keep her safe. What if a dragon came while I was resting?"

I looked at Charlie with a raised eyebrow, and he nodded. "I could watch over you while you rested, Lilly could curl up safely in your arms and you could let down your guard." I could practically hear the next question forming in her head. "And if Lilly wasn't tired, I'd watch her while you rested. I'm not afraid of dragons, and I'd never let any harm come to you or your child."

Nellie's eyes widened. "You'd do that for me?"

"I'd do it for anyone."

A sad smile crept onto her face.

"But I'd do anything for you." As soon as I finished the words, I regretted my forwardness. It was too much to offer so soon after meeting. I could only hope it wouldn't drive her away.

Eyes tearing, she whispered, "Thank you."

I breathed a sigh of relief, thankful my words seemed to please rather than frighten her.

Charlie stood up. "If you'll excuse me," he muttered as he started down the shoreline, "I'm going to stretch my legs."

That didn't make much sense since we'd just walked into the forest and back, but Nellie seemed to appreciate his flimsy excuse as much as I did.

Lifting Lilly off of her lap, Nellie sat her down on the ground and the child immediately started grabbing tiny fistfuls of grass. Nellie turned back to me, smiling timidly with her eyes focused on the ground.

Was it possible that she was nervous? With a sigh of resignation, I crooked a finger beneath her chin and gently tilted her head up. Her pink cheeks were slick with tears. Before I could second guess myself, I brushed a finger over her cheek. "Nellie," I took a shaky breath, "would you consider staying here with me? You wouldn't have to live in fear. I could keep you safe."

She closed her eyes and took a deep breath. When her eyelids lifted, I saw the hesitation in her eyes. "I'd like that very much, if you're sure it wouldn't be too much of an imposition."

"Nothing could please me more than having the most beautiful girl I've ever met join me on this lonely shore. I'd give just about anything for you to stay, Nellie."

Fresh tears streamed down her cheeks as she wrapped her arms around me, prompting my heart to thud. "Thank you."

I hugged her back. "Thank you, for giving my life purpose again. I will keep you safe, Nellie. That's a promise."

45

NELLIE

I dropped my head against Bob's shoulder with a contented sigh. Who would've ever guessed that the grumpy old fool would turn out to be my knight in shining armor? He was beautiful on the inside. The Dream form never lied. *You old fool! You know that's not true.* I ignored the doubts in my head. This sweet man was promising to protect me and my daughter.

Out of the corner of my eye, I caught sight of Charlie walking down the shoreline. Once he'd gone a fair distance, he stopped and looked back at us. I turned my head to get a better look at him. Bob felt the movement against his shoulder and turned his head to follow my gaze.

With a satisfied grin, Charlie gave us a heartfelt salute. I waved, and Bob did the same. Nodding, Charlie moved to the Water's edge and jumped in.

Bob jerked reflexively to go after him, but I put a hand on his arm. "He has other places to go."

Bob looked confused but he settled back down. He still hadn't taken his arms from me and quite frankly, I hoped he wouldn't anytime soon. "He's going to that other world, isn't he?"

"Maybe," I whispered, "or to another part of the Dream World."

Bob thought for a moment. "Is that how he gets from one place to another?"

"Yes."

He looked down at me. "Can you do it, too? Skip between worlds through the water?"

I smiled at him. "Yes."

"Nellie?" he asked softly. "Do you and I know each other in this other world?"

"Yes, Bob. We do."

"Tell me," he murmured, "are we friends there?"

"We're getting there."

"What do you look like there? Charlie said I'm a feeble old man." He brushed a curl from my face, barely touching the skin underneath. "Are you still young and beautiful?"

I felt my smile slip and fade. "No. I haven't looked this way in a very long time."

Instead of the disappointed frown I expected, Bob's mouth curved into a wide smile. "Then there's hope that you and I could become more than friends?"

He was a good man. *Be cautious, you gullible fool.* I could trust him. *Have you learned nothing from the past?* "Yes." *You hopeless idiot!* "There's a very good chance of us becoming more than friends in time."

He smiled. "I've got nothing but time, and I can't think of a better way to spend it."

Feelings that I thought had shriveled and died a lifetime ago stirred inside me. Maybe after all these years, I'd finally be allowed some happiness.

46

EMMA

I t'd been impossible to fall back to sleep after waking from that dream. I didn't wake with vivid images in my head, I woke with my skin tingling from his touch. Restless desire replaced the hopelessness that'd gripped me the night before and an aching need swelled inside me, burning like fire beneath my skin. Too agitated to lie still, I slid out of bed at the first hint of sunlight, wandered distractedly into the bathroom and moved to the shower. Easing the knob with a gentle caress, I held a hand under the faucet and watched the water spill through my fingers. When it was warm enough, I stepped in, dragged the curtain closed and pulled back the knob. As the rush of warm water rained down on me, I closed my eyes, tilted my face toward the spray and pictured his hands on my body. From out of nowhere, a memory washed over me. *I stood alone in the rain. It was dark. And I was afraid.* Heart racing, I opened my eyes. Where did that come from?

As I showered, flashes of that dark night peri-odically pulsed through my mind—but even as the darkness gripped me, my body still ached for his touch—curiously mingling fear with desire. I mas-saged the shampoo through my hair, tipped my head into the stream of water and an image of his hand gripping the back of my head and holding me to his mouth surged back to me. *Another pulse of darkness.* Heart thudding, I picked up the soap and turned it over and over in my hands until a slippery pink froth spilled through my fingers. I slid the suds over my body, remembering the feel of his hands. *Another wave of darkness.* As each pulse of darkness ebbed, I ached for him a little more. Turning so the stream poured down my back, I looked down and watched the pink froth pool in the basin and slip away. When the last of the suds disappeared, I yanked the knob, dragged back the curtain and tugged a towel off the rack. *More darkness.* Heart pounding, I dried off as fast as I could. *More fear.* Dropping the towel, I yanked the door open and raced back to the bedroom as if something was chasing me. Hurrying to the dresser, I grabbed the first clothes my hands touched and as I fumbled with buttons and zippers, I longed for the unwavering strength of my husband's hands.

I didn't want to be alone, so I moved to the door and yanked it open. The hallway was quiet, but faint voices wafted from the television in the large common room. It had to be Bob, up early to stake his claim on the couch. Even watching television with Bob would be better than being alone. I headed toward the common room, reminding myself to take slow deliberate breaths.

As expected, Bob was on the couch in the large room, staring fixedly at the morning news. I stepped into the room and moved around the back of the couch so I wouldn't block his view. Rounding the corner, I sat down on the opposite end and to my surprise, Bob turned his head and greeted me with a welcoming smile.

"Good morning," I muttered.

"Morning," he echoed cordially. Then he returned his attention to the screen, which was fine with me. I wasn't in the mood for conversation.

I tried to focus on the anchorman's words, hoping the distraction would help me calm down. He was discussing a bombing that'd occurred somewhere recently. I vaguely felt as though I should know what he was talking about, but I'd been cut off from the outside world for days. The reporter might as well have been talking about something that'd happened on another planet. I looked down at my hands. *Rain.* They were shaking. *Darkness.* The thudding of my heart was a deafening echo inside my head. *Desperation.* And there was an unbearable ache in my heart.

The television voices dulled to nothing but a monotonous chorus of distant sounds until one familiar name broke through the din. "… Sophie Turner…" I looked up. She was on screen, smartly dressed in a black tailored suit jacket with a strand of black pearls at her throat, smiling seductively as always. "…Though investigators initially suspected foul play, the coroner's report now suggests otherwise." The on-screen image flashed from Sophie's picture to a young policeman commenting on her case. The voice of the newscaster continued to drone as pictures of Sophie's apartment building, followed by the outside of the Talbot law offices, flashed on screen. "…Although foul play was originally suspected, given Ms. Turner's modest age and good health, it was determined yesterday that the cause of death was actually a fatal heart attack. According to the coroner's report, Ms. Turner suffered from a heart defect that tragically remained undetected until after her death."

"He didn't do it," I muttered.

Bob turned and eyed me suspiciously. "Just because they determined the death to be of natural causes, doesn't necessarily mean it wasn't foul play. The smart criminals know how to make a death look like an accident or the result of a medical condition."

Snapped out of oblivion by Bob's unexpected and surprisingly coherent statement, I shifted to face him. "What?"

"You heard me," he answered gruffly. "It still could've been murder. If the killer's smart enough, they might never catch him."

"Thanks," I muttered, begrudging the fact that he'd picked this particular moment to start making sense.

"You're welcome." He kept his focus on me instead of turning back to the television and the attention quickly became unnerving, mostly because it was so out of character, but also because he was radiating that intimidating-police-officer vibe that always made me feel so uncomfortable. "Is there something you wanna say?" he grumbled, like he was a detective investigating Sophie's case.

"Um...no," I muttered, turning to look at the screen and hoping he'd do the same. He kept staring for a few painfully long minutes, but eventually he turned back to the news and we went back to staring at the screen in mutual silence. As the morning sky brightened, other patients and staff filtered into the room, my heart rate slowed and my hands stopped shaking. But I stayed on the couch, cocooned by the dull noises of the others in the room, staring as blankly at the television screen as Bob—maybe more.

Unless I took Bob's word over the coroner and police officer's, David had nothing to do with Sophie's death. Funny thing was, that didn't make me feel any better. I knew I could've forgiven him for murdering Sophie, but not for sleeping with her. I was his. *Just me.* The thought of his hands on another woman's body filled me with so much heartache and rage that I wanted to make someone else hurt as deeply as I did. *He chose me...*

... We sat cross-legged on the carpet. The coffee table between us was set for a tea party. Dolls and stuffed animals surrounded the table, each with a toy cup and saucer at its place. David sat across from me, his hand looking gigantic holding his tiny plastic cup. "You know, Princess, sometimes even daddies make mistakes."

I dropped my eyes to the coffee table. "Sometimes he scares me." When I looked back up, his lovely blue eyes were watching me attentively. "Why does he wish I wasn't here?"

David smiled. It was a melancholy smile and yet, it conveyed more love than any smile from my parents ever seemed to. "It's not that he wishes you weren't here, he just has trouble grasping the concept of loving more than one individual. In his mind, there has to be one special person that you choose to give all of your love to."

I frowned, still confused.

"And your daddy chooses your mommy," he explained softly.

That didn't surprise me, or even upset me. "Who does my mommy choose?" I whispered, afraid I already knew the answer.

He cleared his throat. "Your mommy is very conflicted. She loves you and she wants to do everything she can for you—"

"But she chooses my daddy," I finished, because I knew it'd hurt him to say the words to me.

He sighed regretfully. "Yes. In the end, she chooses your daddy."

Tears pooled in my eyes as I whispered, "Then who chooses me?"

"I do," he assured me, without stopping to consider the question for even a second. "I'll always choose you." Tears shimmered in his eyes, too...

"Emma!" Charlie's voice plucked me from the daydream and the rest of the memory slipped away.

I frowned at the panic in his eyes. "What's wrong?"

He raked a hand through his hair. "I got worried when you didn't answer your door this morning."

"I'm sorry," I whispered, "I didn't mean to worry you."

He sat down between me and Bob. Bob smiled at him then turned back to the television. "Hey, Bob," Charlie muttered.

"Hey, kid," Bob replied, without looking from the screen.

Charlie turned to me. "I was just afraid..." He stopped mid-sentence, eyes tearing.

"Afraid of what?"

"Lately, you've looked like a flower that hasn't had water or sunlight for a little too long. I was afraid you might've done something..."

"I needed to get out of that room," I whispered, "but I'm fine."

He looked at me with a sorrowful smile, then his brow furrowed. "You are, aren't you? Some of your glow is back."

"What?"

He shook his head. "Never mind. You look like you're feeling better, that's all."

Nodding, I whispered, "There was an update on Sophie's death on the news this morning."

Charlie leaned a little closer to me. "What did it say?"

I looked around, finally noticing how crowded the room had become. "Move to a quieter spot with me?" Nodding, he hopped up and I did the same.

Bob looked up at us and smiled. "You kids be good, alright?"

Charlie clapped him on the shoulder. "We will, Bob."

With a satisfied nod, Bob returned his attention to the television.

Frowning, as if a thought had just occurred to him, Charlie looked the room over. "Where's Nellie?"

Bob shrugged. "Not sure, kid. But she's gotta be around here somewhere. She'll turn up soon."

"I'm sure you're right," Charlie muttered as we left the room in search of a private place to talk.

We didn't have to search for long. Our favorite room was unoccupied, a game of checkers angrily spilled across one of the tabletops was the only evidence that it'd ever been otherwise. We sat down on our loveseat and Charlie smiled, wordlessly encouraging me to share what I'd learned.

"Sophie's cause of death was a heart attack," I whispered. "She had a heart defect that the doctors never detected."

Charlie tilted his head. "That's a good thing, right?"

"It is," I agreed numbly, "but it still doesn't tell me whether she lied about the affair."

Charlie's brow furrowed. "Do you believe he cheated, Em? Deep down inside, what does your gut tell you?"

Eyes tearing, I whispered, "I want so badly to believe that he didn't, but there's always this nauseating doubt in the back of my mind."

Charlie considered that for a second. "Worst case scenario, say he did cheat. What would you want to do then?"

"Kill myself...or him," I choked back a sob, "or both of us."

"That's no good, Em," Charlie murmured.

"I couldn't take it," I whispered. "I'm not as strong as you."

"You're stronger than you think. You need to realize your own strength, whether or not you stay with him in the end."

A single tear slid down my cheek. "If I didn't stay with him, I'd want it to be the end."

47

CHARLIE

I wiped the tear from Emma's cheek. But before I had time to say anything, Frank stumbled into the room, fixed his beady eyes on Emma and started toward her. As he moved, he flipped back and forth—between human and swarming-humanoid-mass-of-insects—and each time his Dream form reappeared, it seemed disturbingly larger and darker. It was the first time I'd ever considered Frank to be anything more than just pathetic.

I stood up from the loveseat and planted myself in front of Emma. "What do you want, Frank?"

A slimy discharge drooled from the swarm of insects that raggedly composed the shape of his mouth, but he just kept staring at Emma and moving toward her.

I heard Emma fidget then stand up behind me. I took a step toward Frank and repeated my question in a more demanding tone, "What do you want?"

With a deranged smile, his gaze shifted to me. "We want the girl," his voice buzzed in a maddening chorus of droning insects. "She offered herself."

"Fuck off!" I hollered, heart slamming in my chest, "You sick demented pervert!"

His Dream form snickered, a mind-defiling crescendo of buzzes and chirps. Then he reached out and shoved me hard in the chest. The move was so unexpected that it caught me off guard and knocked me off balance. I jerked to the side, so that I'd topple onto the loveseat behind Emma instead of into her and as I started to get up, the rest seemed to happen in slow motion.

Something dark and unclean and *just plain wrong* glimmered in his Dream form's eyes as he reached a twitching hand toward Emma, but just as he was about to touch her, the dragon reared up from behind the loveseat. Rising to an enormous height on its hind legs, its front legs lunged over the loveseat, landing so that its massive body framed Emma like a doorway. Then the dragon opened its cavernous mouth and bellowed a deafening thunderous roar. When the noise stopped, brilliant blue flames barreled from the creature's mouth, melting the flesh of Frank's extended limb.

Frank flipped back to human form and fell backward with an agonized shriek. He clutched his fire-mangled arm at the wrist as he sat motionless, staring at it. I'd watched it blacken to nothing but a misshapen lump of charred flesh but as staff members scrambled into the room, all they found was greasy old Frank sitting on his ass, gaping in horror at one perfectly good hand grasped in the other.

Tim's facial expression conveyed a mix of pity and annoyance as he cautiously approached the whimpering mental patient. "It's alright. We're here to help." As Tim calmed him down, a nurse snuck up behind Frank, holding a syringe behind her back. All the dark filth gone from his eyes, Frank's lower lip trembled as he listened to Tim. The sorry figure sitting on the floor was once again nothing more than pathetic. Tim patted his shoulder. "We're gonna make it better, Frank."

As Tim finished talking, the nurse crouched down at Frank's side. He sucked in a breath when he noticed the syringe in her hand, but Tim gripped him and held him still while the nurse plunged its contents into his arm. Frank's eyes pleaded for help as he looked up at me. Then he went limp and slumped against Tim as another staff member wheeled in a gurney. They lifted Frank and strapped him to it. Then they wheeled him out, leaving the room silent and still.

Emma stood frozen, exactly where she'd been since she rose from the loveseat. The dragon stayed firmly planted above her and I sat slumped against the back of the couch, acutely aware of the enormous scaled belly above my head. Emma was facing away from me—the skirt of her gauzy white sundress fluttering, golden hair dancing in a breeze I didn't feel—and on each of her pale shoulder blades was a large deep scar, just like Nellie's.

Nellie shoved me into the Waters for asking about hers. But why? What were the scars from?

And how the hell could a Dream form do what the dragon just did?

48

NELLIE

Bob wanted me to sleep while he stood watch. I tried to explain that I was asleep, in the other world. He looked skeptical at first and I can't say I blamed him. It did all sound a bit ridiculous. I suggested we sit and talk until he needed rest, then fall asleep together. He was uncomfortable with the idea. But after I made several promises that we'd wake together in the other world, he eventually agreed and at the end of a magical night beneath the stars, we laid down to sleep with Lilly nestled snugly between us. I closed my eyes and listened to Bob's breathing until his deep steady breaths assured me that the Waters had carried him to the other world. Then I quieted my mind so the Waters could sweep me back to him.

But they didn't.

I woke in Darkness. I could tell without opening my eyes. I felt it. It wasn't the sort of darkness that comes when you turn off the lights. It was the sort of Darkness that dwells in the lowest depths of the soul, where unspeakable thoughts are born—thoughts so Dark that none but the basest creatures alive would dare utter them out loud.

I held my breath, kept my eyes squeezed shut and listened. Leaves rustled in a faint breeze, but it wasn't cool and sweet like the breeze on my beach. It was suffocatingly hot and thick and wherever it touched my skin, it clung like a leach and sucked the life from my soul. The sounds of creatures filled my head from the inside. They were Dark creatures who feared the light and their voices echoed in my head until it became unbearable. Desperation gnawed at me until I begged for death just to make it stop.

I was in the Dark part of the forest.

As the voices magnified inside my head, I squeezed my eyes shut tighter and prayed for the Waters to come and carry me away. But I knew that they wouldn't. I'd have to fall asleep first, and falling asleep in this tangle of nightmares would be impossible.

Time had no meaning where I was. So I couldn't begin to guess how long I stayed there, motionless in the Darkness with my eyes squeezed shut, hoping no creature would discover me. For me, it was an eternity. I lay there listening to the whispering and groaning and wailing in the Darkness and knew in my heart this was where I would die.

Just as I reached the limit of what my feeble mind could bear, one voice cut through the infinite tangle of tormented voices. "Woman, will you come with me?" his rich Dark voice roared inside my head. A shiver that no amount of heat could fix erupted from deep within me, but he was offering to take me away and I needed to leave before the madness took me completely.

I opened my eyes but I might as well have kept them shut. There was nothing but absolute Darkness. I reached out for the voice, but I felt nothing. "I will go with you!" I cried, praying I hadn't waited too long to answer and lost my only chance.

Then something gripped me. Whatever the something was, it wasn't human. It didn't have hands or claws or limbs, but it gripped me all the same and started dragging me through the Darkness. I stayed still and let the thing drag me and focused on re-pressing the scream that fought to escape my throat.

We stopped moving, all the voices were gone and utter silence filled the void that should've been air but didn't feel like it.

"Open your eyes, woman," the thing commanded.

I did as he said. Our surroundings were dimly lit with only enough illumination to see shadows. I couldn't see the thing, but I felt his presence and it made my skin crawl. "I can't see," I whispered hopelessly.

"You can see as much as you need to," the thing answered from the shadows. His Dark voice conjured visions of my deepest fears and darkest desires. I dreaded it, despised it and loved it—in a place deep inside me that I didn't want to know existed—and suddenly I knew who spoke to me.

"Please," I begged, "let me go."

"Promise something first," he insisted, his voice hinting threats of unthinkable pain.

I tried to swallow but my mouth was too dry. "Anything."

"Show respect," he roared, rattling the bones inside me.

"Of course, Sir," I whispered, terrified beyond any point I'd have thought possible.

"Not to me, you foolish hag," he snarled.

Sensations of absolute terror mixed with vile lust overwhelmed me so completely that I had to struggle to comprehend the meaning of his words. "To who?" I pleaded, desperate to be free of him and his hellish nightmare. "I'll do anything. Tell me what to do."

"Stay away from the girl," he growled.

I was sure the booming echo of his voice would split my head open. "Of course. I promise. I will." Thick hot tears streamed down my cheeks. I swiped at them and was horrified to find my fingers streaked with blood.

"If you don't listen, woman," the voice roared, "I will come after you."

I opened my eyes and found myself in bed, soaked in my own piss. The smell of it saturated the stale air in my room, turning my stomach—or maybe that was a sensation the thing had left me with, either way—before I could get out of bed, I puked all over myself, the bedding and down onto the floor.

49

DAVID

I sagged against the leather upholstery and felt some of the tension that'd gripped me for months slip away. Benjamin raised the divider separating his seat from mine, whether he did it as a courtesy—to allow me to vent my emotion in private—or for himself, I couldn't say. Regardless, as the division reached the roof of the car, my eyes stung with unshed tears. We'd made progress but this was far from over. I'd been granted permission to visit my wife, a notion that still struck me as unfathomably ludicrous. Denying me the right to see her because she wished it so, I could respect but denying my visiting because you decided it's best for her was preposterous. As long as Emma desired to see me, I would tear through heaven and earth to reach her.

I'd been sorely tempted to drive directly from the courthouse to the facility, shove the court order in that asinine psychiatrist's face and demand to see my wife immediately. But Emma had to remain in that Godforsaken place, and antagonizing the man who currently controlled her life would undoubtedly not make it easier for her. So I waited impatiently for proper visiting hours and Brian headed straight to the facility in my stead to inform the doctor that his imposed restriction had been legally overturned, long before evening visitation began. I'd not waste a second that could be spent with Emma in the company of that buffoon.

I glanced out the window as we pulled into the garage. As soon as we'd parked, I sprang from the car and headed for the door to the house. Behind me, Benjamin's door opened but I turned the knob and stepped inside without looking back.

The pungent aroma of roasting beef accosted me as I stepped into the foyer and my stomach turned in response. I had absolutely no appetite and even less desire to interact with Sara. Bypassing the kitchen, I headed to my study. Though I had no desire to focus on anything other than my wife, I had plenty of work to fill the hours until I could see her and regrettably, I'd become quite adept at attending to business whilst ignoring the ache in my heart.

I entered the study and absently pulled the door closed behind me. Across the room, the window framed a picture perfect view of the beach at midday. I moved to it and slid the window open. A warm breeze wafted in through the screen, carrying the salty smell of the ocean mixed with fragrant hints of spring flowers in bloom, a welcome alternative to the heavy aroma of cooking meat that currently filled my home. I inhaled deeply as I loosed my tie and rolled up my sleeves, exposing my forearms to the breeze.

I headed to my desk, slid the chair back and dropped into it with a tired sigh. A file thick with papers sat square in the middle of the desktop. I picked it up and opened it, but a knock at my study door hindered me from accomplishing anything more.

I called, "Come in." And the door opened so tentatively that it had to be Sara. Granted, I could be intimidating but her meekness was growing extremely tiresome.

Sara poked her mousey face through the opening. "Sorry to bother you, Mr. Talbot, but I have a message for you and I was asked to deliver it as soon as possible."

I tossed the file on my desk. "What part of 'come in' did you not understand?"

She obligingly widened the opening and stepped inside. "Sorry, Sir."

"It's alright," I replied, though I doubt my facial expression conveyed the same sentiment. "What message did you so urgently need to deliver?"

She took a timid step toward my desk, clutching a folded sheet of paper. Holding her steadily in my gaze, I extended my palm. She looked as though she feared I'd just as likely tear her hand off as take the paper from it, but she took a step closer and dropped the note in my hand. I stared at her, unblinking.

She didn't look away, but her face reddened each second she returned my gaze. Her heart was thudding nervously as she squeaked, "Will that be all, Mr. Talbot? Or is there something else I can do for you?"

"That'll be all," I replied, still holding her in my gaze.

Dipping her head in a subservient nod, she exited the room and closed the door so softly that it barely made a sound.

I unfolded the paper. The message was from my Aunt Louise. She'd phoned to inform me that travel arrangements were being made and Rose would be visiting soon. Rose was the secret I helped Isabella keep with the aid of my family back in England.

Isa had come to me many years prior, young and unwed with a child in her belly, begging for help. Her parents were exceedingly strict and traditional and she feared they'd disown her if she confessed her unintentional pregnancy. I hired her and sent her to stay with my family in England for the duration of her pregnancy, and she told her family she was going to receive training to perform her job in the manner customary in all the Talbot households—which wasn't entirely untrue. She was trained but first and foremost, her pregnancy was tended to. She received the best medical care available from the moment she stepped onto British soil until the moment she flew back home, and her daughter Rose remained in England to be raised by my Aunt Louise.

Due to an unfortunate illness, my father's elder sister had been incapable of conceiving a child. Though she'd played a major role in the upbringing of several Talbot children, myself included, she'd never raised a child of her own. Over the years, Louise sent pictures and word of Rose's progress to Isa. Rose learned something of her birth mother through the letters Isa regularly sent, but Rose and Isa hadn't set eyes on each other since the day Isa flew home.

When she returned to America, Isa moved into my home as a live-in housekeeper and quickly became a dear member of our family. She stayed with us until she married, then she and her husband bought a house nearby. She bore him a son and the threesome lived quite happily together until her husband's passing, and neither Isa's husband nor her son had ever learned of Rose's existence.

Now a young woman, Rose knew that her birth mother was quite possibly on her death bed and she wanted to come see her. Since the day she left England, Isabella had longed to see Rose again but she'd always feared the outcome too much to visit. She said her heart wouldn't be able to take it, if her daughter wanted nothing to do with her.

Feeling more optimistic than I had in a long time, I took out my phone and dialed Louise's number. With any luck, her daughter's voice would finally bring Isa back to us.

50

EMMA

I watched in stunned silence as they wheeled Frank out of the room. Until that point, he'd seemed pretty harmless but the look in his eyes as he walked toward me hadn't seemed harmless at all. If Charlie hadn't been with me, I wasn't sure what I would've done. It suddenly occurred to me that the bedrooms in the facility didn't lock. What if Frank decided to sneak into my room at night? I knew for a fact that it could be done because I'd slipped into Charlie's room and no one had been the wiser. I pictured the crazed look on Frank's face. *She offered herself.* The thought of him sneaking in while I was sleeping sent a wave of nausea through me.

I turned to Charlie. He was sitting on the love-seat, looking just as shaken as I felt. Sitting down beside him, I muttered, "What would I do if Frank came into my room while everyone was sleeping?"

Still dazed from the incident, it took Charlie a minute to process my question and another to respond. "Shit," he finally mumbled, "That's a good question." It wasn't the reassuring response I'd hoped for, and it must've shown on my face because he shook his head. "Sorry, Em. That was a horrible answer."

"Yes, it was," I whispered, the waver in my voice emphasizing just how much the possibility frightened me.

Charlie's expression softened to a sympathetic frown. "I can't believe I'm suggesting this, but maybe you should talk to Spenser. He'll already know about Frank's freak out. If you tell him that Frank was approaching you when it started and repeat what he said about 'wanting you' and 'you offering yourself,' maybe he'll lock Frank away or at least have someone stand guard outside his room at night."

I stared at the loveseat cushions and focused on trying not to cry. "Talking to Dr. Spenser sounds better than just waiting for Frank to sneak in." Looking at it from the sleeper's perspective, I couldn't help but feel guilty. I looked up at Charlie and whispered, "I'm sorry."

His brow furrowed. "What for?"

"I did the same thing to you, slipped into your room while you were sleeping."

Charlie let out a chuckle. "That's not at all the same."

I frowned, wondering whether I should be offended by his laughter. "Why not?"

"Because you're a beautiful girl who I care deeply about. You sneaking to my bed is a dream come true. Frank sneaking to your bed would be a hellish nightmare."

I shook my head. "I shouldn't have done it. It's creepy, and how exactly is sneaking into a sleeping person's bedroom a dream come true?"

His grin widened. "Tell you what. When you get back to the real world, why don't you take a poll? See how many men would be horrified to wake up and find you on their bed. I can save you the trouble. The number would be zero. Then find out how many of them would consider it a fantasy come true."

I raised an eyebrow. "Right. I'll just go around asking random men how they'd feel about me showing up in their bedroom."

"Yeah," Charlie chuckled, "on second thought, that's a really bad idea. You'd probably just get some poor sap all excited and end up with another stalker. Anyway, it doesn't matter because we both know I'm right."

"You're not always right, you know."

He gently grabbed my arm as though sensing I was about to elbow him, which I was. "What kind of asshole do you take me for? I never said I was always right, but I am right about this. Why don't you poll Tim and Spenser?" He let out a laugh at the 'are you crazy?' look I shot him. "Alright. That's probably not a good idea either. Just trust me on this. I speak for the whole of my gender when I say that finding you in bed would be a good thing."

"Whatever you say, Charlie." I bit my lip. "What were we saying before this conversation got sidetracked?"

"We were saying how different you sneaking into a bedroom is from Frank doing it." He raised an eyebrow. "And that I was right and you were wrong." I elbowed him in the arm and his eyes danced with laughter as he flinched, pretending it'd hurt. "But more importantly, we decided telling Spenser about your new stalker was a good idea."

"Right," I muttered. "That, we agree on."

Since we were both mentally exhausted after the whole Frank ordeal, Charlie suggested we play a mindless game of checkers. We sat down at one of the tables, half playing and half talking, keeping the conversation lighthearted and silly, which was exactly what I needed. By the time Tim came to gather us for breakfast, we'd each won a game.

Charlie scanned the faces as we entered the dining room. I knew he was looking for Nellie because he'd asked Bob about her earlier. I had to admit, it did seem strange that she hadn't wandered into the small common room. It was as much her room of choice, as ours.

As we sat down near Bob, I did my own scan of the faces in the room and was relieved to discover that Frank's wasn't one of them. Partway through the meal, I noticed Charlie staring at something near the doorway and followed his gaze. Nellie was shuffling into the room, looking like she'd aged ten years overnight. Tim was beside her, guiding her along. Nellie whispered something in his ear and he nodded then slowly walked her to our table.

Tim slid the empty chair between me and Bob back from the table, and Nellie cautiously lowered herself into it. Everything that she did seemed to require more effort than the day before. Tim stayed, helping Nellie open her juice carton and the little packages of jelly for her toast. He was about to spread the jelly for her when Bob stopped him. "What in God's name are you doin, kid? Get the fuck away and let us eat our breakfast before its lunchtime already. If she needs help, we'll help her."

Tim stared at Bob like a deer caught in headlights, an expression he wore often. Then he looked to the rest of us. Charlie nodded, and Tim shrugged and walked away.

Nellie turned tearfully to Bob. "Thanks."

"Anytime," he answered, in a tone much softer than his usual.

I felt a little uncomfortable sitting next to Nellie after our exchange the day before. She'd said some hurtful things to me and Benjamin hadn't taken kindly to hearing them and hadn't hesitated to make that perfectly clear, but the old woman sitting next to me seemed so frail that it was difficult to hold a grudge. I felt like I needed to say something to make our proximity a little less awkward. "Good morning, Nellie. Did you sleep well?"

Eyes darting fearfully between me and the table, Nellie answered in a frail whisper, "Morning," then bitterly added, "No. I did not sleep well."

"I'm sorry to hear that," I muttered.

"Sure you are!" She seemed to rethink her words, and whimpered, "I'm sorry. I didn't mean that."

Feeling as though I'd somehow managed to make things more awkward, I whispered, "It's alright."

Nellie shook her head and a tear slid down her cheek.

"Relax." Bob placed his wrinkled hand on top of hers. "Everything's alright."

Again, I felt like I'd missed something. When had Nellie and Bob grown so close?

We had more free time after breakfast, so Charlie and I headed back to our checkerboard for a tie-breaking game. Instead of joining us in the small room, Nellie headed to the big room with Bob.

I was down to my last two checkers. Charlie was teasing me about his superior strategizing skills and I was laughing, so neither of us noticed when Tim entered the room. I'm not even sure how long he stood beside our table before we both looked up. Once he had our attention, he cleared his throat and smiled at me. "Hey, Emma."

I smiled back at him. "Hi, Tim. Would you like to play a game?"

"Yeah, I would," he muttered, "but I can't. I'm working."

Obviously, I knew that but I'd felt the need to say something since he was hovering and staring. "Right," I muttered, hoping he'd get to the point.

He grinned down at me. "Dr. Spenser asked me to come get you. He wants to talk to you, and he doesn't want to wait until your session this afternoon."

I stood from the table. This had to be about the incident with Frank. I knew telling the doctor what'd happened was a good idea, but I wasn't looking forward to it. "Okay."

Charlie stood, too. "Do you want me to come, Em?"

I did but if the doctor only asked for me, he probably wouldn't let Charlie join us. "No. I'll be fine," I answered, not at all confident that I would be.

Charlie nodded. "Then I'll walk you to his office."

"Thanks," I whispered, grateful to have his support for as long as I could.

Tim's shoulders drooped. "I guess you're all set then."

"Thank you, Tim." I smiled at him as the three of us headed to the door, and he flashed me a goofy grin as we stepped into the hall.

Tim took a left and Charlie and I took a right, without a word. As we passed the door to the big room, I took a peek in. Nellie was sleeping contentedly with her head on Bob's shoulder while he watched a morning talk show. They looked like a little old couple who'd begun their mornings that way for decades.

We reached the door to Spenser's office and Charlie knocked. "I won't go far."

The doctor called, "Come in," from behind the door, and Charlie pushed it open.

Dr. Spenser sat behind his desk with a pair of wire-rimmed glasses perched low on the bridge of his nose. He was peering over the top of them, studying the papers he held tightly in his hands. He looked up, greeted me with a warm smile and gestured for me to come in. "Hello, Emma." Then he looked at Charlie. "Can I help you, Mr. Oliver?"

"Nope." Charlie raked his hair back from his face. "Just escorting Emma to your door."

Smiling faintly, Dr. Spenser nodded. "I don't anticipate this being a very long conversation. Why don't you wait for Emma in the hall?"

"Sure," Charlie muttered, then turned to me. "I'll be outside the big room."

"See you soon," I whispered, stepping into Spenser's office.

Giving me a wink and an encouraging smile, Charlie shut the door.

Spenser motioned to the chair in front of his desk. "Have a seat, Emma." I wasn't sure why he felt the need to invite me to sit in it, since it was the same chair I always sat in. There was an uncharacteristic nervous energy about him, which was odd. What did he have to be nervous about?

I sat down in the chair and waited for him to say something.

He glanced at the papers in his hand then placed them on his desk, print-side down. With a weary sigh, he took off his spectacles, folded them and set them neatly on top of the papers. After staring at the back side of them for a few seconds, he looked up at me. "How are you doing, Emma?"

"I've had better days," I whispered.

The doctor smiled knowingly. "Yes, I heard you had a run in with Frank this morning."

"A run in," I muttered. "That's one way to put it."

"How would you put it?" he asked in cliché psychiatrist fashion, leaning back and folding his arms across his chest.

I hesitated, considering how to explain the bizarre encounter. "Frank came at me in the common room this morning and when Charlie asked what he wanted, he said he *wanted me* and *I'd offered myself to him*." I felt extremely awkward repeating that to Dr. Spenser but knew it'd be foolish not to. "When Charlie tried to stop him, Frank shoved him. Then right when he was about to touch me, he just fell on the floor and started screaming."

Dr. Spenser nodded. "Frank described the incident a little differently."

"What did he say happened?" I demanded, shocked that the doctor would even consider believing Frank's word over mine.

The doctor gave me a patronizing smile. "There's no need to get defensive, Emma. I have to listen to everyone's story and determine what went on from there. I have a feeling if someone took Charlie aside right now and asked him what happened, he'd say exactly the same thing you just did."

Was he implying that Charlie and I would lie about what happened? Why on earth would we even want to?

Dr. Spenser's patronizing grin widened. "It'd be irresponsible of me not to consider all sides of the story."

"There's no story," I snapped. "That's what happened."

Spenser nodded his head with an agreeable, "Alright." Which only frustrated me more.

"What did Frank say?" I insisted.

Spenser exhaled a tired sigh. "His exact words aren't important, Emma. You need to respect that Frank has long standing emotional issues that he hasn't fully resolved. He was brutally abused as a child and young adult, and he has impulses to do what was done to him to others, but you've heard all that before."

I hadn't. That wasn't the kind of thing you forgot. You forgot someone's favorite color or their favorite song, but you didn't forget stories of brutal abuse. "I haven't actually." Not only had Frank been lurking toward me, saying I *offered myself*, he was an abuse victim with impulses to hurt others, and I slept down the hall from him—in an unlocked room.

"He's talked about it in group sessions, Emma," the doctor confirmed, as if that made anything better.

I nodded, feeling numb, aside from the waves of nausea churning in my stomach. "I must not have been listening," I muttered, struggling to keep from crying.

"He won't hurt you, Emma," Spenser stated, like it was absolute fact. "His parents used to burn him to punish him, and it's so ingrained in his mind that he still feels the fire when he tries to do something he shouldn't. The illusion of abusive punishment overwhelms him before he actually does anything wrong."

"Forgive me if that doesn't make me feel better," I snapped, hating that my eyes were tearing. "I sleep in a bedroom with no lock on the door, and that man sleeps down the hall from me. I don't want him coming into my room and starting to do something wrong, any more than I want him to finish it. This doesn't exactly make me feel safe."

Dr. Spenser smiled, but it was an I'm-dismissing-what-you-have-to-say smile. "You're safe here, Emma. We'll see to that, but you need to be understanding of your fellow patients' struggles. All of you are here to work through your problems. Another patient could just as easily hear that you stabbed your house-keeper and decide they're afraid of you."

I was seriously beginning to wonder if I'd make it out of his office without vomiting.

Dr. Spenser glanced down at the papers on his desk with a weary sigh. "But none of this has any-thing to do with the reason I wanted to see you." I was about to protest the fact that he was changing the subject, until Spenser said something that made all concerns about Frank slip from my mind. "Your husband has acquired a court order demanding that he be allowed visitation rights."

In that moment, it didn't matter whether David had been involved in Sophie's death or even been unfaithful. I needed to see him.

Spenser scrutinized me closely. "So I have to ask, do you feel comfortable with your husband visiting? Because you're still fully within your rights to deny visitation to anyone you're not comfortable seeing."

"Yes," I whispered, tears blurring my vision. I needed to see David's face, hear his voice, feel his arms around me and believe—if only for a little while—that everything could be alright. "When can I see him?"

"He plans to come during visiting hours tonight." Spenser leaned forward, resting his elbows on his desk. "But I'm not convinced you're ready for that, Emma."

I grimaced at the maddening expression of grandfatherly concern on his wrinkled face. "I don't care." Spenser looked taken aback, but he didn't say anything. "I want to see my husband."

The doctor nodded. "Well, that settles it. You'll see him tonight but just remember, you can always ask to have him removed if his visit upsets you."

I wanted to throw something at Spenser. He was perfectly comfortable with a creepy abuse victim who *wanted me* sleeping down the hall, but he didn't feel comfortable letting my own husband visit? "Are we done?"

Dr. Spenser studied me appraisingly. "I think we are for now."

I stood from my chair without being asked to and exited the room, slamming the door behind me.

Charlie hurried to me as the door shut. "How did it go?"

"Not great," I whispered as we headed back to our usual room, without either of us having to suggest it.

"What happened?"

I exhaled, wishing I could shake the queasiness that'd settled in the pit of my stomach. "Did you know that Frank's an abuse victim with impulses to hurt others the way he was hurt?"

Charlie looked at me like I'd just announced I was dying. "No. Fuck. Is Spenser going to move him somewhere else because he went after you?"

Tears pooled in my eyes as I whispered, "No."

Charlie stopped walking. "What the fuck?"

"Spenser said he won't hurt me. Apparently he imagines he's being burned before he actually does something wrong because his abusers used to burn him to punish him."

Charlie gritted his teeth.

"It's alright, Charlie." But the tears streaming down my cheeks didn't confirm the words.

"No," he growled, quickening his pace so that I practically had to run to keep up. "That's not alright at all."

We stepped into our room, found it unoccupied and Charlie immediately started pacing like a caged animal intent on tearing its way out of captivity. If it hadn't been concern for my safety that enraged him, even I might've been scared by the ferocity in his eyes.

I moved alongside him as he paced. "We can't do anything about it."

"You don't understand, Em." He stopped and looked at me. "Frank didn't imagine it."

A bit spooked by the urgency of his stare, I muttered, "What?"

He blew out a breath. "This'll sound crazy, but could you trust me anyway?"

I nodded, although I had no idea what he was talking about.

He took my arm and led me to our loveseat, we sat down and I waited for him to say something. The look on his face reminded me of the way he'd looked back when he worried opening up would scare me off. "Charlie, talk to me. I haven't run away yet, have I?"

"No. I guess you haven't. Something I saw…" he hesitated, watching me closely, "something stopped Frank from getting any closer to you."

"What was it?" I whispered.

Charlie didn't answer. He just kept watching me.

"It was the thing you're always seeing around me, wasn't it?"

Charlie nodded. His expression was starting to make me feel like a character in a horror movie, one scene away from becoming the next victim. "What is it, Charlie? What do you see?"

Charlie shook his head. "Just trust me, Em."

"Is it really so horrible that you can't even tell me?"

"I don't want to scare you," he whispered.

"Too late." I suddenly realized I hadn't told Charlie everything yet, and getting an answer seemed a little less important. "There was more to my conversation with Spenser."

Charlie looked ready to get angry all over again. "What else did the jackass say?"

"My husband got the visitation restriction overturned," I whispered, afraid that if I said it too loud it wouldn't turn out to be true. "David's coming to visit tonight."

Charlie leaned back, studying me. "Is that a good thing?"

"There's a lot I'm unsure about, but I'm sure I need to see him." As I spoke, I started to realize just how nervous I was about seeing David. Our life together—before it all went wrong—seemed like something I'd dreamt a lifetime ago.

"Then I'm happy for you." I practically saw a light bulb click on above Charlie's head. "Your husband is a lawyer."

I nodded, wondering what he was getting at.

"If you tell him what happened with Frank, maybe he can do something about it. If you were my wife, I'd be pissed as hell to hear that some psycho who'd gone after you was down the hall from where you slept."

Maybe it was a good idea, but it was the last thing I wanted to waste time talking about with David. "I wouldn't want to worry him."

Charlie frowned. "Are you afraid he wouldn't be concerned if you told him?"

I shook my head and would've laughed if the whole situation wasn't so completely unfunny. "He'd be *very* concerned. I'm just afraid of what he might do to Frank and Spenser."

"Would he hurt them?"

I bit my lip. "He'd want to."

"Well, of course. After everything that happened today, I would too."

I smiled but quickly dropped the grin. The more I thought about seeing David, the more uneasy I felt. I wanted to see him more than anything, but I still didn't know how to feel about Sophie's accusations or her death. "Charlie, I'm actually nervous about seeing David."

He raked his hair back from his face. "Would it help if I was in the room for moral support? I mean, I understand you probably don't want to introduce us. If Benjamin's reaction was any indication of how your husband would feel about me, I don't imagine he'd be thrilled to meet me. No offense, but I get the feeling he's pretty possessive."

I frowned apologetically. Charlie never did tell me what Benjamin said to him. "It would probably complicate our visit, and there's already so much uncertainty between us… It wouldn't be the ideal time to introduce you."

Charlie smiled. "That's a polite way to say he'd want to beat the crap out of me."

"Be nice."

"I was being nice," he chuckled softly, "I wouldn't blame him. If you were my mine, I wouldn't want another man anywhere near you, especially if I couldn't be around."

I raised an eyebrow. "Are you saying I shouldn't spend time with you?"

"Absolutely not! Then you'd be on your own to deal with Frank. I'm just saying, I understand where he's coming from." I was about to say something nice when he added, "Even if he is a pedophile."

My expression must've indicated how tired I was of those comments because he leaned closer and whispered, "Sorry, Em." I gave him a skeptical look, and he sagged against the back of the loveseat. "I really am. That's the last of those comments I'm going to make, I promise. Besides, I only make them out of jealousy."

"What do you mean?"

"I mean, I'd love to fill his shoes." Charlie took my left hand in his. "The man who put that ring on your finger is a lucky man."

I gave his hand a squeeze. "I'm not so sure about that. My life's a pretty big mess at the moment."

"I am sure," he murmured, brushing his finger over my wedding ring. "I'd trade places with the guy in a heartbeat, even if it did mean giving up about thirty years of my life."

I pulled my hand back and smacked him in the arm. "I thought you said that was the last crack you were going to take at my husband."

"No." He grinned at me as he rubbed his arm. "I said it was the last pedophile comment I was going to make, I didn't say anything about calling him old."

"I give up. You're impossible." I slouched against the back of the loveseat. "But thanks for offering your support tonight. I'm more nervous than I would've guessed I'd be."

"That's what I'm here for," he answered softly, resting his head against mine. "I'll just sit on the other side of the room and pretend I'm reading or something, so you can relax and remember I'm with you."

"I don't think I would've survived this long in here without you, Charlie," I whispered. "You really are a Godsend."

Charlie turned to look at me and smiled. "I'm happy to do anything for you, Em. But I'm not sure God pays much attention to my life."

51

CHARLIE

For each minute marking the time until she saw David, Emma was an incredibly preoccupied bundle of nerves. But who could blame her? Between Frank's psychotic outburst, her frustrating conversation with the toad and worrying about seeing her husband for the first time since she was admitted, she had a lot on her mind. Emma still loved her husband—that much was obvious—just the mention of his name had a visible effect on her. Whenever she talked about him, her eyes would light up and her cheeks would flush, but she didn't know if she could trust him anymore. He could quite possibly be an adulterer and a murderer. In her place, I'd be nervous and preoccupied, too. I did my best to provide whatever she needed—whether that was someone to make her laugh or a supportive shoulder to lean on—Emma knew I was there for her, which was perfect since I wasn't comfortable letting her out of my sight. Just the thought of not being with her if she ran into Frank again made me want to slam my fist through a wall.

Each time I glanced at Emma during lunch, she was staring into space with her food untouched. When I commented on it, she said her stomach was too full of butterflies to eat.

After an almost conversation-free lunch, we headed to the big room to zone out in front of the television with Bob and Nellie. We were midway through an episode of a very dated police drama when Spenser stomped into the room and stopped directly in front of the television. I almost could've sworn he did it intentionally to get a rise out of Bob.

Needless to say, Bob took the bait. "Get the fuck outta the way!"

Startled from a sound slumber, Nellie popped her head up from Bob's shoulder with a squeaky little scream.

Spenser didn't budge an inch, he just stood there glaring at Bob. I half expected Bob to jump up and slug him, but Bob answered his stare with a perfectly calm, "Fuck off."

"There are more constructive ways to express your feelings, Bob," Spenser scolded.

Bob just grinned at him. "You mean like standing up and kicking your pansy ass?" He seemed to be enjoying pushing Spenser's buttons as much as I usually did.

"With words, not with violence," Spenser correct-ed, like he was reprimanding a naughty child.

Bob just kept smiling like he didn't have a care in the world. "Doc, if you're gonna keep standin there, why don't you make yourself useful? Turn around and tell us what's happenin."

You could practically see the steam coming from Spenser's ears as he stepped away from the screen and planted himself in front of Emma.

I cleared my throat to get the toad's attention. "If you're counting on Emma taking your side, I wouldn't hold your breath."

Thick drops of mucous dripped from the toad's swollen lips as he scowled at me. Then human Spenser turned to Emma. "It's time for your appointment."

Emma wasn't thrilled about having to talk with Spenser again and unlike usual, she made no polite attempt to hide it.

I leaned closer to her. "Want me to come wait outside?"

"That won't be necessary, Charlie," Spenser snapped before Emma could answer.

I sat up a little straighter. "I wasn't asking you. I was asking Emma, and I'm pretty sure she's capable of answering for herself."

Spenser's scowl deepened. He was usually much more pleasant around Emma. I couldn't help won-dering if being forced to withdraw her visitation re-striction had triggered his exceptionally foul mood.

"Emma is capable of walking down the hall without you lurking behind her."

"I don't lurk," I growled, "and I'm offering because it doesn't seem like the staff is particularly concerned about Emma's safety."

The elderly doctor flinched, then the toad took a step closer to me. "Of course Emma's safety concerns us, but she's perfectly safe here so there's no need for you to play bodyguard, Mr. Oliver."

I slid to the edge of the couch cushion and leaned forward. "So it's gone from *Charlie* to *Mr. Oliver*? That's when you know you're in trouble, when the teacher calls you by your last name."

"That's enough," Spenser snapped, "or do I need to get someone in here to sedate you?"

I took a look around the room. All eyes were on us, even Bob was focused on our confrontation. I turned back to Spenser. "I'm pretty sure that was a threat, Doc."

"Call it whatever you like, *Charlie*. In my book, it's a warning."

Even I'm not a complete idiot. The only thing continuing would've accomplished would be getting me drugged and making me less capable of protecting Emma, and she needed me to watch out for Frank and for moral support during her husband's visit later. "Consider me warned then." I didn't growl, but my glare expressed exactly how I felt.

Spenser eyed me for a few seconds then turned to Emma and barked, "Come with me." He'd never used a tone like that with her before. I didn't like it, but I suppose that was probably the point. Spenser squinted and wiped his brow as a burst of heat blasted him in the face from behind the couch. Apparently, I wasn't the only one who was less than thrilled with the doctor's tone.

Emma stood without a word, and Dr. Spenser motioned to the door. I stood up beside her and whispered, "Want me to wait in the hall?"

Her eyes moved to Spenser. "No. I'll be okay." As an afterthought, she added, "Thanks."

I nodded. "I'll be here if you need me."

"She won't," Spenser barked.

Ignoring him, I repeated, "I'll be here."

With a melancholy smile, Emma headed to the door and the toad followed, leaving a fresh trail of drool in his wake.

I resisted the urge to follow. If Emma needed me, I could hear her from where I sat and reach her in seconds. I sat down closer to Nellie. "Feel like talking?"

She turned her head to me. "Not really."

What the hell was wrong with her? Why was she so off? "How did the rest of your night go?" I asked, too quietly for Bob to hear over the television.

Cloudy eyes misting, she whispered, "Stop talking to me."

"What the hell did I do?" I wondered aloud. "You and Bob seemed to hit it off great in both worlds. So what's your problem?"

Nellie's milky eyes locked onto mine. "You're my problem."

"Would you mind telling me what I did?" I insisted, feeling more hurt than I'd have liked to admit.

Nellie shook her head. "I'm tired of telling you things that you refuse to listen to."

"Fine," I snapped. "Just tell me one thing. What do you think of your new home?"

I caught a flickering glimpse of young Nellie as she turned to look at the old man, oblivious to the conversation taking place beside him at a volume his aged ears couldn't register. She smiled at him but the smile faded as she turned back to me. "It's a good home." With that, she laid her head on Bob's shoulder and turned her attention to the television.

It seemed a pretty clear signal that our conversation was over. The temptation to question her until I found out what the hell was wrong with her was pretty strong, but I knew she wouldn't answer so I didn't bother.

I glanced at the door just in time to see Tim lumber past the room. With nothing better to do, I decided to try and pump him for information. Hopping up, I went around the back of the couch so I wouldn't block Bob's view and caught up with Tim in the hall, which wasn't hard since he'd only gone a few steps past the door.

"Hey, Tim," I called after him.

He turned and smiled at me. "Hey, Charlie." The big guy was painfully dim, but he was also the friendliest staff member in the place—to me, at least.

"How's it going?" The trick to extracting information from Tim was to work it into the conversation so he'd answer without even realizing he shouldn't.

"Spenser's grumpy as hell today," he whispered, like he was sharing something confidential instead of stating the glaringly obvious.

"That's too bad, buddy. What's his problem?" I asked nonchalantly—well, nonchalantly enough for Tim.

He glanced toward Spenser's office. "He's pissed about Frank's episode this morning. Doc thought he was making better progress than he seems to be now. Frank's still all agitated, even under sedation, he keeps mumbling about claiming Emma and saying she offered herself. But Spenser doesn't want to transfer him outta here because he's a subject in a study, testing a new method of his and he's worried Frank'll mess it all up so he's trying to keep it quiet."

I kept my cool, nodded and did my best to look only casually interested. I might be powerless to do anything about it, but Emma's influential lawyer husband probably wouldn't be. "I'm sorry he's so grumpy," I muttered, with half-assed sympathy.

Tim nodded, looking touched by my concern. "Thanks."

"I'm surprised Spenser's so upset over just that."

With another glance toward the toad's office, Tim shook his head. "He's also edgy because some lawyer who works for Emma's husband showed up today, delivering some papers and saying he can't stop Emma's husband from visiting anymore. He's coming tonight and between you and me, I think Spenser's scared shitless of him."

By the time Tim finished talking, his voice had dropped to a whisper and I'd never been more thankful that the big goon loved to gossip like a nosy old woman. "Sorry he's being such a jerk."

Spenser's office door swung open and Tim muttered, "Gotta go," and took off.

Now I just had to figure out how to get the information about Frank to Emma's husband without terrifying her. She'd already had more than enough scares for one day.

Emma left Spenser's office practically in tears. When I asked her about the session, she just shook her head and said she wanted to freshen up before seeing her husband. So, I walked her to her room and although Frank had yet to make a return appearance, I sat in the hall and waited while she got ready—just in case.

I sat with my head tipped back against the wall, staring blankly at Emma's doorknob, trying to think of a way to get a message to her husband without involving her. Nellie sure as hell wasn't going to do me any favors, and there'd be no telling what Bob would say if I asked him to deliver a message. Benjamin's words echoed in my head. *He is what frightens me.* If Emma's husband really was scarier than Benjamin, I'd probably end up pissing myself if I tried to talk to him, especially since he probably already wanted to kill me after talking to Benjamin. What options did that leave me with? I could only think of two. I could tell Emma what Tim said and hope she'd tell her husband, but I'd probably terrify her in the process. My other option was to risk asking dim-witted Tim to relay a message to him, but that could backfire about fifty different ways.

Emma's door opened and my train of thought evaporated as I watched her step out into the hall—waves of golden hair falling around her, lashes lengthened to accentuate those incredible eyes, lips glossed with a hint of pink—she looked as polished and perfect as the day Tim first brought her to our group. A pale blue sleeveless dress wrapped around her perfect body, clinging to each beautiful curve. She took a step toward me and the hall filled with the scent of her perfume. She'd obviously been joking when she said she didn't wear any, she smelled down right delicious.

At a temporary loss for words, I stood up and smiled at her.

She smiled back then exhaled an unsteady breath. "I can't believe how nervous I am." She closed her generously lashed lids, veiling those magnificent eyes. "It feels like he was just a dream. I'm almost afraid I'll wake up and find out that he was never real." Opening her eyes, she whispered, "That sounds ridiculous, doesn't it?"

"Not at all," I muttered as I drank in the scent of her, "It's been a while since you saw him."

We headed toward the large common room because it was the one guests usually visited in, which is probably why Emma and I tended to avoid it. Until that night, neither of us had anyone to visit with. Well, there was Emma's visit from Benjamin, but I did my best to block that one from memory.

As we stepped into the room, I swore I could hear Emma's heart fluttering. I scanned the room, wondering if they'd released Frank from wherever they'd taken him. Some of the patients were sitting at a table at the far end of the room making a craft with a staff member. I watched old Nellie as she stood beside the table, hovering and watching. Surprisingly, Bob was absent from the room. I couldn't help wondering if Spenser had pulled him out for an evening session to scold him for his smartass attitude earlier. Thankfully, Frank was also a no-show.

With Bob gone, the television was off and it felt wrong not to hear its background noise filling what was otherwise just quiet emptiness. Emma and I settled into two lounge chairs in the corner of the room opposite Nellie and the craft group. The chairs were partially angled to face each other while still allowing a view of the window, and the sky beyond the windowpane was already starting to darken. I glanced at the clock on the far wall. Visiting hours would begin in five minutes. Standing from my chair, I grabbed the first book my hand touched from the bookshelf next to me. "It's about that time," I whispered, looking at the book without really seeing it.

Emma let out a shaky breath. "I still don't know what to feel."

"Just take it as it goes," I whispered, willing some of my calm to spread to her. Then I realized I still hadn't done anything about getting a message to her husband. "Emma, I think you should mention what happened with Frank today."

She looked up at me, wordlessly questioning why.

I bent close to her ear and whispered, "I talked to Tim. He told me Frank was still flipping out and ranting about you offering yourself this afternoon, but Spenser doesn't want to move him because he's part of some study he's working on and it'd mess up his results. If Spenser won't take him out of here, maybe your husband can do something about it."

Emma's eyes drifted to the darkening sky outside the window. "One more thing to add to my list of worries." She was smiling, but she looked ready to burst into tears.

I was such an idiot. My timing couldn't be worse. "Just focus on this visit and we'll deal with the rest later, alright?"

"Alright," she answered so softly that if my head hadn't been beside hers, I doubt I'd have heard.

I pointed to an empty chair across the room. "I'll be right over there."

Eyes brimming with tears, she whispered, "Thanks."

I gave her hand a squeeze then crossed the room and settled into my seat for the evening. Keeping Emma in my peripheral vision, I glanced at the book I'd pulled off the shelf. The title, I AM WOMAN, HEAR ME ROAR, was embossed in big gold letters on the cover. Stifling a laugh, I muttered, "Fabulous."

I looked back at Emma. She sat curled up in the chair like a child with her legs tucked beneath her, staring out the window as the tip of her index finger anxiously traced the curve of her lip. I still found that an insanely hot nervous habit.

I shifted my focus to the door. Maybe some of Emma's nervousness had worn off on me or maybe it was Benjamin's threat that had me suddenly feeling anxious about his arrival. I'd never seen David Talbot, so I wasn't even sure who I was watching for. Two visitors filed into the room. The first was a woman in her mid-thirties, eyes eagerly searching the room for her loved one. Behind her, came a man in his forties with well-worn clothes and scuffed sneakers. I didn't give him a second thought.

A sudden commotion over by the craft table captured my attention. I turned away from the door, and what I saw made my heart ache for poor old Nellie. She stood unmoving, with a stream of piss quite obviously trickling down her legs and a puddle slowly forming at her feet. Some of the crafters were freaking out and the staff member was trying to settle them down so she could attend to Nellie's accident. "Come on, dear," I heard the woman say as she started walking. "Let's get you back to your room and cleaned up." Nodding blankly, Nellie followed. The woman led her out the door and they disappeared from sight.

I glanced back at Emma. Still curled up in that child-like pose, she looked so small and delicate and there was this glow about her, like sunshine on a summer day. It took some serious effort to take my eyes off her but for some stupid reason, I felt the need to keep watch for her visitor.

I knew David Talbot the second he walked through the door. The man looked like money. Every article of clothing he wore looked custom-made and offensively expensive. His tie alone probably cost more than every piece of clothing I owned, combined. He was perfectly polished and put together from head to toe, and there was this self-assured air about him that seemed to defy anyone to challenge him. As much as I'd had it in my head to hate Emma's husband, I found myself in awe of the absolute confidence he carried himself with.

He hardly seemed to scan the room before heading straight toward Emma. As he passed by, others seemed to shrink in size as though just his nearness was enough to make them cower. When he reached the chairs, I expected him to sit in the empty chair that faced Emma's, but he didn't. Rounding her chair, he dropped to his knees on the floor at her feet. Tears slipped from her eyes the moment she saw him, and this larger than life man was moved to tears as he knelt in front of her. Reverently placing his arms at her knees, he spoke too softly for me to hear. Emma lifted a hand to her mouth and nodded, then she answered him. Again, the words were lost to me. A second later, she slid from the chair, buried her face against his chest and sobbed. And he wept like a child as he held her in his arms. Their utter abandon as they moved to each other—completely oblivious to the rest of the world—had me practically in tears myself.

I don't remember blinking, but I don't suppose anyone ever does. One fraction of a second, Emma was wrapped in the arms of the love of her life. The next, she was in the dragon's wings—not the Dream image—the *actual dragon*, solid and massive and rippled with muscle. His scales were black, his wings were a magnificent assortment of dazzling colors, some of which I don't even think there are names for, and blue fire blazed in his enormous eyes. I'm not sure how long I sat there too stunned to move. *He is what frightens me.* For a second, I wondered if I'd pissed myself but I couldn't tell one way or the other because I'd gone completely numb. The pounding of my heart became a deafening echo in my ears as I watched that monstrous creature hold Emma in the shimmering brilliance of his wings.

The beast dipped his head, positioning it just above hers. Monstrous nostrils flared as he inhaled deeply, and a blue-blackish smoke began to seep from Emma's body. I watched in paralyzed terror as he drained her small body of whatever the smoke was. He stopped and pulled his gigantic head back to stare at her for a few pounding heartbeats then he exhaled, bathing her body in licks of blue flame.

Seeing this demonic creature destroy my only friend snapped me out of my trance-like state. A primal scream tore from my lungs as I sprang from my chair and charged at the beast, intent on tearing him apart. With every ounce of strength in me, I seized one mammoth wing. My mind only partially registered the sound of people rushing toward us as the wing that I was feebly attempting to hold swung back and hit me with the force of a mac truck, knocking me to the floor.

As the room went dark, I heard the approaching steps of staff members and the last sensation I consciously registered was the sting of a needle sinking into my flesh.

Then there was nothing but darkness.

52

CHARLIE

I existed. Alone. In the Darkness. I sensed no sound. No smell. No taste. I touched nothing, and nothing touched me.

I don't know how long the Darkness held me. It might've been seconds. It might've been years. It clutched me until I started to question whether I'd ever actually existed at all. Maybe I was nothing but a fleeting thought through another's mind, nothing more than a fragment from a long forgotten Dream. Thoughts drained from me like grains of sand through an hourglass, one by one they slipped from my mind until there was nothing left of me.

And I felt nothing.

Then a voice thundered inside my head, "FOLLOW ME."

The deep rich voice slid like dark molasses down my throat, summoning a Darkness inside that I refused to acknowledge. It stirred, and horrific images of unspeakable acts emerged from that Darkness. The voice beckoned forth thoughts too evil to think from where they hid among the shadows, and I was terrified to discover that the thoughts aroused me as much as they frightened me.

"FOLLOW ME."

I tried to speak, but my throat was filled with fire and I had no voice to answer with. A single conscious thought formed in my head. *How?* But the flames held my tongue and I couldn't speak the thought out loud.

I heard no answer, but the Darkness deepened and swallowed me. We started to move and as we traveled, a long forgotten voice echoed in my head. *He is what frightens me.* I knew this Darkness. He'd come to warn me. *Benjamin.* He was faceless but as soon as I thought the name, I knew it was him. I would've worried about pissing myself, but I no longer knew if I even had a body.

We stopped moving and I waited for Benjamin's voice to thunder inside my head again, but it never did.

This would be the end of me. I would die here alone in the Darkness. I was sure of it.

Slowly, my senses came back to me. The first was my hearing. Whispers and growls and cries of desperation filled the emptiness where no sound had been. The voices all spoke at once—whispering of horrible things they'd done, urging me to do wicked things to others, to myself, to them. The voices reverberated inside my head until the sound nearly drove me mad. In my desperation, I cried out in my head. *Stop! Make it stop!* Immediately, the voices disappeared and the silence returned.

The next sense I regained was smell—the smell of Emma's perfume. *Is Emma here?* Her intoxicating scent hung thick and heavy in the breezeless air, and I hungered for it till it made me drool. *I have to help her.*

"That would be my scent," a voice answered, both aloud and in my head. The voice was deep and thunderous, full of Darkness and strength. This wasn't Benjamin. This voice was stronger—and Darker.

Slowly, my vision returned—hazy and unfocused at first—an immense blurred form was slinking toward me. It moved like a panther sauntering toward its prey, filling me with the urge to scream, but still I had no voice. I wanted to run but something held me in place. As the beast drew nearer, it gradually came into focus.

The dragon.

Rage coursed through me as I recalled the way that beast had tortured Emma right in front of me. An angry roar tore from my throat as I heaved my body in his direction, desperate to rip him apart for what he'd done to her, but I was shackled where I lay. "Let me go, you son of a bitch!"

"You are free to go," the dragon thundered inside my head. Quicker than the blink of an eye, the dragon disappeared and David Talbot stood in his place, dressed in fine black clothes.

"Fuck You!" I spat. "Unchain me!"

David studied me with mild curiosity. "Look at your wrists, there are no chains." His voice was calm and casual, as if we were sitting and chatting on a porch somewhere.

I looked around, uneven rock surrounded us from floor to ceiling. We were in a cave. "Where are we?" I demanded.

He raised an eyebrow. "Don't you know?"

And somehow, I did. "The Dark forest," I whispered, too lost in my own fear to remember to sound angry.

"Very good," he replied, sounding genuinely pleased. "The very heart of the Dark forest to be exact."

"Let me go," I growled.

"You are not bound. Look at your arms."

I looked down. Nothing tethered me in place. "What are you doing to me?"

"The spell that holds you," he replied patiently, "only prevents you from moving if your intention is to attack."

I looked at him skeptically. He nodded, and I knew he was encouraging me to try and move. Expelling a determined sigh, I attempted to rid my body of the desire to rip him apart and watched my right hand lift with ease. As I looked up at his face, another wave of rage swept through me and my arm slammed back against the stone.

He smiled at me. "Angry fellow, aren't you?"

"Fuck you!" I growled.

"So crass," he mused, shaking his head in disapproval.

"Where's Emma?" At the mention of her name, the scent of her perfume grew heavier. "What the hell? Why do I smell her?"

David looked at me like I was mentally slow. "I told you, that's my scent—or rather, mine and Emma's—a marriage of her favorite scents and my favorite flavors. It is an intoxicating blend, isn't it?"

"Your scent? Are you saying…you scent marked her?"

He nodded. "A warning to others that she belongs to a Dragon." Raising an eyebrow, he added, "A warning that certain individuals were too ignorant to heed."

"You scent marked your wife?" I muttered. "You mean…you peed on her?"

David Talbot looked at me like I was the most dim-witted fool he'd ever set eyes on. I'd always taken great pleasure in saying stupid things to irritate Spenser, but David's disapproving stare made me feel ashamed of my stupidity. I had no idea why. What did I care what this man thought of me? "The scent is created by touch," he replied, eyeing me with distaste. "The greater the contact, the stronger the scent becomes."

"The greater the contact?" I repeated, curious despite my anger.

He gave me that look, like he thought I was a moron, again. "The most powerful scent is produced by touch from the inside. If you need a more graphic explanation, perhaps we can find a text book to explain it to you."

"So she smells like…"

"A blend of her favorite flowers and my favorite sweets, and I'll save you the trouble of continuing with your pubescent line of questioning. She tastes like dessert."

"Shit," I blurted before I could filter myself, "That's hot."

I expected him to hurt me. Instead, he smiled. "You have no idea."

I did manage to censor myself before asking if he meant the taste of her mouth or… Better not to even finish that thought. I swore he could hear inside my head. Hadn't he answered a question, I didn't ask out loud?

He arched an eyebrow as he looked down at me. I was pretty sure he'd heard the question forming in my head, but he didn't dignify it with a response.

"Where is Emma?" I demanded. "What did you do to her?"

"Emma is fine," he replied matter-of-factly.

The calmer he remained, the more it enraged me. "I watched you drain some sort of smoke from her and then set her on fire." Rage flooded through me as I recalled the way he'd tortured her.

David smiled at me. "The *smoke* you watched me drain from her was the Darkness that's been forcing its way inside her. I was drawing it from her and taking it into myself, and the *fire* you watched me bathe her in was a reinforcement of the enchantment that protects her from being touched by anyone intending to harm her."

"Enchantment?"

He nodded. "Attempt to lay a finger on her, meaning to harm her, and the enchantment will cause pain. The more severe the hurt you mean to cause, the more intense the pain inflicted."

Was that what the image of the dragon was—an enchantment? Did it hurt Frank because he was about to hurt Emma? "Are you going to kill me?" I wondered aloud.

"If I wanted to kill you, you'd already be dead," he replied, as emotionlessly as you'd respond to an inquiry of the time or the weather.

"What do you want with me?"

"It's my turn to ask questions now." Even in a quiet tone, his voice was potent. This man had such absolute power that there was no need to flaunt it or even display it. You just felt it in his presence. He stepped closer and Benjamin's words came back to me. *He is what frightens me.* Kneeling on the stone beside me, he studied me like an interesting slide beneath a microscope. "How can this be?"

"What?"

"How did you become one of the lost?" he murmured.

I sure felt lost. "I don't know what you're talking about."

"You truly don't, do you?" he replied distantly. "I had to see it for myself."

"See what?" I demanded, unsure whether to be angry or curious or afraid.

"Who are your parents?" It was more command than question.

Did he plan to hurt my mother to punish me?

"I'm not going to hurt your mother," he stated, answering my unspoken question. "I have the utmost respect for any woman who would endure so much suffering to bring another life into the world." Looking somewhat surprised, he added, "Is your mother alive?"

"Yes." I wasn't about to elaborate.

"Then how did you end up at the facility?"

Now he should feel like the stupid one. How do you end up in a place for crazy people? You get diagnosed as crazy. *Duh.* "My mother admitted me because I see things other people don't."

"Of course, you do," he agreed, like I'd just said something as obvious as, 'I have two feet.' "You're Sighted."

Okay, now he had my absolute attention. "Do you have Dream Sight?"

"All of our kind are Sighted, Charlie," he replied in a gentle tone like he was talking to a lost child, which I was starting to feel like I was.

I felt the rest of my rage slip away. "Our kind?"

He studied me curiously. "Dragons."

"What the hell are you talking about? You're the dragon."

"Unbelievable," he murmured. "Why didn't your mother teach you about your Sight?"

"She doesn't have it," I muttered. "She just thinks I'm crazy."

"Then she's not your mother," he stated, almost apologetically.

"How the hell could you know that?" Was I upset because I thought he was nuts, or because deep down it felt like the truth? *But I'm no dragon.*

He looked genuinely sympathetic. "Dragons are only conceived when both parents are Sighted."

"Why do you keep saying that? I'm not a dragon."

"Sit up," he insisted. "I'm tired of hovering over you, and lying on that rock can't be comfortable."

"I can't." Even as I said it, I found that I could. "Did you remove the spell?"

"You're filled with too much curiosity to hold onto the rage." He waved his hand as nonchalantly as if he was shooing a fruit fly and the Waters appeared—vertical and motionless—in the middle of a dry cave.

Okay, that was impressive.

He motioned toward the stationary wall of Water. "Look at your reflection."

I looked, and a magnificent dragon with golden brown scales and huge coppery wings stared back at me. I tilted my head and the dragon mirrored the action, I blinked and enormous eyes blazing with orange flames closed and reopened. I turned to David. "It's another spell. You're trying to trick me."

"Look at your torso," he suggested patiently.

I looked down and saw my normal t-shirt-and-jeans-clad human body. My clothes were a little worse for wear but other than that, I looked the same as always. "Human." He should be feeling stupid now.

"You only see what you want to see, Charlie," he replied quietly. "I look human, too."

Shit. He had a point. "How can you be both? I've never come across a person with more than one Dream form."

He smiled. "And how many Sighted individuals have you come across?"

"One. Well…two counting you," I muttered, feeling like a moron again.

He nodded patiently.

Nellie was the only other Sighted person I'd met and she wasn't exactly an encyclopedia of useful information, but something told me this man was. Whoever David Talbot was, he was someone of importance. "How can you be human and dragon?"

"You can't," he answered. "We are dragon but we're capable of taking human form, and none but the highest of other Dark creatures can sense what we are. Others see what we want them to see, when we want them to see it. You, my friend, are so skilled at concealing what you are that you've hidden it from yourself your entire life."

"That's not possible," I whispered, but a churning in my stomach said otherwise.

"Look again," David insisted.

I looked down. Where my human body had been, sat the monstrous torso of a beast covered in gold and brown scales with subtle flecks of coppery brown glinting in my monstrous wings. *My wings.* I looked up at David in disbelief. How could I have hidden something so incredible from myself?

"The mind is a powerful thing," David replied, answering my unspoken thought, "especially the mind of a dragon."

I sighed and boiling hot steam spewed from my nostrils toward him. "Oh...shit," I babbled, horrified, "Sorry."

But he just smirked, fiery amusement flashing in his eyes. "No need to apologize. I'm fire-proof."

"Right...of course you are," I muttered. After a moment, I asked, "Can we fly?" amazed at how much the possibility excited me.

"You can," he answered, with a sorrowful smile. "Much of my energy is focused elsewhere at the moment. Flying would require more strength than I have to spare."

Something in his voice told me that story was private, so I didn't ask.

He tilted his head appraisingly. "There's really only one more thing to discuss."

One thing? I had about a billion questions.

"They'll all get answered in time," he assured me.

"What's the one thing?" I looked down and couldn't decide whether to be relieved or disappointed that my body looked human again.

"When I learned of you, my first inclination was to rip you to pieces," he stated calmly, "and just so there's no misunderstanding, I'm fully capable of doing so."

I didn't doubt it for a second. *Note to self: don't piss this guy off.*

He raised an eyebrow. "Wise note. You'd do well to remember that one."

No shit. I was starting to wonder why I was bothering to say anything out loud.

"Anyway," he continued, "Emma now carries the slightest trace of honey in her scent—a favorite of yours, I assume?"

Shit.

"Shit, is right," he agreed. "Normally, I'd tear you apart but I know about the incident with the other patient. You protected her and encouraged her to tell me about it."

Thank God. Maybe I'd actually leave in one piece.

"I am grateful that you looked out for her."

For some idiotic reason, I felt compelled to clarify. "Actually your dragon image, or whatever that thing is, stopped him."

"Yes. But you were there to make her feel a little less lost, and for that I am grateful. Had you done more than put a friendly arm around her shoulders, the scent would be stronger. Keep that in mind for the future," he instructed, all kindness disappearing from his eyes.

"Got it." Where Emma was concerned, he had no patience. I could respect that.

"Because that other patient went after Emma," he continued, looking kinder again, "I was able to get a judge to rule that she be allowed to return home under house arrest and be treated by a live-in psychiatrist."

How long had I been unconscious? Wait, this was the Dream World. I still was. "So, that's it then." Emma was the closest friend I'd ever had. I missed her already.

David nodded. "But you weren't ordered to be admitted to the facility by a court decision. You were checked in voluntarily, which means you're perfectly within your rights to check yourself out."

How had I never known that? My initial burst of happiness quickly faded, leaving me feeling worthless and unwanted. "I don't have anywhere else to go." My mother didn't want anything to do with me.

He smiled. "I told you, that woman did not give birth to you."

Even if that was true, where did it leave me?

"The Sighted keep their abilities hidden," he informed me softly. "It is a Sighted parent's responsibility to teach their child about our world, while teaching him to ignore what he sees in the waking world. Occasionally, a Sighted child is born to two Sightless parents and they often end up in mental institutions because no one is there to guide them. We call them the lost. Every effort is made to identify lost children at birth and ensure that a suitable guide is placed in their lives. Had I not guided Emma, she also would have been one of the lost."

"But Emma's not Sighted," I muttered.

Though he remained in human form, David's eyes blazed with blue flames and fury flashed across his face but it quickly softened and turned to sorrow. "That is a story for another time," he whispered, tears glistening where the flames had been.

I nodded, feeling like a total asshole.

"Anyhow," he continued, "a lost dragon is unheard of—for obvious reasons—both parents must be Sighted to conceive a dragon child."

I waited for him to speculate on where I might've come from, if my parents weren't really my parents, but he didn't.

"My employees are almost exclusively Sighted, Charlie. They work for me in both worlds. We are a family where all are free to speak of their entire life." He paused a moment, letting that sink in. "So, only one question remains. Would you be interested in joining our family?"

For the first time in my life, I had a chance to be accepted—to be part of a family that didn't dismiss me as a lunatic. I would say I feared waking to find that it was all just a dream, but I knew better. It was a Dream.

But Dreams were real.

And I was a dragon.

Turn the page for an excerpt from
DREAM WORLD
Book Two of The Dream Waters Series

1

CHARLIE

It was a Tuesday. The day my life changed forever. Just another ordinary day for the rest of the world. I hit the power button on the television as I passed the hotel dresser, but I didn't bother looking at the screen. I was way more interested in the grease-soaked paper bag in my other hand. Plopping down on the queen-sized bed, I shrugged out of my jacket, kicked off my shoes, tossed the room key to the bedside table and tore into the bag like a wolf tearing into fresh prey. Practically salivating, I unwrapped the first double bacon cheeseburger and an almost orgasmic moan escaped my throat as my teeth sank into it. I leaned back against the headboard and looked at the television across the room. The middle-aged man onscreen was proclaiming the wonders of a food processor that no kitchen would be complete without. My eyes darted to the bedside table and did a quick visual sweep of the bed. Then I spotted the remote on the desk across the room and let out a defeated sigh. I was already feeling way too lethargic to get back up. After stuffing in a second burger, a large order of fries and a chocolate shake, I sank back against the pillows, closed my eyes and tuned out the infomercial salesman's obnoxiously cheery voice.

In under two weeks, my life had changed so drastically that it was almost too much to process. I'd gone from being a mental patient in a long-term care psychiatric facility to a lonely hotel patron with nowhere to go and nothing on the horizon. I was diagnosed at a young age as a schizophrenic suffering from paranoid delusions, my *delusions* being the fact that I see things and remember things that other people can't. Unlike the rest of the world, I remember the Waters that carry everyone to the Dream World each night while their bodies sleep. I remember the world where everyone takes an alternate form and lives an alternate life. I can see people flip to their Dream forms in this world and I can jump in the Waters and travel to the Dream World whenever I want to. A few weeks ago, a gorgeous new patient had walked through the door in the middle of a group therapy session and though I didn't know it at the time, her entrance was the first in a series of events that'd change my life forever.

At an almost mindboggling speed, Emma Talbot became the closest friend I'd ever had. And it wasn't long before an elderly fellow patient opened my eyes to the fact that I wasn't the only Dream Sighted person in this world. She opened my eyes to a lot of things, including the fact that my new best friend was constantly shadowed by a second Dream form, an enormous fiery-eyed dragon. After several unsuccessful days spent trying to figure out why Emma had a dragon for a bodyguard, I met the man who was going to change my life—the dragon, Emma's husband, David Talbot. When I first realized he was Emma's dragon, I attacked him full force in the middle of the common room during visiting hours and he knocked me out cold with the flick of a wing. I woke up in the Dream World inside a cave in the Dark Forest, where David patiently explained that he was also Sighted. And that I was also a dragon.

When I woke in the facility the next morning, Emma was already gone. Her husband, who also happened to be a big shot lawyer, had gotten a judge to let her go home under house arrest and be treated by a live-in psychiatrist. He convinced the judge that another patient at the facility posed a threat to Emma's safety, and I wholeheartedly agreed. I'd watched that other patient flip to a writhing man-shaped swarm of insects and go after Emma. I also watched the dragon that shadowed Emma lunge at Frank the bug-man and melt his hand to a lump of charred flesh, but I was the only one who'd been able to see that.

Opening my eyes, I extended a leg and dragged my jacket up from the foot of the bed with my toes. I pulled an envelope from one of the pockets and for about the thousandth time, I opened it and slid out the sheet of expensive-looking pale gray stationary. **David Talbot Attorney at Law** was engraved in thick silver letters at the top of the page. The note was written in black ink and the handwriting was elegant, but not in a girly way.

Dear Mr. Oliver,

Please accept this small token of my gratitude for protecting what I hold most dear. Use it to forge a new path for yourself.

Best of luck in your future endeavors,
David A. Talbot

No phone number. No address. Unless you counted the office information that was engraved at the bottom of the page. But I didn't. When I met David Talbot in the Dream World, he asked if I'd be interested in joining his "family" of Sighted employees. He'd offered a glimmer of hope that I might actually belong to a family that didn't dismiss me as a lunatic but if he'd really wanted me to join the family, wouldn't he have done more than leave an envelope at the facility with instructions to give it to me when I was discharged?

David Talbot's business card from the Law Offices of Talbot and Associates had been tucked inside the letter. No more contact information than the stationary. No private number. No "call my office and tell the secretary you were invited to join the family."

A prepaid credit card with no mention of how much it was worth had also been tucked inside the letter. I used it to buy a few necessities at a corner store, gum, toothbrush, six-pack of soda. When I asked the cashier if she could tell me the balance, her eyes grew three times wider as she whispered the amount. I asked her to repeat it. Twice. When I decided to get a hotel room until I figured out what to do with my life, I got a similar reaction from the guy at the check-in desk.

I turned the business card over in my hand a few times, stupidly hoping to find something new. The silver engraving glinted when it caught the lamplight, but that was it. Tucking the card in the pocket of my jeans, I yanked the blankets up over me and sank back against the foreign comfort of the hotel mattress.

I was used to being alone. Even my own mother wanted nothing to do with me, the woman I'd always believed to be my mother anyway. David said it wasn't possible for an Unsighted mother to give birth to a dragon child. Dragons were only conceived when both parents were Sighted, either way, I was used to going solo and I'd never let myself hope for better or believe that I was worth something. I'd always aimed to convince everybody, including myself, that I was a smartass who didn't give a crap but for some moronic reason, I'd let David Talbot get my hopes up. For a brief moment I actually believed I was special, but it was all just a bunch of bullshit. He'd enchanted Emma with a dragon bodyguard and he'd used an enchantment to chain me to the floor of the cave. He'd probably just used magic to make it look like I was a dragon. Since the day we met, I'd spent hours in the Dream World trying to turn back into the dragon he'd shown me to be, but the reflection staring back at me was never anything more than a human idiot who'd gotten suckered into believing in a fairytale. And now being nothing hurt like hell because I'd let David Talbot convince me to care.

There was a new infomercial on television for a bead-maker that no self-respecting crafter should be without, but I had even less energy to get up and grab the remote after all the fast food I'd wolfed down in a pathetic attempt to stuff down the hurt. As I steadily slipped into a grease-induced food coma, I closed my eyes and let the Waters take me…

…I groggily lifted my eyelids and found myself curled up on a soft patch of earth. The Water was only a few steps away and the sun was lazily sinking toward it. Behind me, the cries of awakening nocturnal creatures echoed through the forest. Rubbing my eyes, I stood up and headed toward a weathered dock that jutted out over the Water a short distance from where I'd slept. I had no idea where I was. Since I didn't see any point to jumping in the Waters lately, I'd been falling asleep naturally like the rest of the world and each time I drifted back to the Dream World, I found myself someplace new. I stepped up onto the dock and the boards groaned in protest as I made my way to the end of it. I took a deep breath, filling my lungs with the earthy evening air, and sat down on the edge of the dock. Forgetting I wasn't in the other world, I reached in my pocket and pulled out the card. Then I realized where I was, and that the card shouldn't be there. I turned it over in my hand a few times. Just the same boring law office business card. It didn't say anything new, but what the heck was it doing in my pocket in the Dream World?

"Penny for your thoughts." I jumped at the nearness of the unfamiliar voice. I guess I'd been too engrossed in studying the stupid card to hear him walk up behind me.

I twisted sideways and watched the old man who belonged to the voice take the remaining steps to the end of the dock. Old bones and weathered boards creaking in protest, he sat down beside me. White-haired, bearded and dressed in a simple dark blue tunic and matching pants, he considered me with a kind smile, waiting for an answer.

"Yeah. Uh," I stammered. "Just admiring the sunset."

His smile widened. "And here I thought you were wondering about that card in your hand."

I glanced down at the card. "Nah. This's nothing important."

His pale blue eyes twinkled with amusement. "Of course. Invitations from the Sarrum are just everyday occurrences."

"I'm sorry?" I looked down at the card, then back at him. "The what?"

He chuckled softly to himself. "I heard you were lost. But I didn't imagine you'd be quite this lost."

No longer finding his smile quite so kind, I scowled at him. "Who exactly are you? And why do you think you know me?"

His smile grew faintly apologetic. "Names aren't important, Charlie. But if you must call me something, call me Arthur."

"Okay Call-me-Arthur, how do you know my name?"

He shifted, trying to make his aged body more comfortable on the wooden planks. "Everyone knows your name. It isn't every day that a lost dragon is discovered."

"So you're Sighted?"

"I am," he agreed with a half-smile on his lips.

Yeah. So far this conversation was annoyingly pointless. But he knew about the card. *An invitation from the Sarrum.* "How do you know about the business card? And what the heck is a Sarrum?"

Call-me-Arthur's gaze shifted toward the Water. "News travels quickly through the Dark Forest. Everyone's quite curious about you, you know."

"No. I don't know. Why don't you enlighten me?"

He looked away from the Water and studied me curiously. "I wouldn't dream of stepping on the Sarrum's toes. He's already offered to do just that, hasn't he?"

If he wasn't an old man, I'd have been sorely tempted to knock the smug smile off his face. "Seriously, what the hell's a Sarrum?"

Raising an eyebrow, he replied, "I believe you know the Dragon King as David Talbot."

"The Dragon King?" I raked a hand through my hair. "David Talbot is the king of the dragons?"

Another soft chuckle escaped his wrinkled lips. "No. David Talbot is the king of Draumer."

I resisted the urge to growl at him. "And Draumer is what? The Dream World term for dragons?"

His grin faltered slightly. "No. Draumer is the Dream World term for *Dream World*. It seems the rumors are wrong. You aren't more man than beast. You're more beast than man. Honestly, how could you live your entire Sighted life without even knowing the name of the world you inhabit?"

Who the hell was this guy? I didn't have to take this. "Listen, I'm not really in the mood for company. So why don't you move along?"

He let out a lingering sigh. "I meant no offense, Charlie. Why don't we start over?"

I looked away from him and turned toward the sunset. "Okay. Start."

"I came here to offer advice before you accepted the Sarrum's offer."

I glanced down at the card. "Then you wasted your time. He didn't give me an offer, just a generic thank you note."

Call-me-Arthur cleared his throat, prompting me to look at him. So I did. "That's no generic thank you, my boy. That piece of cardstock is worth more gold than you could possibly imagine."

Well that definitely peaked my interest. "How do you figure?"

He reached out and took the card from my hand. And worthless as I believed it to be, I snatched it right back. "It only appears ordinary because you haven't accepted the Sarrum's offer."

I traced a finger along the edge of the card. "How exactly do I do that? Call the law office and tell the secretary that the Sarrum of Draumer offered me a job? That'd earn me a one-way ticket back to the loony bin."

Eyes narrowed, he studied me curiously. "You aren't embarrassed about your stay in a mental facility?"

"Why should I be? My closest friends were in that facility. Including my best friend, the Sarrum's wife."

The cordial grin slipped from his face. "You'd best keep that to yourself. Dragons do not share their treasures. She's not yours. She's his. And if you'd like your heart to keep beating, you won't forget that."

Seriously, who the hell was this guy? "Thanks for that totally obvious piece of advice."

"If it was obvious, you wouldn't ever refer to her as *your* anything. Not even your friend. She's his. And only his. Period."

I returned my gaze to the Water and the sky above it. The sun was just barely visible above the horizon and the air was already starting to cool. I opened my mouth, hoping something clever would pop out.

But he didn't give me the chance. "Yes, I know. You aren't stupid. But we've gotten off topic. To accept the Sarrum's offer, you have to toss that card in the Waters."

"Toss something worth more than I could possibly imagine?" Seemed like a pretty stupid suggestion to me.

He answered in a softer voice, as if our whole conversation had taken place in a completely different tone. "It's the invitation that's valuable. Not the piece of cardstock."

Somehow his change in manner softened mine. "So what advice did you come to give me?"

He grinned, more to himself than me. "Your life is about to change dramatically, Charlie. I just thought you should know that not everyone believes the Sarrum walks on water. There are those who don't think he deserves to sit the throne."

I studied his amused expression, unsure what to make of him. "Are you saying I shouldn't accept his invitation?"

Call-me-Arthur's brow furrowed. "No. You'd be a fool not to accept. There is much that the Sarrum and his followers can teach you. You won't find a better education in all the Sighted world. I'm simply suggesting that you keep an open mind, remember not everything they teach you is set in stone and consider what else the world has to offer before you blindly pledge yourself in service to the Sarrum. If you'd like, I could provide a different point of view when you need one."

I absently traced the raised silver letters on the card with my index finger. "What am I supposed to do? Bring you with me and tell them I'm not sure if I can trust them?"

A humorless chuckle erupted from the old man's throat. "No. I'd prefer that my heart keep beating. I'm no friend of the Dragon King."

The sun had disappeared completely and the air was cooler, but still pleasant. "Why is that?" I wondered aloud, genuinely curious.

He regarded me with a sorrowful smile. "Because the last time I saw the Sarrum, I tried to take his life."

"Yeah," I muttered, wondering whether that should make me fear him or the Dragon King. "I guess that would get you kicked off the holiday guest list. So why'd you try to kill him?"

His pale blue eyes misted as he whispered, "Because he'd just killed my sister."

For the first time, I wondered if I would've been better off staying lost. "Go on."

He cleared his throat and blinked the tears from his eyes. "I've got nothing more to say on that subject but you must understand that the traditional way of thinking for a dragon, especially a royal one, is that women are property. And the primary function of a Sighted female is to bear a dragon child."

Dread knotted in my stomach at the thought of what that meant for Emma, but he clearly didn't intend to elaborate. "How would I contact you if I had questions?"

He reached into a pocket and pulled out a softly glowing white stone. Then he held his hand out, offering it.

The glow intensified as I took it from his hand. It felt surprisingly cool to the touch. "What is it?"

"A moonstone." He cleared his throat. "I've taken up enough of your time. I'll leave you to your thoughts. If you have questions, hold the stone in your hand when you jump in the Waters and it will take you to me. I only ask that you not mention me to the Sarrum or his men."

"I won't." I looked up to thank Call-me-Arthur. But he was gone. I stroked a finger over the stone's smooth surface, then stuffed it in my pocket and turned my attention to the card in my other hand. *A business card worth more gold than I could possibly imagine.* Muttering, "What've I got to lose," I tossed it in the Water...

...Another infomercial for knives sharp enough to slice through metal was playing as I opened my eyes. Sitting up, I tossed the covers off me and fished for the business card in my pocket. It was still there. I pulled it out with a disappointed sigh. The same generic information was engraved on its surface. Honestly, what had I expected?

Feeling like an idiot, I tossed the card to the bedside table and it landed blank side up. Only, it wasn't blank anymore. Heart racing, I snatched it off the table. A phone number was penned in perfect handwritten numbers on the back. Just a number, but it hadn't been there the thousand other times I'd studied the card. I stood up and moved to the desk across the room, clutching the card worth more than gold.

Hand trembling, I lifted the hotel phone off the receiver.

Made in the USA
Middletown, DE
30 August 2019